Praise for *Beneath the Flames*

"Renz draws on his years of experience as a firefighter to bring a hardscrabble authenticity to his novel. He packs the tale with plenty of action and a lot of heart. His firefighting sequences are detailed and thrilling, placing readers right in front of the flames. His prose is clean and, at times, poetic..."
—*Kirkus Reviews*

"Gregory Renz's new novel is a triumph of poignancy, compassion, and restraint. In it, a man's regret is transformed to triumph."
—Jacquelyn Mitchard, author of the bestselling novel, *The Deep End of the Ocean*

"Renz's debut novel is exactly the kind of book I want to read right now — one where decency is a virtue, where empathetic people win, and it's full of the complex, hardworking Midwestern folks I enjoy reading and writing about."
—J. Ryan Stradal, best-selling author of *Kitchens of the Great Midwest and Lager Queen of Minnesota.*

"*Beneath the Flames* by Gregory Lee Renz is a mesmerizing story that brims with life and humanity, a story that explores themes of race, love, family, and an adventure within the firefighting department. The prose is gorgeous and, from the very beginning, the author had me captivated by the wonderful imagery and the lyrical nature of the story."
—Readers' Favorite Five-Star Review.

"In his debut novel, Gregory Lee Renz gives us an action-packed story of a Wisconsin farm boy turned Milwaukee firefighter, but that's not all. *Beneath the Flames* lies a tender journey of compassion, redemption, and community that will stick with you for a long time."
—Ann Voss Peterson, author of over thirty novels with millions of books in print all over the globe. Winner of the prestigious Daphne du Maurier Award

"*Beneath the Flames* is an action-packed debut novel with something for every reader: suspense, romance, friendship, forgiveness, family, and more. A novel that like its protagonist, relentlessly presses on into fiery and controversial terrain where many other writers fear to tread.
—NICKOLAS BUTLER, author of *THE HEARTS OF MEN and LITTLE FAITH*

Greg Renz knows firefighting from the inside out, and his heroism got him inducted into the State of Wisconsin Fire and Police Hall of Fame. This novel proves he's equally wise about the vagabond ways of the human heart, with a storytelling gift that keeps the pages turning.
—Doug Moe, coauthor of "*Tommy: My Journey of a Lifetime*," the autobiography of Gov. Tommy G. Thompson.

"Gregory Lee Renz's *Beneath The Flames* tells a vivid tale of Mitch Garner's journey from the farm to inner city Milwaukee. A young man caught between the national horror of 9/11 and personal tragedy becomes a firefighter in a neighborhood wracked with poverty and violence."
—Parks Kugle, Managing Editor for *Lumina Literary Journal.*

"Renz's skill as author is evident in the depth of each character and their dialogue and mannerisms—so much so that we feel as though we've met them all in real life. This is a book with serious themes and subjects; suicide, racism, gang violence, domestic abuse, sexual assault, murder and more. But this is also a story about hope, love, and family. Renz handles them all with a brave pen that isn't squeamish with the tough parts."
—Valerie Biel, author of the award winning book series *Circle of Nine*

"Gregory Lee Renz applies first-hand experience as a decorated firefighter to his searing, emotional debut novel *Beneath the Flames*. With Renz, you are in the hands of a reliable guide and deft writer as he captures the fraternal bond of this unique band of heroes...On one level, *Beneath the Flames* contains moving life lessons, sprinkled with messages about friendship, relationships, race and the perils of a dangerous profession. It's about personal pursuit of excellence, the obstacles in achieving it, and coming to terms with sometimes falling short. It's about getting to the good and moving with convincing, uplifting characters."

"This story vividly transports us to the life of firefighters and the harrowing situations they face almost every day. It focuses on one fireman, Mitch Garner, and his growth as a human being. It also gives us a glimpse of life in the inner city. It illustrates the burden of memories that can traumatize an individual, but how facing them one grows and heals. Greg Renz is a masterful storyteller who keeps your attention from the beginning of the story to its end."

—Tania Friedman, Retired Administrator, Harvard Medical School.

"It would be too easy to say that **Beneath the Flames** is filled with burning passion, but it's the truth. One would expect a novel about a firefighter to be full of fire and flames, and Renz doesn't disappoint. However, to the reader's great delight, he also takes the burning within, to a firefighter who seeks to set things to rights and to put out the most dangerous internal flame of all - guilt. Renz's gripping and sensitive story-telling will take the reader along with Mitch Garner as he walks his road from young farmer and volunteer firefighter to professional firefighter in the inner city streets of Milwaukee, Wisconsin. Renz is the rare writer who can create action-packed scenes and the tenderest of intimacies with the same talented hand."

—Kathie Giorgio, critically acclaimed author of four novels, two story collections and a poetry chapbook.

As a white rookie firefighter in Milwaukee's inner city, Mitch has much to learn, not the least is a bit of advice from his captain - "You'll need to learn to smile at the dying. Your mug might be the last thing they see". Set in the urban Midwest, this poignant story of one man's journey to save lives while helping to save his own life will stay with you well after you read it. Mitch's rural past catches up with his present as he becomes involved in his new life as a hero – and sometimes the most heroic acts are those that happen beyond the firefighting incidents. This is clearly one of the best and most brilliant debut novels I've ever read by first-time novelist Greg Renz. Read this book NOW.

– Laurie Scheer, Writing Mentor, Director-UW-Madison Writers' Institute, UW-Madison

"**Beneath the Flames** is not your typical debut novel. The topics covered are both timely and timeless, giving us some much-needed light in very dark times. The protagonist compels us not only to be better, but to do better. The prose is sharp and modern, the themes and subplots are thought-provoking, and the characters will stick with you for days after you finish reading. In a world where superheroes dominate the box office week after week, it is refreshing to see real heroes performing real miracles. Renz has truly delivered a wholly unique story that will simultaneously bring you to tears and inspire you to make a difference."

—Jeff Hill, faculty member of The Writers Hotel Conference in New York

"Outstanding! **Beneath The Flames** is an intimate combination of love, race, life as a Milwaukee Firefighter from outside the city, and life as an African American family, all trying to coexist in crazy and chaotic urban and rural environments. This is a MUST READ for anyone in the fire service or anyone wanting to get into the fire service!"

—City of Milwaukee Fire Chief Douglas A. Holton Sr.

"A mesmerizing debut novel, written from the heart with a passion and authenticity that leaps out and grabs you on the very first page."

—Joanna Elm, author of *Scandal* (1996) and *Delusion* (1997)

"As a retired fire captain, Gregory Lee Renz artfully weaves in gritty scenes taken from actual fire-fighting tragedies that will leave you breathless. **Beneath the Flames** is one novel you simply can't put down."

—Kristin Oakley, author of the award-winning novel Carpe Diem, Illinois

"In **Beneath the Flames**, Gregory Lee Renz weaves together seemingly disparate story threads— the unflinching account of a rookie fire fighter, the hardships of maintaining a family farm, the culture clash of a young man trading rural life for the inner city, and a love story. Tying these threads together is the story at the heart of this book: a man haunted by his past and trying to make amends. With great compassion and skillful writing, Renz shows us the human side of a tragedy and reminds us that when life doesn't turn out as expected, you can build yourself a new life."

—Jen Rubin, author of *We Are Staying: Eighty Years in the Life of a Family, a Store, and a Neighborhood.*

BENEATH THE FLAMES

(A novel)

BENEATH THE FLAMES

(A novel)

Gregory Lee Renz

Three Towers Press

Milwaukee, Wisconsin

Published by

Three Towers Press

An imprint of HenschelHAUS Publishing, Inc.

www.henschelHAUSbooks.com

ISBN (hardcover): 978159598-687-0
ISBN (paperback): 978159598-688-7
ISBN (e-book): 978159598-689-4
ISBN (audio book): 978159598-690-0

LCCN: 2018965332

Cover design: EM Graphics, LLC

Printed in the United States of America

For Paula.
Our magical journey continues.

Foreword

I had the privilege of working with Greg while he worked for the Milwaukee Fire Department. He brings the experience of being a firefighter in an urban community to life for the readers. You will not have to have fire department experience to enjoy this book.

Without question, you will become emotionally involved with the thrill of victory and the agony of defeat as you live through the trials and tribulations of the main character.

When Greg asked me to proof the book, my immediate reply was, "I am not a reader." In fact, the last book of fiction I read was *Member of the Gang*, as a fifth grader. I obliged, but with hesitation because of my personal lack of motivation for reading. I truly started the task as a favor to my good friend.

My reading experience with *Beneath the Flames* was unbelievable. I laughed, I cried, and I related to almost every single experience that the main character endured. Experiences that did not relate to me, I recognized as experiences and hardships affecting firefighters under my command. The book has a sense of realism that hit home with this 34-year City of Milwaukee employee. Every single chapter kept me magnetized to the novel. For the first time since the fifth grade, this reader enjoyed reading again.

I never looked at how long the book was or the number of chapters within the novel. As I read chapter by chapter, I found myself wanting to know the ending, but as I neared the ending, that desire was replaced by reluctance, because I truly did not want the experience to end.

Greg Renz, I was by your side when you earned induction into the Wisconsin Fire and Police Hall of Fame for your life-saving efforts at the North 67th Street fire.

You have put me by your side again with the words, stories, characters, and real-world experiences of *Beneath the Flames*. Thank You.

—Thomas M. Jones, Milwaukee Fire Department Battalion Chief

AUTHOR'S NOTE

This story was inspired by two adorable little girls, around five and eight years of age, who lived across from Milwaukee Fire Station Five at Thirteenth and Reservoir, an inner-city area referred to as "The Core." I was assigned there as a firefighter for three years.

One night they showed up at the firehouse during the early morning hours. Their mother was being beaten by her boyfriend. She had sent them over to keep them out of danger. While we waited for the police, the girls and I talked. I learned a little of what their lives were like growing up in the crushing poverty and violence of the Core. They shared the disturbing details in an emotionless, matter-of-fact way as if this were simply the way of the world. For someone who grew up in a quiet middle-class neighborhood, this was unimaginable. I remember asking the girls whether they would be going to school after being up most of the night. They told me they were used to it and yes they would go to school. No doubt, these would be two of the inner-city children we often saw sleeping during class when we visited schools.

Years later, I still wonder what their lives have been like. Have they escaped the cycle of poverty or are they two more victims of an unjust childhood?

—Gregory Lee Renz

Red Devil's a ravenous bastard devoid of conscience. He'll devour all you hold dear and more. Dare to dance with him; he'll add you to the ashes.

Chapter 1

Lunch couldn't come soon enough. Mitch Garner had been mowing row after mind-numbing row of hay since early morning. His buzzing pager cut through the rumbling exhaust of the tractor. "All units respond to a report of smoke in the vicinity of 7600 County Q, north of Milroy. Repeat, all units respond—"

Mitch jammed the pager into his grungy overalls and sprinted to the milking parlor, leaving the moss-green John Deere 4020 in the middle of the half-mowed field. He stuck his head inside the parlor where his younger brother, eighteen-year-old Chris, was wiping down the teats of a cow. Mitch shouted over the hammering air compressor, "Hey, Chris, sounds like another grass fire out by the Hillenbrands. I gotta fly. Let Dad know."

"Sure, I'll tell him," Chris said while slipping a set of four cylindrical teat cups onto a stomping cow. "Just don't expect me to finish haying while you're out playing with your hose."

As he ran to his truck, Mitch's thoughts turned to last Sunday's potluck lunch at the Hillenbrands. Neighboring farm families had gathered to celebrate Maggie Hillenbrand's fifth birthday. Mitch had trailered his old pony, Bert, to Maggie's party as a surprise. When he had pulled to a stop, six pintsized children charged across the yard with Maggie out front. The flaxen-haired little girl jumped into his arms, hugging him hard around the neck. To the other children, she announced, "Mitchy's gonna marry me when I grow up. Then Bert'll be mine too. Just so you know." Mitch smiled to himself at the image of her beaming face.

Mitch fishtailed his metallic-gray Dodge Cummins pick-up down the drive, spewing gravel. The truck lurched violently when the enormous tires hit pavement. His heart raced as the speedometer approached ninety. Chest-high rows of corn alongside the road blurred into carpets of green.

Speeding to a scene was the best part of being a volunteer firefighter for the small town of Milroy, Wisconsin.

A half mile from the Hillenbrand farm, Mitch could already see dense black and gray columns of smoke rising over two tall silos, staining the blue sky. What smelled like a massive Saturday night bonfire, flooded through the truck's air vents. Cold beads of sweat trickled down his spine. As the youngest member of the department, the only fires he'd fought were grass fires. Now he'd be "first-in" at a major structure fire.

Mitch rounded the corner to the Hillenbrand's farm. Smoke billowed from the second-floor windows of the white Victorian farmhouse. He skidded the truck to a stop, making sure to leave room for fire rigs. Twelve-year-old Lydia Hillenbrand ran to him from the side of the house, her straggly red hair flying in all directions. Mitch sprang from the truck. Lydia clutched his arm, her body trembling, gasping for breath. "I can't—find Maggie."

"Where's your folks?"

"In town."

"When's the last time you saw her?"

"I don't *know*. I was in the barn, doing chores."

Mitch planted his sweaty John Deere hat on her small head and attempted a reassuring smile. "Stay here."

He ripped his firefighting gear from the aluminum cargo box in the truck bed. He stepped into the boots, pulled up the turnout pants, and snapped the red suspenders over his shoulders. His hands shook as he fastened the clasps of the canary-yellow Kevlar coat and strapped on the heavy helmet. He took a deep breath. "Where's Maggie's room?"

Lydia pointed at dark gray smoke raging from a second-floor window. "Maggie!"

The second-floor windows were too high to reach without a ladder. Mitch bolted into the old farmhouse. Light smoke on the first floor darkened to a dense haze as he climbed the stairs. Blackness engulfed the second-floor hallway.

"Maggie, you here?"

From far down the hallway, a tiny voice called out, "I'm scared." Then coughing.

Thank God. "I'm coming."

Mitch hunkered down and crawled into the darkness, keeping his nose and mouth close to the floor, trying to stay below the caustic blackness. The child's terrified screams pierced the blinding smoke.

He fought to control his breathing. The smoke thickened. The foul soup caught in his throat, gagging him. His arms and legs grew heavy. Flickering lights exploded in his head. He was drowning in smoke. *I have to get out.* The child's screams faded to a whimper, sending a chill through him. *I should know what to do. Why can't I think?*

Sirens echoed through the darkness. He backed down the stairs and stumbled into daylight. Big Jim Nelson, a broad-shouldered captain, leapt from the cab of a crimson fire engine.

Mitch coughed hard, hacking black phlegm onto the ground. He drew in a raspy breath. "Maggie's trapped on the second floor. We'll need masks."

Lydia stood at the edge of the yard with her hands on her head.

More trucks roared into the drive, splashing the house and barn with pulsating red and white lights. Sirens blared. Wide-eyed firefighters jumped from rigs as they rolled to a stop.

Jim called back to the others, "Get a line to the second floor. Me and Mitch are going in. Got a little girl up there. Start drafting from the pond. We'll need water. And get a ladder up to the second floor." He turned back to Mitch. "You okay?"

"Let's go." Mitch slung the mask harness onto his back, and they dashed into the burning home. At the top of the stairs, Mitch slid the facepiece into place and pulled the straps snug. The cold rubber cooled his sweating face. He opened the valve on the air bottle. The *shhhhht—shhhhht—shhhhht* of air coming into the mask calmed him. They pushed through the toxic smoke, past a burning room, to the end of the hallway and into Maggie's bedroom.

"Maggie?" Mitch called into the dark, eerie stillness. Nothing.

Mitch and Jim crawled through the pitch-black room, sweeping the hardwood floor with their arms and legs. Nothing. They found the bed and frantically searched around and under it. Nothing. They retraced their search pattern. Nothing.

"Sure she's here?" Jim said.

"She's gotta be here."

Mitch ripped the blankets from the bed and flipped the mattress over. He thrashed around the room, colliding with nameless shapes. *Where are you?* He found the closet and dug through a pile of clothes on the floor. His hand brushed a tiny bare foot. *A doll?* He lifted the small figure to his facepiece and shouted, "Got her."

Mitch cradled the limp child and ran into the hallway, pushing past firefighters who were dragging a hose line up the stairs. Two EMT's were waiting when he burst onto the porch. Bob, a veteran, pulled Maggie from Mitch's arms. The thick smoke had blackened her blond hair and smudged her face. Mitch's stomach heaved. He stared into her serene face, willing her to open her bright blue eyes. "Is she breathing?"

Jim pulled him back. "C'mon, they got her. We need a second line on the fire."

They ran to the rear of the fire engine where the pump operator piled hose on their shoulders. "Let me know when you want water," he hollered over the roar of the engine.

They tramped back to the house, the heavy hose stretching behind them. Mitch led the way inside and up the stairs. Before they reached the top, the house began to shake. A low rumble intensified to a thunderous roar. Mitch stopped. Jim gave him a light shove. "Med Flight. She's in good hands. Let's go."

A curtain of smoke swallowed them as they climbed the stairs. Garbled shouting rose above the crackle of the fire. They dropped to their hands and knees and crawled into the blackness, pulling hose with them. Barely visible through the smoke was the orange outline of a burning bed and dresser and the shadowy figures of three firefighters crouched low. Flames boiled up the wall, licking across the ceiling.

"Give us water on the second line," Jim said into his radio. The limp hose snapped erect. The nozzle hissed as Mitch bled trapped air from the hose. When water came, he slammed the bail open, nailing flames with a torrent of water.

"C'mon, people," Jim barked, the words muffled by his mask, "step it up, it's getting away from us. The Hillenbrands'll lose everything."

The crew yanked plaster off the wall with axes and pike poles. A ball of flames flashed at them from inside the opened wall, turning the room into a blast furnace. Mitch stayed low like he'd been taught, knowing if he stood, the heat would melt his mask and helmet. One breath of the nearly thousand-degree super-heated smoke only feet above him would be fatal.

4

Searing heat penetrated his gear, stinging his back until he couldn't take it any longer. He dropped the hose and crawled toward the doorway. The open hose line flailed around the floor like a crazed snake.

"It's in the walls. Get 'em open," Jim shouted. "Mitch, where's that second line?—Mitch, where the hell are you?"

The others dragged their hose line over him and blasted the flames, but the fire intensified.

"Someone grab that second line before we lose the whole goddamn place." Jim's booming voice broke through Mitch's panic.

Mitch corralled the flailing hose. "I got it."

Even with both lines on the fire, it showed no sign of surrendering. The tinder-dry wood in the frame of the old farmhouse offered no resistance. Flames licked at them from every freshly opened wall, spreading fire through the second floor.

"You three with Engine Thirty-Six, change your air bottles," Jim said. "We'll change ours when you get back. Make it quick."

Mitch struggled to understand Jim's muffled orders over the roar of the fire.

While Engine Thirty-Six's crew went to their rig to replace the fiberglass air bottles, the others worked to keep fire from engulfing the entire floor. They advanced on the fire, got pushed back, and advanced again, the Red Devil leading the dance.

When Jim and Mitch went to change their bottles, Mitch glanced at the chopper, which had landed in the open field next to the house. "I gotta see if she's okay."

"She's in good hands. C'mon, we gotta get back in there."

"I don't see Lydia."

"Probably in the squad. Let's go."

Mitch followed Jim back into the firefight. The fifty pounds of gear he wore felt like hundreds. He struggled to grip the heavy hose line. They'd been fighting the unrelenting demon for less than forty-five minutes but it seemed like hours. Throughout the firefight, Mitch's thoughts kept spinning back to Maggie, limp and lifeless in his arms.

"Listen up," Jim said. "Dispatch says they got a grass fire in Johnson Crick and a barn fire out on Eighteen. We're on our own. I know you guys are gassed. Let's give her hell one more time for the Hillenbrands. If we can't get it, we'll have to let her burn."

The room erupted with the sound of plaster crashing to the floor as the men ripped at the walls and ceiling with axes and pike poles. The hot smoke-filled room echoed with angry grunts of a weary crew. Mitch hit the fire with the full force of the hose line. He barely heard Jim above the deluge of water blasting against the walls. "We're getting it, guys, keep pounding her."

With the walls open, the fire was exposed with nowhere to hide. Alarms on air bottles blared, warning of only a few more minutes of air.

Jim was at Mitch's back. "C'mon, finish it."

Mitch advanced on the orange glow and drowned the remaining fire with a torrent of water. It flickered and died. The smoke gradually cleared, revealing the burned out second floor, plaster gone from the walls and ceilings. The deeply charred studs and joists resembled black alligator skin.

Mitch pulled off his mask. The acrid stench of smoke stung his nostrils. The family's beds, furniture, and clothing were reduced to smoldering piles of rubble. But the house still stood, the Red Devil denied.

They spent another half-hour shoveling rubble and ashes out windows and extinguishing the last of the dying embers.

Jim grabbed Mitch by the back of the neck. Mitch swallowed hard, figuring he'd be getting a bite in the ass for dropping the hose line. "Nice job, Mitch. A rescue and a fire. Way to hang in there."

Euphoria tickled his insides. Maggie was okay.

Jim surveyed the burned-out room. "Nice job, everyone. Let's pick up."

Mitch carried a load of hose down the stairs. He stepped onto the porch and squinted against the dust storm kicked up by the clattering rotors of Med Flight as it lifted off. When the dust cleared, he saw three EMTs gathered at the side yard beside a bright yellow sheet covering a small bundle.

Mitch dropped the hose and ran, struggling to breathe. Bob, the veteran EMT, stepped in front of him. "Mitch, Mitch! She didn't make it."

The words hit with the force of a sledgehammer.

"Why didn't they take her to the hospital?"

Bob stayed between Mitch and the tiny bundle. "Med Flight worked her for over an hour. They did everything possible. We all did."

"Why didn't they take her?" Mitch couldn't stop shaking.

"She was pronounced at the scene. Coroner has to investigate."

"That's bullcrap." Mitch's heart pounded in his ears. "Why didn't they take her?"

"Sorry, Mitch."

"You guys take her then." He leaned into Bob, his fist clenched.

Jim stepped between them. "She's gone, Mitch. Nothing more anyone can do."

"Please, Jim, tell them to take her." Mitch stared at the motionless sheet.

"Let's get you checked. You took a snoot-full in there."

A faded red Ford pickup sped into the gravel drive and slid to a stop alongside Mitch and Jim. John and Betty Hillenbrand leapt from the truck.

"Holy Christ," John said, scrambling around the truck to Mitch and Jim.

Betty gripped her husband's arm. A vein down the center of her forehead throbbed. "Mitch, where's the kids?"

Mitch couldn't get any words past the knot in his throat.

"Lydia's pretty shook up, but she's okay," Jim said.

"What about Maggie?" The heavy bags under Betty's eyes drooped. "Please say she's okay." She cupped her hands over her mouth.

Jim looked over to the yellow sheet in the yard where the three EMTs were silently putting away gear. His voice cracked. "Betty..."

She ran to the bundle and tore the sheet off. The tiny child was covered in soot with defibrillator pads still pasted to her bare chest. Betty dropped to her knees and wiped the soot from Maggie's face with the bottom of her white blouse.

Jim clutched Mitch's arm. "Let's get you checked out."

Mitch pushed him away, threw down his fire helmet, and stomped toward his truck. A siren wailed. He looked back. It was not a siren. Betty Hillenbrand was kneeling on the lawn, rocking her little girl, holding Maggie's head to her chest.

Chapter 2

Mitch trailed well behind his brother and father into the ancient country church. Warm reds, blues, and greens from stained glass windows washed over the somber assemblage. Pictures of Maggie with Jesus, drawn by the children of the congregation, lined the back wall. She was smiling in all of them.

Sid, Chris, and Mitch slipped into the back pew, their usual seats since the three of them rarely stayed awake through an entire sermon. Sid and Chris could be twins separated by years, stout and fair. Sid's hair was long-gone and Chris's already thinning. Mitch also took after his father's short stature but favored his mother's thick black hair and dark eyes.

Mitch tugged at the collar of his ill-fitting suit. Last time he wore it was four years ago at the Wisconsin High School Wrestling Awards Banquet in Madison. He won the State Championship in the one-hundred-fifty-two pound weight division, having gone undefeated senior year.

The sweltering August afternoon had the parishioners fanning themselves with funeral programs. Mitch shuddered as sweat ran down his forehead. The pastor's impassioned sermon echoed off the thick stone walls. He shared how Maggie was excited to be starting school next week and already had her backpack filled with supplies. He choked up and had to pause, then continued, telling the congregation she was in the hands of the ultimate teacher, Jesus.

Mitch struggled to focus. Images flashed through his mind: cradling infant Maggie in his arms, her squeals of glee when he chased toddler Maggie around the farmyard, and the laughter they shared over nonsensical jokes as she learned to talk.

After Mitch's mom died, the Hillenbrands stopped by every Sunday. Betty made them proper farm meals while John helped with chores. When

Lydia, then Maggie, came along, Mitch took charge of them while Betty worked in the kitchen. There was no better medicine than a hug and an Eskimo kiss from Maggie when he was feeling down.

Mitch's thoughts drifted to memories of his mom: her sad face the last time he saw her alive and her cruel words, *"I wish you were never born."* Her funeral had been held in this same church over twelve years ago. He was only ten.

Lydia's wails rose above the muffled sobs, bringing Mitch back to the sermon. His attention fixed on the tiny white casket with gold handles at the front of the church. On each side of the casket, banners hung from flower-filled vases displaying inscriptions: Precious Daughter, Loving Sister, Cherished Angel. None of this seemed real but it was. Maggie was in that tiny white box.

In the closing prayer, the pastor said, "We are so blessed to have such courageous firefighters serving our community and pray they find peace in knowing they did everything possible to save our beloved Maggie. Let us pray. Our Father, who art in heaven…"

Mitch rose. "I'm gonna start the milking. You guys can stay." Heads turned as he rushed out.

Yeah, right, courageous. Bullcrap. The drive home was a blur.

* * *

Mitch had always found refuge from the outside world in the milking parlor. The hum of the compressor, the steady *kachink—kachink—kachink* of the milking machine, and even the sweet-sour smell of manure mixed with the antiseptic smell of iodine was familiar and comforting. At milking time, the herd comes in from the pasture and lines up at the parlor, each cow waiting her turn to take her place in a stall. There's a rhythm and order to it: the animals, crops, and humans working together to nourish her, the farm.

The parlor door squeaked behind him.

"Need help finishing?" Sid asked.

"Nah, I got it."

"John and Betty wanted me to give you this." Sid held out the grimy baseball cap with the John Deere logo. "Said you left it at their place with Lydia. Poor girl blames herself for Maggie. Walks around in a trance, crying. Just a damn shame."

Mitch flung the cap in the corner. "Yeah, a damn shame."

"You okay?"

"Yeah, fine. Why?"

"You just, I don't know." Sid's voice trailed off. "You don't seem right."

Mitch swabbed the teats of a cow with orange antiseptic.

"For Christ's sake, Mitch. You ain't said more than five words to me or your brother since the fire. And Jennie keeps calling. At least talk to her."

Through clenched teeth, Mitch said, "I don't feel like talking. I need time. I'll handle it."

"Handle what?"

"Dad, let it go."

"You're acting like your mother."

"I'm not her," Mitch whispered.

Sid grunted and left.

* * *

After chores, Mitch walked into the woods bordering the farm. Twigs and decomposing underbrush crunched under his feet. Pine scent saturated the air. He plodded toward a majestic oak that towered above the other trees and saplings as if standing guard over its children. He leaned against the weathered giant's scales of bark and gazed at the elaborate treehouse perched twenty feet up in the thick limbs. They built this together, Mitch and his dad, before Mitch's mom died.

Mitch climbed the metal deer-stand ladder and pushed open the trapdoor, coughing from the dust cloud he stirred as he crawled inside. Dust-covered books were scattered on the floor and bookshelves. The musty smell of aging books took him back to his childhood.

Mitch's mother had scoured used book sales, encouraging him to read. She'd quiz him about the books he read when she wasn't in one of her dark moods. He spotted the copy of *A Tree Grows in Brooklyn*, remembering how she told him that while it wasn't an adventure book, it was her favorite when she was a young girl. When she gave it to him, she told him to wait and read it when he was older. He'd understand it then.

He brushed off the hardcover book and settled back into the old wooden rocker. He paged through the well-worn book, the rickety chair creaking as he rocked. Handwritten words on the last page set off a hollow ache in the pit of his stomach. *Mitch, when you finish reading this let me know what you liked about it. Love Mom.*

She was gone before Mitch had the chance to tell her how much he loved it.

The rectangle of light on the floor from the window was fading. He placed the book back on the bookshelf, climbed down the cold metal ladder, and trudged to the house, the leaves rustling behind him in the cool, evening breeze.

Dinner came after milking and chores. Tonight was Chris's turn to cook, and he put out burgers and chips, his specialty. Sid sat at the head of the solid oak table with Mitch and Chris on each side. The chair across from Sid was left vacant. It was *hers*. The twelve-foot ceiling of the cavernous kitchen echoed with grunts of men devouring chips and burgers. Dirty pots and pans littered one side of the countertop. Opened boxes of cereal, pancake mix, and Hamburger Helper were stacked on the other side.

"Think Sherman can handle being coach and general manager?" Chris asked.

Sid chomped on his hamburger without responding. Mitch had nothing to say. Green Bay Packer football usually prompted a lively discussion.

Headlights swung into the drive and flashed into the kitchen followed by the sound of tires crunching on gravel.

"Guess I'll get that. You two keep talking," Chris said and headed for the door.

"Mitch, it's Jim Nelson," Chris called from the front room.

Mitch hustled to the front room. Big Jim filled the doorway, holding Mitch's charred fire helmet. The once-white front piece was blackened.

Jim handed him the helmet. "That was a hot son of a bitch, eh?"

"What's up?"

Jim took two steps inside. "Chief wants everyone down to the station tomorrow. He's bringing in a psychologist."

"If I can get the hay in."

"Mitch, you're a good fireman. You need to know that."

"Sure."

Jim turned to leave, then stopped. "How you doing? Really?"

"See you tomorrow, Jim."

After Jim's truck rolled down the drive, Mitch went upstairs and flung the charred fire helmet into the corner of the closet alongside the grimy John Deere cap he had brought up from the milking parlor. He stretched out on the small single bed, praying this was all a bad dream.

* * *

Next morning at breakfast, Jennie McAdams strolled into their kitchen wearing blue nursing scrubs, her auburn hair pulled back in a tight ponytail. She wasn't well-endowed nor did she have full lips or a small, perfect nose, but to Mitch, his high-school sweetheart was damn sexy, country sexy. "You guys sure are a lively bunch."

Chris waved her over. "Hey, Jen. Sit. Talk. Forgot what humans sound like."

"Stopped by to say 'hi' to my man on the way to Madison," Jennie said. "Haven't heard much from him lately."

Mitch tried to grin. "Hey, Jen."

"Wow, try to restrain your excitement. Jeez."

Sid rose. "C'mon, Chris, let's get to work."

"He talks," Chris said and followed Sid out.

Jennie moved onto Mitch's lap. "Why won't you talk to me when I call?"

"It's hard for me to talk right now."

"Yeah. I get that. Anything I can do?"

"Just need time."

"Mitch, please, let me help." Jennie lifted his chin, forcing him to look at her. He adored that face: her freckled nose, mouth a bit too wide, and those chocolate-brown eyes.

"I'll be all right."

She clutched his chin. "Please talk to me."

"Talking won't bring Maggie back."

"At least talk to Pastor," she pleaded. "Maybe he can help."

"Sure, accept Jesus Christ as your savior and the peace of the Lord is yours. I sat through those sermons all my life. It's a pile of crap." He couldn't stop himself from shouting. "My dad says just get over it. Well, that's what I'm gonna do—just get over it—if you and everyone else would leave me the hell alone."

She winced. "Fine."

After a long pause, she gently asked, "Mitch, really? Is that what you want?"

No answer. She left.

Mitch plodded to the machine shed and climbed onto the faded red Massey Ferguson tractor. The manure spreader was hooked up and loaded. Out in the field, the antique tractor clattered and belched while struggling to pull the heavy load in the hot sun. Spinning rotors at the rear of the spreader were supposed to fling manure behind it, but the rusty fossil pitched the mess in all directions. Everything within striking distance became splattered, including tractor and driver. Mitch bounced along the field on the metal tractor seat, the pungent smell of manure filling the air. The deafening noise, black oily smoke, and his aching back took his mind off Maggie and his mom.

After spreading manure, he headed to the hay field and baled hay until after dark, missing the meeting at the firehouse. He'd get over this. Just like he did when his mom died.

Chapter 3

A black BMW sports car inched up the long gravel drive toward the farmhouse the following morning. Mitch watched from the machine shed where he was pulling gears from the old Massey Ferguson tractor.

A tall, slim man in a gray suit uncoiled himself from the small car and gazed across the farmyard. He didn't see Mitch and Mitch didn't feel obliged to greet him. The man bounded up the porch steps. Billy, their chunky black Labrador, ambled across the porch, sniffed the man's crotch, then returned to his blanket. The front door opened and the man stepped inside.

Mitch knew it wouldn't be long before Sid sent the salesman packing. When the man didn't come out after half an hour, Mitch's curiosity gnawed at him. Besides, he was ready for some lunch and ice water. It was over ninety degrees and only eleven o'clock.

He trudged to the house, stepped into the mudroom, and slipped off his black muck boots. He hung his grease-stained coveralls from a hook on the once-white wall that was now the color of mud and cow crap. The small room reeked of farm and fermenting sweat. Muffled voices filtered in from the kitchen. Mitch washed up in the metal scrub basin, then went into the kitchen.

The Buddha-like figure of Sid, rotund middle and bald head, was reaching across the table with open palms, asking something of the salesman. Conversation stopped when they spotted Mitch.

The salesman stood and offered his hand. "You must be Mitch. I'm Doctor—"

"Look, I have a tractor to fix. I don't have time." Mitch walked past Sid and snatched a bottle of water from the refrigerator. He pressed the cold plastic bottle against his sweltering forehead. "Any ham left?"

"Talk to the man. I'll take care of chores."

"Your captain asked me to stop by. Can we?" The doctor dropped his outstretched hand and gestured toward the table.

Sid left.

"Suppose, since Jim sent you." Mitch slugged half the bottle of cold water, then slumped into his chair.

"I was at the firehouse yesterday talking to your partners about the fire. Losing that child has been extremely traumatic for everyone."

"Maggie's her name."

"Yes, yes, of course, Maggie. Captain Nelson said you were the one who found her. Tragic."

"Yup, tragic all right. That all you wanted to tell me, Doc—what was it?"

"Mallory, Jeff Mallory. Sorry."

"Yeah, Mallory, Jeff Mallory, we're all sorry, and I don't see how sitting around talking about it's going to change a thing." Mitch pushed away from the table and stood. "I've got work to do."

"Your dad shared some painful details of your past. Please, sit. I know about your mom."

I know about your mom. Mitch slumped back into the chair. "What'd he say?"

"Mitch, I'm a clinical psychologist. I help people deal with post-traumatic stress."

"So, you're a shrink."

"I work with police and fire departments around the state. Things you people see and do can result in the same type of distress as our military people."

I know about your mom. "Still don't know what you want from me."

"I'll try not to sound too clinical, but this posttraumatic stress disorder or PTSD can manifest in numerous ways. When a person experiences a traumatic event, it's like an injury to the brain. The person might shut down, trying to ignore the event or start acting out in anger. They might start drinking heavily or self-medicating with drugs. They might struggle with relationships, alienating from family and friends."

I know about your mom. "I have to get back to work."

The doctor thrust his palm at Mitch. "The result can be serious chronic depression. We see this not only in the fire and police service but also in children who've suffered traumatic events or abuse."

15

Mitch slugged the rest of the cold water. "So, what do you do about it?"

"Early intervention is critical. Some therapists prescribe anti-anxiety drugs. Personally, I believe in cognitive-behavioral therapy. We're starting to see some encouraging results, especially with children."

The water bottle crackled as Mitch pointed it at the doctor. "Yeah? Why couldn't you shrinks help my mom?"

"Your dad said you were only ten. That's a lot to deal with."

"Thought you were here to talk about the fire?"

"I'm concerned the trauma of coping with the tragic death of Maggie could trigger painful memories."

"I'm fine."

"Suicide devastates those left behind, especially children. They tend to blame themselves."

"I'm fine," Mitch said in a whisper, his heart racing.

"Your mother's suicide was not your fault, and from what Captain Nelson said, there was no way you could have saved Maggie. In fact, he said your efforts were extremely heroic."

"Real heroes save lives or die trying so that counts me out."

The doctor rose and handed Mitch his card. "Help's available when you're ready."

Mitch followed him to the porch.

The doctor stopped, faced Mitch, and held out his hand.

Mitch took it and said, "Guess I was kind of a jerk in there."

"According to your partners, you're hardly a jerk. Far from it. You're dealing with devastating issues. Get some help. And you're wrong about heroes."

Chapter 4

Nights became unbearable. During the day, Mitch worked himself to exhaustion but no matter how tired he was, sleep came in short, fitful bursts, interrupted by visions of Maggie's soot-darkened face and piercing screams.

Moonlit shadows crept across Mitch's bedroom wall. The light blue display on the bedside clock flashed 4:15. He gave up on sleep and rode the four-wheeler out to the back pasture. The cows were spread over the pasture, resting peacefully, shadows under the full moon. He shut down the four-wheeler and stretched out, resting his feet on the handlebars. The warm night air was dense with moisture and filled with the scent of cows and ripening crops. Mitch relaxed and soaked in the loud hissing of cicadas and the incessant chirping of katydids and crickets. This is where he always had felt connected and at peace. But no longer. For the last two weeks, he couldn't stop thinking about what the doctor said about his mom's suicide and PTSD. Maybe he *should* get help. Maybe Jennie was right.

The bright moon still owned the sky, but the birds were already chirping in anticipation of another sunrise. To the east, a tinge of orange peeked over the tall ripe cornfields, casting an early morning glow across their farm. Red-winged blackbirds chased each other over the pasture. The clear sky promised another long day in the wheat field.

He went to the house and poured himself a thermos of black coffee and threw together three cheese and salami sandwiches to eat on the run. He dragged himself to the field and went to work.

The sea of golden wheat undulated in hypnotic waves as Mitch plowed the enormous John Deere 7720 combine through row after monotonous row. Dry, hot gusts of wind whistled through the rattling door of the combine. He struggled on. One good downpour could put a halt to the harvest. The greasy sandwiches, sleepless nights, and sweltering afternoon had his head bobbing. The blaring radio no longer helped. He couldn't fight the exhaustion any longer. One last trip to the edge of the field by the ravine, then he'd head back to the house for a short break and to refill the empty coffee thermos.

Before reaching the end of the row, he had to close his eyes, just for a few seconds.

* * *

Mitch slammed against the side of the cab. Then the other side. The steering column rammed him in the chest, knocking the wind out of him. He tumbled over and over and over, helpless as the combine crashed into the ravine. His forehead slammed against the top of the cab.

Everything went still.

Stabbing pain shot through Mitch's chest when he tried to straighten. Flames engulfed the engine compartment, spreading fast. Oily smoke filled the cab. His nostrils burned. The combine was on its side with the door wedged against the ground. Mitch kicked at the side-window escape hatch, sending sparks of pain up his spine. The window didn't budge. There was no other way out. Ignoring the pain, he bashed the window again with a ferocious kick. Nothing. His legs went rubbery.

He drew both legs back, grimaced, and gave it one last desperate blow. "Ahhh."

The window flew into the marsh. He crawled from the cab. The metallic taste of blood gagged him. He hacked up bright red froth, slobbering ribbons of it down the front of his T-shirt.

He scrambled up the ravine, clutching his chest to control the sharp pain that came with each breath. He had no cell phone and no choice but to hobble over the choppy soil of the wheat field to the milking parlor, which was a good quarter mile away.

* * *

Mitch burst into the parlor, trailed by the smell of smoke. He bent low at the waist, gasping for air. Sid and Chris spun around, their mouths gaping open as if he were some bloody apparition.

"Holy Christ," Sid said.

"Call 911. Combine's on fire. It's in the ravine."

"What the hell is it doing down there?"

"Just call, Dad. I'm gonna grab extinguishers."

Mitch limped to the machine shed and threw two dry-chem extinguishers on the four-wheeler. He sped back to the combine to find it engulfed in flames. He shuddered. He could still be in there.

Fire had spread to the wheat field and marsh. With the dry summer, the marsh was a tinderbox patiently waiting for the smallest spark. The extinguishers were useless. He waited helplessly for the fire engines and water tankers to arrive.

Flames tore across the tall marsh grass sending plumes of smoke into the howling winds. By the time the Milroy Department arrived, the fire had already consumed fifty acres of marsh, leaving black, scorched earth behind. The wheat field had been reduced to smoldering stubble.

Big Jim bounced across the open field in the fire department's all-terrain Gator while pumpers and tankers rolled into the farmyard. Jim leapt off the Gator, his head swiveling. "Holy shit." He pointed at Mitch's face. "You need that looked at."

Mitch swiped his clammy forehead. His hand came away smeared with blood. "I'm staying."

"Have it your way. Chief wants everyone in the farmyard."

Mitch raced to the farmyard ahead of Jim. He skidded to a stop at the driveway. Wide-eyed cattle trotted by with Billy running alongside, barking. Sid and Chris jogged behind the herd, hollering at the confused animals, pushing them along. Sid scowled at him as they passed.

The chief shouted orders to a dozen firefighters at the top of the drive. Mitch and Jim hurried to the group.

"Sid's evacuating the herd," the chief said to Jim. "Let's clear the farmyard, anything that can burn. And start wetting down the house with foam."

Mitch stepped forward. "What about a fire line?"

"We'll clear a fire line when I get enough people. Now, everyone, get to work."

The firefighters pulled chainsaws and axes from the rigs. Mitch clutched Jim's arm. "This is bullcrap. We should be setting up a fire line."

"Chief's right."

"But, Jim, if it gets to the woods, it'll take out the whole farm."

"Grab a saw and start in on the bushes surrounding the house."

"I'm not cutting down my mom's bushes."

"Then help with the foam."

Mitch pulled a hose line from the engine and began lobbing foam onto the house. He had to look away from the sight of his mother's cherished lilac bushes being cut down and hauled away.

Neighboring farmers lined the road with cattle haulers. A steady procession of fire rigs lumbered in from surrounding rural departments.

Rigs shuttled water back and forth from town to the farm. Ten rural departments and close to a hundred firefighters spread over the farmland to stop the fire's advance. Crews hollered over the deafening staccato of chainsaws. Firefighters scurried for tools and hose lines. Officers clamped radios to their ears trying to hear commands over the racket.

The rampaging fire closed in on crews who were clearing a fire line in the marsh, forcing them to retreat. Within minutes the fire reached the dense woods. Dry brush and timber exploded into a firestorm, shooting flames high in the air. Less than two hours after the combine went up in flames, fire had covered over three hundred acres and was now hurling through the woods toward the Garner homestead. The spectacle sucked the wind out of Mitch.

"Okay, people," the chief ordered over the radios. "Move the rigs to the road. We can't hold this any longer."

Big Jim traipsed over to Mitch. "That's it, then."

Mitch continued spraying the house.

Jim grabbed him by the arm and yanked him toward the street. "You can thank me for saving your ass later."

Farmers, firefighters, and rigs assembled along the road, powerless to stop the Red Devil from laying waste to everything in its path. Crews posed next to their rigs like mannequins, watching. Chris, Sid, and their dog, Billy, watched with the crew from Johnson Creek. The defeat on the old man's face devastated Mitch. For three generations their family had worked this farm.

The wall of fire thundered toward the house. Mitch's face stung from the radiant heat. At the far end of the property, the machine shed exploded in a ball of flame. The deafening blast sent a shiver through him. This was it. He thought about walking down the road and never coming back but was transfixed by the writhing kaleidoscope of oranges, reds, blues, and greens swirling through the flames. He sat on the running board of the Milroy fire engine paralyzed by the sight, waiting for their home to explode in flames like the shed.

Beneath the Flames

Billowing smoke blotted the sun, casting an eerie orange haze over the landscape. The entire woods was aflame, crackling in the howling wind with only the farmyard separating the raging fire from the house and barn. A cloud of steam rose from the foam blanketing the house.

Chapter 5

By mid-afternoon, the flames faded into a white, smoldering haze. Fire crews descended on the marsh and woods to stomp out any dying embers that could flare up if the wind suddenly changed direction. The tallest trees still stood, but everything else in the woods was reduced to ash by the fast-moving fire.

Mitch went to work shoveling dirt onto hot embers, ignoring the racking pain in his ribs. Throughout the late afternoon, he silently worked alongside his crew from Milroy, staying far away from Sid.

He kept gazing back at the farmyard. It didn't seem real. The side of the white house facing the woods was blackened. Ashes covered the barn and milking parlor. The chief was right. The foam and farmyard clearing saved their home, barn, and milking parlor from the blistering attack of the Red Devil.

Most of the departments pitched in until late in the night. After the last rig left, Mitch walked across the burned wheat field to the ravine. The brittle, charred stubs of wheat crunched under his boots. The smoky stench left by the fire obliterated the farm's earthy smell.

Mitch sat for a long time at the edge of the ravine staring down at the burned-out shell of the combine lying on its side in its barren graveyard. Why did he fight so hard to get out? The bright moon illuminated the desolate earth for as far as he could see. There was no sadness, just a hollow ache for the nightmare to end.

Mitch wandered the property and lost track of time. Morning couldn't be far off. He walked into the woods stirring up noxious ashes with every step, stinging his eyes and leaving an acrid taste in his mouth. The towering oak still stood but was gravely scorched. At the base of the tree, was the burned rubble of his treehouse with piles of burned and half-burned books. Mitch picked through the books until he found the hard copy of *A*

Tree Grows in Brooklyn. The cover was singed, but it had protected the book from burning through. He turned to the inscription on the last page. *Mitch, when you finish reading this, let me know what you liked about it. Love Mom.* He clutched the book to his chest, smearing soot across his blood-stained T-shirt.

After wandering on in a trance, he found himself in front of the remains of the machine shed. In the middle of the ruins stood the blackened skeleton of his treasured Massey Ferguson tractor, the machine he had nursed back to health so many times over the years.

Sid stomped down the porch steps and called across the farmyard, "Mitch, let's get the cattle. They need milking."

A wave of nausea hit him. He fell in behind Sid and Chris as they tramped to the pasture where the neighbors had moved the cattle. They walked in silence. The sun poked over the horizon. Mitch felt no warmth in the dawning of a new day.

"Dad, I don't know what to say. Bad stuff just keeps happening."

"Not now." Sid kept walking as if he were marching to war, hunched forward swinging his arms.

"Dad, you need to know …"

Sid spun. "Now you want to talk. Okay, let's talk. You crash the combine, almost burn us out, destroy the wheat crop, and this just happens? Bullshit."

"Dad, please."

"We've walked on eggshells for the last month. You told us to leave you alone. We did. Now we almost lose the farm. Still might. How we gonna pay the bills with no wheat? How we gonna harvest corn with no combine? Is that just gonna happen? Go ahead, talk." Sid latched onto Mitch's shoulders and shook viciously. Sid's watery bloodshot eyes bored into him. Mitch went numb. Sid shoved him. "Just like your goddamn mother. Get out of my sight."

Chris stepped in front of Sid. "Dad, c'mon. It was an accident. He's your son for God's sake."

"That's no son of mine." Sid pushed Chris. "We got work to do." He pointed at Mitch. "Go."

Mitch drifted back to the house in a fog. Billy greeted him at the porch, panting, wagging his tail. He ignored the dog and went inside.

The image in the dingy mirror in the mudroom shocked him. Streaks of sweat lined his coal-black face. The gash on his forehead had stopped bleeding. He explored the raw flesh lining his mouth, then ripped off his

23

T-shirt and tossed the blood-stained rag into the trash. The noxious smoke had saturated everything: skin, hair, and clothes. The stinging pain of the open gash as the hot water hit comforted him in a strange way. He stood under the shower until the water ran cold, then dried off and pulled on fresh shorts.

He wiped the soot from *A Tree Grows in Brooklyn* and limped upstairs holding the book to his chest. He lay down and opened the book to the last page, focusing on the last two words, *Love Mom*.

"Is this what you felt like before taking those pills?"

Chapter 6

Two days after the fire, Mitch was in the scorched wheat field before daybreak, dragging a twenty-foot disc plow over the ground with the John Deere 8200. He had been getting up early and coming in late to avoid Sid. The stench of burned timber and brush hung over the farm, leaving a bitter taste in his mouth.

The sun lifted over the horizon illuminating the bare trunks, limbs, and branches of the blackened woods, the woods where Mitch hunted deer, the woods he loved to explore as a young boy, alive with squirrels, chipmunks, insects, and shrieking blue jays. He had marveled at the endless shades of green among the ferns, leaves, and thick underbrush, and how it all changed through the seasons. Now everything was shades of gray and black, the color of death, the animals gone.

The tractor's CD player blared, but he wasn't listening. His last thread of hope had died in the fire. All he thought about the last forty-eight hours was the plan. He finally had it all worked out. Mitch's mother had demanded Sid take out life insurance policies on everyone many years ago. Mitch's policy would help pay bills for a while. And they could sell his truck.

After chores, he'd go into the woods to cut down some damaged trees for firewood. He'd carefully notch the giant oak with the chainsaw so it would fall slowly at first, giving him time to get under it before it crashed to the ground. Heavy branches would be strewn about the tree for him to trip on, making it look like a terrible accident. No notes and no lingering guilt left behind for Sid and Chris to struggle with. And no more pain.

The end of the field was in sight. Mitch shut down the tractor. He needed some quiet time to reflect. If the pastor was right, he'd join his mom in heaven and be able to tell Maggie how sorry he was. Mitch never bought into the whole heaven and hell stuff, but what did he know? Lately, he wasn't sure of anything.

Well back in the woods stood the towering oak, visible now that the leaves and branches had burned off most of the trees. Steel cables that had supported the treehouse shimmered in the early morning sun, appearing to be tears streaming down the tree's blackened trunk. The metal deer stand ladder used for climbing into the treehouse led to, nothing.

Mitch shook his head hard, put the tractor in gear, and finished plowing the rest of the field.

* * *

Chris and Sid were at the kitchen table slurping coffee when Mitch came in from the field. He rushed by them to the front room and clicked on the TV. He stretched out on the old brown couch with threadbare arms that smelled like dirty laundry. The shades in the musty room were drawn for napping between chores. After the noon chores, he'd head out to the woods for the last time. Knowing today was the day gave him a strange sense of peace. It would all be over soon.

The dingy screen of the electronic relic warmed to life. Smoke billowed from two high-rise buildings.

"The President has declared this a terrorist attack," Tom Brokaw announced in a somber voice.

Mitch stared at the image on the screen, trying to make sense of what he was seeing. Matt Lauer and Katie Couric said something about hijacked airplanes.

A cloud of gray and white smoke mushroomed from one of the buildings.

"Holy crap!"

Sid and Chris burst into the room.

"What's going on?" Sid asked.

"I don't know, Dad."

"What'd they say?"

"Dad, I don't know."

They huddled around the television, Sid sitting on the edge of the scuffed leather recliner and Chris next to Mitch on the couch.

The mountain of smoke erupting from the building was replayed in slow motion from several angles. Tom Brokaw told Matt Lauer it looked like a chunk of the building had peeled away.

Within minutes, Lauer said they just received a report that the South Tower of the World Trade Center had collapsed.

Mitch sucked in a deep breath.

"Damn," Chris said.

Sid clenched his fists.

Mitch strained to comprehend the frantic reports streaming in: the Pentagon on fire, all air traffic grounded, more possible attacks, evacuations occurring around the country, and live video of the North Tower burning. His thoughts turned to the firefighters. Did they get everyone out of the other tower before it collapsed? And did *they* all get out?

The three of them gasped as the mammoth North Tower collapsed. Their mouths hung open as the tower crumbled to the ground hurling a wall of gray ash through the streets of Manhattan.

Sid sprang to his feet and stomped around the room, his face beet red. "They know who did this?"

"Something about a terrorist attack," Mitch said.

"Time we put an end to them bastards and nuke the whole goddamn Middle East. Turn those deserts to glass. Goddamn towel heads."

Mitch leaned closer to the television. "Dad, we can't hear."

Sid moved in front of him, blocking the television. "What did you say?"

"Nothing, sorry," Mitch whispered.

"I'll be out trying to keep this farm going in case anyone wants to get off their ass and help."

Sid's boots clomped against the hard linoleum of the kitchen floor followed by a loud bang of the screen door.

"Man, one of these days he's gonna blow a gasket," Chris said. "I better go help. You done plowing?"

Mitch gave him a quick nod. He couldn't leave. He had to know what happened to the firefighters.

The afternoon became a blur of videos, endless speeches, and interviews. Images of people jumping to their deaths sickened him.

* * *

The smell of beef stew drifted into the musty living room. It was after eight. Mitch had no appetite.

"Dad cool down?" Mitch asked Chris when he entered the front room, gnawing on a Snickers Bar.

"What do you think? Anything new?"

"They're searching for people in the ruins."

"How many?"

"They figure thousands."

"The firefighters make it out?"

Mitch's stomach knotted.

Chris stopped chewing. "Jesus, what's wrong?"

They sat in silence until Mitch could get the words out. "Those firefighters must have known they might not make it out. They went in anyway." He stretched his arms wide. "Because that's their job, Chris, to save people or die trying. You understand?"

"Yeah, that's awesome, but why you so worked up?"

"Because if I had their balls, Maggie'd still be alive."

Chris frowned. "Or you'd both be dead."

"At least I'd be able to live with myself."

"That's crazy talk. It don't make sense."

"I know, right? Nothing does." Mitch attempted a weak smile. "I'll be fine. Go to bed."

"Okay, just stop that crazy talk."

Mitch drifted off watching the news reports well into the night.

He woke to more reports and videos. Two ghostlike firefighters covered in gray soot were explaining the eerie high-pitched wailing coming from the rubble shortly after the collapse of the buildings. The sound was from the PASS devices, Personal Alert Safety Systems, firefighters wear that give off a piercing wail when a firefighter is motionless for more than thirty seconds or manually triggered by a firefighter in distress. The despair on their ashen faces left no doubt what that meant.

Another video showed a firefighter carrying a woman from the North Tower just before it collapsed. The reporter said she was in a wheelchair on the twenty-fifth floor and the firefighter carried her all the way down. Had he not found her and taken her out, he'd have perished in the tower along with her and the thousands of others.

The intenseness of the firefighter's face and serenity of the woman's face blew Mitch away. In that instant, the hopelessness lifted. He knew what he had to do.

Chapter 7

The tired drone of the mail truck signaled it was noon. The rural carrier was never more than a few minutes off. Mitch jogged down the drive to the mailbox to check for the letter he'd been waiting on since the first of March. He dug through the ads and found it. The return address read *City of Milwaukee Police and Fire Commission*.

After 9/11, the reports of the incredible acts of courage had steeled Mitch's resolve to join the Milwaukee Fire Department. The hope of becoming a professional firefighter silenced the suicidal thoughts, but he continued to struggle with suffocating guilt. Friends had stopped coming by, and Jennie stopped pushing him to talk when they saw each other, which wasn't often. They drifted apart. That would all change once he proved himself as a professional firefighter.

The Milroy Savings and Loan financed their purchase of a used combine that Mitch had to recondition, but warned them the farm was at the limit for future loans. After the fall harvest of corn, the workload on the farm eased over the winter, giving Mitch plenty of time to prepare for the fire department entrance exam. Big Jim supplied him with study materials for the written exam and advice on preparing for the physical agility test and the oral interview. Big Jim had applied to both the Madison and Milwaukee departments but never placed high enough to get hired. He told Mitch that Milwaukee gets thousands of applications for fewer than one hundred openings. Chances of getting on were slim to none. Big Jim was the only one who knew Mitch had applied.

Mitch was sure he aced the written exam, and the physical agility test was no challenge. But he got flustered during the oral exam and was sure he blew it.

He swallowed hard before opening the envelope.

His vision blurred as he read.

Dear Sir,

Your name has been certified for appointment as Firefighter in the Milwaukee Fire Department...

* * *

Sid came in late from the barn and joined Mitch and Chris at the table. Tonight was Mitch's turn to make supper. He prepared Sid's favorite, meatloaf with buttered mashed potatoes.

"Dad, I got something important to tell you," Mitch blurted out.

Through a mouthful of meatloaf, Sid said, "We should start planting end of the month. The planter ready to go?"

"Dad."

"Seed ordered?"

"I got hired by the Milwaukee Fire Department."

"What the hell you talking about?"

Chris choked.

"I start training next month." Mitch talked fast. "Once my wages kick in, I can send money back to help pay bills. And once I get through training, I can come back on my off days and help during planting and harvesting. Dad, I—"

"Twelve years I been raising you myself. And this is how you thank me? By running off to that cesspool to play fireman with those black bastards."

"I have to do this."

"You're only twenty-two. How the hell do you know what you have to do?"

Mitch's voice cracked. "I have to do this."

"Then pack your goddamn bags and get the hell off my farm. And keep your money. I don't want it." Sid rose and flung the heavy oak chair backward. "Make sure you're gone by morning." He stomped up the stairs muttering, "Goddamn ungrateful son of a bitch."

Chris's mouth gaped open. "So what you gonna do?"

"Guess I'll see if Jen will let me stay with her until I move to Milwaukee."

"How we gonna run the farm without you?"

"Talk to the Pulvermachers. I think their oldest kid is looking for work. He's good with machinery."

"My brother, the big-city fireman. Just don't go getting burnt up."

Beneath the Flames

* * *

Mitch shoved a worn duffle bag full of clothes and toiletries. He sighed when he uncovered the scorched fire helmet and weathered John Deere hat. He didn't pack them. When he got to the bed stand, he opened *A Tree Grows in Brooklyn*, read the inscription one more time, and put the book back.

The flooring on the second floor of the old farmhouse creaked as he headed to the stairs in the dark. Chris's door rattled. Mitch stopped and dropped the duffle. The brothers embraced silently in the darkness. Chris choked back a sniffle and went back to his room. The door latch clicked. Mitch slung the duffle over his shoulder and moved to the stairs.

Billy lifted his head off the blanket when Mitch stepped onto the porch. Mitch knelt and hugged the old, plump dog around the neck and buried his face in Billy's earthy coat. A ball of sadness welled in his chest. "You're the best dog on the planet, old boy."

Billy licked the side of Mitch's face with his rough tongue and whined.

Before driving away, Mitch looked back to the porch. Billy tilted his head and wagged his tail.

* * *

Jennie greeted him at the door of her flat wearing the oversized Green Bay Packers T-shirt she slept in. "Kinda late, isn't it?"

"Got something I have to tell you."

She pointed at the green canvas duffle bag. "Going camping?"

"Got any beer?"

She frowned. "Okay? This better be good."

He threw the duffle next to the brown leather sofa she had inherited from her grandmother. The apartment was tiny and spotless, smelling of lemon-scented Pledge with a trace of cinnamon. An antique cuckoo clock and a painting of black and white Holsteins grazing on the side of a hill hung on the far wall. It was a painting of her grandparent's farm where she spent summer days helping milk cows and bale hay, painted by her grandmother before cancer took her.

Mitch settled into the cushy sofa. Jennie wedged herself against him and handed him a bottle of Miller Lite. She took a long drink from hers and leaned back, her T-shirt riding up her bare thighs. She had nothing on underneath. Mitch couldn't help staring.

She clenched his chin. "Is that what you came for?"

"What? No." He attempted to smile. "I had a craving for your cinnamon buns."

"Right."

"Jen…"

"So serious."

His hand shook as he lifted the bottle. The cold amber sizzled down his throat. He chugged half before putting it down. "I'm joining the Milwaukee Fire Department."

"Umm, okay? When?"

"Next month. I get sworn in on the eighth and start training on the ninth."

"So, you're leaving in what, three weeks?" Her face reddened. "And you're just telling me now?" She poked him in the chest. "Christ, you're a piece of work."

She finished her beer and peeled the label off the bottle. "The only time I get your attention is when you're horny. So, go ahead, leave. See what I care." She poked him again, harder. "You're an asshole." She sank back on the couch with her arms clamped across her chest.

"Jen, please. I didn't want to tell anybody until I knew. You saw what I was like after I let—after Maggie died, I was a mess. I almost…"

"Almost what?"

"After mom died, the Hillenbrands treated us like family. I got to hold little Maggie the day after she was born. Her and Lydia were like my kid sisters." Mitch choked back tears. "Why couldn't I save her?"

Jennie smoothed his thick black hair and pressed her forehead against his. "You *have* to stop blaming yourself."

"When I saw what those firefighters did on 9/11, it hit me. If I could do that, just maybe, I could feel normal again. I want to be with you more than anything. But I have to do this."

"How can you be with me if you're in Milwaukee?"

Mitch pulled her close. "Jen, I love you. I do."

"It's been a while since I heard that." Her voice softened. "How we gonna do this? I still have a year to go in nursing school."

She burrowed her head into his chest and sighed. The cuckoo clock chimed once. "What did you almost do?"

"Nothing."

"Didn't look like nothing from that look on your face." Jennie's serene brown eyes soothed him. Their lips met. Her mouth tasted of beer and mint toothpaste. He slid his hand under the Green Bay Packers T-shirt. Her small breast responded to his gentle caress. She slipped her hand inside his jeans. Within seconds she had him hard. He pulled her hand away before it was over.

He lifted her T-shirt over her head. The sight of her bare breasts nearly sent him over the edge. She stretched back on the couch and opened herself to him. He caught the slightest, musky scent of arousal. She gripped his thick hair as he brushed his lips over her breasts. She pulled his face to hers and ran her tongue over his. She leaned back, her eyes glassy. "I want you now."

Mitch tore his clothes off and lowered himself onto her, their bodies fitting together like warm, sensuous pieces of a puzzle, every curve fitting perfectly. She wrapped her legs around him and pulled him inside, whimpering. She stared into his eyes, their faces inches apart, her breath hot against his lips. They started slow. He wanted to make it last. But she pushed faster and harder until he couldn't hold back. They collapsed into one another, sweating, chests heaving.

They had come a long way from the first time, both sixteen, when he was done before they got started.

"Let's go to bed," Jennie said after they caught their breath. "I have classes in the morning, then clinicals in the afternoon. I'm exhausted."

"Got any cinnamon buns?"

"So that is what you came for." She headed for the bedroom swinging her slim hips. She glanced back and smirked. "Get me one."

They sat naked on her small bed and stuffed their mouths with the sweet, pillowy buns like two kids sneaking candy. Jennie licked the cream cheese frosting from his fingers. "What did your dad think about all this?"

"He kicked me out."

Her eyes narrowed. "Soo, you planning on staying here?"

"I was hoping."

"You really are a piece of work. Your dad kicks you out, and you show up on my doorstep telling me you plan on staying here until you move to Milwaukee? How's that supposed to make me feel?"

Mitch clenched his lips.

"Used. That's how it makes me feel." Her eyes blazed.

"I'll get my stuff and leave." He rose from the bed.

She grabbed his arm and pulled him back. "God, you're impossible."

They finished off the buns and slipped under the cool cotton sheets. He buried his nose in her auburn hair, lost in the smell of her lavender-scented shampoo. The warmth of her firm body pressed against him had him hungry for more. He slid his hand down her side and up the inside of her thigh. Her hand moved below his waist, teasing his pubic hair with her fingertips. The taste of cinnamon on her lips was intoxicating. He was ready. She crawled on top and they settled into the blissful rhythm of lovers.

Mitch slept through the night for the first time in months. No tormenting images of Maggie or his mom jerked him awake.

* * *

Mitch woke to the sound of the shower and the smell of fresh-brewed coffee. He pulled the shower curtain open to a cloud of steam. Jennie stopped shampooing and handed him a bar of soap. "Here, get my back."

He worked the soap over her shoulders and back, then around to her breasts. She spun and faced him. "I got those already." He pulled her slippery, soap covered body against his. She pushed him away. "Sweetie, this is really good. But I have to get going."

He reached for the curtain, embarrassed.

"Wait, I can't leave you like that. You'll never get your pants on." She wrapped her long fingers around his hard-on. "This won't take long."

Mitch groaned.

"You're not pushing my hand away now, are you?" She smirked.

He was done in seconds.

She gave him a playful shove out of the shower. "I love you, Mitch Garner. Don't you ever forget that."

Chapter 8

Over the next three weeks, Mitch and Jennie worked out a plan. He promised to come home weekends during training, and she would continue working toward her nursing degree. When his wages kicked in, he'd send Chris money to help pay farm bills.

Mitch was sworn in on April eighth, 2002 at the Bureau of Administration in downtown Milwaukee and ordered to report to the Bureau of Instruction and Training the following day to begin training.

On the drive into Milwaukee, heading east on Good Hope Road, he passed through a tidy suburban neighborhood. The early morning sun filtered through the wooded lots, illuminating neatly landscaped yards. The smell of spring drifted into his truck. He passed a white two-story house bordered by mature lilac bushes that were budding out, stirring memories of the farm when his mom was alive. For two weeks every spring the farmhouse would be drenched in their aroma. His mom loved having a vase of the purple flowers on the kitchen table.

Further along the congested boulevard, he passed rows of strip malls and fast food joints. Further still, he passed massive factories, some with full parking lots, some empty and desolate. The metallic fumes of industry masked the smell of spring.

Beyond the factories, approaching Teutonia Avenue, block after block of deteriorating apartment buildings lined the street. Throngs of black people milled around the bus stops. This was nothing like downtown Milwaukee with the towering buildings along Wisconsin Avenue and the shimmering high-rise lakefront condos he had seen when he came in to get sworn in the day before.

Mitch's stomach tensed when he spotted the three-story City of Milwaukee Safety Academy that stretched over a city block. He wheeled his pickup into the side drive, parking at the rear of the crowded lot.

The inside of the Academy reminded him of Milroy High, but much larger. At the end of the first hallway were the offices of the Police and Fire Academies; police to the left, fire to the right.

Mitch's hard-soled cowboy boots echoed off the gray speckled concrete floor as he passed rows of classrooms. The cool air chilled the nervous sweat on his arms and face. A murmur of voices and laughter drifted from the open door of 206. He stepped inside and paused. The tiered classroom had the same gray plastic chairs with built-in trays and baskets as high school. At the back of the room, on one side, was a group of white guys, on the other side a group of black guys, and in the front, three young women.

The room went quiet with all eyes on him. Even the two instructors dressed in blue jumpsuits at the front of the room were staring. One had a purple scar running down the left side of his face, which forced that eye into a permanent squint.

The *clack, clack, clack* of Mitch's boots rang through the hushed room as he dashed to a seat in the middle of the second row. Laughter trickled from behind him followed by hushed chattering. Mitch had never felt so out-of-place.

The round clock on the wall buzzed. Eight o'clock.

"Okay, people, shut your pie holes and listen up. I'm Lieutenant Hager. I'll be your leader and boss for the next eighteen weeks. You will refer to me as sir or lieutenant." He pointed to the scarred instructor. "This is Captain Stockley. He's my boss. You will not address him unless he addresses you first. If you have questions for him, you will address them to me, and I will address them to him. That is called chain-of-command. And you will follow it. If Captain Stockley addresses you, you will respond to him as sir or captain."

Captain Stockley narrowed his dark, ominous eyes at someone behind Mitch. "Put your hand down. I'll tell you when to ask questions."

Mitch looked back to see a skinny black recruit with elaborate tattoos flowing down both arms, lower his hand.

Hager passed out large white binders. "This will be your Bible for the next eighteen weeks. Take it home with you and get to know it from cover to cover. Sleep with it if you have to. Make love to it. I don't care what you do with it, just know it intimately. It's your training manual. You'll be tested on the material and if you fall below passing grades, you'll be dropped from training."

While Hager passed out binders, Captain Stockley distributed forms. "We need your personal information. That way if you die stupidly during training we know who to contact to pick up your carcass. Don't be dying on us. That's an order. I hate paperwork. If you dare to get injured, I don't want to hear about it unless there's a bone sticking out." He didn't appear to be kidding.

"Work on those forms while we check in with the chief," Hager ordered. "They *will* be done by the time we get back."

The officers left.

A shrill voice from behind Mitch said, "Those dudes is serious, man. Specially Captain Scarface."

Mitch glanced over his shoulder. The voice belonged to the tattooed recruit, who was now pointing at him. "Check out dude's green hat. Who John Deere play for?"

"You fool. That's a tractor," said the recruit next to him.

"What do I know about tractors? Don't see none a that shit around here."

"You one ignorant brother."

"Dude, why you wearing a tractor hat?" asked the tattooed recruit, loud enough for everyone to hear.

Laughter echoed through the room. Even the three young women in front snickered.

Mitch's face burned.

The room quieted as the recruits went back to filling in their paperwork, giving Mitch time to calm down.

Assholes.

* * *

The officers marched in. Hager said, "Pass in the forms, then hustle to the locker room and change into your reds and report to the gym for PT, physical training."

Mitch took a locker away from the others and pulled off his polo shirt.

The skinny tattooed recruit strutted across the room and pointed at Mitch's arm. "What's that spose to be?"

Mitch ignored him.

Three black guys scrambled over, gawking at the tattoo on his arm, a green squared oval with a yellow leaping deer in the middle.

"Dude, I'm talking. What's that shit on your arm?" the tattooed recruit said.

Mitch refused to answer.

"Dude, your girlfriend a deer?" The tattooed recruit turned to the three others. They all laughed. "I heard farm boys fuck animals. That some crazy shit there."

Before he turned back, Mitch had him by the throat and slammed him against the locker. "You need to shut the fuck up."

The recruit's eyes bulged. His three friends moved in. Mitch let go. From the corner of his eye, he saw a group of white guys moving toward them.

The tattooed recruit raised his fists. "Who you think you're fucking with?" He bounced on his toes. "Want some? C'mon then, bitch."

Mitch went into his wrestling crouch.

A dark mountain of a man pushed through the others.

Holy crap, I'm dead.

The huge man turned his back to Mitch and said, "Stop acting a fool, LaMont. You get in a fight, they'll kick you both out. Looks like he could mess you up anyway. Step off."

"But, Jamal."

"Step off, *now*." Jamal scanned the room. "You all might want to get your shit on. I don't think those bosses play."

He leered at Mitch. "And you best watch yourself."

Chapter 9

Hager strolled back and forth across the gym examining the segregated recruits. "You better become one big happy family fast or this will be one hell of a long eighteen weeks. Forget about your stupid cliques. You're not in high school. You need to work as a team. If you do that, you just might get through the drills. When I call your name, stand where I point. This will be where you'll start each day."

After they were all in place, Hager said, "Most of you will be good at some things and suck at others. When one of you struggles, I expect the others to step up and help. When your ass is on the line, it won't matter if your partner is black, white, or plaid, male or female. Only thing matters is they step up. So, first and most important lesson, never leave your partner behind. I'll say it again, never leave your partner behind. You do that during training, you'll be dropped. You do that in the field, we lose a firefighter. At the very least, you get a reputation as a stone. And the chief will be asking me why the hell I let you through."

While Hager led them through the workout, Captain Scar stalked the group, shouting at slackers, shoving them down with his foot when they slowed on the pushups, and kicking their feet when they dropped their legs during the lifts. Before taking a break, Hager made them continue doing burpees until half the class collapsed, groaning. For Mitch, this was like training for a wrestling meet. Captain Scar watched him and nodded. Mitch chuckled to himself. *Who's laughing now, assholes?*

Hager led the group out to the five-story concrete tower. The area above every window opening was blackened, giving it the appearance of a burned-out medieval castle. "This is the training tower. We'll be climbing it, crawling through it, and puking in it. This is where you'll see the gates of hell up close. We'll be busting your weak asses so when the shit hits the fan, and it will, you don't panic and screw up. Now, form a single line." He pointed to the narrow, metal ladder that went straight up the fire escape connecting all the landings. "We'll start each day by climbing the cat ladder. When you get to the top, come down the steps on the other side, then go up again. Climbing that needs to become second nature so when we start training in full gear, you don't fall and wreck our schedule."

The recruits gawked at the top of the imposing tower. Mitch wasn't impressed. He'd been climbing ladders on silos and in haylofts since he was a kid.

Captain Scar stood next to the ladder holding a clipboard. "Shout your name when you get to the ladder."

The first recruit approached the ladder. "Murphy."

"You some kind of idiot, Murphy?" Hager asked.

Murphy glanced at the recruits.

"Look at me, not them. What did I tell you about addressing the captain? My five-year-old has a longer attention span."

"Murphy, sir."

"Better, now go." Hager turned to the line of recruits. "Keep one floor between you. If you panic and can't make it, get to the next landing and get off. Turn in your gear and have a good life."

The fleshy white guy in front of Mitch, who struggled through calisthenics, stepped from the line. Mitch was now behind LaMont, who sneered at him.

Screw you, too.

Hager pointed the recruit toward the main building. "Turn in your gear at the office." To the rest, he said, "There's no shame in walking away. This job isn't for everyone. In fact, it isn't for normal people. Now, back to work." Hagger nodded at Jamal.

"Jackson, sir," the big man said. He attacked the ladder, scaling it with ease.

The others followed, shouting their names to Captain Scar. It was obvious most had never been on a ladder, at least not one going straight up five stories. Two recruits stepped off the ladder before reaching the top.

Mitch followed LaMont up the ladder. They covered the first three floors at a good pace. Between the third and fourth floor landings, LaMont slowed. Just below the fifth-floor landing, he stopped.

"Damn it, Franklin, you're almost to the top. Keep going," Hager hollered from the ground.

Captain Scar made for the stairwell.

LaMont looked down at Mitch with the terrified look of a wounded deer, his eyes wide and glazed. This was the same look Chris had the first time he climbed the ladder to the hayloft and froze near the top. After Mitch talked him into climbing the rest of the way, Chris never had a fear of heights again.

LaMont's legs quivered. As much as Mitch wanted to beat the crap out of this guy, he couldn't let him fall. "Listen, LaMont, only one floor to go. Look up and take one rung at a time."

LaMont pulled himself tight to the ladder.

Mitch climbed to him and tried to pry one of LaMont's hands off the ladder and run it up the outside beam. LaMont had a death grip on it. A surge of adrenaline crashed through Mitch. If LaMont fell, he'd take them both down. "You some kind of pussy? Guess you ain't so tough, huh? C'mon, get pissed and stop screwing around. Goddamit, stop looking down."

Captain Scar was one landing below and closing fast.

"Go. Now." Mitch swatted him on the ass. "Snap out of it."

LaMont's eyes cleared like he was seeing Mitch for the first time. He blinked hard and looked up. LaMont slid his hands along the beam of the ladder and climbed, slow at first, then faster until he was over the top. He hurried down the stairs without looking back.

Mitch passed Captain Scar on the way down the stairs. The captain squinted his good eye at him. "Solid."

After the recruits climbed the cat ladder a second time, Hager took them to the utility building at the far edge of the parking lot where the equipment, apparatus, and turnout were kept. It was designed like a fire-house with a hose tower for hanging wet hose and a classroom for lectures and demonstrations.

The rest of the morning the recruits were instructed in the proper use of the SCBA, self-contained breathing apparatus, and turnout gear. Hager demonstrated how to pull on the gear and how to don the breathing apparatus. Mitch watched the others struggle to don the SCBAs in under twenty seconds. He had drilled on this hundreds of times with the volunteer department.

Watch this, assholes. He did it in ten seconds, getting stares from the group, including Captain Scar.

After lunch, they gathered at a stack of old telephone poles smelling of tar. Hager picked up a long fire axe, examining the thick steel blade "You'll become well acquainted with this technological miracle. It starts every time and never fails. You need to be like this axe and never fail." He leered at the recruits. "I need a volunteer."

They all gazed at their shoes except Mitch. "I'll give it a try, sir." He heard a few groans from the others. Yes, he was sucking up to the boss. Screw them.

"Okay, Farm Boy. Let's see what you got. Chop through that pole."

Mitch lit into it, sending wood chips flying. Hager stood back with folded arms, watching. Halfway through the creosote hardened pole, Mitch's arms burned. He gasped for air but kept chopping, barely able to grip the axe.

Hager tapped him on the back. "You can stop. Nice job." He turned to the recruits. "Garner showed you how it's done. Now it's your turn. Have at it."

The recruits banged away with most making little progress.

"I see people giving up. If you're chopping a ventilation hole in a roof, you can't give up, ever. The crew in the attic will be relying on you to get it open so they don't get their asses burned. You need to keep chopping like Garner did when he was gassed."

Mitch got some nasty looks. It wasn't his fault they sucked. And maybe he was showing off. With the way they had laughed at him, he didn't much care what they thought.

* * *

Before leaving for the day, they assembled in the classroom. Hager informed them there will be timed drills, and anyone not able to accomplish a task in the allotted time will be dropped from training. No grading curve, just pass or fail. Hager finished by saying, "Now go shower. And read the first chapter. You'll be tested on it tomorrow."

The subdued locker room clanged with slamming lockers. Mitch caught LaMont eyeballing him. "You're welcome," Mitch said.

LaMont's head jerked sideways.

Figures.

Jamal lumbered over to Mitch. "Why'd you do that?"

Mitch's body tensed. "LaMont said some things that pissed me off."

Lockers stopped banging.

"I ain't talking about that. He's always peacockin' and flapping his big ol' Gumby lips."

"I don't—"

"What you did on the ladder. I passed you on the way down. Heard what you say to LaMont. Get what you did. Don't get why."

"The lieutenant said we're supposed to help each other." Mitch forced a smile. "You know, like one big happy family?"

"The way he messed with you this morning?" Jamal cocked an eyebrow. "Man, you one strange dude." He went back to his locker.

I'm strange?

On the way out to the parking lot, a white recruit stopped Mitch. "Might want to think twice about helping them. If it wasn't for the dual list, most of them wouldn't even be here. And more of us would have jobs." The recruit walked away before Mitch could say anything.

Mitch hurried to his truck, anxious to get away from this place.

"Hey, Farm Boy," Jamal said, crossing his arms over the top of a rusted Bonneville two cars over. "How'd you get that scar on your head?"

"Combine accident."

"What the hell is a—ah, don't matter. Where you staying?"

"Out on Silver Spring, at the Bel Air. Thought I'd stay there until I know my way around."

"My momma's got a upper flat for rent. Don't know if she'll rent to a white boy, but I'll tell her what you did for LaMont." Jamal raised his palms. "So, Farm Boy, what about it?"

"I don't think so."

"Got something against living with blacks?"

Mitch climbed into his truck, cranked the diesel to life, and pulled away, thinking about things Sid had said about black people. After today, he wondered if Sid was right about them.

Chapter 10

The next morning, Mitch stepped inside the empty, chilly locker room that was ripe with the smell of stale sweat. He was an hour early for the second day of training, giving him time to go over the first chapter of the training manual. Recruits quietly filtered in while he studied. None of them approached the showoff and he didn't care.

After PT and the cat ladder, the bosses led them inside the training tower to a small room reeking of smoke, the walls and ceiling black as charcoal. Both windows were covered with plywood. In the middle of the room, Captain Scar and Lieutenant Hager stood next to a fifty-five-gallon drum overflowing with wood shavings.

"Today we'll see who can take smoke," Hager said. "No masks. If you can't take the smoke, the door's right there. Once you go through that door, there's no coming back."

Hager threw a match into the drum. The wood shavings crackled. "See how the smoke curls across the ceiling and down the walls."

Captain Scar paced the room scrutinizing the recruits as the smoke banked down, darkening the room. Mitch could feel Jamal next to him but couldn't see him as the room went black. The smoke choked off his breath. His heart raced. He was back in that burning farmhouse, panicking, Maggie crying out for help.

A flash of light cut through the smoke as a shadow dashed out. Mitch took two steps toward the door. A thick arm went across his chest and pushed him back against the wall, pinning him.

Two more flashes of light as two more recruits bailed.

"That's enough," Hager said. "Get the widows open."

The recruits ripped the plywood from the windows. Everyone stuck their heads into the open air, black snot running from their noses.

Mitch nodded at Jamal. "Thanks."

"One big happy family, remember?"

The rest of the day was spent raising ladders and chopping more telephone poles.

Jamal sidled up to Mitch in the locker room after they had showered at the end of the day. He pointed at the red welts on Mitch's shoulder. "Looks like that Bel Air's providing free bedbugs."

He was right. The itching had kept Mitch up most of the night. He had to find a place soon. Mitch looked up at the big man. "Thanks again. I owe you."

"Then rent my momma's flat. She needs the money, bad."

Bedbugs or blacks? "I'll take a look at it."

* * *

Mitch followed Jamal into the city. He was stunned by how rapidly things changed as they drove from the academy into the inner-city neighborhoods. Cracked concrete walkways and steps led to sagging porches with rotting wood that hadn't seen paint in decades. The massive houses were similar to the old farmhouses around Milroy but most of these were badly deteriorated. Weed-covered lots peppered areas where houses once stood. They passed people lounging on porches with small kids tearing around the bare dirt yards, all of them black and all staring as Mitch roared by. He caught a whiff of rotting garbage. After driving for several miles, he noticed the bold black outline of a scripted *"19"* painted on the side of an abandoned church like some kind religious symbol.

Jamal stopped in front of a three-story house with peeling gray paint. It was one of the few houses with a grass yard. Purple petunias bordered the house.

A petite woman, as dark as Jamal, burst onto the wide porch. "Why you bring a white boy here?"

"This Mitch. He's a recruit. Helped LaMont today. Wants to rent the upper."

"Well, I surely don't know. Renting to a white?"

"Mitch, this my mom, Bernice. Everybody call her Miss Bernie."

Miss Bernie studied him. "You be the only white around here."

"C'mon, I'll take you in," Jamal said.

They went up the back stairwell to the second floor and entered the sparse kitchen. The flat smelled like a country church on a hot day, like the musty smell of aging hymnals. An antique gas stove and refrigerator stood against the faded yellow back wall. A narrow hallway led to the front room, containing a dark brown threadbare couch and splintery wooden coffee table. A rust-colored water stain circled the light fixture on the ceiling.

Jamal opened the front window. "Kinda ripe. It'll clear out. What you think? Only three hundred a month."

Mitch chewed his lower lip. It was roomy and lots cheaper than the Bel Air, but this neighborhood?

"Momma can't work no more since her back give out. She needs the rent."

The sound of shattering glass drew Mitch to the window. Five kids were rifling through his truck. He raced by Jamal and down the steps. The kids scattered. He tore after them and snatched a girl by the arm before she got to the end of the block. She shrieked and clawed at him like an angry bobcat. "Get the fuck off me, motherfucker." Her long, black braids and flimsy, silver-colored necklace whipped back and forth. Her blazing emerald eyes startled him.

Mitch told Jamal to call the cops. The girl landed a crushing kick to his groin, bending him over. He let go and grabbed his crotch, taking short, shallow breaths. She ran to the end of the block, turned, and flashed her middle finger at him. Then she was gone.

Jamal laughed. "Better get back to the house before she comes back. And don't be locking your truck no more. They just gonna break the window again. Not locked, they take a look inside. Find nothing, they leave it be."

"I'm calling the cops."

"Cops won't do nothin'."

"You know those kids?"

"The girl that jacked you? Jasmine Richardson. Lives over by the firehouse. That girl's trouble. Won't be long and she'll be running with the One-Niners."

"One-Niners?"

"Bangers. This they hood. All the way from Nineteenth to Second Street."

Miss Bernie was waiting for them on the porch with her arms clamped to her chest. Mitch didn't want to spend another night at the Bel Air but out there he wouldn't have to worry about kids breaking into his truck.

"So, you want it?" Jamal asked. "I'll make sure nobody messes with your shit."

Mitch's gut told him no.

Miss Bernie scowled at Jamal. "Watch that mouth of yours, Boy."

"Try it for a month," Jamal said to Mitch. "Don't work out. You leave."

Miss Bernie continued scowling at Jamal.

"Don't worry, Momma. Everything's good. You need the rent."

Mitch caved. "Okay. I'll try it for a month if it's okay with your mom."

Miss Bernie fished the keys from her apron pocket and slapped the keys in his hand. "You watch yourself. This the Devil's playground."

Before Mitch left to get his things from the Bel Air, Jamal pointed at his left arm. "What's the story behind the ink?"

"It's the John Deere emblem."

"Oh, yeah, tractors. You country dudes is strange."

No stranger than any of this. "Where do I go to file a police report?"

"Won't do much good. But Fifth District is where you do that. Best draw you a map. Don't want you ending up in the wrong neighborhood." Jamal laughed.

* * *

The officer at the front desk told him, off the record, he'd be better off just filing a claim with his insurance. Mitch pressed him to file a report and the officer reluctantly took his statement. Two hours later he was on his way to the Bel Air.

It was after ten when he got back to Miss Bernie's house. He moved his few belongings upstairs. A bedspread and fresh linens were on the bed. He was exhausted from training and dozed off as soon as he hit the sheets.

* * *

The next morning Mitch was studying the training manual in the locker room. Jamal lumbered over. "Any nappy-headed little girls kick your ass today?"

"She didn't—"

"Dude, lighten up." He gave Mitch a thump on the back. "How things go with Momma?"

"I didn't get back 'til late. Where'd you go?"

"I don't live there, dude. Momma don't approve of sisters staying over. And I got needs." Jamal waved a finger at him. "You best behave around her." Jamal's booming laughter ricocheted off the lockers.

* * *

Mitch lingered at his locker Friday after training. He was anxious to see Jennie and tell her about the first week but queasy about returning to Milroy.

Jamal slid alongside him. "You stopping at Roscoe's?"

"Nah, I'm going home for the weekend."

"Can you stop for one? I've got some serious shit to tell you."

Roscoe's was a neighborhood bar frequented by the diverse staff and recruits from the Police and Fire Academy. Lighted beer signs and wooden plaques with quotations like "In God We Trust, All Others Pay Cash" adorned the dark paneled walls along with racks of beer steins.

Jamal and Mitch clinked their cans of Miller Light together.

"Only seventeen more weeks to go," Mitch said.

Jamal looked like Mitch slugged him in the gut.

"What?" Mitch asked.

"Don't think I'm gonna make it."

"No way."

"I messed up two written tests. Captain said I got to take them over on Monday. If I don't pass, I'm done."

"Crap."

"Don't know what I'll tell Momma. Never give her much to be proud of, always had problems with reading. School said I was dyslexic or some shit." Jamal gazed at the floor. "I'm motherfucking scared."

LaMont pushed between them and said to Mitch, "Dude, what you done for me is tight, man. Just wanna say you a stand-up cracker. And what I said that first day is fucked. Didn't mean nothing by it." He reached out his hand. They grasped thumbs and shook.

Jamal turned LaMont around and gave him a push away from the bar. "He gets it, LaMont, now go." Jamal frowned. "Even that fool's doing better'n me on the tests."

They sat in silence while the others laughed and talked.

"Jamal, come over to your mom's tomorrow. I'll tutor you."

"Ain't you going home?"

"One big happy family, remember?"

"Thanks," the big man said in a small voice.

Jennie would understand.

* * *

Next morning, after being out late with Jamal, Mitch called Jennie. "Hey, Jen, sorry about last night."

"Would have been nice to call."

"I had to help a friend. It got late."

"Yeah? Okay, I get that. What time you coming today?"

"That's just it. This friend kind of saved my job and he needs me to help him with his tests."

The line went quiet.

"Jen?"

"You promised you'd come back every weekend."

"Once all this settles down, I'll be back every weekend."

"Promise?"

"Promise."

* * *

Mitch didn't make it back the next weekend or the next. He dreaded calling Jennie to tell her he couldn't come in. When he put off calling her, she called him. He desperately wanted to see her but as time passed, it became easier to rationalize staying in Milwaukee. Jennie's calls went from pleading, to anger, then stopped.

He never made it back to Milroy during training.

Chapter 11

Lieutenant Hager wasn't lying when he said things would get much tougher. The instructors pushed them to the limits of physical and mental endurance. Through the first six weeks, ten recruits dropped out. Four more couldn't complete the training evolutions in the required time and were dropped. Two recruits succumbed to the sweltering heat of July and had to be transported to the emergency room. They never rejoined the class, leaving only sixteen of the original thirty-two candidates to complete training in August.

The recruits filed onto the graduation stage, dressed in blues: dark blue pants, polished black shoes, and powder blue button-down shirts with the red and white Maltese emblem of the Milwaukee Fire Department on the left shoulder. No more red jumpsuits. Friends and family in the audience rose, cheering and clapping. Throughout the ceremony, Mitch focused on the doors to the auditorium. His brother, Chris, had promised to spread the word about his graduation. Nobody from Milroy showed. Not Jennie and not even his own brother. He barely heard Captain Scar introduce him.

He approached the captain to receive his diploma and badge. Captain Scar stopped him. "Every once in a while we get an extraordinary recruit come through training. When recruit Garner walked into class the first day fresh off the farm, I thought there was no way this cocky young man would fit in. As we got into training and started breaking into small groups to fight fires, raise ladders, and open roofs, this recruit excelled at every drill and pulled along others who were struggling. He never left anyone behind and did his best to help the group accomplish their tasks. And that is what our job is all about. Working together as a team. Our lives depend on it."

For the first time since they started training, Captain Scar smiled. "Welcome to the Milwaukee Fire Department, Firefighter Garner." Captain

Scar shook Mitch's hand vigorously and handed him the diploma and badge. The room exploded in applause. Mitch felt like a golf ball lodged in his throat.

Family and guests were invited to join the newest members of the Milwaukee Fire Department at Roscoe's after the ceremony. With no family or friends from back home to celebrate with, Mitch just wanted to go back to his flat. But Jamal demanded he join him and his mom. When they entered the bar, it was jammed and noisy. Jamal led Mitch toward a table where Miss Bernie was waiting. Before they got to her, a voice from the back of the bar called out, "Mitch, over here."

He raced to Jennie and lifted her off the floor. His brother, Chris, and Big Jim, the captain from Milroy, rose from their seats.

"We almost didn't make it," Chris said. "Bad pileup on I-94 outside Waukesha. By the time we got here, the auditorium was filled. We had to stand outside, but we heard it all. Holy crap, Brother. You ruled."

Jennie leaned back. "Okay, you can put me down now."

Everything was making sense again. Jennie filled Mitch in on Milroy gossip, like how Carol Barker had cheated on Ray Bunzell with his brother Jack. Now the whole Bunzell clan was in an uproar, taking sides in the family drama.

Chris told him they lost corn to the hail storm last month. Sid didn't buy crop insurance again so getting through winter with enough feed would be a struggle.

"Dad ever ask about me?" Mitch asked.

Chris shrugged. "You should know there's no way we'd make it without that five hundred you've been sending us."

Jamal ambled to their table with a pitcher of beer. "Who needs a refill?"

Mitch sprang to his feet. "This is the man who schooled this farm boy on the big city."

The others stared at the dark man towering over them.

Jamal rested his hand on Mitch's back. "Just a couple of brothers watching out for each other."

Jamal told them how Mitch tutored him and two other recruits. And how Jamal's mother brought Kool-Aid and chocolate chip cookies up to the flat while they studied. When they finished studying, they'd go for a jog, getting stares as they ran through the hood.

Other classmates drifted over to introduce themselves and share stories of how Mitch pulled them through drills.

"You have a lot of admirers," Jennie said flatly.

"Sure didn't start that way."

LaMont stepped in front of Jamal. "Mitch, dude. This your crew?"

"This is my brother Chris. And these are my friends Jim and Jen."

"Wooo, girl, you hot. Ever get tired of this country boy you come look me up."

Jennie's eyebrows shot up.

Jamal pulled LaMont away. "These people don't want to hear your nonsense." Jamal gave him a gentle push away from the table.

"Mitch knows I'm playing."

Across the room, Miss Bernie was holding court with two heavy women and an immense, nattily dressed bald man. She was tiny next to them.

"Your mom got a boyfriend?" Mitch asked.

"Nah, he's a church friend, Brother Williams." Jamal waved to the others. "Nice meetin' you all. Let you get back to your visit."

"Bet he can swing an axe," Big Jim said after Jamal left.

"Jen, I need to talk. Let's go outside." To the others, Mitch said, "We'll be back." He led her to his truck.

"Been a long time since I got a ride in this," Jennie said.

"I missed the hell out of you." He hugged her and pressed his lips to hers.

She pulled back. "Who you seeing?"

"What? Nobody. Why?"

"Dammit. I didn't want to do this today."

"Do what?"

"I'm proud of you. I am. I've seen a side of you today I haven't seen in a long time."

Mitch took her hands in his. "Why you so pissed?"

"In four months, you couldn't come back once? Come on, be honest. Who you seeing?"

"I told you I had to stay and help Jamal and his friends on the weekends."

She rammed her finger into his chest. "You promised you'd come back and see me. You lied, Mitch Garner. Damn you." She shoved him with both hands. "You promised."

He reached for her. "How about you stay for the weekend? We can talk."

"Talk? Right. You talk?" She wiped at her eyes with the back of her hand. "Anyway, I have to work tonight, then clinicals Saturday and Sunday."

"Can't you call in sick tonight?"

"If you cared about me, nothing would have stopped you from coming back. Nothing."

"I couldn't come back."

"Not even once?"

"Jen, it's not you. I wasn't ready."

"Ready? Ready for what?"

Mitch clenched his lips.

"I'm done," Jennie said and stomped off.

She climbed into Big Jim's truck and slammed the door.

* * *

Shortly after Mitch told the others that Jennie was waiting in Jim's truck, they left. He had several rounds of shots with his classmates, then went back to the flat, agonizing over Jennie's words. Did she mean she was done talking or done forever?

The following afternoon, he headed to the quarters of Engine Fifteen to meet his crew and get a quick orientation before reporting for his first twenty-four-hour shift on Monday, August twelfth, a red-shift day. The other shifts in the three-day cycle are green and blue.

On the short drive from Miss Bernie's house to the firehouse, most blocks had at least one decaying, boarded-up house, some had several. The streets were deserted. Papers and trash fluttered over empty lots. The muggy August breeze carried the faint odor of rotting waste. Two blocks from the firehouse, mounds of charred roofing and shingles smoldered next to a burned-out house.

* * *

The cream-colored brick firehouse stood alone in the middle of the block, bordered by a green, manicured lawn. An American flag snapped in the breeze from a tall flagpole. Through the two open overhead garage doors, Mitch saw three men scrubbing flattened hose with wide brooms while another hosed it off. On the cement platform in front of the firehouse, the cherry-red fire engine shimmered in the afternoon sunlight. The four men stopped working and rubber-necked as he turned into the side drive.

He pulled around back and parked in the fenced-in lot. Razor wire lined the top of the fence. Mitch took a deep breath and walked around front.

The firehouse smelled of tires, diesel, and wet concrete. A broad man with a pockmarked face and bulging thyroid eyes met him on the platform, scrutinizing him. "You the new paperboy?"

"I'm the new cub."

"Yeah? What stunted your growth?"

"I, uh..."

The man pointed at the door. "Office is in there. Hope you're sharper than you look."

The three others leaned on their broom handles, smirking.

Inside the doorway was a desk referred to as the joker stand, containing a red telephone, desktop paging microphone, computer, and printer. Opposite the joker stand was a small room containing a twin bed and television. Past that was another room with a closed door, then a long hallway. Mitch knocked on the closed door, praying this was the boss's office.

"Enter."

Behind a wide cluttered desk, sat a stocky man with thick, graying eyebrows. "Ah, our new cub." He came around the desk and extended a hand. "I'm Stan Reemer. Stockley said you were quite the star at the academy, hey?"

"Just glad to make it through, sir."

"Humble. Good. These guys'll eat you up if you come in here spouting off. I'll show you around. Crew's busy with hose work. We caught an attic fire this morning just down the block."

"I saw it on the way in. Looks like it was a good fire," Mitch said, trying not to sound stupid.

"Just a squib attic fire in a vacant. Stockley work you guys over pretty good at the academy?"

"It wasn't too bad." Mitch tried to think of something intelligent to say. "How'd he get that scar?"

"Caught an axe in the face. What about you? How'd you get the ding on your forehead?"

"Crashed a combine."

"Don't see much of that around here."

Captain Reemer took him upstairs and showed him the locker room, showers, and dormitory. The shower area smelled of Ivory soap. Bars of it were everywhere. The dormitory had four beds, all neatly covered with army-green bedspreads.

Captain Reemer took him to the basement where the turnout gear was stored in racks. The canary yellow gear was blackened and had saturated the basement with the smell of hundreds of fires. The captain pointed to the workout area. "Good idea to keep yourself in shape. The way we eat around here can balloon you up in a hurry. You'll see when you meet our driver."

When the recruits received their assignments the last week of training, Hager informed Mitch he would be working at the busiest firehouse in the city with one of the best officers. Of course, Hager had to add that he sure as hell better not make him look bad.

The captain headed to the stairs. "Let's go meet your partners."

Mitch followed the captain into the cavernous kitchen that smelled of baking ham mingled with cigar smoke. Four men were seated at a long solid-oak table with wooden benches on each side. Thyroid Eyes puffed a fat stogie. "See that fucking stone from Ladder Nine go ass over tea kettle?" The three others laughed hysterically.

Captain Reemer rapped his knuckles on the table. "This is our new man, Mitch Garner."

The laughter stopped. Mitch stood at the end of the table, not sure what to do.

A stout, burly man whose T-shirt strained to cover his rotund belly pointed to the bench next to him. "Grab a seat."

The man pressed against Mitch when he sat. "Stick close. I'll protect you from these animals."

"That's Crusher, our driver," the captain said, shaking his head. He motioned toward the man with bulging eyes and five-o'clock shadow. "And this is Ralph Eberhardt, our resident grouch." The others laughed.

"Or Mr. Angry, as he's known around the battalion," Crusher said. More laughter.

Ralph ignored them. He studied Mitch with the look of a man waiting for an answer. Mitch didn't know the question.

Captain Reemer continued, "This is the man you're replacing, Al Jenkins. He's dumping us to work over on the east side."

"Hey, boss, wasn't my idea." The lanky, black firefighter with a short afro extended a hand to Mitch. "You lucked out. These old fucks know their stuff. Just have to put up with their shit." He grinned at the captain. "No offense, honorable, all-exalted leader."

The captain pointed toward a gaunt man with red, wavy hair and a putty nose plastered in the middle of his face. "This is our resident nut bag and cook extraordinaire, Kenny Slowinski."

Kenny reached across the table and pumped Mitch's hand. His eyes flicked around the room like a rabid dog. "I wouldn't trust any of these assholes. You need to know anything, you come to me."

More laughter.

They asked Mitch what he did before joining. He told them about the farm and the small community of Milroy. They seemed interested, except Ralph, who stared at the ceiling while puffing his cigar.

At three o'clock Kenny rose from the table. "Enough bullshitting. To the alligator pit." He left.

Ralph followed, scowling at Mitch with a look of pure disgust.

"They call the dorm the alligator pit," Captain Reemer said. "Best to catch an afternoon nap. Things heat up down here after dark." The captain nodded. "Glad to have you aboard." They shook and the captain headed to the office.

Al escorted Mitch outside. "We call this area the Core, where hot bricks fly. You'll be right in the middle of some of the most incredible drama you could imagine: gang shootings, knifings, accidents where people are dismembered, and raging fires that'll scare the fuck out of you. Just know you're working with some of the best firefighters in the city. Learn from them." Al stepped back. "Hang on a second."

Mitch heard rattling from above. He glanced up in time to see Crusher and Kenny leaning over the top of the roof with buckets. Before he could move, he was struck by an icy waterfall.

Al grinned. "You've now been baptized with the holy water of Engine Fifteen. You're now absolved of all your civilian sins and accepted into the brotherhood of firefighters. Bless you, and may Saint Florian, the patron saint of firefighters, keep you safe. Or some shit like that."

Mitch stood dripping at the front of the firehouse.

Chapter 12

The early morning sun cast an orange hue over the cream-colored firehouse. Mitch was relieved to find the front door open. The last thing he wanted to do was ring the bell and disturb the blue shift on his first day. All he thought about the last two days was what he did to piss Ralph off.

The apparatus floor of Engine Fifteen was eerily silent and deserted. He walked around the front of the rig and found a young woman bent over a pile of turnout gear alongside Engine Fifteen. Her strawberry blond braid fell to the top of her back. A red, orange, and black tattoo of flaming wings peeked between the top of her navy blue Dickie work pants and the bottom of her matching T-shirt. He didn't want to startle her but felt stupid standing there. "Morning," he said.

She straightened and spun. "Jesus, you always creep up on people?"

Mitch gulped. She looked like she should be riding waves in Malibu, not sorting dirty turnout gear in the hood. His eyes were drawn to her snug T-shirt.

"Hey, buster, up here," she said, pointing two fingers at her turquoise eyes.

His face burned.

She smirked. "Nice to meet a man I can embarrass. Not like the pervs around here. I'm Nicole. You can call me Nic."

"I'm ah, Mitch," he said, trying to avoid staring. "Who do I take down?"

"What time they tell you to report for duty?"

"Seven-thirty at the latest."

"Okay, you're one of those. You do know it's only six-thirty. Your crew won't be here for another hour." She shook her head. "DeWayne's the cub on the blue. That's his gear. I'll show you where to take it."

Mitch collected the gear and followed her down the stairs mesmerized by the sway of her Dickies.

"Here's DeWayne's cubby hole," she said.

He stashed the gear. When he turned around, he caught Nic checking *him* out.

"I'm up here," he said pointing at his eyes. Her smoky laugh was intoxicating.

"How long you been on?" Mitch asked.

"Five years." She raised her eyebrows. "You seeing anybody?"

"Ahh …"

"Not an essay question. Yes or no?"

"I think I still have a girlfriend back home."

"Shame. Stay safe, Cub Mitch. Don't let the red shift get to you, especially that dickhead, Ralph." She trotted up the stairs. He resisted the urge to watch. She called down, "Lose interest already?" Her seductive laugh trailed off.

DeWayne, a buff black guy with short-cropped hair and a trace of a mustache, met him by the rig. "Get the bread rolls?"

"Yeah, a dozen."

"Wait 'til your crew comes in to put 'em out or the blue shift'll pound 'em down and deny it. Then you'll be in deep shit."

DeWayne went into the long list of cub duties which included checking the air pressure on the masks, going over equipment on the rig, cleaning the boss's office, swabbing toilets, ensuring the coffee pot was never empty, and on and on.

"Don't worry, miss anything, they'll let you know. Man, will they let you know." DeWayne wasn't smiling.

Mitch started by checking the masks, then checked over the hose lays. He was checking the extinguishers when Ralph marched through the open overhead doors smoking a fat stogie.

"Everything squared away, kid?" Ralph said through the side of his mouth, his voice sounding like tires on gravel.

"One of the masks was a little low, so I changed the bottle. Everything else looks good."

"Better be or it'll be your ass."

Ralph flicked a large ash onto Mitch's shoe. "Make sure you clean that up."

Mitch shook the ash off his shoe.

Ralph flicked another ash onto his shoe and blew a cloud of cigar smoke in his face.

Mitch stared at the ash, balling his fists.

After several long seconds of glowering at Mitch, Ralph left.

Mitch continued with morning duties, stewing about Ralph. He was at the joker stand reading the entries in the company journal when Crusher, the pot-bellied driver, came up behind him. "How's it going so far, kid?"

"Hope I'm not missing anything."

"Got the rolls?"

"Yup. A dozen."

"Good, put 'em out."

The others were waiting when he entered the kitchen. Kenny snatched the bag of rolls and pulled one from the bag and examined it. "Where'd you get these hockey pucks?"

"Value Mart over on Vine Street."

Captain Reemer buried his face in the newspaper.

"We got discriminating tastes around here, kid," Crusher said. "We don't eat just any swill thrown at us."

Kenny pointed at Crusher's belly. "Couldn't tell by that Milwaukee goiter you're growing. Looks like you're sitting on a slow leaking air hose."

"Hey, asshole, I'm building reserves for when I'm an old fuck and start wasting away."

Crusher waved his middle finger at Kenny, then said to Mitch, "You want to keep us happy, you bring us Sciortino's rolls. And you do want to keep us happy, don't you?"

Before Mitch could reply, five rings of the alarm system chimed over the loudspeakers.

Mitch was surprised by how fast they all moved, especially the aging captain and portly Crusher. The captain rushed down the hallway to get the computer printout while the others dashed to the rig. They were in their turnout gear and on the rig in seconds. Mitch struggled to straighten his bunker pants that had snagged on his boots.

"Jesus, kid, get your ass on the rig," Ralph hollered.

Mitch climbed into the jump seat behind the captain and before he closed the rig door they were flying down the street, siren screaming. Adrenaline electrified every cell of his body.

"Give her hell, Crusher. Don't let those jags from Thirty's beat us in," Ralph said.

They raced up Fond du Lac Avenue in the opposite lane of traffic. A car stopped in the middle of the road.

"Get the fuck out of the way," Crusher shouted into the windshield as he swung around the panicked driver, the rig seeming to go onto two wheels. "Goddamn morons." He flailed his arm out the side widow waving oncoming cars to the side of the road. The fire engine's air horn sounded like a freight train roaring down the tracks.

The exhilaration of racing to an alarm through busy city streets with the screaming siren, blaring air horn, and stormy crew had Mitch's insides jumping.

"Try breathing, kid," Ralph said, shaking his head.

Kenny laughed. "Couldn't drive a penny nail up his sphincter right now." He pulled a package of chewing tobacco from an inside pocket and stuffed a wad into his mouth.

A fire engine and ladder truck were positioned at the front of an eight-story apartment building when they arrived on scene.

Ralph slapped the back of Crusher's seat. "Fuck. Thirty's beat us in."

"Kenny, you and Mitch grab the hotel pack," the captain ordered. "Ralph stay with the rig. Crusher, secure the hydrant."

When the rig stopped, they jumped off. Mitch and Kenny pulled the portable hose pack off the back of the rig and followed the captain. Kenny paused and spit the wad of tobacco onto the sidewalk. They pushed through occupants scrambling by them and stopped in the lobby while the captain talked into the radio. Mitch couldn't hear what he was saying over the deafening wail of the fire alarm.

The captain raised his hand. "Somebody pulled a hook. Thirty's is checking it out. Stand by."

Mitch's breathing returned to normal while they waited.

The alarm stopped blaring. The captain headed to the entrance. "False alarm, fellas. Let's pick up."

Mitch and Kenny followed the captain down the sidewalk, stopping at the wad of tobacco Kenny had spit out. It looked like a brown dog turd.

Kenny sneered at him with a mischievous grin. "Watch this." He bent over the wad, picked it up and examined it. Eyes widened as Kenny sniffed it and then plopped it into his mouth. The crowd gasped, some covering their mouths, others turning away. They cleared a wide path for Kenny as he strutted to the rig.

Back on the rig, Kenny said to Mitch. "Enjoy that?" Before he could reply, Kenny leaned forward. "Hey, boss, how about we stop at the store on the way back?"

"What's on the menu?"

"Cub's first day. Let him pick."

How would he know what they liked? "Um, chicken?"

Ralph and Crusher groaned.

"First you put shit rolls in front of us and now you want us to eat ridge runners?" Crusher said. "Jesus, kid."

"Screw these guys. You want chicken, you'll get chicken," Kenny said.

Ralph glared at Mitch.

On the slow drive to the store, the rig radio came alive. "Engine Fifteen, your location?"

Captain Reemer keyed the mic. "Twenty-third and Fond du Lac."

"Engine Fifteen, respond to an unresponsive party at 1919 West Clarke Street."

The siren activated and they were tearing over the narrow inner-city streets again.

"Puke run, kid. Take your coat off," Kenny said.

The two-and-a-half story house appeared vacant with half the windows of the first floor boarded. 1919 was an upper flat, so they went to the back entrance with Crusher staying behind to guard the rig. A scripted *"19"* was scrawled in black paint across the gray, warped door. Captain Reemer pounded on it. "Fire department." No answer. The captain tried the door handle. "It's locked." He moved aside and Ralph bashed it open with a fierce mule kick.

"Up here," came from inside. The stairwell reeked of stale urine.

A haze of tobacco smoke greeted them on the second floor. Three black men and a pregnant young woman hunkered around a yellowed laminate table, sucking on cigarettes and arguing. Empty forty-ounce bottles of Olde English Malt Liquor littered the small table.

A shirtless man with gold front teeth pointed down the hall. "Back there."

"Why'd you call?" The captain asked.

"Go see yourself. Got no time for this shit."

Ralph took a step toward the man.

"Ralph, let it go," the captain said. "Let's see what we got."

Halfway down the hallway, Mitch smelled rotting flesh, like the carcass pit at the farm, but this was different, a sickening, sweet odor he could taste in the back of his mouth. From behind the closed bedroom door came what sounded like the hum of a barn fan. Captain Reemer pushed it open to the drone of a thick cloud of flies. The smell of rancid feces and rotting flesh in the small hot room gagged Mitch. He fought the urge to vomit. He was used to the heady smells of the farm but this foul stench was beyond anything like that.

"Mouth breathe, kid, or you'll lose it," Kenny said.

Ralph approached the bed of a shriveled old woman with matted, gray hair. He lifted the sheet which was stained dark yellow and brown. "Holy shit, she's breathing."

Her paper-thin lips parted with random, haunting moans.

Ralph yanked off the sheet. Maggots squirmed in the loose folds of her skin and cockroaches scurried from beneath her legs. "They're eating her alive for Christ's sake."

There was no stopping the sour bile shooting up Mitch's throat. He dropped the med kit, bent over and retched.

"C'mon people, she's breathing. We gotta work her," Captain Reemer said. "Med unit's on the way."

"Open the window," Kenny shouted at Mitch. "And bring the kit."

Mitch couldn't stop gagging.

Ralph scowled at him and rammed the window open. "Fucking useless cub."

The captain stepped in and took vital signs, Mitch's job, while Ralph slid an oxygen tube down her throat. Kenny brushed the fly larvae from her wrinkled chest and pasted the defibrillator pads on her.

Mitch hung his head out the open window.

By the time the paramedic unit arrived, his spasms calmed. The first paramedic choked when he saw their patient. Mitch couldn't look away from the tiny creatures devouring the helpless old woman. The sole of her left foot flopped open exposing muscle, bone, and more writhing maggots.

Once the med unit left, they silently organized their equipment. Mitch was still queasy but not from the old lady. He let his crew down.

The four people in the kitchen hadn't moved.

"I'll need some information. Who knows her?" the captain asked.

The man with gold teeth examined the smoking cigarette between his fingers. "We don't know shit."

A black scripted *"19"* tattooed on the man's neck caught Mitch's attention.

In an even tone, the captain said, "Just need her name and anything else you can tell me."

"Said, I don't know shit," The man said, grinding out his cigarette in the full ashtray. "Now get the fuck out my crib."

Ralph pushed in front of the captain. The man rose from the table and pressed his bare chest into him. Ralph's bulging eyes threatened to leave his skull. "You miserable piece of shit."

The other two men slammed their chairs to the floor. The skinny one with spiked black braids and a scraggly goatee leered at Mitch with a toothless grin. Mitch peered into eyes he had never seen on a living creature, dark and vacant. The man reached around his back. The blood drained from Mitch's face.

The captain shoved Ralph toward the stairway. "Sorry to bother you gentlemen."

Mitch followed, breathing hard.

Ralph sneered at the gold-toothed man, who looked like a hungry predator eyeing prey.

At the rig, the captain called in a request for the police. After explaining the situation to the dispatcher, he pointed at Ralph. "You'll get us killed flapping your jaw like that. From now on keep your mouth shut.—That's an order. Got it?"

Ralph glared at the back of Crusher's seat.

They drove to the grocery store in silence.

Chapter 13

Back at the firehouse, Mitch went to work mopping the second-floor locker room, trying to get the images and smells out of his head. Someone stomped up the stairs. The door slammed open, and Ralph marched across the room. Mitch backed away. Ralph bashed his hand into the locker inches from Mitch's ear. "Fucking useless cub. The boss should be pissed at you, not me."

"I—"

"Shut the fuck up." Ralph's bloodshot, bulging eyes had the manic look of a rabid dog. "9/11 comes along and now everyone wants to be a goddamn hero. Go back to Podunk, cub. This ain't no place for you."

Ralph went downstairs leaving Mitch shaken. Ralph was right. He was useless.

Mitch made sure to have the kitchen table set and coffee brewing well before lunch. The comforting smell of fresh coffee and chicken baking in the oven couldn't eliminate the foul smell of that small hot room lingering in his brain.

At exactly noon, Kenny served the one-pot meal, a combination of chunks of chicken, white rice, and black-eyed peas all mixed with cream of mushroom soup. Crusher viewed the concoction, smirked and said, "Hey, Kenny, nice job with those maggots you scooped off the old blister." Crusher shoveled a heaping mound of casserole into his mouth. "Excellent fricassee of maggot."

Kenny and Crusher laughed. Ralph and the captain ignored them.

"Mitch, I made this for you," Kenny said. "What's wrong? They still wiggling?"

Mitch forced a weak smile.

After lunch, Mitch cleared the table. He went to empty the ashtray that was heaped with Ralph's cigar ashes. The irregular clay ashtray looked like a grade school project, painted bright red like the fire engine. He banged it on the inside of the trash can.

"Bust that and I'll bust your ass," Ralph said.

After dishes were washed, the crew deserted the kitchen. While mopping the floor, Mitch couldn't stop agonizing over the old woman and how useless he had been.

"Firefighter Garner to the office," sounded from the PA system.

Mitch tensed. He was going to get an ass-chewing, and he deserved it. He hustled to the office.

A dark brown briarwood pipe hung from the side of the captain's mouth. "Mitch, have a seat." The sweet smell of pipe tobacco was much more agreeable than Ralph's bitter cigar smoke. "Tough morning, heh?"

"Yes, sir."

"That was a bad one. You're not the first to lose it. I've seen veteran paramedics fall apart down here. You'll see plenty more." Captain Reemer tapped the pipe on the ashtray. "I need you to keep it together. If she required resuscitation, we would have needed another set of hands." He paused, studying Mitch. "I need to count on you. Can I?"

Mitch wanted to tell the captain he was sorry for letting him and the crew down. Shame blocked the words. All he got out was, "Yes, sir."

"Good, let's forget about this morning. Need to have a short memory, or you'll drive yourself batty." The captain stuffed his pipe with fresh tobacco and lit it with a wooden match, sending a cloud of sulfur and tobacco smoke into the air. "Any questions?"

"I was wondering about that lady."

"Just got off the phone with the meds. She was a diabetic with lousy circulation. The maggots were eating the dead flesh, keeping her from dying of septic shock. She won't live much longer. Too far gone."

"How could they let her get that way?"

"Don't know. We patch them up best we can and send them off to the hospital or the morgue." The captain pointed the tip of the pipe at Mitch. "You'll need to learn to smile at the dying. Your mug might be the last thing they see."

"Yes, sir."

"One more thing. We have this program called the Literacy Project where inner-city firehouses invite neighborhood kids over in the afternoon.

Around three, some kids'll show up here. Since you're the cub, it'll be your job to tutor them." Captain Reemer chuckled. "Lucky you, heh?"

"What am I supposed to do with them?"

"Doesn't matter. Most can't read yet. Al just gave them firehouse coloring books."

* * *

Mitch waited at the joker stand, listening to dispatchers call out runs to other companies.

The heavy glass door rattled. A knobby-kneed little girl in a bright yellow sundress squinted at him. Black braids lined her head in neat rows. She waved and grinned wide, her two front teeth missing. Four pint-sized children jostled around her. Behind them stood a scowling older girl, her arms clamped to her chest.

Mitch opened the door and the children ran to the apparatus floor. The older girl leered at him as she walked by.

The kids scraped chairs up to the oval table at the back of the apparatus floor. The older girl stood behind them twisting a thin, silver-colored chain necklace.

"Okay, kids. What do you want to do?" Mitch said.

The girl in the yellow dress raised her hand. "Where's Firefighter Al?"

"How about telling me your names so I know who you are?"

The girl in the yellow dress said, "I'm Alexus. People call me Lexus. Wish they call me Lexi, but nobody listen to me." She pointed to the older girl. "She my sister, Jasmine. Takes care of me. We live across the street. And these my friends. This here Kyle."

"Why don't we let them introduce themselves. And, Lexi, glad to meet you and your big sister."

The children sorted through the coloring books, grabbing the few unbroken crayons, ignoring Mitch. Kyle snatched a red one from the girl next to him. She kicked him. "Kyle, that mine. Give it back." He tipped her and the chair over backward. She shot to her feet and wrestled him to the ground, biting the hand holding the crayon. He howled and let go. She got back in her chair and colored as if nothing happened.

"That bitch bite me," Kyle said rubbing the red crescent on his hand. He punched the side of her head. She sprang from her chair and the two clawed at each other.

Before Mitch could separate them, Jasmine pulled them apart. "Kyle, sit your behind down. Mess with Peaches again and I'll tell her dad."

Kyle and Peaches stuck their tongues out at each other and went back to coloring.

"I can see you real good with kids," Jasmine said, frowning at Mitch.

"Thanks for helping."

"Just make sure no one messes with my Lexus."

"What grade you all in?" Mitch asked.

"We starting kinner garden, except Kyle. He starting first grade," Alexus said.

Mitch cringed. Maggie would have been going into first grade this year.

Alexus nodded at Jasmine. "My sister starting eighth grade."

"Anyone else ever get to talk?" Mitch asked, glancing around the table.

The small heads shook in unison. He liked this little girl already.

"How about I read a story?"

"Can't we just color?" Kyle said.

"What kinda story?" Alexus asked.

"There's some kid's books on the back bench. Go ahead and pick one out."

"They all about white kids," Kyle said. "Just let us color."

"Okay, go ahead, color." Mitch stood off to the side, observing the kids, feeling helpless.

* * *

Captain Reemer's voice blared over the PA system, "Four o'clock. Class over."

The five children threw down their crayons and ran outside. Jasmine stayed, studying Mitch.

Mitch smiled at her while collecting the crayons. Her flimsy silver-colored necklace was kinked where she twisted it. Then he saw them. Those fiery jade eyes. He dropped the crayons.

"Now I know who you are," she said. "Wasn't me broke your mother-fucking window. Cops come to my house and tell Momma she got to pay for it. That crackhead she got for a boyfriend beat my ass good. Hope that makes you happy, goddamn cracker."

"You shouldn't be breaking into people's trucks."

Jasmine stepped into him, their faces inches apart. Her lips and cheeks puffed in and out. "Come in here acting like you all that. Acting like you care about those kids. What you know about us?" Her green eyes blazed. "Lock your truck like an ignorant cracker and wonder why people break your window. You don't know nothing about nothing."

"How the hell do you know what I care about? You know nothing about me."

"I know you white. That's all I need to know." She clutched the tarnished silver-colored necklace, spun and left.

Chapter 14

Mitch was relieved to see hamburgers for supper and not chicken and rice again. He was still queasy. Watching the crew eat was like feeding time on the farm.

"Cops called with an update on the investigation from this morning," Captain Reemer said between bites. "The lady was a retired teacher from Chicago. Had medical issues, so she moved here to be with her loving daughter. This daughter has an impressive rap sheet: prostitution, drugs, violence. Known to hang with the One-Niners. Anyway, those assholes were cashing the old lady's social security and pension checks. That's why they didn't want her going to a nursing home. Checks would stop."

Ralph sneered. "Bastards are a fucking waste of skin."

Through the early evening, they responded to two false fire alarms, a diabetic with low blood sugar, and an asthmatic whose inhaler was empty. After the ten o'clock news, the crew filtered into the dormitory carrying their boots and bunker pants. They kept them at their bedside so when an alarm came in they could jump into the boots and pull up the bunker pants before sliding the pole to the rig.

Mitch stayed up, reading the training manual until his eyes blurred. He crept into the dorm, trying not to disturb the others. The dorm smelled like a dank calf barn. Ralph and Crusher snored a loud duet. Mitch crawled under the sheets and felt small, hard lumps scattered around him. He reached under the sheet and found a dinner roll. He collected the rolls from the bed and piled them on the floor. The rolls left the bed full of scratchy crumbs. Mitch tried to sleep on top of the bedspread but couldn't stop reliving the day, his first day on the job. Ralph was right. He was useless.

* * *

Six rings chimed over the alarm system. "Engine Fifteen respond to a report of a shooting at 845 West Meinecke Avenue."

Mitch slid the chrome pole to the apparatus floor before the dispatcher repeated the message.

"Damn, kid, you sleeping on the rig?" Kenny said as he climbed into the cab.

Approaching the scene, Crusher slowed the rig. The street was alive with a carnival of flashing lights from a swarm of police cars. Throngs of half-dressed people, some in nightgowns and some in shorts, milled about the adjacent yard. Kids ran around as if it were the middle of the day instead of middle of the night.

Mitch followed the captain up the crumbling steps of the small one-story bungalow, carrying the med kit and the oxygen. He had to hold it together this time. Prove he wasn't a total loser.

A disinterested, stocky police officer met them in the entryway. "Over there." He pointed to a group of cops in the front room.

"Oh, Lord. Not my baby boy. Please, Lord," echoed from down the hallway, followed by guttural wailing.

The cops parted, exposing a young man reclining in a brown leather lounger. A white-haired officer stepped in front of the captain. "Don't move anything until we're done with the investigation."

Captain Reemer pushed by the officer. "*We'll* decide what we need to do after we assess the patient."

"Fine. Have at it. Just don't touch the gun."

The patient was a young black man in his teens or early twenties with a smooth face and short stubble on his head. He appeared to be sleeping peacefully. A silver .357 caliber handgun lay at the side of the recliner.

Mitch snapped open the med kit and fished out the blood pressure cuff. A cop clicked on a lamp next to the recliner, illuminating the wall behind. Mitch gasped. The wall resembled an abstract painting, a rainbow of gray and red. The back of the young man's skull was gone.

Ralph pushed on Mitch's back. "Get in there, kid. Check vitals."

Mitch got a metallic whiff of blood and brain. He mouth breathed like Kenny told him. He could not let himself puke.

The young man sucked in a loud gurgling breath. Mitch jumped back. Kenny snickered.

"Ralph's working on you," the captain said. "We don't work patients with their brains blown out."

"He's breathing."

"Agonal breaths, the death rattle."

Kenny and Ralph inspected the artwork created from the man's blood and gray matter.

"Think he was shooting for Monet or Matisse?" Kenny said.

Ralph shoved Kenny. "Stop talking like a jag." He faced the white-haired officer. "Took the route, hey?"

The officer shrugged one shoulder.

Crushing sadness gripped Mitch. This kid had killed himself. Mitch didn't know a thing about him, just the horrible, relentless agony and hopelessness he must have been feeling right before he wrapped his lips around the cold barrel.

"Hey, kid? How about spaghetti next day for lunch?" Kenny said with a wise-ass grin.

The captain frowned. "Let's get you ghouls out of here. The M.E.'s got this."

* * *

On the way back to the firehouse, Mitch kept flashing from the image of the young man's serene face to the image of blood and brain on the wall.

"Hear that mother?" Ralph said to Kenny. "Fucked her up good splattering his brains against the wall. Goddamned coward. Life sucks and then you die. Have the balls to stick it out."

Coward. The word jolted Mitch. Was Ralph talking about him?

Thinking back to 9/11 and how close he had come to killing himself terrified him. And more terrifying was the fear of hopelessness returning. What do you do when every day is filled with one excruciating thought after another? How could death be worse? The young man knew about that. Mitch knew about that. He also knew returning to the farm would bring it all back.

"See the gray matter hanging from the roof of his mouth?" Kenny said to Ralph. "That's how you speak your mind." He turned to Mitch. "Hey, kid, you should have seen the guy who committed suicide by drinking furniture polish. It was a terrible end, but a beautiful finish." Kenny laughed alone at the joke. "Or what about the guy who swallowed a bottle of Midol? Didn't kill him but never got another cramp."

Mitch was relieved he kept it together this time. But a young man had taken his life. The crew's reaction sickened him.

Before they made it back to quarters, the dispatcher sent them to extinguish a dumpster fire followed by another one and yet another. Someone was having a good time keeping them busy.

They finally got back around 4 a.m. and trudged to the dormitory. Ralph and Crusher went into their duet as soon as their heads hit linen. Mitch couldn't sleep. He lay in bed agonizing about that day on the farm and whether he could have gone through with it. This guy had. His mom had.

Two gunshots rang out from the street below. The others never stirred. Mitch waited for the run that never came.

Mitch got up early and was soaping himself in the shower when the curtain opened and a naked Kenny climbed in behind him.

"We shower together around here to save on water," Kenny said. "We're real environmentalists." Kenny rubbed a bar of soap across Mitch's back.

Mitch jumped out of the shower and fled toward his locker, slipping on the cold tile floor.

Crusher and Ralph watched from the locker room bench.

Kenny leapt from the shower, naked and dripping. He was not a well-built man with his chicken legs and knobby knees. He strutted over to Mitch with hands on hips. "Well, I've never been so humiliated. Time I teach you a lesson."

Kenny pulled a bullwhip from an open locker. A loud crack echoed through the locker room as he snapped it at Mitch.

Mitch stepped back. "What the hell?"

Kenny came at Mitch. Not knowing what else to do, Mitch ran through the locker room with Kenny in hot pursuit, snapping the whip. Crusher snorted with laughter. Kenny charged after Mitch like an old lion, his saggy balls flopping back and forth. After circling the locker room twice, Kenny tossed the whip and bent over in laughter. "Mitch, you gotta lighten up and have some fun around here. It's not all blood and guts."

Mitch was now convinced there was something seriously wrong with all of them.

Crusher pointed at Mitch's bare arm. "What's that?"

"John Deere emblem."

"That's a jumping deer?"

Mitch pointed at the head. "Actually, it's a buck. See the rack?"

Ralph squinted at the tattoo. "Fuck that. Looks like Bambi to me."

Kenny and Crusher stepped back.

Ralph rammed a finger into Mitch's chest. "You weren't worth a shit yesterday. You're an embarrassment. Don't come back."

Chapter 15

"*Don't come back,*" resonated in Mitch's head on the drive home. How was he going survive the next eight months of the probationary period? April 8th was an eternity away.

By the time he reached the flat, he was drained and collapsed onto the couch. Visions of the young man's serene dark face and Maggie's soot-darkened face tormented his dreams. One wanted to die. One fought to live. One succeeded.

Banging on the door startled him. "Hey, Mitch. I know you in there. C'mon, get your ass up. It's after six." Jamal stepped inside and waved for Mitch to follow him. "Momma wants us to eat supper with her."

The fog cleared. "I'll be right down."

The aroma of roasting beef, bacon, and cinnamon drifting from Miss Bernie's flat had Mitch salivating like he hadn't eaten in a week. Jamal and Miss Bernie were waiting for him at a shiny gray Linoleum table with polished chrome legs. Black Jesus looked down on them from the light purple wall. White dish towels with purple embroidery hung from the towel rack.

Miss Bernie pointed to the empty chair. "Mitch, honey, set yourself down."

The table brimmed with a platter of roast beef swimming in brown gravy along with potatoes, carrots and onions, a pan of cornbread, a pot of greens with bacon, and a deep-dish apple pie.

Jamal reached for a carving knife. Miss Bernie slapped his hand and bowed her head. "Lord, bless this bounty we're about to share."

Jamal and Mitch bowed along.

"And thank you, Lord, for protecting these two young men as they seek to do good in your world, amen."

"Amen," Jamal and Mitch said in unison.

74

Jamal went to work carving the roast beef.

Miss Bernie rattled ice cubes and grape Kool-Aid into tall glasses. "So, Mitch, how that first day go?"

"Fine."

"Your mouth ain't saying the same as your eyes."

"Best be straight," Jamal said. "She'll take you to church."

"Had a couple of bad runs." Mitch took a long swallow of the sweet purple liquid. "A kid killed himself and nobody cared. They even joked about it."

"A black boy?" Miss Bernie asked.

"Yeah."

"Your people white?"

Mitch nodded. "I don't think they're racist, though."

"Umm-hmm. They tell you who they are if you watch close. My daddy told me haters didn't hide behind fake smiles down in Alabama. Think I prefer knowing."

"You grow up in Alabama, Miss Bernie?"

"Nah. Daddy move here right after I was born. They was factories all over hiring and not much down south. These streets was full a families with young'uns. We'd run the streets 'til the crickets chirped. I had so many friends. Families celebrated every little thing together." She closed her eyes. "Oh, Mitch, I wish you could of seen what it was like back then."

"What was your mom like?"

"Never knew her." Miss Bernie gazed out the window.

Mitch waited for an explanation. None came. "Oh, hey, Jamal, the girl who broke into my truck showed up at the firehouse with her little sister. Man, did she rip into me about turning her in. And she has these spooky green eyes."

"Jasmine. Think her daddy was mixed. Anyways, won't be long, she'll be hooking up with the One-Niners. They like 'em young when they brains soft, so they can mold them into little hoes."

Miss Bernie slapped Jamal's hand. "You keep talking foul language, boy, and I'll lay a knot on that big old head of yours."

"It's true, Momma."

"I don't need to hear about that foulness in my home."

"Miss Bernie, I'm supposed to tutor those kids and I don't have a clue," Mitch said.

Miss Bernie narrowed her eyes at Jamal. "You talking about the Richerson girl?"

Jamal nodded.

"Umm, umm, umm. That family sure know what the devil look like up close."

She turned to Mitch. "Why you wanna help those children?"

"I want to show my captain I can do something right."

"Don't care nothing about them children, just showing off to your boss?"

"I don't know. They sure don't like me much."

Miss Bernie pointed her fork at Mitch. "You best decide what you wanna do, help those children, or show off to the boss."

They ate in silence while Mitch's mind wandered back to the farm and how Maggie and the other neighbor kids flocked around him at social functions. When Mitch was around children, he was a kid again, full of fun and mischief.

"Miss Bernie, how *do* I help them? I really don't have a clue."

"Show them you care. Black kids no different than white."

After they finished eating, Miss Bernie sent them to the porch while she washed dishes.

"Got any brothers or sisters?" Mitch asked Jamal.

"A sister, Latonya. We called her Lettie. She run off over eight years ago. Her and Momma butt heads bad when she got to be a teenager. She smart and stubborn like Momma and look just like her, small and pretty. I take after my daddy, big and dumb."

"Dumb? Yeah, right. Look what you taught this dumb farm boy."

"True that."

"Whatever happened to your dad?"

"Pains Momma that Lettie gone but not that *he* left. Hey, what was the other bad run?"

"It was sickening. An old lady was rotting in a back bedroom, covered in maggots."

"That some nasty shit. Nobody know she dead?"

"She wasn't dead."

Jamal's mouth gaped open. "Damn."

"And there were people in the house who didn't give a crap about her. One had gold teeth and a One-Niner's tattoo on his neck."

"Over on Clarke, around Nineteenth?" Jamal asked.

"How'd you know?"

"One-Niner's crack house. They all suck the glass dick. Dude with the gold teeth is DeAndre. Used to call him DeeDee when we back in school. Momma took him in as a foster child when his momma went away. Dude's mind is gone. Who else there?"

"Two rough-looking guys and a young girl."

"She knocked up?"

"Big as a house."

"Oh, man. That LaMont's baby sister, Chirelle. She only fifteen."

"LaMont know?"

"He know better than to say something."

"What about the cops?" Mitch asked.

"People who talk end up a blood stain on the sidewalk."

"That's insane."

"Soon's I get ahead, I'm getting Momma out."

* * *

Mitch reported for duty before sunrise. The firehouse was dark. Two small round holes in one of the aluminum overhead doors caught his attention. The engine and crew were out, so he headed to the kitchen.

While scouring a baking pan, he heard the *rat-a-tat-tat-tat* of the rig's Jake brake as it slowed. Mitch trotted to the front and opened the overheads. The blue-shift crew rolled up in a battered fire engine that looked like it should be parked in a museum. They backed into quarters, *the teedle—teedle—teedle* of the backup warning system chiming. The crew jumped off, reeking of smoke, their faces streaked with sweaty soot.

"We used ten sections," the driver called back to the others.

DeWayne, Nic, and a firefighter Mitch didn't know went to work yanking sections of dirty, wet hose off the fire engine.

Mitch climbed into the hose bed and Nic followed. They worked shoulder to shoulder arranging fresh hose into neat folds. He tried to give her room, but she kept rubbing against him and smiling to herself. Mitch knew what she was trying to do and it was working. He adjusted himself to hide his arousal.

"What did you guys have?" Mitch asked, glancing at her clinging T-shirt.

"Another squib vacant. Somebody ought to show these assholes how to start a real fire. We should have been first in, but Thirty's ran by us before we could get to our masks."

"The masks?"

"They're in a side compartment on this old piece of shit. The other crews are masked up before we even get to ours. Sucks. Get anything last shift?"

"Just dumpsters."

Nic pressed her warm, wet T-shirt against Mitch's arm. She whispered, "Join me in the shower? You can wash my back."

Her hot breath in his ear turned his brain to mush.

Nic leaned back and laughed. "Or would you rather get in the shower with Kenny?" She cupped Mitch's ass. "Nice." She climbed off the rig. Mitch had to wait for the embarrassing bulge to fade.

Mitch stopped by the office to see if Lieutenant Laubner, the blue-shift officer, needed anything. His black hair was neatly combed, his face clean, no soot.

"Anything you need me to do?" Mitch asked.

"What the hell did you buffoons do to get the rig shot up?"

"I don't remember anybody shooting at us. I think I'd remember that."

"Don't be a smartass. You didn't see the holes in the overhead?"

"Saw them when I came in."

"The rounds went through and hit the front of our rig. Now we got this old Mack while they fix ours, thanks to you idiots."

Lieutenant Laubner waved him off. "Get the hell out of my sight."

* * *

Mitch's crew filtered in. His stomach jumped when Ralph ambled over. "See you didn't take my advice."

"Nope."

Ralph chewed on his cigar, squinting at him, challenging him. "Shame."

Mitch's jangled nerves had him on edge, but he refused to respond.

Ralph flicked cigar ashes on Mitch's shoes and walked away. "Fucking cub."

The captain, Ralph, Crusher, and Kenny were scarfing down rolls when Mitch stopped by the kitchen to make coffee. Tobacco smoke hung over the crew. Department rules against smoking in the firehouse were ignored on the red shift.

"Mitch, you hear any gunshots last shift?" The captain asked.

"Yeah, it was early in the morning after our last run."

"Keep the overheads closed from now on. Cops think it was the One-Niners. They shook them down over that old lady." The captain peered over his reading glasses at Ralph. "And loud-mouth over there had to jump in their shit."

Ralph chewed on his cigar like he didn't hear, then mouthed, "Fucking assholes."

The captain raised his eyebrows. "What, Ralph?"

"Nothing, boss."

"Good."

* * *

Late in the morning, Mitch checked in with Kenny to help prepare the noon meal.

"Hey, wanna see my dick?" Kenny asked.

"I don't think so."

He handed Mitch a huge stainless steel butcher knife. "Read the inscription on the blade."

It read *Dick Cutlery.*

Kenny chuckled. "Like the feel of my dick in your hand?"

Mitch grinned.

"Careful, it's got an edge like a straight razor." Kenny pointed to a long scar from his thumb to the middle finger. "Did that last year. Had to go in for stitches. When the doc asked what happened, I told him I laid my hand open with my dick. Should have seen the look on the nurse's face. Almost as good as yours." He handed Mitch a box of mushrooms. "Here, cut the jibas for the stroganoff." He winked at Mitch. "Be careful with my dick."

Chapter 16

Over the next two weeks, Mitch's shift had two minor kitchen fires, one dryer fire, and two garage fires. Even these minor fires were challenging in the August heat. The heavy gear trapped body heat and quickly sapped energy. Crusher hosed them down with cool water when they emerged from the fires to keep them from passing out.

Mitch got the pipe—the nozzle—at these smaller fires. Any serious fires would have Ralph on the pipe with the boss and Kenny backing him up. Mitch would be outside feeding hose.

Mitch got comfortable with the long list of duties but was frustrated by Ralph's constant nagging. Toilets and sinks were never clean enough, the fire engine never shiny enough, floors never swabbed properly, and grass never mowed right. On EMS runs, he bitched that Mitch was too slow with vitals or setting up the oxygen. When Mitch got the pipe at minor fires, he opened it too early or too late or too fast. The only way he was going to prove himself to the crew and the captain was at a good working fire.

Another day passed without that fire and without kids to tutor.

On the way home, he thought about giving Jennie another call. He'd been calling, hoping she had cooled off and was ready to talk but all she'd say is he knew where to find her, then hang up.

* * *

When Mitch returned from work in the morning, Miss Bernie met him on the porch with her arms clamped over her chest. "C'mon up here and set yourself down."

The porch swing creaked as Miss Bernie lowered herself onto it. Mitch sat across from her in the wicker loveseat padded with bright purple floral cushions.

"Seem like you been steering clear of me."

What could he say? She was right.

"You helping those kids or not?" The weathered swing squeaked while she rocked.

"No, ma'am. They haven't been back."

"Why not?

"I don't—"

"You don't what? Don't care?"

"No. It's not. I don't know."

"You giving up on those children?"

"Well, maybe they gave up on me," he said louder than intended.

Miss Bernie heaved herself from the swing and wagged her finger. "Well, let me tell you something, Mr. Mitch. Think the only way to save people is pulling them out of burning buildings? These kids around here are dying just like if they in a fire. They just dying slower." Miss Bernie stood over him and jammed her fists onto her hips. "Want to be a hero, figure how to help those young'uns. Might help put out what's burning inside you. You think you hiding all that pain? It's written all over your face. That's all I got to say. Now go sleep on it. Then do something before it's too late for them or you."

The screen door slammed behind her.

* * *

Miss Bernie was bent at the waist in the sweltering August heat, pulling weeds from her vegetable and flower garden when Mitch came down after catching a morning nap. Neat rows of tomatoes, peppers, cucumbers, zucchini, and acorn squash brightened the small plot with vibrant reds and greens. The edge of the garden blazed with blooming lavender bushes. The scent of lavender reminded Mitch of the smell of Jennie's hair. He pictured her freckled face and warm eyes. God, how he missed her. Would they ever be together again?

Miss Bernie wore a wide-brimmed straw hat with a purple scarf trailing off the back. She continued pulling weeds from around the tomato plants as if Mitch wasn't there. Pearls of sweat dripped from her petite nose.

It dawned on Mitch that purple was everywhere. "Miss Bernie, you sure like purple a lot."

"Umm-hmm. Color of hope. Used to be green lawns, flowers, an' houses painted all colors around here. Kids everywhere. Working folks coming and going at all hours to A.O.Smith. My daddy welded car frames there until they started shuttin' down. Jobs dried up. Daddy didn't last long after they laid him off. He took to the bottle 'til it took him."

"Sorry, Miss Bernie."

"Think about what I told you?"

"I do want to help those kids. I don't know how though."

Miss Bernie stopped pulling weeds and faced him. "Mitch, you smart and you got a gift. If it wasn't for you schoolin' him, Jamal would never got through training. You see, you use your gift to lift him. And I love you for that, Mitch Garner." She draped her sweaty arms around him. "You give my boy his pride back."

He tried to remember what his mother's hugs felt like.

Miss Bernie held him at arm's length. "You want that devil out your head, figure a way to lift those children like you did Jamal."

Chapter 17

Over the next two days, Mitch struggled for ideas on how to get the children to come back and still had nothing when he reported for duty. Nic met him at the front of the rig wearing sandals, tight black shorts, and a white lace blouse knotted across her slim waist. "Interested?" she asked as she swayed her bottom at him.

"In what?"

"Tell me you're not that dense."

Nic kept him off balance. Some days she ignored him and other days acted like she wanted to jump his bones. As much as he missed Jennie, he couldn't help fantasizing about what it would be like with Nic.

"I'm leaving for Cancun this morning. Shame you can't come along."

Before he could think of anything clever to say, she was gone.

Mitch spent the quiet morning mowing the firehouse lawn and anguishing over what to do about the kids. Jasmine and Alexus lived across from the firehouse, so he saw them come and go. If he was outside he waved. Alexus always waved back, but Jasmine ignored him and hurried Alexus along. On occasion, Mitch saw their mom's boyfriend leave the house wearing a long trench coat, no matter how hot the weather. Jasmine's mom usually came home late in the evening. She walked bent like she was climbing a steep hill.

Alexus burst onto the porch and hopped down the steps. Jasmine was right behind. He had to do something *now*. He sprinted across the street and knelt in front of Alexus. "Hi, Lexi, when you coming back to do some more coloring?"

"We can't come no more."

"I thought we were having fun."

Alexus looked up to Jasmine.

Jasmine glared at Mitch. "Get your honky ass back across the street."

"At least tell me why the kids won't come around."

"Told them not to."

"Why'd you tell them that?"

"Lexus, go back inside." Alexus ran into the house.

"You ignorant motherfucker. You fucked my shit up when you turn me in. Momma still paying for that stupid window. She working two shifts at the laundry to pay it off, leaving us alone with that worthless crackhead of hers. So I got no time for your silly-assed shit."

Through the fury and foul language, there was sadness in her green eyes.

Mitch tried to think of something to say before she marched off.

"I didn't do nothing to your truck." Jasmine was on the verge of tears. "I was just hanging with those kids when they did it. Ain't right I got to take the shit for it."

"Why didn't you tell the cops?"

"You *are* ignorant. I tell them who did it, I end up like my sister."

"What happened to your sister?"

The rage drained from her face. "Don't matter."

Miss Bernie's words came back to him. *They just dying slower.*

"Jasmine, would you get those kids back if I paid your mom for my window?"

She studied Mitch. "What I got to do? You one of those sick dudes into young girls?"

"No, no, no. Jesus, no. I feel bad you got blamed. That wasn't right. I can see it was my fault for being such a cracker." He grinned, hoping to convince her.

Her lips curled into a slight smile. "You a cracker all right."

"We got a deal?" Mitch asked.

She cocked her head and twisted the cheap silver-colored necklace between her thumb and finger. "How I know I can trust you?"

"Seems like I'm the only one who has anything to lose. Your mom could take my money and leave me hanging."

"Damn, you're ignorant. I catch serious shit if word gets on the street I'm helping some honky-assed fireman."

"What about helping the kids?"

"From what I seen, you ain't so good with kids."

"We got a deal?"

Mitch noticed flecks of gold in her emerald eyes as she studied him. "I got to kick it around some." She went to the porch and hollered, "Lexus, c'mon, we goin'."

"Okay. Let me know," Mitch said to her back.

* * *

Mitch waited by the front door, watching their house. At three-thirty he gave up and went to the kitchen to help Kenny. He dreaded telling Miss Bernie the kids wouldn't come back.

After supper, he took some study materials outside to the worn bench in front of the firehouse. Mitch stretched out and soaked in the laughter and shouts of children playing in the vast, empty lot behind the firehouse. Rusted abandoned cars, appliances, and piles of junk served as their jungle gyms. It could be the laughter of children anywhere. The smell of fresh-cut grass in the still air masked the stench of hopelessness.

Mitch closed his eyes and pictured lush green fields of ripening corn with golden tassels. He missed the smell of the farm, the smell of life. And Jennie. He ached to gaze into her soft brown eyes and to feel her body pressed against him.

The vision of the farm faded and he opened his eyes, focusing on the girls' house. The roof was missing shingles. The porch had holes and badly warped boards. One step was completely missing. The bleached gray siding showed no sign of what color it had once been. The dying house screamed for attention.

* * *

Mitch spent the next day off consumed by thoughts of Jasmine. He felt awful about causing her so much misery. He'd make it right somehow. The steamy August afternoon forced Mitch outside to the porch swing.

"Sup, little bro?" Jamal said from the sidewalk, carrying a twelve pack of Miller Light. "Thought you could use a taste." Jamal bounded up the steps.

Miss Bernie was inside. A heart-rending version of *Without You* was blaring from the television.

Jamal clinked his can against Mitch's. "Here's to you, Firefighter Garner."

"And to you, Firefighter Jackson." Mitch snapped the pop tab and took a sip. "Your mom's not happy with me."

"Don't feel like you the only one. Thinks I need me a family. Right now I'm a popular man. Got me light skins and dark skins waiting for me to sample the goods. Don't care much for those bony-assed bitches though, prefer a thick girl. I mean look at the size of me. What would I do with one a those lollipops?"

Jamal took a long swallow and belched. "What's up with that lanky girl from back home?"

"Messed that up, bad."

"Then get your ass out there and get yourself a little sumpin sumpin. I know some light skins wouldn't mind getting under a white boy."

Jamal's roaring laughter had Mitch laughing along.

"You boys keep it down," Miss Bernie said from inside. "I'm trying to hear this."

Mitch leaned toward Jamal so Miss Bernie couldn't hear. "There's a smoking hot firefighter on the blue shift who seems interested, but I can't tell if she's just screwing with me."

"Then put your game on her."

"I don't know. I want to get back together with Jen."

"Don't tell her."

"I can't lie."

"You best tap that smoking booty before she loses interest."

A captivating voice coming from the television caught their attention. The audience erupted in applause. The announcer said, "Kelly Clarkson, ladies and gentlemen."

"What's Momma preaching on you about?"

"I told her I don't think the kids are coming back. You know, the ones I'm supposed to tutor? Said I needed to figure something out."

"She'll keep pecking at you 'til you do."

* * *

After Jamal left, Mitch drove to North Avenue and parked a block from the Laundromat where Jasmine's mom works. She usually walked home around eleven.

He recognized her by the way she walked, bent, her shoulders stooped. He stepped in front of the stout bulldog of a woman as she ambled along.

"Get the fuck out the way." She pushed at him and scooted around.

"No, wait. I wanted to talk to you about Jasmine."

She spun and jutted her chin. "Don't you be fussin' with that child. Ain't even formed yet." Her droopy eyes went wide. They were Jasmine's green eyes, but hollow. "Get the fuck out my way before I call poh—leese."

"Wait, wait, wait. I'm a firefighter. I work across the street from your house."

She looked at Mitch's truck. "Ohhh. You the one with the truck. I oughta beat your ass." Her listless eyes showed no sign of the anger in her voice.

"I want to pay for the window. Jasmine told me she didn't break it."

"Why you do that?"

"Just want to make things right."

The woman's mouth twisted to the side. "What else you want?"

"I'm supposed to tutor Alexus and some other kids. It's part of my job, but I can't get them to come. I need Jasmine's help."

"Sound like some bullshit to me."

"How about I fix your roof? Must leak bad when it rains."

The woman narrowed her eyes, studying Mitch as he pulled a check-book from his back pocket.

"Who should I make it out to?" Mitch asked.

"Benita Richardson, spell with BE, not BO," she said, cocking her head while she watched him fill in the amount, $450.

Mitch ripped off the check. "Extra's for your trouble. I really am sorry."

Benita snatched the check and strode down the sidewalk.

Chapter 18

Next day at work, three o'clock came and went with no kids. Hope faded. Later that night, the fire alarm chimed. The dormitory clock read three-thirteen. "Engine Fifteen, Engine Thirty, Engine Thirty-two, Trucks Twelve and Nine, Battalion Two, and Battalion Five respond to a report of a fire…"

Mitch slid the pole and raced for the rig. After two weeks and countless runs, gearing up was automatic. He was always first on the rig.

The biting smell of an angry fire filled the cab as they rolled out of quarters. An orange glow lit up the sky. The captain shouted over his shoulder, "We got a worker. Thirty's will be right on our ass. Mitch, lay out the line to the back while Ralph and Kenny mask up. You mask up after they take the line."

Adrenalin was on full flow. Mitch would get to lay out the first line to a working fire.

They were first on scene. Flames licked from the doorway of the first-floor tavern. Dark smoke heaved from second-floor windows. Mitch leapt off the rig. Intense heat stung the side of his face. The captain radioed in a report to the dispatcher while Ralph and Kenny ran to the side of the fire engine for their air packs. Rigs barreled down the block toward them, sirens blaring, red and white strobes reflecting off the houses.

"Get that goddamn line laid out before Thirty's gets here," Ralph hollered.

Mitch pulled the quick attack line off the side of the engine and ran it to the back of the building. He looped several sections around the back lot so it would play out smoothly. He went to the nozzle and waited.

Engine Thirty's crew stormed up to him. "We'll take that line," the lieutenant said.

"That's our line."

"I don't give a fuck. We're taking the line. Now move. That's an order."

A tall, lanky firefighter shoved Mitch and jerked the nozzle away from him. The firefighter sneered and took off for the back door, leaving Mitch speechless.

"Tell your loser crew they can back us up anytime," Engine Thirty's lieutenant said as he and two firefighters crawled into the black smoke churning from the open doorway.

Seconds later Mitch's crew tore around the side of the blazing structure.

Ralph frowned at Mitch. "Where's our line?"

"Engine Thirty took it."

"Goddamn it. You never give up the line. That was our fire."

"All right, all right, all right," the captain said. "Settle down. Mitch, get your mask. Ralph, you and me will see about taking our line back from those bastards. Kenny, you and Mitch get a line to the second floor."

Mitch wasted no time masking up and followed Kenny up the blinding stairwell with the hose.

"Mitch, stay at the top of the stairs and feed me hose."

Mitch wrestled the hose up the stairs as Kenny disappeared into the smoke. The hose stopped advancing. Muffled cries penetrated the darkness. "Kenny, hear that? —Kenny?"

Mitch dropped the hose and crawled into the hallway, trying to get a fix on the faint sound. The cry intensified to a chilling moan, sounding like it came from the first room off to his left.

"Kenny. Kenny. I got someone here."

Mitch froze as the panic and confusion took him back to that burning farmhouse, and Maggie. *No, not again.* He fought through the paralyzing panic and crawled into the ink-black room toward the guttural moans. Sweeping the floor with his arms, he hit something that yowled. He pulled it close to his facepiece. It clawed at him. *Crap.* He clutched the cat and ran it down the stairwell and let it go into the night, then raced back to the top of the stairs. Kenny was hollering for him. Mitch followed the hose line into the blackness, down the long hall, and into a small room, bumping into Kenny. "I'm here."

"Where the hell you been? My back gave out pulling this tub of lard out of bed. You'll have to get him out. I can barely crawl."

Mitch slid his arms under the armpits of the limp body and dragged him down the hall.

Clomping from the stairwell. The captain's voice cut through the darkness, "Got anything?"

"Got a man down," Kenny said. "Mitch needs help getting him out. My back fucked up again."

Mitch and Ralph wrestled the man down the stairs and outside where the paramedics were waiting.

"Let's get another line on the fire," the captain said.

Kenny limped toward the doorway. The captain stopped him. "Not you. You get checked out."

Inside the burning tavern, Mitch fed Ralph and Captain Reemer hose as they advanced through the building, hosing down hot spots, backing up Engine Thirty's attack on the fire. While they sprayed water, Mitch pulled plaster from the ceiling and walls like a maniac. The harder he worked, the less he thought about screwing up. *A stupid cat.*

After the fire was out, they spent a good hour overhauling the building, making sure every last dying ember had been extinguished. They were told to leave as much intact as possible. The police arson team would be investigating.

Back at the rig, the chief approached them. "I'll need statements from all of you on what you saw when you got here. The occupant on the second floor was the owner of the bar. He's DOA."

Mitch swallowed hard.

Kenny was inside the rig waiting, bent forward, his face ashen.

"You okay?" the captain asked Kenny.

Kenny nodded.

"Fucking cub," Ralph said as they pulled away from the scene.

Nobody said anything on the way to quarters.

* * *

Back at the firehouse, Crusher, Ralph, and the boss silently went about repacking fresh hose while Mitch sanitized and checked the masks. By the time they were done, it was after six in the morning. They plodded to the kitchen for coffee before showering. Mitch went to the sink to wash dishes while Ralph fired up a stogie. Kenny was hunched over the table.

The captain waved Mitch over to the table. "Sit down."

Mitch swallowed back sour bile and moved to the bench, away from the others.

The captain shook the end of his pipe at Mitch. "My top priority as an officer is to ensure everyone goes home in the morning in one piece. So when we get a worker, we talk it over afterward. If somebody screws up, we all learn from it. And we've all screwed up." The captain pointed at Ralph. "Right, Ralph?"

Ralph blew bitter cigar smoke at the ceiling.

"Anyway, companies in the Core think they're the gods of fire. We all feel like we're the best and we'll do anything to show up the other companies. It's fierce. So when Engine Thirty took our line, that was an insult, an attack on us. You get that, Mitch?"

"Yeah, I get it. But the lieutenant ordered me to give them the line."

He could have murdered a baby from their expressions.

"Next time tell the boss you've been ordered by me not to give up the line. And fight like hell for it. Tell him to go fuck himself. I'll back you."

Mitch stared at his folded hands.

"We'll hear about that one for a long time. Not much we can do now."

"Oh, I don't know. I got an idea," Kenny said.

"Oh for Christ's sake, don't do anything stupid." The captain's eyes narrowed. "How'd you wrench your back?"

Kenny glanced at Mitch and back at the captain. "You saw the size of that bastard. Me and Mitch found him and were pulling him out. I got careless, should have used my legs."

Mitch couldn't let Kenny lie. He took a deep breath and told them about the cat and leaving Kenny alone.

The captain rubbed his chin. "Get cleaned up and meet me in my office." He headed down the hallway.

Ralph jammed his cigar into the red clay ashtray. "I knew you'd screw up. A man died while you were rescuing a fucking cat."

The others said nothing. Mitch took a quick shower and trudged to the captain's office with his badge.

The captain motioned for Mitch to sit. "Took guts to admit that."

Mitch laid the badge on the desk.

"Kenny should have kept in voice contact. But, and this is a big but, you should not have left him. Things turn to shit in a flash. Learn from this."

The captain examined Mitch's badge. "I'll keep this until next shift. You give this some serious thought. None of us can say we never screwed up.

God knows I've had my share of fuck-ups. We all have. It's the nature of our job. We're forced to make split-second, life and death decisions. Can't exactly call a meeting to discuss options. Sometimes bad things come from those decisions and we have to live with it. You'll have to decide whether you can live with yourself after a bad one. Some can't."

Chapter 19

The pungent sweet-sour aroma of manure blew in through the open window of Mitch's truck on the way to the farm. He forgot how good it felt to breathe the fresh stew of the farmland, the sweet smell of home.

The fields should have been bursting with tall green stalks of corn ripening in the late August sun. Instead, shriveled yellow spears swayed in the sweltering afternoon wind. Even farms with irrigation systems had stunted corn. Mitch never imagined the drought had been this bad.

He idled up the long drive to their farmhouse, scanning the fields for signs of Sid or Chris. Billy watched from the porch. When Mitch jumped down from the truck, the chunky black lab bolted at him, knocked him over, and lathered Mitch's face with saliva. Mitch wrestled with his old friend, then headed to the house.

The house was quiet. Not much had changed since he left. Dirty pots and pans lined the counter, and the cavernous kitchen still smelled funky. He stared at his mom's chair, overcome with the emotion of being home, but not being home.

The porch boards creaked. Chris bounded into the kitchen. "Thought I heard your truck." Chris pulled Mitch into a bear hug. "Damn, it's good to see your ugly face."

Mitch choked.

"Whoa. What's wrong?" Chris asked.

"Dad around?"

"What am I, Swiss cheese?"

Mitch forced a weak smile. "How's Pulvermacher working out?"

"You saw the corn. Total loss. We didn't get much hay either. After the fire, we didn't have money for crop insurance." Chris paused. "Even with the money you send us, we're falling behind. Had to let Pulvermacher go. Dad's at the bank right now, begging for extensions on our loans."

"Damn, he must hate me."

"Enough of our troubles. What about you? Save any lives?"

"You see Jen around?"

"Once in a while at the Hideaway. She's bartending Saturday nights."

"She seeing anyone?"

Chris clenched his lips.

"Who?"

"Some guy nursing student. I don't know. Ain't from around here."

"Crap." Mitch headed to the door.

"Sorry, brother."

Mitch took a long walk around the farm. Instead of grazing on green fertile pastures, the cows were feeding on dry bales of hay. The woods was still blackened from the fire. Many of the trees were barren, but the massive oak had sprouted leaves on its upper branches. Mitch sat at the base of the old oak for hours convincing himself he was ready to come back.

* * *

Sid's rusted, gray pick-up rattled into the drive. Mitch traipsed to the house fantasizing about Sid telling him how much he missed him, pleading with him to come back to the farm.

Sid was hunched over a folder of papers at the kitchen table.

"Hi, Dad," Mitch said, lowering himself into his old spot at the table.

"Why you here?" Sid said while shuffling papers.

"Wanted to stop by for a visit. See how things are going."

"Things are fine."

"Chris said the farm might be in trouble."

"Things are fine."

"I was thinking, maybe I'd quit the fire department and come back."

"Said things are fine. Don't need your help."

"But, Chris said…"

"I don't give a shit what Chris said." Sid looked up from the papers, his face reddening. "Go help those black bastards in Milwaukee that were more important than your own family."

Sid's fierce scowl burned away any thought of coming back to the farm. Billy followed Mitch outside. "Sorry, Boy. You can't come." The dog whimpered as Mitch climbed into his truck.

He didn't know where else to go, so he drove to the Milroy Firehouse. The place was deserted. He went inside and lay down on a cot. After working most of the night at the tavern fire, driving to Milroy, and then getting run off the farm, he was spent. He had to get some rest before heading out to the Rock River Hideaway to see Jennie. If he could get her back, everything else would work out. They were only taking a break, after all.

He awoke to thunder and pounding rain. *Sure. Now it rains. Must be God's twisted sense of humor.*

* * *

Saturday nights the Rock River Hideaway was the place to be. It was the only bar for miles around, located three miles from Milroy. Mounted deer heads with wide racks adorned the wood-paneled walls. A giant shoulder mount of a moose watched over the pool table. A loud chorus of the song *Where I Come From* rang out as Mitch made his way to the bar. Some in the raucous crowd waved cans of beer in the air while singing along to Alan Jackson on the jukebox. A cloud of cigarette smoke hung over the rowdy group of young people. The cigarettes, stale beer, sweating bodies, and too much cologne blended into a heady mixture.

Mitch gazed around the bar. It all felt different, strange somehow. Jennie was at the far end with her back to Mitch, talking to a neatly dressed young man wearing a light gray blazer. The sight of her disheveled auburn hair, loose-fitting T-shirt, and denim shorts filled him with a familiar yearning.

He swung a leg over a round wooden bar stool. Mitch's old friend, Danny Mueller, ambled over. "About time you showed your ugly face."

Jennie marched toward them, her cowboy boots clacking on the concrete floor.

Danny clapped Mitch on the back. "Talk later. Jennie looks pissed."

"Jen, I need to tell you…"

She slid a can of Miller Light at him. "Not now." And then she was gone, working her way around the bar, taking orders and filling drinks.

She paused when she got to the neatly dressed young man. The man laughed and grinned with his face close to hers. She patted his arm. Before turning back to the bar, she rubbed his cheek.

Mitch ground his teeth together.

Every time Jennie made her way to Mitch, he wanted to jump over the bar and take her in his arms. When he tried to say something, she raised her hand, slid another beer at him, and walked away.

A steady stream of old friends came by, asking him about Milwaukee. He tried to listen to what they were saying, but he was locked onto Jennie. He answered their questions with, "It's a tough job. Things are going good. I'm fine." The friends drifted away as the night wore on. By closing time he was alone at the end of the bar nursing his beer.

"Mitch, c'mon. I'll take you home," Jennie said from behind him. "You shouldn't drive."

"I'm not drunk."

"Well, you look like hell."

"I can't go back to the farm."

"No, I mean my place."

"Your fancy friend okay with that?"

"Shut up before I change my mind."

When they got into her truck, Mitch said, "Jen, I have to tell you something."

"Not now."

* * *

Mitch followed her into the apartment. Lemon Pledge never smelled so good. Jennie led him into her cozy living room, stopped, and pressed her lips to his. She leaned back. Her warm brown eyes glistened. "You gonna kiss me or just stand there?"

He pulled her close. Her hair smelled like the smoky bar with a hint of lavender shampoo. They kissed and groaned, tongues probing. They tugged each other's clothes off, tossing them to the floor. Her warm, smooth skin against his sent a luxurious rush through him. As soon as they hit the carpet he pushed inside her. It was over fast. He collapsed on top of her. She held him until he faded and their breathing slowed. Why had he waited so long to come back?

She led him back to the bedroom. "Like the view?"

"Nicest ass in Milroy."

"And Milwaukee?"

"Nothing even close."

She raised an eyebrow. "Right."

They rediscovered each other with their hands and tongues and settled into the slow rhythm of lovers trying to make it last as long as possible. This is where Mitch belonged. Everything would be fine.

Mitch woke to the smell of cinnamon buns and brewing coffee. The thought of spending the day with Jennie, lounging and talking, gave him a warm glow. She was at the plastic folding card table in the kitchen, wearing his dark blue MFD T-shirt and nothing else. The shirt barely covered her slim hips. He couldn't help but stare at her long legs.

Jennie frowned. "Jesus, didn't you get enough last night?"

"Didn't hear any complaints."

She pointed to a platter of golden brown buns slathered with white frosting. "Stuff a bun in it, dickwad," she said, smiling.

He wolfed down a cinnamon bun in three bites, savoring the rich cream-cheese frosting.

"Hey, what's going on with that guy you were hanging all over last night?"

"Last night you couldn't wait to talk. Now talk."

Jennie's smile disappeared. Mitch froze. The apartment was still, except for the *click clack, click clack* of the pendulum clock in the living room.

"Mitch." She cupped her hands over his. "If you're not going to tell me what's going on you can leave. I've been through this before. I can't do it again."

He took a breath and began. The words came slowly. He told her about the treatment he was getting from Ralph, about leaving Kenny in the fire and the guy dying, and his miserable failure of tutoring the neighbor kids. He choked up telling her about the young man's suicide and how the crew joked about it.

"That's sick," Jennie said.

"I can't go back."

"What would you do if you quit?"

"All I know is I want to be with you."

Mitch studied her face for a sign. She chewed her lower lip while wringing her hands. "You hurt me bad, Mitch."

"What about last night. What was that all about?"

"If you quit and came back, why would anything be different? What's changed?" She shook her head frantically. "If you think by being with me, you'll be fine again, that somehow I have the power to keep you from getting depressed, from thinking about..."

"What if I stay on the department and you come live with me?" Desperate, he said, "Marry me."

She went to him. He held her until she pulled away.

"I can't do this, Mitch. I have exams tomorrow. I have to finish nursing school. You need to finish what you started in Milwaukee. You were so full of hope and pride at your graduation. You need to get that back." She pressed her lips to his so very gently. "Bye, Mitch."

Chapter 20

The drive back from Milroy was a blur. He'd been on autopilot, replaying the last twenty-four hours over and over again. Every time he heard Jennie say, "Bye, Mitch," his chest ached.

Both sides of Hawkins Street were lined with cars. Mitch had to park a block away from the flat. A crowd milled around Miss Bernie's yard. Two police cars were parked across the street from her house. Getting closer, he saw people arm in arm, staring at the ground.

He sprinted toward the house where a group of older women had gathered on the porch. The top of Miss Bernie's head was barely visible through the gathering. He blew out a sigh of relief and shuffled up the steps. The older women stepped aside. Miss Bernie looked up, her eyes dark and watery, her chin quivering. "They kilt him, Mitch. Shot him in the street like a stray dog."

"Who?"

"My boy gone." She looked to the blue sky. "Ohh, Lord, Lord, Lord. Why?"

She couldn't be talking about Jamal. No.

"They took my baby boy." Her body shook.

Mitch choked as the words sunk in.

The heavy woman behind Miss Bernie rubbed her back. "Bernice, c'mon and set yourself down."

Miss Bernie reached for Mitch. They hugged. "Jamal love you like a brother," she whispered, then followed the heavy woman to the porch swing, sobbing.

Mitch wandered around the yard, numb.

LaMont edged up to him. "This the shits, man."

"Who did this?"

LaMont glanced back at a group of young black men. "Nobody knows nothin'."

"Who did this?"

LaMont shifted on his feet. "Don't know, man. Bad shit happens around here."

Mitch shook him by the shoulders. "Who did this? He was your friend, for Christ's sake."

"Let it go or you'll end up..." LaMont lowered his head.

Red flares flickered behind Mitch's eyes. His ears rang. "Fuck that, LaMont. Fuck that. I'll hunt the bastard down. Jamal deserves that. So fucking tell me who did this."

LaMont pushed Mitch away. "Let it go. Things not like where you come from. Jamal gone. Nothin' gonna fix that." LaMont slinked over to the group of young black men.

"Fuck you, LaMont." Heads jerked in Mitch's direction.

* * *

Late-night news reports on television repeated the same information. "Milwaukee Firefighter Jamal Jackson was found dead in the seventeen hundred block of Wright Street with multiple gunshot wounds. Police have no leads at this point. Anyone with information is urged to contact the Milwaukee Police Department hotline." Mitch stayed up, hoping to hear more, but the newscasts were playing footage from 9/11 with the first anniversary only two weeks away.

Mitch thought back to their first meeting when he was sure the big guy was going to kick his ass in the locker room of the academy. And how they became close friends. Saturdays, after studying for exams, Jamal would show Mitch around Milwaukee. They'd hit the popular bars on the fashionable East Side and enjoy the lakefront festivals. They'd wind down late in the evening with long talks, usually about women, sometimes sharing their excitement of what it would be like when they graduated and got assigned to a firehouse. Mitch stopped thinking of him as his black friend. He was Jamal's little bro'.

Soft knocking pulled him from his thoughts. It was after midnight.

Miss Bernie stood in the open doorway. Her normally tidy hair hung in dark shreds.

"I can't sleep either," Mitch said.

They settled onto the couch. "Oh, Mitch, what we gonna do without our Jamal?" Her whispery voice was distant.

"Miss Bernie, you have any idea who did this?"

"Got nobody left."

"No other family?"

"When Daddy move us up here they all turn their back on us. We the only ones come north. Daddy said he was the black sheep. Never told me why. And I never dared ask him again." Miss Bernie rubbed her forehead. "Why bad things always gotta be black?"

Mitch lowered his head, not knowing what to say.

Miss Bernie continued. "Anyways, we never had nothing to do with relation down in Alabama, so I never did get to know them while Daddy was alive. He wouldn't allow it. Just a shame he let his stubbornness pull us away from all that family."

This reminded Mitch of his own stubborn father. "You have any brothers or sisters?"

She blew out a weary breath. "After Daddy passed I got ahold of a cousin down there. She told me Momma died birthin' me. Said Daddy refuse to take her to the doctor. Didn't believe in them." She paused. "Shame Momma's family couldn't find it in their hearts to forgive him. He was a good man." She held her face in her hands. "Got nobody."

Mitch rubbed her bony arm. "I'm here."

"The devil's got a hold down here an' he ain't giving it up. You go on back to the farm before he take you too."

A siren ran through the night. On the farm, nights were filled with symphonies of nocturnal insects, the sounds of life. Here it was the sounds of violence, suffering, and death.

"I can't leave," Mitch whispered, not sure if she heard him.

Chapter 21

The department flag was at half-staff when Mitch pulled up to the firehouse to report for work the next morning. He started in on the daily routine by going over the masks.

Ralph came around the side of the rig. "Jackson in your class?"

"Yup."

"Why didn't he move out of this cesspool?"

"Don't know."

"Well, he should have been smarter."

Mitch stepped into Ralph. "Shut the fuck up. Say whatever you want about me. Just shut the fuck up about Jamal. He was smart."

Ralph took a step back. His eyes widened. "Didn't say he wasn't." He reeled and left.

The captain called Mitch into the office. He came around the desk and handed Mitch his badge. "Glad you're back."

"I won't let you down again."

Captain Reemer waved his palm. "I understand Jackson was your classmate."

"He was a good friend."

"We're family and Firefighter Jackson was part of that family. You're not alone. We grieve together." The captain stepped back. "You gonna be okay? I can get you some time off."

"Rather keep working if that's okay."

The captain nodded.

* * *

Late in the morning, Crusher, Kenny, and Ralph emerged from the basement. Kenny said, "Best you don't know anything, kid."

The day dragged on with three EMS runs and a kitchen fire by afternoon. Mitch struggled to focus. He got the pipe at the kitchen fire and quickly extinguished it. The boss congratulated him on a job well done, and Ralph kept his mouth shut. This should have felt good.

During the afternoon Mitch studied the training manual at the joker stand where he could hear radio transmissions and watch people come and go in the neighborhood.

Rattling at the front door startled him. Chief Corliss yanked on it, scowling. The chief's hair was as black and shiny as his patent leather shoes. Mitch had heard from the others the chief was not well respected. His nickname was Slick Dick because he was always screwing with people. Mitch unlocked the door.

The chief pushed by him. "Where's your boss?"

"Should be in the office, sir."

The chief barged into Captain Reemer's office without knocking. Several minutes later, the captain's voice came over the PA system. "All members to the kitchen, immediately."

Crusher, Kenny, and Ralph were waiting in the kitchen when Mitch got there. Kenny grinned at Mitch. "Wait 'til you hear this, kid. It's a masterpiece."

The chief marched into the kitchen and slammed a glossy eight by ten photograph on the table of three men mooning the camera with doughnuts dangling from their butt cracks. "What the hell is wrong with you people?"

The faces weren't visible, but Mitch could see it was Crusher's broad ass, Kenny's scrawny ass, and Ralph's dark, wooly ass.

Captain Reemer stood behind the chief, gazing at the ceiling. Crusher, Kenny, and Ralph exchanged glances, shaking their heads.

"I'd say those are some mighty fine tushies there," Kenny said. "But I can't say I recognize them." The others snickered.

The chief poked his finger at them. "Goddamnit. I don't need this shit in my battalion." He turned to Captain Reemer. "Captain, a report. I want somebody on charges. Try to control these misfits. Jesus Christ." The chief threw up his hands and stomped down the hallway.

Captain Reemer leaned over the table. "So this is how you jags get back at Thirty's?" He glared at the giggling group. "You guys are unbelievable. I'm in awe. I don't know how you came up with that one. It's genius."

Laughter bounced off the walls.

"Kenny, fill Mitch in. He looks confused," the captain said.

"We had a box of doughnuts delivered to Thirty's this morning with a note from the neighbors of the tavern thanking them for protecting their house." Kenny smirked. "Then we had *that* picture delivered in the afternoon mail addressed to Engine Thirty with a note that said 'Tasty?'."

As sick as this was, Mitch couldn't resist laughing along.

"So, boss. We all on charges?" Crusher asked.

"If this goes upstairs it makes the battalion look bad and he'll catch hell. I'll tell him you misfits will write personal letters of apology to anyone who ate the doughnuts. I'm pretty certain nobody's going to fess up to eating doughnuts from your wrinkled asses. So, miraculously, nobody ate them. Problem solved."

Kenny, Crusher, and Ralph headed to the alligator pit, clapping each other on the back.

After supper, Mitch took the training manual to the bench in front of the firehouse. The familiar odor of ripe garbage hung in the muggy air, but he barely noticed anymore.

Mitch felt the booming bass before the dark blue Mercury Cougar with huge chrome wheels and low profile tires slowed to a stop across from the firehouse. The tinted window slid down. The driver sneered at him, flashing his gold teeth. Alexus ran out of the house as Jasmine emerged from the back of the car. The little girl hugged her big sister. The two of them hopped up the steps and went inside. As the car pulled away, DeAndre stuck his arm out the window, splaying fingers in the One-Niner's gang sign.

Chapter 22

"A glorious day for the funeral," Mitch heard someone say when he went downstairs in the morning to ask Miss Bernie if she needed help with anything. Seemed a strange thing to say. The crowded kitchen buzzed with activity, thick with the smells of baking casseroles and pies and the chatter of finely dressed ladies.

The funeral was being held one week after Jamal's passing to allow estranged relatives from Alabama to make the trip north for the services. Miss Bernie had the funeral parlor place an obituary in the Tuscaloosa newspaper. Late in the week, four cousins arrived. They stayed with her and pitched in. Stories were shared of aunts and uncles Miss Bernie never met. Miss Bernie came up to Mitch's flat in the evenings to get away from them. She knew they meant well, but she didn't much like people fussing over her. She told Mitch it helped take the sadness away to be with someone who shared her love of Jamal. None of the cousins or church friends had known him. When he was a kid, he hated going to church. Once he was a grown man, Miss Bernie couldn't get him to go anymore. And she didn't push him. She believed everyone comes to the Lord in their own time.

The night before the funeral, Miss Bernie came up and took her seat on the couch. She rested her head on his shoulder and sobbed. "Oh, Mitch. How can there be another tear left in me?"

After the tears ebbed, Miss Bernie wiped her eyes and kissed the back of Mitch's hand. "I have so many proud memories of my boy. I was remembering back when DeAndre stayed with us and came home crying because the older kids were beating on him after school. Jamal walked DeAndre home every day after that." She smiled somberly. "I was so proud of my boy. It's easy for a child to stand back when somebody else getting picked on. Easy for grown folk too. We all need someone standing up for us. That's what Jamal would do. That was his gift."

Mitch thought back to the training academy and how Jamal got between him and LaMont and saved their jobs. Now he understood. Jamal couldn't stand to see anybody getting messed with.

* * *

It *was* a glorious morning. A warm September breeze blew through the Core. Mitch pulled the truck to the front of the house and waited for Miss Bernie with the engine rattling, filling the air with diesel fumes. Miss Bernie ambled down the steps accompanied by three heavy ladies, all dressed in brightly colored dresses, wearing crimson lipstick and wide floppy hats. It surprised Mitch to see such vibrant clothing for a funeral.

One woman urged Miss Bernie to ride with them, telling her she can't be riding to her son's funeral in that noisy, smelly truck.

"I'm going with Mitch. And that's that," she said. The other women scoffed, but nobody argued.

Cars, fire engines, and ladder trucks jammed the street in front of a faded white one-story brick building that could have been a corner store at one time. A small sign in front said: *New Hope Baptist Church, Reverend Turner Presiding, Sunday Services 8:00 A.M. and Noon.*

Engine Fifteen was parked behind Engine Twenty-Seven, Jamal's company. Firefighters congregated around the rigs, some in dark blue dress uniforms and others in their on-duty powder blue shirts with badges.

Miss Bernie sniffled and wiped at her nose with a purple handkerchief. "Lookit all the people. Oh, Lord, give me strength."

Mitch needed a hanky himself. With nowhere to park, he pulled to a stop in the middle of the street and helped Miss Bernie down from the cab. A flock of brightly dressed ladies swarmed to her and hustled her into the church.

Mitch drove three blocks before finding an open spot to park. He trotted back to the church. Captain Reemer, Kenny, and Crusher greeted him by the rig. They were in street clothes since it was their off day. Ralph was nowhere to be seen, which didn't surprise Mitch. Captain Stockley and Lieutenant Hager from the academy were off to the side talking to a group of battalion chiefs. Half the department must have been there to pay their respects.

As Mitch's crew made awkward small talk, a deep voice resonated through the crowd, "Is there a Mitch Garner here?"

Mitch rushed to the steps and found the voice belonged to a short, corpulent man with a trim goatee, wearing a long black robe. The loose coal-black skin of his neck spilled over the white collar.

"You Mista Garner?" the minister asked.

"Yes, sir."

"Come with me. Bernice will not let the service begin until she has you next to her."

Mitch followed the minister as he pushed past people crowding around the front of the small church. Inside, every seat appeared to be taken. Parishioners lined the walls. A heady mix of aftershave and perfume saturated the stuffy room. People fanned their faces with the funeral programs. Heads turned as the minister led him down the aisle. The legs of brown metal chairs screeched on the bare concrete floor as people adjusted themselves. There were no pews or benches, just rows of folding chairs.

A bright red flag with *Milwaukee Fire Department* inscribed in white, draped the mahogany casket at the front of the church. A solitary stone-faced firefighter dressed in dark blue honor guard colors, his white-gloved hands crossed at the waist below a brass buckle, stood guard at the head of Jamal's casket.

The minister steered Mitch to two open chairs next to Miss Bernie. "Here he is, Bernice. We should get started before we lose the congregation to the heat."

Miss Bernie struggled to rise.

Mitch bent and hugged her, gently sitting her back down.

She nodded at the minister. "Okay then."

Mitch nodded at Miss Bernie's cousins and church friends seated in the first row. Glancing around the church, it struck him that he was one of only several white people in the crowd.

The minister took his place at the black metal music stand serving as the pulpit and signaled to the back of the room. *Amazing Grace* wailed from three bagpipes. The Honor Guard solemnly marched down the narrow aisle and lined up at the front of the church. Two of them meticulously folded the flag that had draped Jamal's casket. They handed the folded triangle to Miss Bernie, thanking her for her son's service. They stepped back and the entire line of firefighters pivoted to Jamal and slowly raised their white-gloved right hands to their foreheads and saluted a lost brother. They spun back in unison and methodically marched up the aisle accompanied by sniffles and blowing noses. Miss Bernie stared at the flag that had covered her son's casket. Mitch struggled to hold it together.

"What a blessing to have these noble members of the Milwaukee Fire Department honor our brother Jamal in such an inspiring fashion," the reverend said. "Praaaise Jesus."

"Praaaise Jesus," the congregation answered.

"Welcome brothers and sisters in Christ. I welcome you to the New Hope Baptist Church to rejoice in Jamal Jackson's journey to meet our Lord and Savior, Jesus Christ."

"Amen, brother. Preach, brother. Tell it," erupted from the congregation, irritating Mitch. This seemed disrespectful. The reverend's voice thundered through the small church, then lowered to a whisper. He waved his hands to the heavens, then dropped them to the side. He was the conductor and the spirited mourners the symphony. As the service continued, Mitch realized the reverend invited the loud responses.

The reverend paused and motioned to a tall bald man dressed in a dapper gray suit. "Brother Williams will sing for us." Mitch remembered seeing him with Miss Bernie at the graduation.

Brother Williams swaggered to the small stage. His bald head shimmered under the harsh fluorescent ceiling lights. He looked over the mourners, cleared his throat and sang soft and slow. The congregation raised their hands in the air with fingers spread wide, waving as he sang. Brother Williams' velvet voice swelled to a melodic roar. Tears flowed down the huge man's face as he repeated the song's request to just stand, each chorus louder and louder until his voice cracked. The entire congregation stood, swaying back and forth with hands in the air. Mitch helped Miss Bernie up, and they swayed together. The exhilarating music filled Mitch with a strange, radiant mixture of joy and sadness.

When Brother Williams finished, the reverend resumed the sermon with impassioned pleas to praise Jesus and rejoice in Jamal's journey home. Sweat drenched the top of his robe. He swabbed at his face with an oversized black handkerchief. When it appeared there was no way he could continue, he asked them to sing. While they sang, he sat, pursing his lips, struggling for air. They sang joyful gospel songs, not the melancholy hymns Mitch knew from the Lutheran Hymnal. When they finished, the minister rose and continued the service with renewed vigor.

Throughout the marathon sermon, Miss Bernie kept gazing back up the aisle. Mitch knew who she was looking for. The empty chair was for Lettie, Miss Bernie's lost daughter.

* * *

Mitch jogged to the truck when the service concluded. Miss Bernie's church friends tried to persuade her to ride with them in the procession to the graveyard. She was having none of it. She'd ride with Mitch.

Mitch followed the hearse as the procession wound through the inner city. Miss Bernie pointed to an empty rail yard surrounded by vacant parking lots. "That's where Daddy worked. Them lots was filled back then." She bowed her head.

They drove on in silence, slowing when Jamal's firehouse came into view. Out front, Jamal's boots, turnout gear, and helmet were neatly stacked with the helmet's black and white frontpiece facing the street. The members of Engine Twenty-Seven stood at attention behind the solitary gear, saluting the procession as it approached.

Miss Bernie stared at the display. "Those Jamal's?"

"Yes, Ma'am."

"Stop for a minute and help me down."

He stopped. The hearse kept going. "Miss Bernie, what about the others?"

"They gone have to wait. Get me down from here."

Mitch lowered her to the pavement and followed her to the line of nine firefighters standing at attention behind Jamal's turnout gear.

"Y'all work with my boy?" She asked them.

Their captain stepped forward. "Yes, Ma'am. This is his crew."

Miss Bernie hugged him. "Bless you. Bless you. Bless you." The captain awkwardly patted her on the back. She gave the captain a kiss on the cheek, leaving a bright red trail of lipstick.

Miss Bernie worked her way down the line of firefighters, hugging and blessing each one in turn. Mitch stood in awe of her grace.

When she got to the end of the line, Miss Bernie asked the captain, "Can I take my son's fire hat?"

He handed her the shiny black helmet.

The long line of cars in the procession waited.

Back in the truck, Miss Bernie ran her hand over Jamal's helmet. She brought the liner of the helmet to her face. "I can smell my boy in there." She smiled. "Let's get this done."

The line of firefighters snapped to attention, saluting as the procession inched away.

This tribute for a fallen comrade, a fallen brother, his friend, reignited Mitch's desire to be a part of this fraternity. In spite of all the craziness he had seen, these were honorable people with a tremendous amount of pride and respect for one another. He ached to be one of them.

Chapter 23

"Firefighter Garner to the office," blared over the PA system. Mitch tried to remember whether he had scrubbed the captain's toilet this morning. After the funeral yesterday, he was struggling to keep it together.

"Mitch, have a seat," the captain said when Mitch entered.

"Boss, sorry if I missed anything."

"You doing okay?"

"One minute I'm down, the next I'm so pissed I feel like I'll explode. District Five keeps saying there's no leads."

"Yeah, not surprising."

"Jamal gets murdered and nobody gives a crap?" He realized he was yelling at the captain. "Sorry, boss."

"Aach." The captain waved him off. "I'm supposed to tell you we have an employee assistance program if you need it. Here's the number." He held out a small card.

Mitch reached for the card. The captain pointed to flecks of light purple paint on his forearms. "Doing some painting?"

"Jamal's mom's house."

"How she doing?"

"Not good. She only had two children. And her daughter ran off years ago."

"Sad. Painting the house yourself?"

"Keeps my mind off things."

"What else she need done?"

"Roof's shot and the porch is falling apart."

"I'll give Twenty-Sevens a call. They'll want to help. And we'll take a department-wide collection. She's one of the family now. Tell her that."

"I will, boss. Thanks."

"Oh, Mitch. That tavern fire two weeks ago? The cops want to know if any of us saw anything suspicious. You see anything?"

Mitch shook his head. *I was too busy screwing up.* "Why?"

"It was a homicide. The crispy critter Kenny found inside was the owner. M.E. said he died from gunshot wounds, not the fire. And get this, earlier that night he kicked some One-Niners out for harassing a customer." The captain tapped his pipe in the ashtray and rocked back in his chair. "Of course nobody knows anything."

"He was shot?" Mitch resisted the urge to pump his fist in the air.

The captain refilled the pipe. "Watch yourself out there."

* * *

Twelve firefighters with tool belts and ladders descended on Miss Bernie's home in the morning. Six of them swarmed to the roof, stripping shingles. The others scraped and sanded the wood siding. Mitch went to Home Depot on Capitol Drive to get paint and planking for the porch. A father of one of the firefighters who owns a roofing company had arranged to have shingles delivered after lunch.

Miss Bernie busied herself feeding the crew with casseroles left over from the funeral. Mitch was glad to see her out of the recliner where she had been spending so much time since the funeral.

After two days, the home had a new roof, a rebuilt porch, and a coat of light purple paint. Before the firefighters packed up and left, Miss Bernie called them together. "I thank the Lord for each and every one of you. You can't know how much this lifted me. Not so much what you done here but the love you showed doing it. This is truly the good Lord's work, whites and blacks working together. And I pray you keep finding ways to do His work. The peace of the Lord comes to those who help others."

Several firefighters said, "Amen."

Miss Bernie made sure to hug every one of them. After the last ones left, Mitch and Miss Bernie soaked in the return to glory of the proud Victorian now painted her favorite color, the color of hope.

"Mitch, honey, you're surely a blessing." She pulled him close.

* * *

Mitch lingered in the firehouse basement before work the following morning.

"See you're still getting here at the crack of dawn," Nic said, trotting down the stairs. The Mexican sun had darkened her face and lightened her hair, accenting her turquoise eyes. "That's awful about Firefighter Jackson. How you doing with that?"

"I'm okay."

"Don't look okay. What can I do to help?"

"You guys get anything yesterday?"

"Nah, a few false alarms. Oh, last night during the rainstorm we got called across the street. The lights were flickering and water was dripping from the ceiling fixture. We pulled the breakers and opened the ceiling. They're lucky the attic didn't go up." She headed to the stairs. "Mitch, really. Let me know if you need to talk or anything."

* * *

Mitch was upstairs dust-mopping the dorm when he heard hollering coming through the pole holes. "Goddamn shop. Can't fix shit."

He ran downstairs and found the crew standing by the pump panel of the rig watching Crusher manipulate the controls. "This damn thing ain't gonna pump."

Kenny stood behind Crusher with his arms folded. "Fuck, we're back to that old spare piece-of-shit."

"Our rig's going back to the shop," the boss said to Mitch. "Start stripping the gear off."

"What's wrong?" Mitch asked.

"Won't go into PTO."

Mitch frowned. "That all?"

"That's pretty major. Won't pump if it won't go into PTO."

"Mind if I take a look?"

The captain rubbed the back of his neck, arched his thick, graying eyebrows and said, "Have at it."

Mitch rolled under the rig on a creeper, pulling the toolbox along. The others chuckled. Fifteen minutes later he rolled back out. "Give her a try."

Crusher started the rig and engaged the PTO, the power take-off. "Nice job, kid. You're hired."

"What was it?" the captain asked.

"I checked the PTO clutch first. It wasn't hung up, so I traced the wiring harness to the ground. Pretty corroded. Cleaned it, and hoped for the best."

"Where'd you learn that?"

"All part of farming."

Kenny patted Mitch on the back. "You saved our ass. C'mon to the kitchen. Forget cub duties. Okay, boss?"

"Just be on the platform by 8:30. We'll be having a moment of silence at 8:46.

While joining the crew for coffee, Mitch avoided Ralph who was gnawing on a cigar and studying him.

At 8:30 they headed to the concrete platform and formed a straight line in front of the fire engine. At 8:46 they raised their hands in a silent salute. It was only one year ago that Mitch watched the horror of 9/11 unfold. If it wasn't for that day...

* * *

Mitch spent the afternoon at the joker stand trying to concentrate on the training manual. He couldn't stop staring at the decaying house across the street that was now without electricity. No kids should have to live like that. Alexus was such a cute, rambunctious child. And although Jasmine had ripped into him, he shouldn't have lost it. She was just a kid. It sickened him that Jamal was probably right about her hooking up with the One-Niners. How long before she'd be on the street selling her body for them?

They had a half dozen minor runs before midnight. At four in the morning, they responded to a woman in labor. The rig pulled to a stop in front of a one-story bungalow with overgrown vacant lots on each side. A muffled scream came from the dilapidated home.

"You get to catch, kid," Ralph said. "Try not to puke."

A stooped black woman wearing a fuzzy blue bathrobe flung the door open before the captain could knock. The heady aroma of marijuana drifted out. She pointed down the hallway. "In the back."

They hurried past the front room where a teenaged girl rocked a crying infant in an old wooden rocking chair. Five small children sprawled around her on the bare hardwood floor.

Two young women were standing by the bed when they entered the room.

Ralph pushed one of them away with the back of his hand. Both went for the doorway. A small table by the bed contained a full ashtray and the remnants of a joint. Next to that a glass pipe.

Ralph sneered at the women. "Smoking dope with her? Unfucking real."

"Ralph, cool it," the boss said.

The expectant mother looked like she should be playing with dolls, not delivering the real thing. Her legs were spread wide and the sheets were soaked. The top of the baby's head was visible. She arched her back. "Owww. Owww. Owww. Make it stop."

Kenny rifled through the EMS supplies. "I got the OB kit."

Mitch crouched next to the bed and leaned in with a small penlight, the copper smell of blood filling his nostrils. "I need more light."

Glaring white light from Ralph's handheld spotlight lit up the room. Cockroaches scurried over the walls, fleeing from the light.

"Crap. Head's blue," Mitch said. "Cord's pinched."

The elderly lady and two women crowded the doorway, clasping their hands over their mouths.

Kenny leaned in. "Shit."

"Dispatch, Engine Fifteen requesting a med unit," Captain Reemer said into the radio. "We got a hypoxic baby being delivered."

The girl's deafening screams had Mitch gritting his teeth. Ralph pushed the women back from the door and slammed it shut.

The baby's head and cord were pinched tight against the cervix. Mitch pushed on the baby's slippery head to get it off the cord. It didn't move. "Ma'am, listen, try not to push. Help's on the way. You and the baby will be fine. I've seen this lots of times." He nodded at Kenny. "I need a four by four."

Mitch took the square of gauze from Kenny and wiped the slick fluid away. He cupped the baby's blue head and tried to force it back in. It was him against the intense force of the uterus that was doing everything it could to push the baby out. But it would be dead before it delivered. Mitch adjusted his footing and pushed harder, holding his breath. The head moved just enough for him to force two fingers along the cord between the baby's head and mother's cervix.

Mitch breathed. "Got it. Cord's free."

The girl's screams diminished to moans and sobs along with the contraction. Less than a minute later, the pressure increased, pinching Mitch's fingers between baby's head and mother's cervix. The cord was safe between his two fingers. With the other hand, he held a firm grip on the baby's head while the mother pleaded to make it stop. Mitch peered over the top of her distended abdomen. "You're doing great. Hang in there."

Kenny and Ralph watched in silence as the contractions came faster. The screams turned to breathless moans. Mitch continued to comfort her. Beads of sweat stung his eyes.

Paramedics burst into the room, slamming the yellow gurney down to bed-level. Without looking up, Mitch said, "Cord's pinched."

The paramedic lieutenant got down next to Mitch. "Nice call." He turned to his crew. "Get an IV going and a set of vitals."

After they stabilized her, one of the paramedics took over supporting the cord.

Mitch stepped back. Why was he so nervous *now*? It was over.

After they loaded the young girl in the med unit, the paramedic lieutenant said, "Nice work, Engine Fifteen."

The med unit sped off with the siren blaring. The captain nodded at Mitch. "Made us look good. Nice job." The praise from the boss should have left him ecstatic, but what he needed more than anything was to share this with his best friend on Miss Bernie's porch, with a cold beer.

* * *

It was after five when they got back to the firehouse. They shuffled to the kitchen for coffee.

"You saw that lots of times before?" Kenny asked. "You some redneck midwife?"

Mitch grinned. "We deliver a couple of calves a week on the farm. Sometimes the cord gets pinched. Then we gotta get them out quick. We have a puller where we wrap a rope around them and yank them out."

"Good she didn't know you were talking about cows," Kenny said. "Hey, boss, we need one of those puller things. Wouldn't have to wait for the meds."

"You're amazing, kid," Crusher said.

"Yeah, fucking amazing," Ralph said gnawing on his stogie.

Mitch furrowed his brow. "One question. How could she be having a white baby?"

Crusher and Kenny erupted in laughter.

Mitch raised his open palms.

Crusher stopped laughing. "Must not get many black babies in God's country."

This got Crusher and Kenny going again.

"What?" Mitch asked.

The captain waved his pipe. "Since these ladies won't tell you, lots of black babies are born with light skin. Takes a while for them to darken up."

Ralph followed Mitch to the parking lot at the end of the shift. "Think you're pretty hot shit? Let me fill you in. You ain't." The stench of Ralph's early morning cigar breath turned Mitch's stomach. Ralph rammed his cigar into Mitch's chest. "I let it slide when you told me to get fucked. Ever talk to me like that again, I'll rip your head off and shit down your throat."

Ralph ground his cigar into the pavement and left.

Screw you. You don't scare me anymore.

On the way home, he forgot about Ralph. He had more important things to do today.

Chapter 24

From the roof of Benita Richardson's house, he could see the green-shift crew inside the firehouse going through their morning routine. It was strange watching the activity from across the street. He had bundles of shingles left over from Miss Bernie's house and plenty of lumber. Maybe he couldn't tutor those kids, but he could fix their roof. He stripped weathered and brittle shingles from around the bare areas and one by one replaced them with fresh ones.

From below someone shouted, "What the fuck you doing up there?"

Mitch edged down the roof. A gaunt black face looked up at him.

"Patching the roof."

"Who hired you? We got no money."

"Don't owe me anything. I told Ms. Richardson I'd do this for her."

"Who the fuck you?"

"I work across the street. I'm a firefighter."

"How you know my woman? Ah, fuck. I ain't got time for this shit. Keep the noise down."

Mitch was still on the roof when Jasmine and Alexus came home from school. Alexus waved at him. Jasmine shook her head and went inside.

"What you doing up there?" Alexus shouted.

"Fixing your roof."

"Can you cut the lights back on when you done? I can't watch my shows."

"See what I can do."

Alexus clapped her hands and ran into the house.

* * *

He finished in the moonlight. The wiring would have to wait until tomorrow. He never did see Benita Richardson come home.

Next morning he started work on the porch, replacing rotting planks and framing. He tried to be as quiet as possible so he didn't wake the boyfriend or whatever he was. The man's sunken face gave him the willies.

While struggling with a rotting plank, Mitch turned to get a pry bar and was startled by Benita Richardson standing over him with her arms crossed. "What you doing?"

He stood, met by her hollow eyes. This must be the thousand-mile stare Mitch had read about, except she was obviously not a Viet Nam vet.

"Told you I'd fix your place up."

"Never said I'd get Jasmine to help with those kids. Child has a mind of her own."

"Don't matter."

Her hands went to her hips. "Why you wanna do all that? Don't make no sense."

"Should I leave?"

"You wanna fix shit. You go right ahead and fix shit."

She shuffled into the house, muttering, "Crazy motherfucker."

By noon the porch was done.

"Want me to check the wiring?" Mitch called through the screen.

"Do whatever you gotta do."

The sight of the spotless front room shocked him. The walls were painted bright yellow, the wood floors glowed, and a sectional couch spanned two walls. The place had a soapy fresh smell. This woman took pride in her home. Mitch had her wrong.

He found her on the back porch, smoking. "I'll need to get in the attic and the basement."

"The stairs is right there."

"I don't want to disturb your boyfriend."

"Maurice? Never come home last night." The woman spoke in a bleak monotone.

Mitch went upstairs and found where the blue shifters had opened the ceiling. The room was tidy and dry, the plaster and wet insulation gone. Along the inside wall was a neatly made single bed covered by a pink comforter emblazoned with a bright blue pony. The pillowcase said *My Little Pony*. Against the opposite wall stood a dresser with an array of random framed photos spread over it. He recognized Alexus and Jasmine in many of them. Some pictures had a third girl. She was older than Jasmine. Mitch spotted a picture of a black man and a little girl smiling at the camera, their cheeks pressed together. Looking closer, he saw the emerald eyes of the little girl. She was clasping a thin silver-colored chain necklace.

* * *

Over the years they had rewired much of the farm so replacing deteriorating wiring in this house was no challenge. He spent the afternoon crawling through the stifling attic, yanking out old wiring and running fresh wires to new junction boxes. He was covered in gray insulation when he came down and went to the basement to upgrade the fuse box. He paid for all this but didn't plan on telling them. After installing the new circuit breakers, he went upstairs.

Before he could get outside and brush the insulation off, Alexus ran at him and hugged him hard. "You lookin' like some kinda big bird."

Jasmine stood in the center of the room with her hands on her hips, looking like her mother just then, except Jasmine's green eyes sparkled. "Yeah, maybe you should be on Sesame Street." She was not smiling. "Who say you could go in my room?"

"I had to get in there to fix the wires. Sorry."

Alexus looked up at him with her almond Disney princess eyes. "She glad you fix our house. She just can't tell you."

Jasmine pulled Alexus away. She kneeled down and put her arms around her sister, frowned at Mitch and said, "Next time ask."

Maybe there won't be a next time.

He headed to the front door and heard Jasmine whisper, "Thanks."

* * *

On the way home Mitch stopped at the Burger King to get Miss Bernie a Whopper and some fries. She loved those fries. He couldn't wait to tell her how he helped the Richardson girls. Miss Bernie was right. The peace of the Lord does come to those who help others. Fixing things felt good.

The lights were out in Miss Bernie's flat when he got home. He didn't want to wake her and headed up the creaking stairs.

"Mitch?"

He backed down and stepped inside. "Thought you were in bed already."

"Can't sleep." She clicked on the floor lamp next to her recliner.

"Want some Burger King?"

She clutched a photo to her chest. "Can't eat nothing." She wiped at her nose with her hanky. "Police come by today telling me they still don't know who kilt Jamal."

Mitch pulled a chair next to her and held her hand.

Miss Bernie sighed. "I know the good Lord got a reason for taking him, but it pains me so." She choked and drew in a deep breath. "I been praying for Him to show my baby girl the way home. She been gone eight years now."

"Any idea where she is?"

"She told Jamal she was running off to Chicago soon as she got a chance."

Mitch rubbed her hand.

"She was the sweetest thing. Tickled my bones with her nonsense. Once she started formin' I knew the boys would be after her. See how pretty she was." Miss Bernie pointed to a young girl in the photo who was around Jasmine's age. She was small and slight like Miss Bernie. A young Jamal towered over her, both of them grinning.

"Looks just like you."

Miss Bernie stared at the photo. "I was hard on her. Too hard. I see that now. The more I tried to hold her down, the more she pull away. We couldn't be in the same room without fussin' at each other. Oh, that girl got a mouth on her. Cuss me out good. I couldn't take it no more and slapped her foul mouth." She hugged the photo to her chest. "That's when she run off."

"You never heard from her?"

"I push that girl too hard. So hard I push her away. I was scared to death." Miss Bernie lowered her faraway gaze to Mitch. "See what fear do? Make you stupid. That's what I was, stupid and prideful, thinking I had all the answers. I shoulda been loving that girl through those times and listening to her instead of hounding at her. Now she gone."

She wiped at her eyes with the hanky, sniffling. "Go on up to bed. You don't need to set all night holding my hand."

"I'll keep pestering the police. I won't let them give up."

"Imagine they already did. Too much giving up around here. You go on now."

I'm not giving up.

Chapter 25

In the morning, Mitch drove to work through a light drizzle, thinking about Miss Bernie and her daughter. *Eight years.*

Was this how Sid looked at his leaving, as running away from him and the farm? He didn't run away, though. Sid ordered him off the farm. Was Sid acting out of fear like Miss Bernie did with her daughter? But fear of what? Losing Mitch? Losing the farm? What?

Late in the afternoon, Mitch was at the joker stand, studying the training manual. Rattling. Alexus stood at the glass door of the firehouse wearing a fluorescent pink T-shirt, smiling wide, exposing two missing front teeth. Tight black braids hung over her face. Her pencil-thin legs peaked from her baggy shorts which hung to her knobby knees. Mitch recognized the four other kids crowding around her. They were the same ones who were there last month. He remembered the name of one of the boys, Kyle, but couldn't remember the others. Kyle's face was as grimy as the last time. He wore a grungy Green Bay Packer jersey that hung past his knees. The faded "80" and the name "Driver" were barely visible.

Jasmine hovered behind the group. She had straightened her jet-black hair that now hung past her shoulders and accented her smooth, coffee-colored complexion. She didn't appear twelve anymore.

Mitch swung the door open and Jasmine said, "About time. We're getting wet out here."

Alexus giggled. "We back."

The elation Mitch felt from seeing them was tempered by Jasmine's unsettling appearance. Was this DeAndre's work?

The children scampered past him to the apparatus floor. He caught a whiff of Kyle as he ran by. The boy smelled like Mitch's high school locker room.

Jasmine pointed at his chest. "Hope you better with them than last time."

By the time he locked the door and followed them in, Kyle was on top of a smaller boy trying to wrestle an unbroken crayon from him. The three girls chased each other around the table, squealing. Mitch went to the end of the table. "Hey, guys, guys, listen."

They ignored him.

"Kyle kick me in the nuts," shouted the smaller boy.

"C'mon, listen up. We should work on school stuff."

The kids paid him no attention.

The smaller boy twisted and squirmed under Kyle, who grinned deviously. Mitch yanked Kyle off the sobbing child. "Okay, that's enough."

Kyle whirled and punched Mitch square in the groin, bending him at the waist, sucking the wind out of him. He instinctively clenched his fist but caught himself. "Damn, you. Don't you ever do that again."

Jasmine giggled. "Yup, I can see you sure know kids."

He had never seen her smile, much less laugh. "You teach him that?"

He dragged the two boys to the table and plunked them down. As soon as he turned to rein in the girls, the boys were back at it.

"Any suggestions?" Mitch asked Jasmine over the loud squealing and shouting.

"Not *my* job."

"Thanks."

"Just chill. Suppose I owe you."

"Don't owe me anything. I know your mom made you bring the kids back."

"Don't know as much as you think."

Jasmine snatched Kyle off the other boy, dragged them both to the table, and jammed them in the miniature chairs. "Now sit." One mean look from her and the girls ran to their seats. "Now keep your behinds in those chairs and listen to the man. He got something to teach y'all." She flashed Mitch a mocking grin. "They all yours, Mr. Teacher."

Now what? "I forgot some of your names. Can you introduce yourselves?"

The kids looked at each other with scrunched brows.

"He mean, tell him your name," Jasmine said.

Alexus sprang from her chair. "I'm Alexus. Everybody call me Lexus. Rather be called Lexi though and this here—"

"Why don't we let the other kids tell me their own names?" He raised his hand. "Wait, I've got an idea. Stay put. I'll be right back." Mitch rushed to the study room and brought back a large whiteboard they used for training.

"Okay, Lexi. What's your favorite color?"

"Like me some red."

In large red letters, he printed "Alexus" followed by a dash then "Lexi."

He handed the marker to Alexus. "Now copy what I wrote right below it."

Alexus neatly printed her name and nickname. Before she got back to her seat, Kyle snatched the red marker from her hand.

Mitch grabbed the boy's wrist. Kyle punched at him. He caught the boy's hand and squeezed hard. This kid was beyond pissing him off.

The boy struggled to get free. Jasmine covered her mouth, trying not to giggle.

"Soon as you cool down you can take your turn," Mitch said.

The boy stopped struggling.

Mitch released his hand. "Ready for your turn now?"

The boy nodded. Mitch wrote Kyle's name on the board and handed him the red marker. Kyle hesitated, so Mitch wrapped the boy's hand in his and together they wrote his name. Kyle smiled at the board.

The other children all took their turns printing their names in their favorite colors.

"You all know how to write your names now. Nice job."

Kyle arched his back and tilted his head to the ceiling. He clenched his fists and whimpered, "Uh, uh, uh." His eyes went wide and mouth gaped open. The moaning stopped abruptly along with his breathing.

A chill shot through Mitch. He lifted the stiff boy from the chair and carefully laid him on the floor. "I gotta get help," he said to Jasmine. "Can you watch him?"

"Kyle was a crack baby. He has fits. He'll sleep a while when it stops," Jasmine said in a matter-of-fact way as if she were telling him the boy was born with black hair.

The other kids were oblivious to Kyle's seizure.

"Doesn't he go to the hospital?"

"Nope. His momma probably forgot to give him medicine again."

"I gotta let the boss know. Keep an eye on him."

"He ain't gonna do nothing."

The captain told Mitch the boy had seizures here before. As long as it subsided quickly, there was no need for medical attention. He usually recovered pretty fast. If not, they'd call in a med unit. The first time it happened they took him in, and the mother went ballistic about how she had to go all the way downtown to Sinai Hospital and pick him up. She said the next time she'd leave him there; the fire department could get him home.

Mitch raced to the dorm and brought down a pillow and blanket. He lifted the boy off the cold concrete floor and slid the blanket under him, gently lowering his head onto the pillow.

"Sure he's okay?" Mitch asked Jasmine.

"Just leave him be."

He was taking advice from a young girl, a kid. How smart was this? But this young girl seemed wise about things he knew nothing about. Seizures had been covered in the EMT manual and he saw calves having seizures but never a person.

"Jasmine, can you stay with Kyle while I show them the truck?"

She sat down next to the softly snoring boy.

Mitch stood. "Guys, c'mon over to the fire truck. I'll let you sit in the driver's seat."

The children sprang from their chairs and dashed to the rig. He lined them up and lifted each one into the driver's seat when it was their turn. They grabbed the steering wheel, swinging it back and forth, pretending to drive. The warning lights washed the apparatus floor with beams of red and white.

Mitch was lifting Alexus into the rig when Jasmine and Kyle shuffled over. "Do I get a turn?" Kyle slurred.

"Is it okay if Kyle goes next?" Mitch asked.

Alexus nodded. He put her down and lifted Kyle into the cab.

Kyle wanted to know what all the controls and dials were for. When Mitch showed him the cable for the air horn, Kyle yanked it. The deafening blast rattled the inside of the firehouse. A broad smile broke across Kyle's face.

Crusher burst from the kitchen. "Get those kids off my rig."

"Okay, guys. We're done for today. See you Monday."

It was worth getting a bite in the ass from Crusher to see the smile on Kyle's face. He ushered the kids to the door.

Jasmine stopped. "You one strange cracker."

Chapter 26

Before getting off work the following morning, Crusher invited Mitch for a drink, telling him to stop by Norby's Squeezebox on Lincoln Avenue around seven. He and Kenny wanted to take him out to show their appreciation for fixing the rig on Wednesday.

This had to be another prank.

* * *

The solid white door was darkened with smudges around the pitted chrome handle. Above it, a flickering neon sign read *Norby's Squeezebox*. At eye level were the handwritten words *Polka Spoken Here*. Mitch took a deep breath before pulling the heavy door open.

Inside he was assaulted by a fog of tobacco, the smell of stale beer, and oompah music playing from a jukebox in the corner. Four men and two women seated at the mahogany bar eyed him suspiciously. At the back of the dingy room, five men sat around a small table studying their cards and flicking cigarette ashes into clear glass ashtrays. This was nothing like the lively crowd at the Rock River Hideaway. He spotted Crusher's wide ass hanging over the back of a round barstool at the far end of the bar. Kenny stood next to him in serious conversation, his hands flailing in the air.

Crusher waved Mitch over and pointed toward an empty stool. "Well, well, well. Look who showed."

Mitch glanced around the bar. "Ahh, nice place."

"Yeah, a real four-star lounge. The maître d' show you in?"

Kenny slapped him on the back. "Hey, kid. What'll you have? I'm buying."

Mitch took the stool between them. "Beer's fine."

Kenny hollered to the beet-faced bartender at the far end of the bar, "Norb, a round of boilermakers."

The portly man waddled to their end of the bar, lined up three shot glasses, and filled them to the brim with Jim Beam. He poured three mugs of foaming Miller High Life from the tap and placed one in front of each of them. Crusher and Kenny splashed the whiskey into their beers. Mitch followed suit. Crusher lifted his mug. "Here's to our ace mechanic."

They clinked their mugs together and chugged.

"You come over the Sixteenth Street Bridge?" Kenny asked.

"Yup."

"You know that's the longest bridge in the world?"

"What you talking about?"

Kenny raised his eyebrows. "How many bridges connect Africa and Poland?"

Crusher scowled. "Jesus, you're such a knob."

Kenny thrust a finger in the air. "Norb, set us up again." Kenny winked at Mitch. "When we drink, we drink. We don't fuck around."

Two rounds later the booze took effect, and Mitch couldn't hold back. "What you did with those donuts was nasty."

Crusher frowned. "Listen, kid. Things aren't always what they seem."

"You jam donuts in your asses and trick those guys into eating them. How's that not nasty?" Feeling bold from a belly full of whiskey and beer, he went on. "And how can you guys joke about people dying?"

"Look," Crusher said. "We see shit nobody should have to see. I know it's sick, but if we sat around feeling grooblick about it we'd all take the route, or end up dribbling down our chins. That's how we deal with it." Crusher stared at the bar. "Lost some good firefighters over the years who couldn't. Most quit. A few took the route. Lost a good friend that way." Crusher paused. "Okay, enough."

Crusher's words cut through the alcohol fog. *A few took the route.*

"Should I tell him?" Crusher asked Kenny.

"Probably better."

"The doughnuts we sent over weren't the ones we had sticking out of our asses. But those jags don't need to know that. We're sick, but we do have limits."

Mitch had to laugh. Nic was right. These guys were masters.

Kenny belched. "So, kid, you getting laid or jagging off?"

Mitch's face throbbed. "I have a girlfriend back home." *At least I used to.*

Kenny frowned. "Not what I asked."

He didn't want to piss these guys off, so he answered with another lie, "Well, yeah we're having sex. Why'd you ask that?"

"Wanted to see if you'd bullshit me and say something stupid like you weren't doing either one. Listen up and learn from the oracle in your presence. Forget that snapper back home. You're young. Never miss a chance to get your cane polished. No such thing as a bad piece of ass. Love is something dreamed up by Hallmark." He belched again. "They're all bipolar. Every one of 'em."

Kenny pulled a wallet from his back pocket and slammed it on the bar. "There's true love." He pointed at the faded leather wallet. "Right there."

Mitch held onto the cracked black vinyl padding lining the front of the bar. The beer and whiskey had him reeling. "You married?" he asked Kenny.

Crusher choked on his beer. "Who could stay married to a dickhead like him?" He grinned at Kenny. "And I mean that in the nicest way." He turned back to Mitch. "The man's been divorced three times; pays child support and alimony to all of them. So the oracle here might not be all that full of wisdom."

Kenny waved his middle finger at Crusher.

"You meet anyone here yet?" Crusher asked.

"I'm thinking of asking Nic out. Seems like she's interested."

Kenny and Crusher howled with laughter.

"What?"

Kenny restrained a belch. "That girl ain't interested in dick. She's a carpet muncher, for Christ's sake. Gotta love you, kid. You crack me up."

"Crap," Mitch said. "She's really hot."

Crusher waved his palms. "Hot's overrated. Now listen to *my* advice. Forget what the oracle told you. Find yourself someone to laugh with. You can laugh all day, but you can't screw all day. My sweet Brunhilda ain't much to look at; in fact, she looks like she's smuggling apples in her jeans. But not a day goes by we don't have a laugh. Even when she went through her cancer, we'd find something to laugh about together. Best medicine in the world."

"Your wife's name is Brunhilda?"

"Course not. That stays in the firehouse."

Me and Jen used to laugh a lot.

Crusher wiped the foam from his lips. "My advice is find yourself a gal with thick ankles who you can laugh through life with." Crusher took a sip of beer. "Ignore the oracle unless you want to end up like him."

Kenny let out a loud breath. "Why do I waste my time drinking with you?"

128

"Because nobody else will."

They all laughed.

"What the fuck is he doing here?" Ralph stomped toward them.

A jolt shot up Mitch's spine.

Crusher sprang off the barstool. "Ralph, c'mon cool it. We're just having a few drinks."

"Since when do we drink with cubs?" Ralph pressed against Crusher.

Crusher hung his thick arm on Ralph's shoulder. "C'mon, sit, have a drink. Kenny's buying. You know that don't ever happen, hey?"

Ralph swung onto a stool on the other side of Crusher, glowering at Mitch.

Mitch looked away from Ralph, trying to calm the pounding in his chest.

"I hate fucking cubs, especially that one," Ralph said to Crusher, loud enough for Mitch to hear. "Come out of the academy all full of themselves thinking they're fire-eating warriors. But they ain't shit. Know just enough to get their asses burned."

"Wasn't *he* ever a cub?" Mitch said to Crusher.

Ralph leaned around Crusher. "Got something to say, Bambi?"

"You heard me. I asked if you were ever a cub."

"I was pissing out fires when you were shitting yellow." Ralph's gravelly voice deepened. "Goddamned piss pot."

"Well fuck you, just fuck you." Mitch charged around Crusher.

Ralph spun off the barstool to meet him. They went chest to chest. Before Mitch could react, Ralph's hand went to Mitch's throat. "What'd I tell you about talking to me like that?"

Mitch struggled to turn away from Ralph's hot, sour breath.

Ralph tightened his grip. His bulging eyes bore into Mitch, their faces inches apart. "You want to dance, Bambi, we'll fucking dance." He slammed Mitch against the back wall.

Mitch tried to pry Ralph's leathery hands loose, but the man's grip was relentless. Mitch's knees buckled. The lights dimmed.

Crusher and Kenny pulled them apart. The card players rushed toward them. Crusher shouted, "We got this. Go back to your game." He looked from Ralph to Mitch. "You two. Stop. You want the cops here?"

Ralph shoved Crusher. "You want to drink with this jag, go ahead." He marched to the door and kicked it open.

"You didn't tell me he'd be here," Mitch said, rubbing his raw neck, his voice hoarse.

"Ralph didn't know either. The oracle there thought if we got you two together, had a few beers and a few laughs, you'd both lighten up."

Kenny shrugged.

Mitch's head cleared, but he wasn't ready to trust his rubbery legs. "What the hell is Ralph's problem? I should have kicked his ass. He's lucky I was drunk."

Kenny chuckled. "Yeah, you had him right where you wanted him. Clever how you wrapped his hands around your neck." Kenny turned serious. "You should know Ralph was an Army Ranger before coming on the job. They don't fuck around. They called him the Jawbreaker of South Milwaukee when he got out."

"I'm not scared of him." The words didn't even sound convincing to Mitch.

Crusher narrowed his eyes. "You sure didn't help things. Might want to work on that short fuse of yours."

"He started it."

Crusher snapped his fingers in front of Mitch's face. "Pipe down and listen. You need to know some things about Ralph. The man's had a tough go of it. He's third-generation firefighter. Family tradition. His only son's been trying to get on the job for years, but the kid's not very sharp. Ralph blames the minority hiring and outsiders for the kid's struggle to get on. Says you're taking jobs away from Milwaukee people. You're not the first cub Ralph's tried to drive off the job but you sure get to him."

"Why do I piss him off so much?"

"Ralph fancies himself quite the mechanic. When the rig broke down the other day, he worked on it and gave up. You come down and fix it in what, ten minutes? Of course, we had to give him some shit. That probably didn't help."

"So I shouldn't have fixed it?"

"You showed him up. You're a threat, and that stubborn kraut will do anything to beat you. He can't stand to lose. That's what makes him a damn good firefighter. Where others back out, he'll keep pushing deeper into the fire."

"So, what do I do?"

"Might not want to tell him to get fucked anymore." A faint grin spread across Crusher's lips.

"Why does he have to be such an asshole? He couldn't even come to Jamal's funeral?"

"That asshole is my friend."

"I didn't mean..."

Crusher drained his beer, then said, "One more thing about Ralph. Five years ago his wife was diagnosed with MS. When she has a bad bout, she's bedridden. He has to do everything for her; you know, bedpans and all that fun stuff. So Ralph's pissed at the world. Oh, and that's why he didn't show at Jamal's funeral. The wife was in pretty bad shape."

"I shouldn't have said that."

"Assumptions will bite you in the ass. Okay, enough about Ralph. I better fill you in on the blue-shift boss, Lieutenant Laubner. If you work on his shift, or if he works on ours, watch your ass. The man's pert near a perfect imbecile. Course, nobody's perfect, hey?"

"Why'd they make him a boss?"

"Ohhh, he talks a good fire. Great with books. But the man couldn't extinguish a match. So when he gives an order, we ignore it. You do the same if you don't want to get your ass burned."

"Won't he write me up?"

"Doesn't have the balls. When he gives a bone-headed order, act like you're gonna do it, then put the fire out the way Ralph and the boss show you."

Crusher shifted his gaze to the back of the bar. "Three years ago the fucking idiot lost a cub in a fire. The place was charged. Him and the cub laid a line to the first floor. Never checked the basement. The idiot didn't know there was fire rolling right below them, so they crawled into the first floor directly above the fire. The kid fell through into the burning basement. Didn't stand a chance." Crusher sighed. "Shitty way to die."

Kenny nodded while Crusher told the story. When Crusher finished, the three sat in silence listening to polkas play on the jukebox.

Crusher took a deep breath. "You want to know what you can do? Don't get yourself killed."

Chapter 27

There was no morning bull-session over coffee the next shift. After Mitch finished with the morning routine, he headed to the kitchen. He heard Kenny's knife hammering the wooden cutting board. Inside, Mitch saw him violently hacking carrots.

"What can I help with?" Mitch asked.

"Might be best to make yourself scarce for a while."

"Sorry about the other night."

"Ralph's still smoldering."

"Don't know why *he's* pissed. He jumped on me."

Kenny pointed the knife at him. "Just stay out of his way."

Mitch kept busy through the morning spray-painting tools. He kept watching for Crusher and Kenny, hoping they would start working on him again, play a prank, anything to lighten the mood.

* * *

Crusher, Kenny, Ralph, and Mitch were silently eating lunch when the captain strolled in. They couldn't be sitting any farther apart.

The captain glanced around the table and stopped at Mitch. "What the hell's on your neck?"

Before anyone answered, Mitch said, "Some kind of rash."

The captain furrowed his brow. "Strange looking rash." He went to the large kettle on the stove and slopped goulash into an oversized bowl. He was halfway through when he slammed the end of his oversized spoon against the table. They all jumped. "Okay, what the hell is going on?"

The captain scrutinized his crew. "Nobody's got anything to say? That's a first. I don't know what's up, but you ladies need to settle your hissy fit. Any of you don't like it here; I'll be glad to get you a ride out." He dumped the rest of his goulash into the garbage and ambled back to the office, mumbling.

Ralph pointed a finger at Mitch while facing Crusher. "He needs to go. And you two need to stop sucking up to him like a couple of butt buddies."

Fuck you, Ralph. The words were on Mitch's lips, but he held back.

Ralph stomped off to the TV room.

Crusher clicked his tongue. "Not your fault, kid."

He was coming between these old friends and pissing off the boss. It *was* his fault.

* * *

After lunch, Mitch was studying at the joker stand when Maggie suddenly appeared in his thoughts without warning. Never a day passed without Mitch tormenting himself by playing the fire over in his head. As he sank into the all-too-familiar hopeless pit, a throbbing headache set in.

Tapping at the front door. The image faded. Jasmine and the five children stood outside, staring at him. As soon as he let them in, they scrambled by. Jasmine tilted her head. "You okay?"

"I have something for the kids."

Jasmine raised an eyebrow, then followed the children inside.

When Mitch got to the table, Alexus pinched her nose. "What stinks?"

"I was painting tools this morning."

"Hey, can we paint something?"

Mitch rapped on the table. "Guys, I have something for all of you."

The chattering stopped.

Clear plastic containers were stacked against the back wall. Mitch placed one in front of each child. "Go ahead, open them."

The kids peeled back the covers and squealed. Mitch's headache eased.

The containers were crammed with crayons and coloring books and markers. To get his mind off Ralph, he had gone shopping yesterday and found coloring books picturing black children.

"Dude," Kyle said holding up a bright green and gold jersey with "Driver" printed across the top and the number "80" below it.

"Go ahead, put it on. It's yours."

Kyle slid it over his filthy T-shirt, swiveling his hips and pumping his skinny arms like he scored a touchdown. The children snickered.

"There's one for each of you. You can take them home. Just make sure to wear them when you come here. We'll be Team Driver, the Eight-Ohs."

"We like a gang? Get to mess with people?" Kyle asked.

"No. We're a team. We help each other."

Kyle wrinkled his grimy forehead. "Rather be a gang."

A flurry of squirming arms and heads popped through the jerseys.

Jasmine folded her arms and grinned.

After they went through the containers and settled down, as much as five and six-year-olds can settle down, Mitch told them how Donald Driver had lived in the hood when he was a kid. And how Donald's family was homeless and lived in their old car. Donald knew he needed to work hard at school if he wanted to play football someday. If he quit school he would never have gone to college and would never have played for the Packers.

"He the man," Kyle said.

"You can be too, Kyle." Mitch glanced around the table. "You guys ready to learn something?"

Kyle rested his chin in his hands. "Can't we just color in our new books?"

The others joined in. "Yeah, let's color."

Mitch threw up his hands.

"Ever think of asking for help?" Jasmine asked.

"Didn't think you'd want to."

"Maybe you don't know as much as you think."

"Any ideas?" Mitch asked Jasmine.

She smirked. "Asking for help?"

"Ah, forget it."

"Dude, chill. I'm playing. These kids been in school all day. They all schooled out."

"They're all yours."

Jasmine went to the boom box on the workbench and tuned it to hip-hop. She cranked the volume. "C'mon, shorties. Let's shake some booty."

Mitch couldn't make out the words over the heavy bass.

The kids jumped up and wiggled their bodies to the music. Jasmine joined them, her moves fluid and rhythmic.

Alexus grabbed Mitch's hand. "We been doing what you want. Now you gotta do what we want."

Mitch swung his hips to the music, nowhere near the beat. The kids squealed with laughter.

Jasmine giggled. "Man, watching white people dance is painful."

When the song ended, Jasmine said, "Now, listen up and do what the man say."

Mitch had the children write their names on the plastic containers and let them color in their new coloring books. When time ran out and they were putting their things back in the containers, Mitch went to the kitchen and came back with Snickers bars. "Nice job, Team Driver."

The kids snatched the candy and ran out the door, except Alexus and Jasmine. Alexus hugged Mitch's waist and said, "You da bomb."

As they left, Jasmine turned to him with a confused expression on her face, "I don't get you."

"I'm the bomb. Didn't you know?"

He watched the pint-sized Eight-Ohs scatter through the neighborhood, then went back to the watch desk, basking in the excitement of the children and Alexus's beaming face, the headache gone.

* * *

Mitch was anxious to get home in the morning to tell Miss Bernie about the children, hoping it would cheer her up. It was getting hard to visit her. She rarely had anything to say. He had been harvesting the ripening vegetables from her garden and leaving them on her countertop. After several days, he'd find the vegetables untouched. She told him not to bother, so he stopped and the garden filled with weeds.

Mitch smelled something rotten coming from Miss Bernie's flat. He slipped inside to grab the garbage, not wanting to disturb her in case she was napping. The stench caught in his throat; the same putrid stench of the old woman infested with maggots. Not as intense but even more sickening coming from Miss Bernie's flat. He ran to the darkened front room and stopped in the entryway. The windows were closed and shades drawn. She was in her easy chair, head tilted back, and mouth gaped open. He froze. An intense wave of sorrow washed over him. He was inundated with visions: their talks on the front porch, her warm hugs, and her radiant face. From the smell in the flat, she had been gone for some time. There was no rush to dial 911. He collapsed in the hard wooden chair next to her, feeling hollow and alone. He put his hand on hers.

Her eyes snapped open. They both shrieked.

"Good Lord, Mitch. You give me a fright. My heart's a poundin'."

"I thought you were…"

"Thought what? I passed?" She rubbed her temples. "I'm surely ready, but that's up to the good Lord."

Mitch caught his breath. "God, I'm sorry. Something smelled bad. I thought…"

She furrowed her brow. "Thought it was my dead body?"

"I didn't know what to think. You've been so down. Just wish I could help."

"Mitch, honey, only one can help me is the good Lord. I been praying hard for him to show my daughter the way back."

He searched the flat for the source of the odor. When he opened the cabinet under the sink, he gagged. At the back of the cabinet, behind a bucket and a bottle of Pine-Sol, was a colony of decaying mice and a box of D-Con. He had to laugh at himself. *Dead mice. You're quite the EMT.* After scraping up the slimy mess and bleaching the cabinet, he went to tell Miss Bernie. Her head was bowed and hands folded. She jerked when she noticed him. "Oh, Mitch. Seems I'm not even here most of the time. I keep thinking back to when Lettie and Jamal were kids and the love we had in this house. If I could only go back to them times and forget all this mess. It pains me so."

Mitch nodded. If only they could both go back.

He told Miss Bernie how he repaired the Richardson house and how Jasmine brought the kids back. And how he bought supplies and Green Bay Packer jerseys for them. It felt good telling her and to see it lift her spirits.

"Benita used to come to our church," Miss Bernie said when he finished. "She was always so full of the spirit, smiling and praisin' the Lord. She'd have her three girls dressed all fine. They had the prettiest skin. Daddy was mixed. And that oldest one, such a beauty." Miss Bernie gazed at the ceiling while telling him this as if she could see them all up there. "We used to be good friends, me and Benita, until the devil took that oldest one. Her man couldn't take the pain. He left her with those two girls. It broke her. Lost the will to mother them. I tried to help, but she push us all away."

Mitch remembered seeing the photos of the three girls in Jasmine's room.

Miss Bernie closed her eyes and nodded slowly. "I never could understand how she gave up like that when she had two little ones. Now I do. I feel like I'm ready to break just like Benita. If my girl don't come home soon, I'm afraid I will." Miss Bernie gave him a warm kiss on the cheek. "You go on now and get some rest. God bless you Mitch, honey. You a good man."

He wasn't so sure. But her words felt good.

Chapter 28

Mitch reported for duty at six a.m. His whole life he had been getting up at five to milk cows and still found it hard to sleep in. Coming in this early gave him quiet time to get himself together before his crew came in at seven-thirty. He lingered in the basement trying to think of something he could do to cheer Miss Bernie up. After thirty minutes and no ideas, he headed upstairs to check the rig. While checking his mask, he felt her breasts press against his back. She ran her fingers through his hair. "Sorry. Can't help myself. You have the thickest black hair."

"Hi, Nic," he said, spinning around. Her tight jeans and low cut V-neck sweater hugged her curves. A black lace bra was visible under the loose knit of the sweater. It looked like one of the Victoria's Secret bras from the catalogs that came to the farm. This was the first time he had seen her with her hair down. On duty, she had to keep it tied up. She was stunning, but the sexual tension was gone now that he knew she wasn't into guys. In a way, it was a relief because he was hanging onto a thread of hope he could get Jennie back. In another way, he was disappointed. No more erotic fantasies.

"You ready yet?" Her lips turned up seductively.

"You didn't work yesterday?"

She jutted out her hip. "Does it look like I worked yesterday, Einstein?"

He grinned sheepishly. She had a knack for making him feel stupid.

"I flipped days with Ralph so he could take his wife to the doctor. Today you're *my* cub." She cupped her hand on his crotch and squeezed. She pulled her hand away and dashed off to the locker room before he could react.

When Mitch finished his morning duties, he reported to the kitchen to help Kenny.

Kenny waved the huge butcher knife in the air. "Me and my dick can handle it. Making Woof-n-Poof."

Several times a month Kenny made this firehouse dish of hamburger, potatoes, onions, carrots, and celery mixed with tomato soup and baked in an industrial-sized casserole pan.

Mitch went to the locker room to get the training manual. Nic sashayed up to him in baggy red shorts, a blue T-shirt, and tennis shoes. "C'mon, I need somebody to spot me. You can study later. Throw on some sweatpants and meet me in the basement."

The cool, damp basement reeked of smoke from the soot-stained turn-out gear along the wall. A single fluorescent fixture hung from the ceiling, dimly lighting the large room and the bare gray concrete walls. Nic was sitting on a faded gold carpet remnant with her legs spread, stretching her hands toward her feet. He watched her loose-fitting workout shorts ride up her tan legs. He wondered if she had gone down to Mexico with a girlfriend. He imagined the two of them sunbathing in the nude and later...

"Mitch, let's go before a run comes in, hey?" She got two jump ropes off the back table and handed one to him. "You jump?"

"Let's go."

Nic started off slow and built up speed, the rope clacking off the concrete floor. Mitch struggled to keep up. She snorted every time he tripped on the rope. She spun the rope faster, skipping from foot to foot. The rope became a blur as it made two revolutions with each jump. Mitch stopped, frustrated and pissed that she was laughing at him. Her breasts barely budged. She was not wearing a Victoria's Secret bra.

By the time she stopped, the sweaty T-shirt was plastered to her body. "Hope I didn't damage your frail male ego." Her smoky laugh made it hard to stay pissed.

She went to the weight rack and grabbed two twenty-five-pound dumb-bells that once must have been black but were now gray and mottled. Mitch lifted two dumbbells marked forty pounds off the rack.

"Can't let a girl beat you, hey?" She laughed and alternated curling each dumbbell to her chest.

They stood side by side facing the six-foot mirror on the back wall so they could watch themselves, except Mitch wasn't watching himself.

She smiled smugly. "You aren't bad either."

Still playing the game.

When they finished, she went to the weight bench. "Help me load a hundred-fifty."

"No kidding?"

They slapped the weights on the bar, and she lowered herself onto the bench.

He helped lift the bar off the rack and watched as she lowered it. When it hit her chest just above her breasts, she blew out a loud breath, then rammed the bar upward, gritting her teeth. Each time she lowered the bar her thighs stiffened. When she pushed the bar up, her breasts pressed together. Her T-shirt rode up, exposing rippling abs. The view was almost too much, lesbian or not. He was helpless to stop the excitement swelling below his waist, and she was staring at the evidence. "Hey, cub, you're supposed to be spotting not gawking."

He guided the bar into the rack. The moment was over.

"How much you want?" she asked.

"Two-eighty."

"No shit?"

They loaded the plates, and Mitch slid under the bar. Nic stood directly over his face to spot him. He couldn't help staring up her loose-fitting work-out shorts. *Stop.* He closed his eyes and grunted off fifteen reps. She helped guide the bar back to the rack.

"You farm boys bench press cows when you get bored?"

As he sat up, Nic straddled him and said, "Let me see that ink on your arm." She lifted off his T-shirt. "Damn, Garner, you have one hell of a bod." She rested her warm hand on his tense stomach and examined the jumping green deer. "The guys said that's a tractor emblem? I don't get it. A tractor instead of your high school sweetheart?"

"I guess you think it's pretty stupid, but I've seen some pretty stupid tattoos around here too."

"Oh, settle the fuck down. I'm just asking." Her face reddened. "You talking about mine?"

"I'm just saying. I don't know what I'm saying."

She pulled down the front of her T-shirt and red sports bra exposing a tattoo of a small white dove above her left breast.

"Looks like a pigeon," Mitch said. "Why wouldn't you have a tattoo of your high school sweetheart?"

She laughed. "It's supposed to be a dove, idiot. But you're right. It looks like a stupid pigeon."

"What about the one on your ahh…"

"My ass? Bad mistake."

She ran her hands up and down his arms. Her eyes turned glassy. She ripped off her T-shirt and red sports bra in one motion. Mitch gulped. His erotic fantasies didn't do her justice. Nic grasped the back of his head and kissed him hard, running her tongue over his. Her hand moved over his chest, down to his waist, and into his sweatpants. She gazed into his eyes as she gripped his hard-on.

He pulled her hand away. "Okay, okay, okay. You had your fun."

"What you talking about?"

"These games you're playing. This is getting crazy."

"What games? I just wanna fuck."

"Wait, what?"

Her turquoise eyes glistened. She slid her hand back inside his sweatpants.

What the hell? He grabbed the back of her neck and pressed his lips to hers.

He stopped. "What if we get caught?"

"I know, hey? Now shut up." She pushed him back on the bench and tugged off his sweatpants. "I see I got your attention."

She slid her shorts down her thighs. Mitch sucked in a deep breath. This was really happening. As she was stepping out of her shorts, the fire alarm chimed with a report of a house fire only two blocks away. She pulled her shorts up and slipped on her T-Shirt, leaving the red bra on the floor. She nodded at Mitch's erection and said, "Don't trip on that thing." She laughed and sprinted to the stairs.

Mitch snatched his scattered clothing off the floor. After yanking on his sweatpants, he flew up the stairs, ran to the rig, and geared up. Nic was on the other side of the rig. Together they jumped into the cab.

The rig left without Kenny. As soon as they hit the street, Mitch smelled smoke. A dark cloud of brown and black smoke mushroomed high in the sky. Captain Reemer leaned around his tall seat and said, "We got a worker. Kenny had to run out for supplies. You two will have the fire. I gotta take command. The chief and Truck Twelve are at another fire."

Nic nodded at Mitch, her expression scary serious. "Ready to rock and roll?"

Adrenaline electrified every cell of Mitch's body as they approached the dilapidated Victorian. Most windows were boarded. The ones that weren't spewed churning, angry smoke. The boss keyed the rig radio, "Dispatch, Engine Fifteen reporting fire in a three-story wood-frame vacant. Smoke coming from all floors." He handed Nic his portable radio. "Take this. I'll use Crusher's."

"Let's go, Garner."

Mitch and Nic hoisted hose onto their shoulders, allowing it to play out as they rushed to the back of the smoking house.

Nic kicked open the back door. Hot ink-black smoke gushed at them, the kind of smoke that could ignite in a deadly flashover without warning if not vented. They'd have to wait for backup before going in. The hose line snapped rigid behind them. Air hissed from the nozzle as Nic bled the line until water flowed. She shut it down. "Mask up. We got water."

Mitch couldn't believe what he heard. The idea of crawling into this blinding hot blackness had his guts churning. She disappeared into the smoke. He had no choice. He followed, keeping one hand on her back.

"Help me find the basement door," she said, her voice muffled by the face piece. "It should be around here somewhere."

He slid his free hand along one side of the wall and then the other. "Think I found it."

"Okay, stay off to the side and open it." Her hand was now on *his* back.

Scorching heat blasted at them. "Close it," she hollered. "I hate fucking basement fires." Into her radio, she said, "Hey, boss, we'll need the basement windows out."

Mitch's heart hammered at his ribcage, and she sounded like she was placing an order for pizza. He remembered Crusher telling him how Lt. Laubner screwed up and lost a cub because he made a bad call at a basement fire. He looked back to where he thought the back door was.

Shattering glass. "Windows are out," Nic said. "Open it. Let's go."

He hesitated.

"Goddammit, Garner, get that basement door open."

He yanked it open. "Too hot. We gotta back out."

"No way. This is *our* fire. Stay low."

"It's too hot."

"Fire's waiting."

When they got to the bottom, it was hot, but nothing like the top of the stairs. Nic stopped. "Listen for it. Most of these basements are loaded with shit. Makes it a bitch to find the fire. Hear it? Off to the left. Let's get the son of a bitch."

He struggled to stay with her while dragging the heavy hose behind him in the pitch-black darkness. He kept getting hung up on abstract shapes. The searing heat bled through his turnout coat as they blindly crawled deeper into the maze. He hunched lower.

"It's just ahead. See the orange glow?" Nic said. "Here, take the line."

Mitch slammed open the bail. The water rip-rapped through the hose. He blasted the orange glow, swirling the nozzle in a figure eight pattern, chasing fire through the basement until it banked down and went out. He finally felt the exhilaration of knocking down a working fire.

The fire was extinguished by the time Engine Thirty's crew came down to back them up. When the smoke cleared and masks were off, Engine Thirty's lieutenant poked Mitch in the chest. "Tell your asshole crew we didn't forget about those doughnuts. Payback's a bitch."

"Eat shit, dickhead," Nic said from behind Mitch. "You and your crew would be experts on that, hey?"

"We're done here," the lieutenant barked to his crew. "Let the dyke and her cub finish." His crew followed him up the stairs.

Mitch faced Nic and they both broke out in belly laughs.

Captain Reemer trotted down the stairs. "See you got to Nowicki. Good." He surveyed the charred basement. "Nice job."

"It was all your cub," Nic said.

The captain nodded. "Wet it down one more time and pick up. I gotta give the chief a report. Meet you at the rig."

"Why'd you say that?" Mitch asked Nic.

"You got the fire, didn't you?"

"Yeah, but you're the one who—"

"Look, we're all scared shitless at our first basement fire."

If they had backed out and Engine Thirty took the fire, Mitch knew he could never have faced Ralph and the crew.

When they finished in the basement, Mitch went to the bottle rig for fresh air bottles. Jamal's friend, LaMont, shuffled up to him, his head hanging.

"I didn't know your company was here," Mitch said.

Tear tracks lined LaMont's soot-covered face. "Shoulda never told Jamal about my sister."

"What the hell you talking about?"

LaMont didn't answer.

"C'mon, let's get away from the rig." Mitch pulled LaMont between two houses. "Now, what?"

"My baby sister, Chirelle, been hanging with that One-Niner, DeAndre. She come home beat bad, her face all angry. An' here she carrying his baby." He paused. "Momma was crying an' I got agitated. What could *I* do? Can't go messing with that bunch."

Mitch shook LaMont by the shoulders. "What about Jamal?"

"Never shoulda told him."

He shook him harder, then let go. "Why…"

LaMont rubbed his shoulders. "You and Jamal tight. Figure you got a right to know."

"Why didn't you go to the cops?"

"Chirelle be dead before they ever got to him. An' me too." He slumped away.

* * *

While cleaning hose back at the firehouse, Nic asked Mitch why he was so quiet. He told her he was exhausted from the fire. He didn't know what he was going to do but knew he had to keep it to himself. There would be an investigation.

After lunch, he went to the joker stand. At two-thirty, the dark blue Mercury Cougar stopped across the street and Jasmine got out. DeAndre leaned his head out the window, flashing his gold front teeth in a sneering grin at Mitch. The car pulled away, trailed by thumping bass.

Mitch had asked Jasmine about DeAndre once. She told him she got rides home from him, that's all. Mitch needed to mind his own business.

"Always study with your books closed?" Nic asked from behind him.

"I was such a wuss at the fire."

"Forget that." She waved her red sports bra in his face. "How about we go out tomorrow night?"

"Okay? Hey, want to help with the kids this afternoon?"

"Can't stand kids." She headed to the hallway. "Keep an eye on those little shits. They'll steal you blind."

As soon as she left, he went back to thinking about DeAndre. Jamal deserved justice. And Jasmine deserved to be free of that miserable bastard before it was too late.

Chapter 29

Mitch pulled his high powered .30-06 Browning hunting rifle from the closet. He'd gone up to his flat without stopping to visit Miss Bernie this morning. She'd know something was wrong.

He tore the rifle down and went about cleaning and oiling it. The smell of light oil and feel of cold steel quickened his pulse. He snapped the Browning together and put the smooth wood stock to his shoulder. Pointing it out the window, he focused the scope and clicked the trigger. On the farm when a predator tormented their herds, Mitch hunted it down and killed it. The rifle was ready. He was ready. But first, he had a date.

* * *

Nic's apartment was on Knapp Street, not far from Water Street, on Milwaukee's trendy East Side, where he and Jamal had spent many nights drinking. He knocked on her tenth-floor apartment door. He waited and knocked again. He rapped harder and the door flew open. A large red bath towel covered her dripping body. "Jesus, Garner. You always gotta be early?"

"Wasn't sure if I could find the place."

She wagged her finger in his face. "Hoping to catch me in the shower, you perv?"

"I can come back."

"Don't be stupid. I got a bottle over there. Whiskey's what you country boys like to swill, isn't it?"

"Prefer Courvoisier, but I'll settle for your cheap whiskey."

"You should smile more. Looks good on you."

He stepped inside the one-room studio apartment. Along the back wall were folding closet doors. A small sofa bed took up one whole side of the room. On the other side was a narrow counter with a sink, a half-sized fridge, and four small cabinets; everything white. It was no larger than the bedroom of his flat. Dirty clothes were piled in the corner. Crusted dishes littered the sink and counter. A touch of mildew hung in the air.

"Feel free to tidy up while I finish getting ready." Nic disappeared into the bathroom, trailed by her smoky laughter.

Mitch rinsed a dirty water glass and poured himself some Jack Daniels. He settled onto the sofa bed.

He fought the anger boiling below the surface. *Fucking DeAndre.*

She emerged from the bathroom rubbing her strawberry blond hair with the red towel, naked.

DeAndre can wait.

She smirked as she passed him on her way to the closet.

The flaming orange and black wings on her lower back belonged to an eagle staring at the crack of her ass. Watching her dig through the closet had him craving her naked body. He pretended to examine the glass of whiskey as she slipped into her powder blue lace bra and panties, then slithered into some faded jeans that had holes in interesting places.

She smoothed her beige, tight-fitting V-neck sweater over her curves. "Ready?"

"Can't afford new pants?"

She crossed her arms. "You some kind of fashion expert?"

"I've thrown out jeans with fewer holes."

"Very flattering, thanks."

"Sorry, I didn't mean ..."

"I'm fucking with you." She grabbed his drink and threw down the rest of the straight whiskey without flinching. "Let's go."

Mitch followed her out. The exquisitely placed holes in her jeans exposed the back of her tanned thighs and the edge of her blue panties. They strolled down the well-manicured streets lined with high rises. A cool September breeze blew in from Lake Michigan, carrying the fishy smell of the shoreline. The area was alive, nothing like Miss Bernie's neighborhood where people locked themselves away after dark.

While walking to Water Street, Mitch told her about the crap he was getting from Ralph.

She listened and when he was done tousled his hair. "Oh, poor boy. Try fitting in when you don't have a cock and balls."

She told him how she got hit on, talked about, and ridiculed. They were careful not to push her too far since her dad was a chief. The wives and girlfriends of her crew despised her because they didn't want their men sleeping in the same room and using the same showers. Her looks didn't help.

"Okay. I'm confused. The guys told me you were gay. Then we make out in the basement. And now we're going out."

She laughed hard and rested her forehead against his. "Those animals were all over me when I came on. They'd rub up against my ass while I washed dishes and try to sneak peeks when I dressed. And the stupid shit they'd say. They thought they were so fucking clever." She sneered. "I couldn't go to my dad. And I didn't want to go sniveling to the boss."

"What about sexual harassment rules?"

"Rules? Companies in the Core make their own rules."

"So you're not gay?"

She snickered. "Okay, listen close. I faked being gay to get them off me. I had a friend drop by one afternoon, a very sexy girlfriend. Took her behind the firehouse and I knew they'd be watching. We groped each other and swapped spit. Can't say I minded it and she got into it. We went at it pretty hot and heavy, put on quite a show." She pulled him close and ran her tongue up his neck, nibbled his ear, and ended on his lips. "But I like to feel a man inside me." She leaned back. "Get it now?"

"Aren't you afraid I'll blab your secret to the others?"

She squeezed his balls. "You wouldn't do that, would you?"

"Doesn't it bother you what people think?"

"What do I give a shit what people think? After that, I got treated like one of the guys, and the wives actually talked to me when they came to visit their sweet hubbies."

* * *

They made the rounds. Nic could drink as well as she fought fires. Every stop she was greeted by friends, most of them well-dressed and attractive. She made sure to introduce Mitch. She was showing him off, and he was liking the attention. When no one was looking, she'd brush her breasts against him and run her hands up the inside of his thigh. The music, pulsing crowds, and this seductive woman had him deliciously intoxicated and horny by closing.

Staggering back to her apartment, they stopped and groped each other, their tongues jousting. Nic pulled back. "Mitch, why so sad all the time?"

"Miss Jamal."

"You never seemed happy before, though."

"I don't know, Jen."

"I'm Nic."

His face flushed. "Sorry, I'm drunk." He turned to walk away.

Nic grabbed his arm. "Oh, no you don't. You're not bailing on me now."

Once inside the apartment, she pulled the sofa into a bed which was spread with sapphire-blue sheets. When she turned back to Mitch, he lifted her snug sweater over her head and guided her onto the bed. "Tonight *you're* the cub." He tugged her jeans off while she watched him, smirking.

She unclasped her powder blue lace bra and tossed it across the room, then stretched her arms behind her head and lay back. He slid her lace panties down her legs.

He started at the nape of her neck, nibbling with a feather-light touch until she moaned. She turned her head to the side and closed her eyes exposing more of her neck. He lifted her hand to his face and lightly kissed her wrist and palm. He moved over her body with his lips, tongue, and fingertips, lingering when she trembled. Her moaning turned to gasps. Mitch's excitement rose along with hers. She clutched his hair and pushed his head between her legs. He teased her until he felt her thighs tighten, then pushed his tongue inside. Her hips ground into him. She shuddered violently.

She looked down at him, gasping for breath. "Where'd you learn that? Holy shit."

"You approve?"

"Jen taught you well. Now get your clothes off."

She watched Mitch strip. "Stand there a minute. I just want to look at you." She blew out a loud whistle while scanning his naked body. "Okay, my turn. Lay down on your belly."

"I'm not into any of that anal stuff."

"Relax."

He stretched out on the smooth satin sheets.

Nic took a small bottle from her bed stand and lathered her hands with lavender-scented oil. The oil smelled like Jennie's hair. He shook the memory from his head and lost himself in the pleasure of Nic's strong hands working the oil into his back and thighs.

"Now turn over," she whispered in his ear. Her hot breath sent a spark down his spine.

She started at his forehead, then worked her way down his neck and chest, taking her time. She went to his feet where she massaged each toe. He couldn't remember feeling this relaxed. As she moved up his thigh, arousal replaced relaxation. Mitch arched his back as she massaged his hard-on with the warm oil.

"Slow down, cowboy," Nic said as she moved on top of him and guided him inside. She gasped. "Ahh, fuck, you feel good, Garner." She went slow, taking her time. He pressed deep into her. He was close.

She wrapped her warm, oily hands around his neck. "Not yet. Wait for me."

She rocked, keeping her hands on his neck. She moaned from deep inside. She squeezed his neck so hard the room went dim. He grabbed her wrists as he went rigid followed by a mind-blowing orgasm.

Nic collapsed on top of him while he settled into the balmy afterglow. When she finally moved off him and snuggled into his arms, he ran his hand down her back, cupping her ass. "Ever going to tell me about that eagle?"

"Ever going to tell me why you're always so sad?" She kissed him on the neck and lightly brushed the hair on his chest. "You okay?"

"I'm fine."

She propped herself up on one elbow. "I hooked up with this biker dude when I was eighteen. He talked me into getting that tat. It's the Harley Davidson Eagle." She lifted his chin. "Sure you want to know all this?"

"Go on."

"He was like thirty years old, and I thought he was a god. He was the vice president of the Freedom Riders. Nickname was Bronson. He loved fucking me from behind so he could see that damn eagle while we did it. I think the eagle got him off more than I did." She paused. "The horny cocksucker never could get enough strange pussy, so I finally bailed. End of story. Now, what's your story?"

"Just a horny farm boy."

Nic ran her fingers over the scar on his forehead. "Bar fight?"

"Nothing that exciting."

"Okay, I'll stop asking questions, for now."

Mitch lay next to her for what seemed like hours listening to her light snoring. Unbearable visions of Jamal's dead body and Jasmine walking the streets as a prostitute made sleep impossible. He dressed and left. He drove home through the dark, empty streets and got the Browning.

Chapter 30

Lying in the tall grass of the open field, fifty yards from the crack house, Mitch's veins surged with the thrill of the hunt. The dried grass smelled like the ripening wheat fields back home, the autumn air still and crisp; a perfect night for hunting. Through the night scope, he watched the house where they had imprisoned the old woman in that horrific bedroom, bringing back in nauseating detail the cloud of flies, the maggots feeding off her, and that putrid smell. The vision of DeAndre's partners, one with dreadlocks and the other with spiked hair, was burned into his memory.

He waited. They would come to him eventually. He needed to be patient, like hunting predators on the farm.

Through the night, people came and went, never staying long. DeAndre didn't show. The sun would be up in an hour. He'd have to come back. Before reaching the road, Mitch heard thumping bass. He ran back in time to see the front door of the dark blue Mercury Cougar open. His breathing quickened. It was like the first time he bagged a buck and struggled with the panic of deer fever. He slid the rifle from under his jacket and peered through the night scope, watching for the gold teeth. This was it. Focusing the scope he saw the spiked hair and scraggly goatee, but no gold teeth. Mitch's heart raced. He took a deep breath and squeezed off six rounds.

* * *

Back in his flat, the visions of the night played over and over and over. He should have waited until his head cleared. This was a bad mistake.

Knocking. It was almost noon. He'd been tormenting himself for over seven hours. He cracked the door. LaMont was leaning against the wall, his eyes cloudy and bloodshot. "DeAndre's car got shot up last night. Said he knows I had something to do with it."

Mitch's entire body tensed. "Why'd he think that?"

"Made Chirelle tell him about complaining at me when he beat on her. He took me upstairs and there she was crying, side of her face all swoll up. I had a gun I'd a shot DeAndre dead right there. He knew it too. Then he puts a gun to her head and says I best tell him." LaMont sobbed.

Mitch's knees went weak. "Did he..."

"I kept telling him, I didn't do it. Then he says he knows I went to Jamal. Cussed me out good saying, 'who the fuck else you tell?' He grab Chirelle by the throat. Has the gun in her mouth. She twisting all over, her eyes all bugged out. Says tell him now or she dead." LaMont covered his face.

Mitch yanked his hands away. "You tell him?"

"I had to. He'd a killed her."

"Fuck."

"Told me to tell you he's coming for you." He gawked at the rifle lying on the coffee table with the cleaning oil and rags. "Why you do that?"

"Why didn't you get your sister the hell out of here?"

LaMont's cloudy eyes turned to ice. "Dude's gonna pay."

* * *

Mitch didn't pay much attention to the department flag at half-staff the next morning. They were routinely flown at half-staff when a retiree passed away.

Nic met him at the joker stand, wide-eyed. "Mitch. Things are really fucked up."

"Yeah, I'm sorry I left the other night."

"Another firefighter was killed last night, LaMont Franklin. All the firehouses are on lockdown."

He had to sit.

Nic bent over him. "Wasn't he in your class?"

What the hell did I do?

Nic lifted his chin. "Talk to me. Please. Do you know what the fuck is going on?" He never heard fear in her voice before.

"I gotta go. Can you work my shift today?"

Mitch was out the door before she could answer. He should have dropped the gangbanger when he had the chance. He had him in the sights, but Jamal's deep voice had shouted, "nooo," inside Mitch's head. The high powered bullets tore into DeAndre's car. The spiked-hair One-Niner had gawked at the shattering glass and fled to the house.

* * *

Mitch was barely inside his flat when three police officers barged into the room through the open door. Two uniform officers spread out while the suit stepped forward. "You Mitch Garner?"

"What you doing here?"

The officer glanced at the rifle on his coffee table. "Planning something?"

"Just cleaning my rifle."

The suit picked it up and examined it. "Smells like it's been fired. Get anything?"

Mitch didn't answer.

"Let's cut the shit. You knew both victims." The corners of the officer's mouth turned up. "Shoot up that crack house; you'll end up dead or behind bars."

"If you know it's the One-Niners, why aren't *they* behind bars?"

"We got nothing. But I think you do. Give us anything. We'll get them off the streets."

The officer was right. If he killed DeAndre, he'd be their prime suspect. So far all he'd done was make things worse. He told them everything.

The suit finished scribbling notes. "That should be enough to put DeAndre away while we build a case."

"And the rest?"

"Can't arrest any of them from what you said."

"Great. So I'm their next target?"

"They're not stupid enough to do that."

"What? Kill a *white* firefighter?"

"Got nothing to do with it. We'll be so far up their asses, they won't be able to shit without us knowing."

"Get that murdering bastard off the street or I will."

"I didn't hear that. Stay low until we make an arrest."

* * *

Mitch plodded downstairs. He found Miss Bernie rocking in her easy chair, staring at the television, gripping a purple hanky. "They sayin' another fireman kilt."

He gritted his teeth.

"That why the police here?"

What could he tell her? That he shot up DeAndre's car and DeAndre killed LaMont.

"Mitch, honey. I can see you hurtin'."

"It was LaMont," he blurted.

"Oh, dear Lord. Not my LaMont. I love that boy." Guttural sobs racked her body.

Mitch stared at the wall, throbbing with rage.

Her sobbing slowed. "Mitch, get on back to that farm before the devil take you too."

"Not until DeAndre's gone."

"That who they think killed LaMont?"

"He did. And Jamal too."

"DeeDee?" Her face sagged as the words sunk in. "Him and Jamal, they good friends when they kids. How could he…?"

"They're arresting him today for both murders."

Her chin collapsed onto her chest. "Should a known. His momma in and out of prison." Mitch could barely hear her. "Hard for kids growing up with no daddy around here and near impossible to grow up without a momma. Children need a momma's love. DeeDee never had that." She sighed. "Opens the way for the devil to get in their heads. That Devil use DeeDee to kill my boy. I won't hate DeeDee. I won't. That's what the devil feast on is hate. I won't give him that."

I'll hate him enough for both of us.

* * *

Miss Bernie had asked Mitch to join her for dinner. She didn't want to be alone. The aroma of meatloaf and buttered potatoes greeted him in the stairwell on the way down. He thought about the first time he was invited to dinner with her and Jamal and how they made him feel like family and the laughter they shared. Her kitchen was a place of comfort.

"Miss Bernie, what we—"

"Let's say grace." She bowed her head. "Lord, thank you for providing this bounty. And thank you for bringing this young man into my life. I know you got a plan for us but we're at our end. Please give us a sign and lead us to your glory. Amen."

They ate in silence, both picking at their food.

Miss Bernie laid her fork next to her plate and folded her hands. "Mitch, we need to share our pain. No good keeping it to ourselves. Only festers. All our time together you never talk about your momma or daddy. I never push you. It's time."

He couldn't admit what he left behind in Milroy. Not yet.

She rested her chin on her folded hands and waited.

Mitch stopped shifting food around and gazed through the window searching for words. "I should go. Supper was great." He rose.

Her eyes ordered him to sit.

"I can't, Miss Bernie."

"All right then. You set and listen to my pain. I told you how people need their mommas. Mine died birthing me. I knew it was my fault she died. Now ain't that some foolish thinking, that it was a child's fault her momma died?"

Mitch's jaw tightened.

She went on. "I carried that guilt most of my life. The good Lord finally convince me to let it go. You go around carrying all that guilt and hating yourself, another way for the devil to get a hold."

"How did you stop it, the guilt and all?"

"Started doing for others instead of pitying myself. I used to take in all manner of foster children. Even took DeeDee in for a while. Doing for those children brought me joy until my back got to grippin' me bad. It was hard, specially with the babies. I had to stop taking 'em in. Oh, I surely miss that." She lowered her head. "I still fret over running my Lettie off. Hard to let that go. And I been hurtin' real bad about Jamal. And now LaMont. But I can't let that devil put hatred in my heart. Gotta forgive. Only way to find peace."

She paused. He thought about what she said but telling her about his mom and dad after fighting so long to keep it buried terrified him.

"Mitch, you want that devil out your head, need to forgive yourself."

"How?"

"Start by telling me." She waited, her face grave.

After an uncomfortable silence, he gritted his teeth, took a deep breath, and told her about not being able to save Maggie and almost burning the farm down.

When he finished, she said, "And your folks?"

The question paralyzed him.

Miss Bernie pulled her chair around so they were facing each other. "Just let it out."

Mitch hesitated but couldn't turn away. "My mom died when I was ten. After she died, me and my dad didn't get along. I tried hard to please him, but after a while, I gave up. I guess we just didn't like each other much."

"And your momma? What was she like?"

"We'd read together and talk. I loved being with her when she wasn't feeling sad."

"I can tell by that look on your face, you must have loved her plenty. How'd she die?"

Mitch's temples throbbed.

"This where your pain come from, ain't it?"

He nodded.

Miss Bernie leaned in. "Let it out."

Mitch exhaled slowly. "She killed herself."

Miss Bernie's eyes widened. "And you blame yourself. Just like I blamed myself for my momma dying. Now, ain't we a pair?"

He bit his lower lip.

"Honey, that ain't no more your fault than me causing my momma's passing."

"How could she do that?"

Miss Bernie wiped her watering eyes with her purple hanky. "She must have struggled with some awful misery. Guess you'd have to know that kind of pain to understand."

Mitch did know.

Miss Bernie straightened in her chair. "Don't let the devil get you hating yourself. You a good man. It's time you accept that and stop frettin' over things you can't change. Use your pain to change what you can. Like those children you teaching."

They rose together and hugged. She was right. It did feel good to share this. Nobody else could have dragged it out of him.

* * *

Back upstairs, the night wore on. The police hadn't called to tell him they arrested DeAndre. Mitch jumped at every car going by, every shout, and every banging door in the neighborhood. He imagined sounds, racing from window to window with his rifle. He had locked Miss Bernie's door but left the downstairs door to his flat open, praying DeAndre would come for him.

A volatile mixture of adrenaline and fear kept him awake through the night. That and hatred. He understood what Miss Bernie said. It all made sense, but he wasn't ready to forgive.

The Core grew still as morning approached. Sitting by the back window he fought off sleep, jerking awake every time his chin dropped to his chest. Footsteps on the back stairway rocked his jangled nerves. He tried to shake the cobwebs loose.

Mitch jumped out onto the landing, leveling the rifle at the figure coming up the dark stairway.

"Jesus!—Police—Put the gun down." The words were a jumble of confusion.

The figure dove around the wall of the stairwell. A handgun appeared, pointed at Mitch. "I said, put it down. Now."

Mitch stared down the gun barrel, trying to comprehend what was happening. His finger went to the trigger of his rifle.

From below, Miss Bernie shouted, "Mitch, what in the world going on?"

Mitch was shocked to see the rifle in his hands. He immediately laid it down and sat on the landing with his hands in the air, horrified by what almost happened.

Two officers vaulted up the stairs with guns drawn. The first officer, a young white man, grabbed the rifle. "What the fuck's wrong with you?"

A gray-haired black officer was right behind him. "Let's all take it easy." He pushed by the white officer and leaned over Mitch. "Greet all your guests like that?"

"I'm. I'm. I don't know what I'm doing."

The white officer holstered his gun. "Lucky I didn't shoot your ass."

The gray-haired officer waved at the other one while watching Mitch. "The boss wanted us to let you know DeAndre's on the run."

Miss Bernie clomped up the stairs. "Leave that boy be."

The gray-haired officer turned to her. "Just a minor misunderstanding, Ma'am. Everything's fine. Right, Mr. Garner?"

Mitch's brain cleared. "Yeah, everything's perfect." He called down to Miss Bernie, "DeAndre got away."

The white officer said, "We'll need to confiscate the gun."

"What gun?" the gray-haired officer said. Then to Mitch, he said, "Took a lot of guts to come forward. Anyway, the boss wanted to assure you DeAndre won't be showing his face around here any time soon. We'll keep combing the streets until we get him."

Mitch stared at the rifle on the floor and trembled.

Chapter 31

Mitch's blind hatred nearly cost a police officer his life. He had to get a grip on his emotions; take Miss Bernie's advice and let the hatred go. Keep the devil out of his head.

Through the rest of September and October, he battled bouts of guilt and hatred, always coming back to Miss Bernie's words, "Use your pain to change what you can."

Team Driver grew to over a dozen children by the end of October. Jasmine and Mitch made a great team. Jasmine's quick wit and humor kept him on his toes. Twice a week he'd let her lead the group, and the kids loved it. Helping the kids and working with Jasmine took the edge off his dark thoughts. Miss Bernie had been right again.

* * *

Mitch waited at the front of the firehouse for the kids to arrive, enjoying the crisp November breeze. This had always been his favorite time of year on the farm. The crops were in and deer hunting season underway.

Thanksgiving was only two days away. Mitch thought back to three months ago when Jasmine was in his face, raging at him with ghetto profanities. Now she spoke with correct grammar, most of the time. She explained how "talking white" was not that hard. After all, television shows were mostly white people. Even the Huxtables talked white. It wasn't that most kids in the hood couldn't talk that way; they talked ghetto to survive.

Mitch stepped outside when Alexus came skipping across the street, her long braids bouncing. Jasmine trailed close behind. Alexus crashed into him and wrapped her arms around his waist. "You my boyfriend. You best know that."

Mitch's chest tightened. That's what little Maggie used to say.

Jasmine grinned. "So, Mr. Teacher, what's planned for today?"

"Thought we'd all get down and bust some moves."

"You're too funny." She pulled a notebook from her book bag and thrust it at him. "Check it out."

At the top of the page was an A+ in red and a note: "Jasmine, you are doing such great work. Keep it up." It was a book report on *A Tree Grows in Brooklyn*.

He lowered the paper to see her broad gap-toothed smile. Her face glowed.

"I'm not surprised. You're a smart young lady."

After the tutoring sessions, Jasmine had been staying behind to talk about school and what she was reading. Mitch had suggested she read *A Tree Grows in Brooklyn*. He told her how it was his mother's favorite book when she was Jasmine's age. Jasmine loved it and couldn't talk enough about this story of a young girl growing up in poverty. Reading it made her feel like Francie even though Francie was a white girl growing up a long time ago.

Jasmine crammed the notebook back in her bag. "My teacher said if I keep doing well I might get into Riverside next year. Says that's where you need to go if you want to get into college."

"You'll get in. What do you want to be?"

"Um, teacher maybe?"

"Not maybe. You'll make a great teacher."

A group of children filed into the firehouse, giving Mitch high-fives as they passed. He looked down the street and back at Jasmine. "Seen Kyle yet?"

"Won't be seeing him anymore. Had a bad fit. They got him at the nursing home over on Hopkins." Jasmine nodded toward the firehouse. "Better get in there before those kids tear your firehouse apart."

Mitch choked. Kyle had become his little buddy. He lived in the Donald Driver jersey, and when it got nasty, Mitch exchanged it for a clean one. The boy would thank him by resting his head against him, but pull back if Mitch tried to hug him.

* * *

The next morning Mitch went to see Kyle. He walked down the long hallway of the Orchard Manor Nursing Home looking for Kyle's room. The strong odor of bleach stung his nostrils. The bleach barely masked what? Urine? Feces? Decaying flesh?

Kyle appeared tiny in the full-sized hospital bed. His head swayed back and forth, his mouth in a perpetual "O". The boy's eyes were open but vacant. When Mitch was able to talk, he said, "Hey, Kyle. Heard you needed another jersey. Donald Driver, he's the man, remember?"

Mitch held out the green and gold jersey with the number "80" on it. He pried the boy's stiff arm up and slid the jersey under it. He kissed the top of Kyle's head. The boy's hair was matted and sour smelling. "I need you to come back. You're my man."

Nobody came by during the two hours Mitch was at Kyle's bedside.

* * *

Before going up to his flat, Mitch stopped by Miss Bernie's to see what she had planned for Thanksgiving. This would be her first Thanksgiving without Jamal. Mitch suggested they have a fancy Thanksgiving dinner at a restaurant of her choice. She said she wasn't up to going anywhere. Said she'd be glad to cook if he wanted to join her. He couldn't say no.

* * *

Miss Bernie had prepared a feast for them. Her kitchen was saturated with the cozy smell of turkey, buttermilk biscuits, and sweet potato pie. Enough turkey and trimmings for a dozen.

While they ate, Miss Bernie told him how Jamal would invite friends over for Thanksgiving. They'd have a houseful. The young people would gather in the front room and cut up with each other while watching the football games. And she'd keep pushing more food at them. When they got older, there was beer and drinking, but they behaved themselves. She even had a beer or two with them on occasion.

This got him thinking about Thanksgivings on the farm. After his mom died, Betty Hillenbrand, Maggie's mother, demanded the three Garner men join them for Thanksgiving dinner. Spending Thanksgiving with the Hillenbrands became a tradition. And Mitch's place was always next to Maggie's. It started when she was a toddler, pushing anyone aside who dared sit next to her Mitch.

He ached to be back there but knew, for him, that world no longer existed. He imagined the table loaded with turkey, mashed potatoes, stuffing, green bean casserole, and homemade loaves of sourdough bread. They'd be gathered around that farm table right now, without him, without Maggie.

Miss Bernie sighed. "Ain't we a pair? All wrapped up in ourselves. You don't have to set here with me."

Mitch pointed at Miss Bernie. "You told me we need to share our pain."

"You right. I ain't so good at taking my own advice." She placed her fork across her plate. Her lips quivered. "Can't turn away from the pain no more. It's taking me down. Jamal's gone, and it pains me bad, but I accept it." Her eyelids drooped. "But my Lettie, where my sweet Lettie? Oh, Lord, why can't you give me an answer?"

Mitch squeezed her hand.

Her voice faded. "Used to feel better after a good cry but can't cry no more. It's like I'm all dried up."

Mitch studied his white hand entwined with her small, dark hand, wondering what he could say or do to comfort her. He'd been making such great progress with the children, and Jasmine had grown in so many ways the last few months. But he was powerless to help this woman who had been like a mother to him.

"Pack up this food and give it to them children you teaching. Imagine some ain't getting a proper meal today."

He talked her into letting him clean the kitchen. She agreed as long as when he finished he got out for a while. After drying the dishes, he found her dozing in her easy chair.

He headed over to Nic's apartment. She had invited him to have Thanksgiving dinner with her and her family. He declined. There was no way he was leaving Miss Bernie alone all day. Nic said to at least stop by her place later for a Thanksgiving drink.

She greeted him in a black lace camisole. He had become hopelessly addicted to that body, that face, that sex. He constantly craved more.

After a final round of volcanic sex, he drifted off.

* * *

Mitch's eyes snapped open to Nic's face inches from his. She whispered, "Love watching you sleep." She planted a warm kiss on his forehead. "Your scar is sexy."

"What time is it?"

"Almost five."

"Crap. I gotta get ready for work."

"Of course. Always have to be the first one in." She kissed his mouth, her morning breath a touch sour. "Call in sick. I'll make it worth your while." She went to the bed and patted a spot next to her.

He yanked on his jeans, tightened the belt, and clasped the brass John Deere buckle.

She watched him from the bed, lying naked on her stomach. "You need to move in with me."

He pulled on his shirt and laughed. "Right. You'd get sick of me and toss me aside like a used dish rag. Add me to the pile."

"I mean it, Mitch." She went to him and pressed her naked body against him. "I love you."

He kissed her and left.

Chapter 32

Mitch lingered in the parking lot before reporting for duty, stewing over Nic. She was drop-dead gorgeous. He loved being with her. And the sex was incredible. What the hell stopped him from telling her he loved her?

He went inside.

He had told the kids he'd be here if they wanted to come in for a fun session since it was the day after Thanksgiving.

At three o'clock he stepped outside in the light drizzle, waiting for the children to arrive. The battered screen door on the Richardson house slammed. Alexus ran across the street and crashed into him. Jasmine shuffled well behind. Mitch told Alexus to go on in.

"Jasmine, you okay?"

"I'm fine."

Mitch pointed to a darkened bruise on her neck. "What's that?"

She slapped her hand over the bruise. "Ain't nothin'." She pushed past him.

Eight more children showed. Mitch had Alexus select one of the hip-hop CDs he purchased that didn't carry the adult advisory warning. The children jumped up, busting their best moves to the thumping bass. Jasmine stood back, her arms folded, staring at the back wall. Mitch went to her side. "Don't feel like dancing?"

She continued staring at the wall.

He knew better than to push her and went back to the others. They danced around him, challenging him to mimic their moves. He looked silly exaggerating their rhythmic movements. This had them squealing with laughter. They danced to two more tracks on the CD and then played some word games. This is where Jasmine would normally step in and help. Not today.

When it was time to go, Mitch handed the children the brown paper bags of food Miss Bernie sent along. The bags rustled as the kids inspected the contents. They weren't impressed with the turkey and biscuits.

Mitch pulled giant chocolate chip cookies from a white paper bag. "How about these?"

"Dude!" the kids hollered. The cookies were frosted in green with "80" written in gold frosting. Each child gave him a high-five as they ran by. Alexus buried the side of her face in his waist.

"C'mon, we need to go," Jasmine said.

Mitch raised his hand. "Wait. Lexi, go to the kitchen. You can eat your cookie in there. Tell Kenny to give you some milk." She skipped to the kitchen.

Mitch gripped her slender shoulders. "Jasmine. Talk to me. What happened?"

"Don't matter."

"What don't matter?"

"Don't matter." She shook her head while looking past him.

"Please, Jasmine. Talk to me. You get in a fight?" He lifted her chin. Her eyes dilated. "C'mon. Let me help."

"That crackhead of Momma's. That's who did it. That what you wanna hear?"

"He hurt you bad?"

"Don't matter."

"Your mother know?"

"Says kids need a good beating once in a while so they grow up right." Her face pinched into a scowl. "Guess she needs a good beating too, because he sure beats on her plenty."

"Why doesn't she kick him out?"

"Says it's hard to keep a man, so you gotta put up with their shit."

Alexus skipped into the room. "You done?"

Jasmine stepped toward Alexus. "We're going."

"Lexi, go back in the kitchen," Mitch said.

He clasped Jasmine's clammy hands. "When did he do this?"

Her scowl wilted. "Yesterday. He was drinking forties and smoking that pipe after Momma left. She had to work: double time on Thanksgiving. Now that DeAndre gone away we need the money."

"Wait. What? What's DeAndre got to do with anything?"

"He used to help Momma. Said the One-Niners owed it to her."

"Why? Why would they owe her money?"

"It was about my sister Preddy."

Mitch hunched forward, their faces inches apart. "You know DeAndre killed two firefighters, two of my friends?"

Her head dropped. "I know they saying he killed Miss Bernie's son."

"He did. He's a killer, Jasmine. You know that, don't you?"

"All I know is he kept Momma's crackhead off us. Told him he'd cut his heart out if he messed with us." Her voice trailed off. "Now that DeAndre gone, that crackhead says he'll take what he wants."

A vision of Jasmine in DeAndre's car flashed in his head. He had to know. "DeAndre ever, you know, try anything?"

Her emerald eyes flared. "You mean, he try to fuck me?"

"Jesus. No."

"Well, he didn't."

Mitch let go of her hands and stepped back, figuring it was time to change the subject. "What happened after your mother went to work?"

She groaned, then said, "That crackhead keep giving me the bug eye while I cleaned up. I got Lexi settled and went to bed. Woke up to that nigger standing over me holding his…" She gagged.

It took a second for her words to register. Mitch's voice cracked as he asked, "Jasmine, what did he do to you?"

Her head twitched. "I gotta go."

He gripped her shoulders again. "Jasmine. Tell me what happened so we can put him away."

"What you know about anything? You come from the farm."

"What if he tries that with Alexus?"

Her emerald eyes turned steely cold, sending a shiver through him. In a deep voice he didn't recognize, she said, "I cut his heart out myself."

Alexus peeked around the corner, "Now?"

Jasmine took Alexus by the hand. Mitch followed them to the door and watched Alexus skip across the street, clutching what was left of her giant cookie. Jasmine trudged behind, her shoulders slumped and head hanging. She stopped on their porch and looked back at him, slowly shaking her head before disappearing into the house. The screen door slammed shut.

* * *

A haze of tobacco smoke watered Mitch's eyes as he shuffled into the firehouse kitchen. Crusher, Kenny, and Ralph were seated at the long oak table puffing on cigars and laughing.

Crusher studied him. "Why so grooblick, kid?" The others stopped laughing.

"The older girl from across the street, the one who's helping with the kids? She was molested by her mom's boyfriend."

"That the scumbag wears the long coat?" Crusher asked.

"Name's Maurice. Bastard needs to be put away. And get this. The girl said he left them alone until DeAndre took off. Said DeAndre protected her and her family."

Ralph exhaled a cloud of smoke at the ceiling. "Protect? Bullshit. He's grooming her." He pointed the cigar at Mitch. "Get used to the shit that goes on down here. Think you're gonna save those porch monkeys? Forget it. Ain't happening."

Mitch's face burned. "That's such bullshit."

"Bullshit? Get some time on the job, then tell me what's bullshit."

"So I should let that creep...? That's total crap."

Ralph ground out his cigar in the clay ashtray that looked like a grade school project, painted red like the fire trucks. He stood and rammed his finger into Mitch's chest. "You got a lot to learn. Most of these animals around here are a waste of skin. Don't think you're gonna come down here and save the world. The girl you think you're saving? Once she grows tits, she'll be on the street selling her body for another rock."

Mitch shoved Ralph's leathery hand away. "Why don't you transfer out if you hate them so much?"

The captain stormed from the office. "Hey, you two. Back off. Now."

Ralph stepped back. "Screw you, Bambi. You're an ignorant jag."

"Yeah, well you're an ignorant bigot."

"You're talking out of your ass." Ralph stomped past the boss, turned and grabbed his crotch. "I got your bigot right here, jag."

Mitch glared at Ralph through a red mist of rage and punched the wall.

Crusher chuckled, rolling a cigar around in his mouth. "Nice shot, kid. I think you got to the cranky, old pus bag. Won't be seeing him the rest of the day. He'll be off to the dungeon worshiping at the altar of Fox News. Think I'll go see if I can settle him down." He grinned at the captain.

Captain Reemer shook the end of his pipe at Crusher. "Leave the man alone. Don't need you stirring the pot."

"Ya vol, Herr Commandant." Crusher saluted and left, laughing. Kenny followed.

Mitch couldn't stop shaking.

The captain motioned him to the table. "Sit. Those kids from across the street ever tell you about their older sister?"

"God, he gets to me. *He's* the jag."

"Mitch!"

"Sorry, boss. I heard they had a sister who died."

The captain shook the pipe into the red clay ashtray and refilled it. He lit the fresh tobacco with a wooden farmer's match, sending a cloud of sulfur and tobacco smoke toward the ceiling. After three short puffs, he ran his fingers through thinning, silver hair and said, "Name was Preddy. Quite a while back, long before you got assigned here, there was a fire in the basement of their house. Not much of a fire really, but Ralph found Preddy in a back bedroom and carried her out. She started coming over to the firehouse wanting to know if Ralph was working. If he was she'd follow him around pestering him with questions about anything and everything. He tried to act like she irritated him, but that cute kid broke through his thick hide."

"Why does he talk that way?"

The captain puffed on his pipe and continued. "Ralph's worked in the Core over twenty years. It changes you. Changes the way you think. Some of us put up walls and act all macho; I guess to hide our emotions. I don't know. I'm not a damned psychologist. When you get more time on you'll understand."

"How long you worked in the Core?" Mitch asked.

"Too long."

"You feel the same way Ralph does?"

"Listen, Ralph's made impossible saves. Risked his ass umpteen times to save these people you think he hates, the people he wants us to think he hates. Why? Damned if I know. But I'd rather have that man next to me when all hell breaks loose than anyone else. And you're right, he can be a jag, but a he's damn fine firefighting jag. You could learn a lot from him."

"Why—"

"Let me finish. When Preddy got older, she started hanging with the One-Niners and stopped coming around. We'd see her on the streets and then she disappeared. Ralph wouldn't admit it, but it tore him up to lose his little friend. Around two years ago Preddy's body was found in a dumpster. She'd been beaten, raped, and strangled."

Captain Reemer waited while Mitch absorbed the gruesome details.

He handed Mitch the red clay ashtray. "Turn it over."

Mitch emptied the ashtray and ran his hand over the coarse inscription scratched on the underside *for my frend Ralf luv Preddy*. His anger faded.

"One more thing. The shit bag who killed Preddy turned up in the same dumpster two weeks later. Someone beat him, threw him in there, poured gas on him, and lit it. Burned him alive."

"Holy crap. Who did *that*?"

"Nobody knows."

Captain Reemer relaxed back in his chair. "I'll call police dispatch and get a squad over here. You can tell them what's going on across the street." The captain shrugged. "Maybe they'll do something."

* * *

"So the older girl, Jasmine, was sexually assaulted?" The burly officer with dark, sunken eyes asked Mitch.

"She didn't say that exactly. She did say the man beats her and her mom."

"See any marks or signs she's being beaten?"

"Looked like a bruise on her neck, but she covered it before I could get a good look."

The officer scowled. "That's it? I got other calls waiting."

"What happened to protect and serve? Or doesn't that apply to black kids?"

The officer narrowed his eyes. "That's a shitty thing to say."

"No. What's shitty is what's happening to those kids."

"All right, all right, all right. Take it easy." The officer's thick black eyebrows knit together. "So here's what I'll do. I'll take a run at the asshole, pretend I know some things."

Mitch stood by the window at the front of the firehouse and watched the officer march across the street. His thoughts drifted to the horrific story of Jasmine's sister. He was still at the window when the officer ambled back across the street thirty minutes later.

The officer shrugged. "I tried."

"So?"

"Asshole denied everything. And the mother of the year got pissed when I got her alone and asked if she knew her daughter was being sexually assaulted. Told me to get the fuck out of her house when I pressed."

"So that's it?"

"Get the girl to tell you what he did to her and I'll run his ass in."

After the officer left, Mitch remained by the front window. How would he get her to tell him about something that sick?

The screen door slammed. Maurice trotted down the steps, the steps Mitch had rebuilt and painted. Maurice strutted down the sidewalk waving his middle finger at the firehouse and mouthing the words that go with it. Mitch fought to control the overpowering urge to run him down and bash his face into the sidewalk.

Chapter 33

Mitch sat night-watch in the room adjacent to the front entrance, reeling from the miserable day and thinking about things Jasmine had told him over the last few months. She told him how her momma used to be happy. Now all she did was work, drink, and sleep. Jasmine took over the house, keeping it clean, cooking, and taking care of Alexus. She hadn't seen her dad in years. When she was little, her dad called her his little princess and gave her a necklace to wear instead of a crown since she couldn't wear a crown all the time. She never took the necklace off. She wished he'd come back and kick Maurice out. While sharing the heart-wrenching details, she never seemed emotional or sad.

Mitch's imagination ran wild with sickening visions of Maurice on top of Jasmine. Somehow he'd get the son of a bitch away from her. Loud rattling startled him. He glanced at the round wall clock on the way to the door. It read 2:30 a.m.

Alexus's tiny body was plastered to the glass door trying to push it open. She was in Barney pajamas, nothing on her feet, her gaping mouth and chestnut eyes wide. Mitch yanked the door open. A biting, acrid smell swept into the firehouse. Smoke blanketed the street.

"Our house," Alexus struggled to say, "on fire."

"Stay here!" Mitch rang the alarm and shouted over the PA system, "Working fire across the street." In one motion he stepped into his boots, pulled up the bunker pants, and snapped the red suspenders over his shoulders. He slipped on his Kevlar coat while rushing across the street. He'd get his helmet and mask from the rig when Crusher drove it over.

Gray and black smoke gushed from every crack and crevice of the old house. Benita Richardson stood on the back porch howling like a wounded animal. Her only clothing was a white robe, blackened with soot, which barely covered her ample frame.

He vaulted up the porch steps and grasped her doughy arms. "Is Jasmine *in* there?"

"Oh, Lord, don't take my babies. They all I have. Oh, Lord, please, please, please..."

He shook her. "Is Jasmine in there?"

She nodded, moaning hysterically.

Mitch looked into her bulging eyes. "Get over to the firehouse. Alexus is there, she's safe."

Benita moaned louder. She didn't move.

"Go! And close your robe." He shoved her down the steps. She staggered toward the firehouse.

Captain Scar's incessant command during the academy blared in Mitch's head, *"Never enter a burning building alone."* Screw that. The others would be coming. Mitch flung the door open. Smoke billowed out, stinging his eyes. He crawled into the caustic blackness, keeping his face close to the floor, below the scorching heat.

"Jasmine," he called into the darkness. "Where are you?" The eerie crackle of hidden fire answered. He crawled deeper into the burning home, sweeping the floor with his arms and legs, desperate to get to the child before it was too late. Nothing. The cool linoleum of the kitchen floor changed to the coarse carpeting of the hallway. He called her name again. Nothing.

Mitch backed into the stairwell. The smoke thickened as he scaled the stairs. The first bedroom off the stairwell was Jasmine's. He searched frantically under and around the bed and inside the closet. Nothing. Where was she?

Back into the hallway to Alexus's room. He fought to control his breathing. Every breath of the foul soup was torture. His lungs screamed for oxygen as he choked and gagged. His arms and legs grew heavy. Needles of light flickered behind his eyes. Paralyzing fear gripped him.

I gotta get out. No.—Not this time.

He pushed through the panic, crawling deeper into the guts of the house.

Heroes save lives or die trying.

The house groaned from the ravenous beast feeding on it.

Mitch's hand brushed a small bare foot.

* * *

Mitch woke to a piercing headache, squinting against bright lights. Someone behind him said, "Pulse-ox is low." Cold, dry oxygen hissed through the facepiece covering his nose and mouth.

The back doors of the paramedic unit flew open, and Kenny jumped in. "What the hell were you thinking, going in without a mask?"

Mitch pushed the facepiece away. The fog cleared, but the excruciating pounding in his head intensified. His body smelled like smoldering charcoal, every pore oozing smoky venom. He could taste it. The back of his neck was on fire. "Is Jasmine okay?" he croaked, startled by the biting pain in his throat.

"According to the mom, they thought the little one was in there. The older girl went back in for her. Fucking amazing."

"Jasmine," Mitch said.

Kenny nodded. "You were only five feet from the back door when Ralph got to you."

"Where is she?"

"Ralph said you were draped over the girl."

"Where is she?" Mitch hollered, ignoring his raw throat.

"She was barely alive. Meds had to intubate. And she's got some serious burns. The place was rolling. If you hadn't covered her..."

His carbon monoxide-saturated brain struggled to understand. He barely remembered finding her on the second floor; nothing after that. Random images of Jasmine overwhelmed him: her gap-toothed smile, dancing in the firehouse, her excitement over school, and how she liked to mess with him and call him Mr. Teacher.

He struggled to sit, collapsing back onto the cot, his insides churning. "I know, kid. Hurts like hell."

He reached for Kenny. "That scum Maurice get out?"

"The mom said he never came home last night."

"That bastard should be the one burned."

The paramedic slid the oxygen mask back over Mitch's mouth and nose. "We gotta go. Now."

Kenny leaned into Mitch and whispered, "You got balls, kid." Kenny jumped off the rig and slammed the door shut.

The paramedic unit pulled away from the still-smoldering house. Through the back window, Mitch caught a glimpse of a solitary figure standing under a street lamp, wearing a long trench coat, flicking a lighter in front of his smirking face.

Chapter 34

Mitch was floating on the farm pond with the worst sunburn ever on his neck. Someone called his name from far away. *Leave me alone.* Someone grabbed his hand and pulled. *Leave me alone.*

"Mitch, it's me."

His vision cleared. Nic had his hand in both of hers.

"What the hell?" he asked, the words stinging his raw throat.

"You're at Saint Mary's. They brought you in last night."

"I'm—numb."

"Morphine. They hit you with a pretty good dose. You've been out all morning. Here, drink some water. You sound terrible."

He pushed the plastic cup aside. "Jasmine."

"She's detoxifying in the hyperbaric. You kept hollering her name until they put you under."

"She okay?"

"They won't know for a while. She had some burns on the side of her face and down her back. They're not all that bad thanks to you. But they're worried about brain damage from the smoke inhalation."

Brain damage. Kyle. Now Jasmine. Mitch collapsed back onto the bed.

"If it wasn't for you, she wouldn't have a chance," Nic said. "The story's all over the news. You're a hero, Garner."

"Jasmine's the hero."

Nic kissed him gently, then rested her head on his chest.

Mitch's brother Chris, Jennie, and his old friend Danny appeared in the doorway. The sight of Jennie sucked the wind out of Mitch. She gave him a weak wave, then studied Nic. Her eyes watered.

Chris shuffled to his bed. He smelled like the farm; like home. "You made the news in Milroy. Whole town's talking. You okay?"

"Got a neck redder than old Danny there, but yeah I'm okay," he said while watching Jennie. She scanned the room, avoiding eye contact.

Nic rose. "I'll let you guys visit. The crew's down in the cafeteria. I'll tell them you're awake." She eyed Jennie as she left.

Danny moved alongside Chris. "Hey, little buddy, you sound like Yoda."

Mitch reached for Jennie. She went to the bed and took his hand. A familiar glow spread through him. So many things he wanted to tell her. All he could think to say was, "Jen, you look great."

She pulled her hand away and nodded toward the hallway. "Nothing like her, though."

"Jen, she's just…"

"Don't. I only came to make sure you were okay. I'm sure you'll make real pretty babies together." She turned to Chris. "I can't do this. I'll be in the truck when you're done." She left, sobbing.

"She couldn't wait to see you," Chris said.

Mitch exhaled loudly. "Crap. I keep screwing things up with her."

They all stared at the blank TV screen.

Mitch waited for one of them to say something. He finally cleared the phlegm from his raw throat and said, "So, how's Dad doing?"

"Sure you want to know?"

"How could things get any worse?" As soon as the words crossed his lips, he regretted saying them.

"It's bad. Got no money for feed. Dad's turned over all the finances to me and doesn't want to hear we're broke. When I try to tell him we need to sell off some of the herd, he goes ballistic. I don't know what to do." Chris bit his lower lip.

"How much you need?"

"Figure around twenty grand will get us by for a while, but the bank won't give us any more credit."

Mitch pointed to a small closet. "My pants should be in there. Get the keys. Take my truck. Ray Bunzell's been horny for it; said he'd give me twenty-five grand for it last year."

"Can't sell your truck."

"It's my fault the farm is going under." He forced the words past the stinging in his throat. "Dad's got a right to hate my guts. Take the truck. And don't tell him where the money came from."

"Dad doesn't hate you."

"Sure."

Before leaving, Chris and Danny filled him in on the gossip around Milroy: who was dating, who was cheating, and who got drunk and raised hell at the Rock River Hideaway. He wasn't listening. He kept watching the hallway.

Shortly after they left, his crew filed into the room.

"See the Red Devil gave you a peck on the neck," Kenny said.

Ralph made his way to the foot of the bed. "Next time wear a mask."

Kenny stepped alongside Ralph at the foot of the bed. "You missed all the excitement. We were picking up after the fire. The mom and kid were in the firehouse. All of a sudden the crazy bitch comes flying out the door screaming like a wild banshee about how that motherfucker would never lay another hand on her babies. She laid the boyfriend open with my dick."

Mitch's jaw dropped.

Kenny pointed to the scar on his hand. "You know? My knife? Spilled the bastard's guts all over the sidewalk. He's staring at his insides with those crazy eyes, and she's standing over him screaming. Everyone froze, then all hell broke loose. Think the cops would have shot her if she hadn't dropped my dick."

"Gutted him like a dead carp," Crusher said.

Kenny pointed at Mitch. "And the goddamn cops won't give my dick back. Evidence."

Captain Reemer patted Mitch's knee. "Nice job, son." To the others, he said, "All right, let the man get some rest."

Ralph lingered at the foot of the bed, squinting at Mitch. "Maybe I got you wrong."

* * *

Nic came back after supper with cinnamon rolls from Sciortino's Bakery. They watched television together without talking. He kept thinking how excited he felt when he saw Jennie and how shitty he felt when she left.

Nic rubbed his chest, then turned his face to hers. "I should go. It's blue shift tomorrow."

"Thanks, Nic. You're a great…"

"What, Mitch? A great friend? A great fuck? Sorry I didn't mean that."

He clenched his jaw.

"That was Jen today wasn't it? Wish I could make you smile like that."

"Sorry."

"Me too."

Chapter 35

Jasmine's neck and left ear were dressed in gauze, her face swollen and eyes shut. Mitch gently straightened the girl's tangled hair to frame her soft brown face. Jasmine's chest rose and fell as the ventilator hissed oxygen through the clear plastic tube. The nurses encouraged him to talk to her, explaining how coma patients can sometimes hear and understand what's being said.

Mitch spent the morning telling Jasmine how excited he was over the progress they were making with the kids. And telling her what a great teacher she had become. He struggled through waves of grief but refused to let it stop him from comforting this young girl who just taught him how the power of love overcomes fear.

It was almost noon when a young nurse rolled a cart into the room. "I have to change her dressings. You'll have to leave. Sorry."

"Jasmine, I need you to get better." He rubbed her smooth forehead. "You know I can't handle all those kids myself. Who's going to teach me to dance? You know us white dudes got no rhythm. Get better. Please."

* * *

Mitch shuffled to his room.

"Miss Bernie, how'd you get here?"

Her full body hug was soothing. "Mitch, honey. I worried myself sick over you." She stepped back, examining his neck. "How bad you burned?"

"Just my neck. How'd you get here?"

She guided him to the bed. "When I cut the TV on this morning and saw the news, I nearly fell out." She smoothed the white bed sheet.

Mitch reclined onto the bed.

"How's Jasmine?" Miss Bernie asked.

Mitch took her through the tragic events. "She wouldn't be here if I kept my mouth shut."

Miss Bernie scowled. "From what I see, you the only one tried to help that poor girl. You weren't the one abusing that girl. You weren't the one lit their house on fire. That one in hell alongside the devil." She wagged her finger. "You sure got a notion to blame yourself for anything bad happens."

Mitch turned the television on and tuned it to *Days of Our Lives*, Miss Bernie's favorite.

"Okay, I'll let you be," she said.

The Price is Right came on after *Days of Our Lives*. For Mitch, it was all background noise. When *The Price is Right* was over, Miss Bernie heaved herself from the chair. "I best go. Take me three buses to get home. They might be running late with the snow."

"I'll pay for a cab."

"I been riding those buses all my life. You spend that money on those children you teaching. And make sure that little one, Alexus, is looked after. She must be in a state."

Where *was* Alexus? If she knew what happened, she had to be terrified.

* * *

After Miss Bernie left, Mitch went to Jasmine's bedside. The thought that she might end up like Kyle with her body curled into a fetal position, mouth gaping open, and head endlessly swiveling, sickened him.

Is this what God does? Takes away the people you love? Miss Bernie worships this God and what does He do? Takes away her son and daughter. Well, fuck you, God.

Jasmine was going to wake up and he'd be there when she did. He told her stories of the farm and his pony, Bert, and dog, Billy. He promised if she woke up he'd take her there. He stayed by her bed through the night.

* * *

Mitch's throbbing neck woke him. He stretched and glanced at Jasmine, jerking when he saw her green eyes.

"Oh, my God. Jasmine." Her listless eyes didn't respond. "You're in the hospital. It's me, Mitch. I'll be right back. I have to let the nurse know you're awake."

He froze when he entered the hallway. The spiked-hair One-Niner and two other gangbangers crowded the nurse's station. They all turned, glaring when he rushed at them.

"What the fuck you pieces of shit doing here?"

The spiked-hair banger stepped forward. "Here to see Jasmine."

"Stay away from her."

Spiked Hair's eyes narrowed. "You the one turn DeAndre in. Best hope he don't find you."

"I'm not the one running."

The other two sneered while Mitch and Spiked Hair measured each other.

"You gentlemen need to leave now," the nurse at the desk said, her voice cracking. "Only immediate family is allowed to visit."

Spiked Hair continued glaring at Mitch. "He ain't family."

Mitch grabbed the front of the banger's shirt. "Get the fuck out of here."

"Doctor Brown to BICU STAT. Doctor Brown to BICU STAT," echoed through the hallway as the nurse shouted into the intercom mic.

The banger studied Mitch's fist. "We ain't done." He pushed Mitch's hand away. "Next time, cracker."

"Yeah? Next time it won't be a car that gets shot up," Mitch said.

The man's dead eyes flickered.

The nurse stared at Mitch, slack-jawed.

Mitch felt surprisingly calm.

A doctor was at Jasmine's bedside when Mitch and the nurse rushed in. The tracheal tube had been removed.

"Pulse ox is holding," the doctor said to the nurse. "Keep an eye on her airway."

"What about brain function?" Mitch asked.

The doctor threw up his hands. "We've done all we can."

Mitch spent the morning at Jasmine's bedside. After running out of things to say, he called Nic to ask if she could get a copy of Jasmine's favorite book from the library.

* * *

Nic read to Jasmine from *A Tree Grows in Brooklyn* when Mitch's voice gave out. At lunchtime, they went to the cafeteria. Nic reached for Mitch's hand across the tiny table. "Forgot how much I loved that book. Thanks for letting me read to her."

"You've been great." He forced a grin. "Things are just so messed up right now."

180

"You ever get over Jen…" She kissed the back of his hand. "We better get back."

Mitch spent the night listening to Jasmine's soft breathing. In the morning he read to her some more. His throat was feeling better, but the burn on his neck throbbed. Later that afternoon, a serious lady in a dark blue business suit stepped into the room. She studied him. "Your picture in the paper didn't do you justice."

"You are?"

She reached out her hand. "Sarah Johnson. Social services. I've been assigned to Jasmine's case. I'll be in charge of her care until she's transferred to a care center."

"She's not going to a nursing home."

Sarah pulled her hand back. "The doctor said she'll need special care."

"She won't need a nursing home."

"Even if that were true she needs somewhere to go."

Mitch stared at Jasmine. "What if I found a place for her?"

"It'd have to be to a licensed foster parent."

"Bernice Jackson was a foster parent. She knows Jasmine. Where's Alexus?"

"I got her an emergency placement."

"They both have to be with Ms. Jackson."

"I can't promise anything. These things take time."

"No." Mitch pointed at her. "Tell your boss to make it work, or I'll grant an interview with these reporters who've been hounding me and let them know Social Services is dropping the ball on these poor kids."

"I'll tell him." She grinned. "Shame more kids in our system don't have you fighting for them."

* * *

Mitch spent the rest of the day and night at Jasmine's bedside. He prayed to a God he didn't believe in, making promises he wouldn't keep. The next morning he finished reading *A Tree Grows in Brooklyn* to her. After lunch, he was discharged from the hospital and paid Miss Bernie a visit.

The smell of cinnamon and chocolate filled the back stairwell to her flat. He heard something he hadn't heard in a long time, Miss Bernie's robust laugh. He knocked once and stepped inside. Miss Bernie and Alexus were at the small kitchen table with their hands in a large metal mixing bowl.

Alexus squealed, ran at him, and jumped into his arms. She grabbed his neck with her sticky hands. "We making chocat chip cookies. If you good you get some." She kissed him on the cheek. He ignored the stinging pain from her small hands clutching his raw neck.

Thank you, God. I owe you.

He gave her a firm hug and put her down. "Better keep working or Miss Bernie will get after you."

She went back to work rolling balls of dough, carefully spacing them onto the darkened aluminum cookie sheet. "See how you do this? Miss Bernie teach me."

Miss Bernie didn't look happy.

Mitch rubbed the back of his neck and grimaced. "When she get here?"

"That social worker drop her off early this morning. Said you put her up to it. That true?"

"She said it would take time. I wanted to ask before she came. If your back bothers you too much, I'll tell her—"

"Hush now. Jasmine coming too?"

"If it's okay."

"Stop with that foolishness."

"Anything I can do?"

"Pull those cookies out the oven and taste one."

The soft, gooey mixture of butter, sugar, flour, cinnamon, and chocolate tasted like heaven.

Miss Bernie got Alexus chattering about school and flashed Mitch a knowing smile while Alexus told them about every kid in her class and all about her teacher and what they were learning.

After Alexus wound down and stuffed her mouth with warm cookies, Mitch asked Miss Bernie if any of her church friends had a cheap car for sale. She told him Odyssey School has an old van for sale. The superintendent is Brother Williams, the man who sang at Jamal's funeral. Miss Bernie asked what happened to Mitch's fancy truck. He told her it was sold to pay farm bills.

When he finished, she said, "Someday you'll see all this you do, for these girls, for your family, for me, is all God's work. Might not always go the way you think it should, but you doing His work, and you'll be rewarded."

Mitch had trouble buying into God's plan. "Where's the van?"

"At the school six blocks down. Don't look like a school though. Used to be a grocery store. Has one of those curvy roofs. Tell Brother Williams I sent you."

Mitch kissed the top of Alexus's head. "Take care of Miss Bernie."

"When Jasmine coming?"

"Soon, Lexi, soon."

"Wish Momma could come too. That lady told me she gone away for a long time. And Maurice gone forever. He mean."

Mitch stopped at the doorway and glimpsed back at the woman and child who were laughing at each other's chocolate-smeared faces.

Chapter 36

In black letters, *Odyssey Alternative School-All Are Welcome* was printed on the double doors. Mitch stepped inside to an expansive room with groups of black children of all ages. Some sat in rows in front of green chalkboards while others sat in circles around an adult. Sheets of drywall and two-by-fours were stacked against a side wall. The children stared at him like he was an alien. He waved, not knowing what else to do.

An immense hand grasped him from behind. The man's face had a mouth brimming with teeth that jutted out in a massive overbite, displaying most of his pink gum line, giving Brother Williams a perpetual smile. The large black man was wearing gray slacks and a black button-down shirt. His bald head glistened under the fluorescent lighting.

"What brings you to our modest school?" Brother Williams' deep bass echoed off the tall ceiling.

"I'm a friend of Miss Bernie's."

"I know who you are, my brother. What can I do for you?"

"She said you had a van for sale."

"Motor smokes bad. Brakes are shot. The wheelchair lift stopped working a long time ago."

"I don't have any cash right now."

"Miss Bernie said you're handy." He pointed to the children scattered around the large open space. "Gets noisy in here. Makes it hard for the children to focus on their studies. If you can give us a hand putting up walls, the van's yours."

"I can't right now. But, yeah, I can do that."

"Excellent. Do these kids good to see a friendly white face. Stay by that girl as long as she needs you. Miss Bernie was right. You're a good man. I can feel it."

Before heading to the hospital, Mitch stopped by Miss Bernie's house, driving the rusted white Chevy van with *Odyssey School* scrawled along its side in faded gray lettering. He told her how impressed he was with Brother Williams. She told him Brother Williams had been a One-Niner when he was a teenager. He got involved in a drug deal gone bad. A young man lost his life, and Brother Williams went away for ten years. He found Jesus in prison and has been working with kids ever since.

On the drive to the hospital, Mitch couldn't stop thinking about Brother Williams. This man killed someone?

* * *

When he approached the nurses' station, the chief nurse motioned for him. "It's Jasmine."

"Is she...?"

"She's asking for you."

He sprinted to the room, greeted by her glimmering green eyes. "Where—is—Lexus?" Jasmine said, her raspy voice barely above a whisper. She sat up. "Say something."

"She's fine," Mitch said after the shock wore off.

Her words were slow and slurred. "I know that. Where *is* she?"

"With Miss Bernie."

Jasmine relaxed back into her pillow. "What about Momma?"

Mitch grasped for the right words. "You'll be staying with Miss Bernie."

"Where *is* Momma? Tell me." Her green eyes blazed.

Mitch gritted his teeth. "Your mom killed Maurice."

"Good. He deserve killin'. Where is she?"

"They arrested her."

"She done nothing wrong." Her breathing quickened. The electronic monitor next to the bed beeped.

A nurse hurried to the bedside, checking the monitor. "Her pulse is racing. She's due for morphine."

Jasmine ran her hand over her neck. "Where's my necklace?"

"Paramedics never saw it."

Mitch pulled a glistening white gold necklace from his shirt pocket. He cradled the delicate necklace, displaying the gold pendant shaped like a tiny oak leaf. "I know this isn't from your father, but I think he'd want you to have it."

"That was all I had—from my daddy." She sniffled and gave in to the morphine.

Mitch placed the necklace next to her.

* * *

Over the next week, Jasmine sank into silence. Her listless expression tore at Mitch. The burns were healing nicely, but the psychologist was having no luck. She told him Jasmine suffered from acute PTSD. Mitch remembered what the psychologist back in Milroy said to him about PTSD after Maggie's death; that it's like an injury to the brain. If left untreated, it can get worse. The patient needs strong family support, counseling, and sometimes anti-anxiety drugs.

After pleading with Jasmine's physician and promising to follow his orders, Mitch was allowed to take her to Miss Bernie's home. If anyone could lift Jasmine out of her funk, it would be Miss Bernie. On the drive, Jasmine stared into the distance. Covered in an early December blanket of sparkling snow, the Core appeared pristine.

The old van sputtered to a stop in front of Miss Bernie's house. Mitch helped Jasmine down from the passenger seat. The burns on her back and thigh made it hard for her to walk. But it was the burn on her neck that devastated her. Mitch had seen her disgust when she looked into a mirror at the hospital.

Alexus dashed down the porch steps and laid her head against her big sister's waist.

Miss Bernie shuffled down the steps with open arms. "Ain't this the best Christmas present ever? Both these girls together again. C'mon now, let's get inside before we all catch our death." She steered them toward the house. "Alexus made a batch of cookies just for you." Miss Bernie ushered the girls inside.

From down the street came a rumbling bass. Mitch stopped at the foot of the stairs. A faded green Buick Riviera stopped in front of the house. The window glided down, and Spiked Hair pointed a finger at him as if he were pulling a trigger. Mitch lifted his arms as if he were holding a rifle and pulled the imaginary trigger three times, once for each gangbanger in the ghetto cruiser. Spiked Hair gunned the old Buick and sped off.

The front room had Christmas lights looped along the ceiling and around the front window. Pine scent from the densely trimmed tree saturated the room.

Alexus led Jasmine to the tree. "Look what we done. Ain't it just the best tree ever?"

Jasmine glanced at the star on top, then lowered her gaze to the floor. "You did real good, Lexi."

"Why this make you sad?"

"Let's eat some of those cookies you made, Alexus," Miss Bernie said.

"Can I go to my room?" Jasmine asked.

"Surely can. I'll bring some cookies along." Miss Bernie showed her to her room.

Alexus's lips quivered.

Mitch knelt and pulled her close. "It's going to take a while before Jasmine is like she used to be. All we can do is love her and give her time. It'll be hard, but hey, we're the Eight Ohs."

"Wish she was better now."

"Me too, Lexi. Me too."

* * *

In the morning Miss Bernie showed Mitch how to change Jasmine's dressings while Jasmine watched in silence.

"Where'd you learn all that?" He asked after they left Jasmine's room.

"Back in the day when I worked at the nursing home, we changing dressings all day long. Folks with the sugar diabetes would get those ulcers and terrible bed sores."

Mitch pinched his lips together.

"So much misery," Miss Bernie said. "Sometime it helped to just set with them. Show them someone care. We need to do that for Jasmine. Don't push her, just give her time. We got to leave our sadness at the door."

"I keep thinking if I would have been smarter none of this…"

Miss Bernie leveled her finger at him. "Stop that hurtful talk right now. This God's answer to my prayers. And He worked through you. Don't you see? You doing God's work bringing those girls to me." She pulled Mitch into her arms. "I'm so full of joy with them here." She kissed his forehead.

Mitch headed to the Odyssey School on foot. The green Buick slowed and inched alongside him. "Hey, Snow White, you lost? C'mon in the car, we give you a ride." Mitch nonchalantly flashed his middle finger at Spiked Hair. The others in the car whooped as they sped off.

The lead inspector on Jamal and LaMont's murders had assured Mitch these assholes wouldn't screw with him. The last time they raided their crack house, he warned them if they so much as spit at a firefighter, the trigger-happy tactical squad would be all over their asses and there'd be no arrests, just work for the coroner.

Mitch kept busy with the construction project at the school throughout the rest of December. He wasn't allowed to return to work until the burns healed. Mitch taught the older children the proper use of power tools and how to square up a wall. After the first week, he allowed the kids to do most of the work while he supervised. Brother Williams used Firefighter Mitch as motivation for school work. Only students who completed their assignments were allowed to help him each day. By the second week, all the older students were helping.

Mitch spent mornings taking care of chores for Miss Bernie. After Jasmine's burn dressings were changed, he read to her from books Brother Williams sent over. She showed no interest, but Miss Bernie encouraged him to keep at it. Later, he'd visit Kyle, then head over to the school to work on the walls with the students.

He stopped by the firehouse on red-shift days to work with the Eight Ohs. When the kids left, he worked on the old van. The firehouse was equipped with lifts and a full assortment of mechanic's tools.

A hot meal would be waiting for him when he got home. In the evening, the patchwork family settled in the front room to watch television, with Alexus snuggled next to her big sister on the couch. Mitch noticed how Jasmine's hand always covered the burn on her neck, her thumb constantly rubbing where the necklace had hung for all those years. She never wore the necklace he gave her. He didn't ask why.

Three times a week he took Jasmine to the hospital to see both a clinical psychologist and a physical therapist. Tears flowed down her face during physical therapy, but she never complained. The therapist had a puke bucket close at hand for the grueling sessions designed to keep the burn tissue from scarring and limiting motion. When Jasmine reached the point of retching, Mitch's insides tensed along with hers. As hard as this was to watch, it was her sadness that crushed him.

Chapter 37

Crowds of young people roamed Mayfair Mall, a popular mall located in Wauwatosa, a western suburb of Milwaukee. It was the last Sunday of winter break. Raucous shouting and laughter thundered through the tall corridors. Jasmine's burns had healed enough for her to return to school on Monday. Miss Bernie and Mitch thought it would cheer her up to get some trendy new school clothes. And Alexus too.

They trekked from store to store with Alexus stuffing shopping bags with brightly colored child's wear. Jasmine's eyes flittered back and forth as they walked through the mall. Her hand never left the scar on her neck. When Miss Bernie asked if she liked something, Jasmine said, "I suppose."

After no more than an hour, Jasmine asked, "Can we go now? I don't feel good."

When they got home, Jasmine dashed to her room, sobbing. Mitch followed but was stopped by Miss Bernie. "Let her cry. She need to get it out."

* * *

Monday morning Alexus waited patiently by the front door wearing her bright blue winter coat. The hood was snugged around her head, and her Sponge Bob backpack was hanging on her back. Her hands were covered with matching mittens.

Miss Bernie came out of Jasmine's room, frowning. "Said she can't go back to that school." Miss Bernie kissed Alexus on the cheek. "You scoot off to school."

Mitch walked Alexus the three blocks to school in the light snow. He got to hear who her best friend was and who her second best friend was, right on down the list of all the kids in the class. She told him she was going to pick Elan for her boyfriend. She giggled and covered her mouth with her mitten.

Miss Bernie was in the recliner waiting for him when he got back. "Mitch, that girl got me worried."

"Why won't she go?"

"Said those kids at school would torment her over the scars and what that man done to her."

"Now what?"

"If we can't get her to school, Social Service will take her away. Oh, Lord, what we gonna do?"

Mitch knocked on Jasmine's door. Silence. He opened it a crack. She was curled under the covers. "Need anything?" She didn't stir. "Okay, then. See you at supper."

Mitch walked to the Odyssey Alternative School. The students were back at school after their winter break and anxious to start hanging drywall on the framing they had built. Mitch organized the four-by-eight-foot sections, containers of joint compound, drywall screws, and drywall knives while the students worked on their morning lessons. After lunch, they went to work. Brother Williams helped lift the heavy sheets of drywall into place as Mitch showed the students how to screw them to the studs. Their spirited banter didn't quiet Mitch's disturbing thoughts about Jasmine. In his short time on the job, he'd already responded to suicides of three young people.

When school let out, Mitch followed Brother Williams to the office. "I need your help."

"Anything for you, my brother."

"It's Jasmine. She won't go to school."

Mitch filled him in on all she'd been through and how her psychologist wasn't having much success treating her depression.

"It's like a plague," Brother Williams said. "The youngest ones come to school all bright-eyed and eager to learn. But that glow fades. You start to see the pain and sadness in their eyes. Seen too much already in their short lives." Brother Williams paused. "Sadly, our city is the most segregated in the country with our black students suffering abysmal graduation rates. Our teachers are in the trenches down here fighting to give them some tools and some hope."

"How do I give Jasmine hope?"

"She won't get better staying in that room. And she can't go back to her school. Too many of those kids are running wild. They have no empathy for others and think nothing of ganging up on one another. We don't allow that here."

190

"How do you stop it?"

"We demand respect and teach empathy." Brother Williams waved his arms as if he were preaching from the pulpit. "We have some children with learning disabilities. The more advanced students work as tutors for the ones who are struggling. This forces children who would otherwise never have contact to connect and eases the workload of our teachers. When problems arise, we have peer counseling where the students create their own solutions. And do they come up with ingenious ones."

"This works?"

"We send children off to college who never dreamed it possible. Around here that's a mighty fine miracle."

"How do you handle the really bad ones?"

"Those get some one on one with me. Put the fear of God in them. They know I was a pretty bad dude back in the day. I still have the street cred. Sometimes fear's not such a bad tool." Brother Williams laughed.

Mitch had to ask, "Miss Bernie said you went to prison?"

Bother Williams' massive brow creased. "I got in the middle of a bad situation, and a young man lost his life. Terrible tragedy. I didn't do it, but I got sent away." He took a deep breath before continuing. "Some law students heard of my case and spent two years collecting evidence until the truth came out. After ten years in prison, my conviction was overturned. I would never have been allowed to work with these kids if not for those wonderful students. God bless them all."

"Prison for ten years? For something you didn't do?"

"The good Lord had to show me darkness before He allowed me to see the light. I know that now. The only way out of the darkness was to forgive those who put me there and forgive myself for turning to the streets."

"Ten years."

"Enough of my sad story. What we doing about Jasmine?"

"Could she come here?"

Bother Williams grunted and said, "They're shutting us down. Don't want the children to know yet. They've been so excited building those walls, I wanted to let them finish before I told them."

"How can they do that?"

"Last month the roof started leaking. We've been told the rafters are rotting and the whole roof needs replacing."

"Won't the city fix it?"

"We're a private school. We rely on vouchers and donations."

"How much it going to cost?"

"Over eighty thousand, mostly labor. Our teachers all agreed to go without pay for a few months if it would keep the school going, but it won't be near enough."

"When does it have to be fixed?"

"The building inspector gave us a month to make repairs before he condemns the building. Don't see any way that's happening."

"Anyone you can go to?"

"Went to our alderman. Off the record, he said Victory Schools had lobbied the common council to allow them to set up their private voucher schools here. He said Victory Schools wants the vouchers of my students in their schools."

"That's total bullcrap."

"I spent the weekend on my knees. I'll have to trust in the good Lord."

* * *

Cars and trucks streamed into the parking lot of Odyssey Alternative School two days later. The early morning sun sparkled off the powdery snow cover. Fumes from a tar boiler filled the frosty January air. A flatbed loaded with lumber pulled into the lot. Off-duty firefighters threw ladders up and cleared snow from the leaking roof.

Mitch found Brother Williams in the makeshift office in the boiler room. Against the wall, opposite the ancient, rattling boiler, stood three battered metal file cabinets and a cot strewn with disheveled blankets. Brother Williams was seated behind a small desk scattered with papers and manila folders. He pressed his massive frame from the listing office chair. "Hope you're not intimidated by my fancy crib." Brother Williams pointed to an old kitchen chair. "Sit."

"I got you some help. We should have a new roof on by next week."

"Mitch, I told you we don't have the money."

"It's taken care of."

Brother Williams threw out his arms. "How?"

"Once word of your school spread through the department, firefighters from all over the city volunteered to help. The project manager is a firefighter whose dad owns a roofing company. Said they'd give you all the materials at cost, and you can pay them when your next voucher payments come in." Mitch paused as Brother Williams' mouth gaped open. "When this firefighter's dad heard about the great work you were doing with these kids, he was excited to help. He grew up in the Core."

Tears formed at the corners of Brother Williams' eyes. His mouth widened into a broad grin.

Mitch grinned along with him. "Can Jasmine come here now?"

"Oh, my Lord, yes. I'll stop by tonight and invite her myself."

Mitch stood. "Oh, something I wanted to ask. Why don't these kids talk like the other kids around the neighborhood?"

"When those children walk through the doors of *this* school, they leave Ebonics, ghetto talk, behind. Only proper English is allowed. They call it talking white. I call it talking freedom."

Mitch called Miss Bernie with the news, then joined the crowd of firefighters attacking the roof. They stripped the roof to the joists and removed the rotting ones. As darkness set in, they attached giant blue tarps to cover the open areas. Tomorrow they'd begin rebuilding the roof.

* * *

From outside the house, Mitch smelled roasting beef and baking biscuits. The clacking he heard would be the potato masher banging the tall aluminum kettle Miss Bernie boiled potatoes in. It reminded him of when they were in training and how it was Jamal's job to mash potatoes for their evening meal.

Miss Bernie stopped mashing and wiped her sweaty brow when Mitch stepped inside. The small table was set and pulled away from the wall. His mouth watered at the sight of Miss Bernie's meatloaf. This was not the anemic meatloaf he made back at the farm. She rolled ham and Swiss cheese into the loaf and covered it with a homemade tomato sauce made from her canned tomatoes. He wasn't a fan of her collard greens; too salty for him. But those buttermilk biscuits and the sweet potato pie were pure heaven.

"Jasmine come out of her room today?" Mitch asked.

Miss Bernie shook her head. "I'm at a loss with that poor girl."

The *Sponge Bob Square Pants* theme played from the front room with Alexus singing along.

Mitch went to get Jasmine when Brother Williams arrived a few minutes later. She was curled under her covers. "Jasmine, we have company for supper. It's Brother Williams. He runs the Odyssey School and wants you to come there."

She turned to the wall. "I don't want to go to no school."

"I know how you feel, but won't you at least listen to him?"

"You don't know how I feel. Leave me alone."

He did know how she felt. The tormenting guilt of Maggie's death was never far from his thoughts. He saw her face every morning when he woke. Mitch trudged back to the kitchen. "She won't come."

Miss Bernie folded her hands. "Oh, my Lord."

Brother Williams lifted his massive body from the small chair. "Let me see what I can do."

Miss Bernie closed her eyes and rested her forehead in her hand. Mitch was sure she was making some serious prayer requests. He did some praying himself while they waited. Alexus squirmed in her chair.

Thirty minutes later, Bother Williams emerged from Jasmine's room holding her hand. Jasmine had a brightly colored silk-like scarf looped around her neck so it covered the scars on her neck. Geometric patterns of black with bright stripes of greens, yellows, and blues adorned the scarf. Alexus ran to Jasmine, hugged her, and squealed, "Yaaay."

Mitch thought he saw a trace of a smile from Jasmine.

When they were all seated, Miss Bernie bowed her head. "Lord, thank you for providing this wonderful bounty for us tonight and thank you for bringing Brother Williams to our table. And thank you for blessing me with these precious children. I promise to lead them in your loving ways."

Everyone except Jasmine chanted, "Amen."

Alexus took over the conversation with the latest kindergarten dramas. Jasmine ate in silence, never looking away from her plate. Miss Bernie, Mitch, and Brother Williams grinned at each other as Alexus ran on. After they finished with the sweet potato pie and whipped cream, Miss Bernie made some coffee. Jasmine returned to her room and Alexus went to the front room for more television.

"Miss Bernie, you always could lay out a tempting table," Brother Williams said. "Delicious. Can't remember the last time I overindulged like that."

Miss Bernie poured him coffee. "Well, then you best be stopping by more. Now, how you get Jasmine to join us?"

"I've been saving that Kente scarf for some time. Got it from a student of ours who's now a teacher herself, teaching at a mission down in Ghana. The scarf was given to her by the mother of one of her students."

Miss Bernie pushed away from the table. "How about another slice of pie?"

Brother Williams' overbite spread into a broad grin. "You sure know how to take care of an old man."

"Oh, hush now."

Mitch chuckled to himself. They were flirting.

"There's a story behind that scarf," Brother Williams said. "The colors have deep cultural meaning. The yellows, like the rays of sunlight, remind us of divine goodness. Blue is the color of the sea and the sky which provides tranquility and balance. Black represents maturation and intensified spiritual energy. And green is the symbol of life, growth, and harmony. It represents the forest, the trees, birth, and spiritual growth."

Miss Bernie squinted. "That scarf come all the way from Africa?"

"Yes, Ma'am. I told Jasmine the history of the scarf and how I was waiting for the right student to come along. The way she risked her life to save her sister told me there was nobody more deserving."

"Ain't you something, Brother Williams."

"What about school?" Mitch asked.

"She knows she'll be taken away from her sister if she doesn't go to school. That terrifies her. But going back to school is equally terrifying."

"She say yes?" Miss Bernie asked.

"Mitch told me how she wants to be a teacher."

Miss Bernie scowled at Brother Williams. "You gonna tell me or not?"

"Let me finish, Bernice. I asked Jasmine if she could help us with three girls who were way behind in their studies. I asked if she could put her pain aside and work with them. They desperately need a good tutor like her."

"That true?" Miss Bernie asked.

"What I didn't tell her is those three girls have also been molested. A psychologist volunteers her time twice a week with them. She's a woman who was molested as a child. I'm hoping Jasmine will connect with them and join in on the counseling."

Miss Bernie shook her head. "You one sly old dog. She said yes, didn't she?"

"I told her if she was worried about her burns she could wear that scarf to school. We'd tell the children it was from Africa and she was honoring her heritage by wearing it."

"She say yes?"

"Said she'd give it a try."

"Brother Williams, you a true blessing."

"No. It's that young man next to you. He's the blessing."

"Lord, if that ain't the truth."

Their words melted into Mitch.

Chapter 38

The following morning, news crews began showing up at the school. Firefighters were interviewed to explain why they were helping, but the most compelling interviews were with Brother Williams. The local stations and newspapers ran with the story of a prior gang member who was dedicated to helping inner-city children. His fight for the school in the face of a takeover by a national private school organization sparked public debate. When reporters learned about the school's accomplishments with children from the most impoverished area of the city, they turned their focus to the mayor and alderpersons. Questions were asked about donations of campaign funds from Victory Schools. A local interview aired on the *Today Show*. Donations poured into the school.

* * *

Snow clouds darkened the late afternoon sky. The firefighters stopped for the day. They'd have the school roof finished Tuesday. Mitch headed home, walking the dark streets. The snow cover and early evening quiet gave the Core a rare touch of serenity. He knew he should be feeling good with all he had done for the school and Brother Williams, but Jasmine worried him. Brother Williams told him she was tutoring the three younger girls but refused to join in the counseling sessions with the psychologist. At home, she remained quiet, detached, and sad.

Mitch cut through an alley while trying to focus on the school renovations. With all the donations flowing in, cost was no longer a factor. Booming bass from the end of the alley echoed off the dilapidated garages. Headlights inched toward him. He backed against a crumbling garage to allow the car to pass. It stopped. Another car flew in from the opposite end, sliding to a stop on the snow-covered surface. The two cars, ten feet on each side of him bathed him in headlights. When his eyes adjusted to the glare, he saw the green Buick Riviera.

His first instinct was to run. Instead, he stood his ground glaring at the green beater. The doors of both cars flung open. Six gangbangers formed a semi-circle around him. Spiked Hair swaggered toward him. Mitch went into a wrestling crouch ready to charge him as soon as he got close enough. He sucked in a deep breath. Three of the gangbangers raised their AR-15s. Spiked Hair flashed an open palm at them while watching Mitch. "How 'bout you open that coat?"

"Fuck you."

"Aight then. Best not be strapped. Know you country boys love your guns."

Why didn't they shoot him already?

Spiked Hair turned to the others. "Y'all get back in the rides. I got business to talk wit dis man." When he turned back, he looked at Mitch's empty hands. "Good."

A strange calmness settled over Mitch. "What do you murdering bastards want?"

"Heard you save that school of Junior's."

"Junior?"

"Y'all call him Brother Williams. He Junior back in the day. No matter. He doing good wit those kids. My baby girl goes there." The man's dead eyes flickered.

"What's any of that got to do with me?"

"My Peaches been going to your firehouse. Didn't know before. Told me you give them Packer jerseys and school stuff."

Peaches was the spirited little girl who wrestled Kyle to the ground when he tried taking her red crayon.

"Only reason I'm here is to say we done wit you. Won't bother you none."

Mitch didn't know what to say.

Spiked Hair continued. "But DeAndre? Best hope he stay away."

"I'm not worried."

"Should be. Dude's crazed." He glanced back at the cars. "You need to know some things. Wasn't us had anything to do with those firemen got killed. Before DeAndre took over, we just took care of providin' drugs. Never to kids. None of that prostitutin' young girls or killin'."

"Yeah. I can see you fellas just doing business with the arsenal you got."

"Those burners keep the niggas out."

"And the bar owner? That just business too?"

Spiked Hair snarled. "DeAndre kill that man. We was acting out in there. Wasn't right what he did. Can't say I'd be tore up if DeAndre never come back."

"Then go to the cops. Tell them what he did."

"Don't work that way." He stepped closer. "Just thought you should know."

Spiked Hair swaggered to the green Riviera and turned back to Mitch. "We only wanted to check on Jasmine that day you run us off. She a good kid."

A shiver shot up Mitch's spine. He had almost killed Peaches' dad that night.

Chapter 39

The department doctor finally allowed Mitch to return to duty on Thursday, January ninth. When the charcoal skeleton of the Richardson home came into view, he thought back to how tidy Jasmine kept the house; the pride she had in her home. He shook off the grief as he pulled the rusted van into the firehouse parking lot. Stepping from the van, he exhaled white vapor clouds. The frigid air stung his nostrils.

Nic was sitting on the bumper of the rig when he went inside. "Hey there, Farm Boy. Been a while."

"Yeah, things got crazy lately."

"Laubner's working a trade for your captain today. Thought I better warn you."

"Crap."

"He's been spouting off how reckless you were, going into that fire with no mask. Said he would have put you on charges if he was the boss."

"Maybe he's right."

"Bullshit. By the time you masked up, that girl would have been dead. Laubner's an imbecile."

"Working today?" Mitch asked.

"No, but I can come back for a workout later." She raised an eyebrow seductively.

"Nic, you're—"

"Sexy?" She laughed. "Hey, I'm fucking with you. How about stopping by tomorrow night? We can finish that bottle of Jack."

"I don't know."

"Hey, I'm not asking for your hand in marriage. Just want to have a drink, and you know…"

"It might be late." Like Jamal always said, a man's got his needs. "I'll be at the Odyssey School most of the day. I could use help with the shop class I'm teaching."

"Nah. You know kids irritate the hell out of me." She kissed him on the cheek. "I told your crew you turned me. Told them after you, I'll never go back to women." She grinned. "I love screwing with those old fucks, they're so easy."

* * *

Mitch fell into the morning routine, laughing to himself over Nic. It felt good to be back.

Crusher was the first one in. "Glad to have you back, kid. Missed your sorry ass."

Kenny wasn't far behind. He tried to kiss Mitch on the lips. Kenny folded his arms. "Sure, now that you're tapping Nic, you toss me aside like a used rubber."

"How can I make it up to you?"

"Get my dick back."

They laughed.

Cigar smoke clouded the kitchen. The three old friends roared with laughter over some story Kenny was telling. Mitch got another pot of coffee brewing on the Bunn machine, adding the smell of fresh-brewed coffee to the bite of cigar smoke. As soon as the coffee started flowing, he headed to the sink to finish the morning dishes.

"Hey, kid. Come on over. Join us," Crusher said.

Mitch hesitated, uneasy about what they had in mind for him.

"It's okay, c'mon. Sit. Have some coffee. Even gulags had breaks."

Ralph nodded once.

Kenny slid next to him on the bench. "What do you farm boys know that we don't? You know how many Romeos tried to get in Nic's pants?"

"Not allowed to share country secrets with city guys."

"At least tell me if she's got a chia pet between her legs. Or better yet, she shave?"

"Jesus, you ain't right," Ralph said. They all hooted.

The banter felt good.

"Hey, cub. Off your ass." Lieutenant Laubner stood in the kitchen entryway, hands on his hips.

Ralph pointed his cigar at Laubner. "Listen, asshole. We're drilling here. Talking fire tactics. Try it sometime. Maybe you'd be worth a shit."

"I'm gonna write your ass up, Eberhardt. You're over the line."

"Pension number 47389. Make sure you spell my name right. See you downtown."

Laubner stomped to the office.

Mitch rose from the table. "I should get back to work."

"Firefighter Garner to the office, immediately," blared over the loudspeakers.

Laubner was pacing when Mitch entered the office. "You want a career on this job, you ignore the shit those guys feed you. They're a bunch of outlaws." Laubner's face turned crimson as he ranted. "We get a fire today, you'll follow my orders or I'll have your ass. Got it? None of that cowboy shit like you pulled across the street. Any questions?"

"No, sir."

"Good. Get out of my sight."

After lunch, Mitch headed to the joker stand to hit the books and stay clear of Laubner. He was well into the chapter on the Jaws of Life when he heard shouting from the apparatus floor. "Goddamn piece of shit."

Mitch peeked out at the apparatus floor in time to see a crescent wrench skip across the concrete. Ralph stood in front of the open hood of his old gray Chevy Cavalier with his hands on his hips.

Mitch knew he should steer clear of Ralph, but his curiosity trumped caution. He joined Ralph at the car. "What's wrong with it?"

"Why you want to know? So you can show me up again?"

"Sorry. Just wanted to help."

"After all the shit I gave you? You want to help? Seriously?"

"Sorry, I'll leave you alone."

Ralph sighed. "Wait. Can't keep the son of a bitch running. Gotta keep giving her gas or she dies. Replaced the plugs, distributor cap, and plug wires. Didn't help."

"This an eighty-nine?"

"Yeah, you want it?"

Mitch rubbed his temple. "I had a buddy with one of these. Fuel injectors went bad. They're pretty easy to replace." They leaned under the hood, standing side by side, resting their elbows on the fender.

"Now who's the butt buddies?" Kenny said from behind them.

Ralph flipped him off without looking back. "How do you know which ones are bad?"

"I got a tester that picks up the tapping of the injectors."

"I don't get it. Why you want to help?"

"Just hoping to keep the Jawbreaker of South Milwaukee from strangling me."

"Yeah, that." Ralph straightened and faced Mitch. "You got balls, kid. Crawling into that fire with no mask was damn impressive. But you gotta learn when to pull back on the throttle. Need smarts to go with those gonads."

Feeling bold, Mitch asked, "How about teaching me to be smarter?"

"When's your probation up?"

"In three months, April eighth."

"You're one stubborn son of a bitch. I'll give you that."

Ralph stepped back and rubbed his chin.

Mitch waited.

"From now on, you'll be with me on the pipe. Kenny will be third man. I'll clear it with the boss. He should be good with it. Thinks you could make a solid firefighter." Ralph paused. "We'll see."

"Sorry about getting you in trouble with Laubner."

"If we get a fire today listen to me, not that idiot. He couldn't piss out a wastebasket fire." Ralph surprised him with an evil grin. "It wouldn't go well for Laubner to go after me, and he knows it. The deputy chief was my cub."

"I won't let you down."

"You do, I'll remove those oversized gonads."

* * *

Ralph pushed Mitch relentlessly over the next three months. He was as ornery as ever but now Mitch was intent on impressing him. Ralph had the boss get them access to vacant homes and businesses. They addressed different construction types and the best tactics to use on them. Ralph stressed the dangers of balloon construction in many of the older Milwaukee structures as there are no fire stops in the walls. Fire can spread from the basement to the attic in seconds when it gets in the walls. Plenty of crews had been fooled into thinking fire on a lower floor was out, only to have the attic explode in flames.

They practiced laying hose lines into these structures while Ralph peppered him with impossible scenarios that would have Mitch's brain swimming. While laying out the lines, Ralph would shout questions: "The house is closed up tight, no ventilation, smoke is puffing in and out of the cracks. Now what? Thick black smoke is gushing from a basement window, what's your first move? Fire's blowing out the roof. Where you gonna take the first line? Fire's impinging on a propane tank, now what?" When he faltered and grasped for an answer, Ralph would hammer him about focusing through the panic and chaos.

After fires, they'd go over what Mitch did right and what he could do better, mostly what he could do better. He pushed Mitch to think beyond what's in front of him; to anticipate the worst possible outcomes. He needed to be smart because there was nothing more unforgiving than the fireground. Ralph warned him you can do everything right and still die. Just don't die being stupid.

Chapter 40

On April eighth, Mitch's recruit class planned to celebrate their year-on at Roscoe's. They would no longer be probationers. They would be professional Milwaukee firefighters. With Jamal and LaMont gone, Mitch could not go back to the bar where the three had spent so many Fridays celebrating another week of training. He made a trade to work on the blue shift, the day of the party.

Before heading to the firehouse that morning, Mitch picked up Kyle from the nursing home. He had begun taking him to the school at the end of January. Brother Williams had agreed that bringing him to the school would be good for him and the students. Mitch had repaired the wheelchair lift in the old van so he could transport the boy. Each day a different student was in charge of taking care of him. Brother Williams explained how critical it was for them to learn how to care for someone with greater challenges than they have. Kyle taught them well. He became an adored member of the school community.

On the way to the firehouse, Mitch rolled down the van window to let in the fresh April air. The Core smelled alive. Abandoned trash hadn't begun to ferment. Back home, Chris would be busy plowing fields to ready them for planting in May. He had been checking with Chris through the winter. Their phone calls were usually short with Chris assuring him the farm was doing okay. Mitch sensed something wasn't quite right, but he didn't press him. He'd have to trust Chris to take care of things. Mitch was busy teaching a shop class at the Odyssey School, mentoring kids at the firehouse, and spending as much time with Jasmine as he could. She went to school every day and helped tutor the three girls but remained distant and sad.

Mitch dreaded working with Lieutenant Laubner but working with Nic and DeWayne, her partner on the blue shift, would be fun. The morning went by smoothly with Laubner only bitching about how his bed wasn't made properly. It was.

At lunchtime, Laubner pranced into the kitchen, spotted the tray of burgers and the bag of chips and said to Nic, "Don't you know how to make anything else?"

"Sorry, boss. Not all girls can cook. Some of us are good at other things." She winked at Mitch. He had to look away to keep from cracking up. They ate in silence; nothing like the raucous meals on his shift. Nic kicked Mitch in the shin. She ran her tongue over a potato chip. He bit his lip to keep from laughing.

Mitch headed to the watch room after lunch for some quiet time. He was no longer a probationer and no longer had to study the training manual for the monthly tests. Besides, Ralph told him to forget most of that shit. He now had time to read about his favorite hero, Dirk Pitt, in Clive Cussler's *Valhalla Rising*.

Nic sauntered into the room. "Mitch, read later. I need you to spot me."

"What if Laubner catches us?"

"Catches us what? Working out?"

Mitch raised his brows.

"Jesus, Garner. Get your mind out of the gutter?" She grinned.

The fire alarm chimed. "Report of a fire, 2145 West Wright Street. Engine Fifteen, Engine Thirty-Two, Engine Thirty, Ladder Nine, Ladder Twelve, Battalion Five, and Battalion Two responding."

They met DeWayne at the rig. The three young firefighters hustled into their turnout gear, then waited along with the driver in the idling rig while Laubner strolled across the apparatus floor and pulled on his gear.

"We should be first-in but not with that slug," Nic said, spitting the words. "Could he go any slower? Fuck."

The blue-shift driver rarely exceeded the speed limit, pausing at every red light. Nothing like Crusher who finessed the engine like a shiny red twenty-ton stock car.

Two engines, a ladder truck, and battalion chief were on scene by the time they pulled up. Smoke billowed from the basement windows of a rectangular four-story brick building that covered half the block. A Miller Light sign in front read *Ebony Lounge*. Mitch knew the layout from training with Ralph. Businesses would occupy the first floor with the top three floors divided into apartments.

Laubner keyed the radio, "Incident command, Engine Fifteen on scene."

"Engine Fifteen, check the second floor for occupants."

"Engine Fifteen, ten-four," Laubner said in a cheery voice.

Mitch went for the hose.

"Fire's in the basement. Forget the line," Laubner barked.

They entered through the back exit. Heavy smoke from the basement choked the stairwell. They donned their masks and followed Laubner as he squeezed past Engine Thirty's crew who was pulling hose to the first-floor bar. Engine Thirty-Two would be working their way to the fire in the basement with Ladder Nine forcing entry and taking out windows for ventilation.

Mitch's crew completed a quick search of the second floor and found nothing. The third floor was vacant, much of it gutted, the studs bare.

As they searched the fourth floor, a tsunami of greasy brown and black smoke cascaded into the apartment. Flames erupted from the stairwell.

"Hey, boss! Better let the chief know we got fire up here," Nic said, her voice muffled by the mask.

"I can't find my radio," Laubner said.

The heavy smoke banked to the floor. Total darkness set in.

Mitch flared. "How could you lose it?"

"Put it down to glove up."

"Nic, you got a radio?" Mitch called into the darkness.

"Boss has the only one."

"Ralph's right, you're an idiot, Laubner. Jesus."

Air horns sounded from the rigs below, signaling all companies to evacuate. They were losing the building.

A warning bell rang. "I gotta get out," DeWayne said, his voice wavering.

Another bell rang. "Fuck, fuck, fuck," Nic yelled.

They only had minutes of air left. Mitch's stomach squeezed into a nauseating ball. Fire crackled from the stairwell. He crawled to the window, praying to see a ladder. Flames shot up the side of the building from a lower window. They were trapped.

Think.

Sheets of plaster and insulation rained down on them. Orange and red swirled over their heads. Mitch dropped to the floor to stay below the searing heat. If the others were calling for him, he couldn't hear them over the roaring fire. He was going to die being stupid. Why did he listen to that idiot? He should have grabbed a line.

Mitch's vision reddened with rage. He'd never see Jennie again. And Jasmine. What would happen to her?

Think.

He crawled back toward the stairwell, hugging the floor. The heat bled through his turnout, stinging his back.

Think.

It struck him that the third-floor walls had been opened. Had the fire traveled up the walls and come out on the third floor right below them? Could he make it to the next landing before being incinerated? His mind reeled from the adrenaline surging through his body. The nearly thousand-degree heat would burn through the turnout within seconds, and he'd die an agonizing death if the stairwell was in flames from top to bottom.

Wait for the rapid intervention team. No. Nobody knows we're here.

He fought the urge to vomit in his mask, clenching his teeth against the sour bile in his mouth.

Ralph's words punched through the chaos. *Focus through the panic.* Mitch swallowed hard and launched himself headfirst at the flaming stairwell. The steps dug into his chest as he clawed and kicked his way down. *Too many steps. Too hot.*

The blistering heat gave way to dense smoke just below the third-floor landing. He tumbled down the stairwell and outside where the crew of Engine Thirty-two was changing their air bottles. Their mouths dropped at the sight of his smoldering turnout.

"My crew's trapped on the fourth floor," Mitch hollered through his mask.

"Mayday, mayday, mayday," the shocked officer shouted into his radio. "Engine Fifteen trapped on the fourth floor. Engine Thirty-two taking a line up the back stairwell. We'll need backup."

They scrambled up the stairs and encountered heavy fire on the third-floor landing. They blasted it with their hose line and tried to fight their way through. The high-pitched blaring of PASS devises from above sent a chill through Mitch, bringing back the scene of 9/11 where the eerie silence after the towers collapsed was shattered by the high-low chorus of these devices.

Mitch's bell rang.

"You need to back out," the boss ordered.

"I gotta show you where they're at."

"Back out."

Mitch would suck the last breath of air from the bottle before he'd back out. His company was up there.

The wall of flames forced them back.

"Give me the line," Mitch hollered.

"Gotta wait for backup," the officer hollered back.

"No. We gotta get to them. Now." Mitch yanked the hose from Engine Thirty-two's pipeman and crawled into the scorching heat. He'd get to his crew or die trying. He whipped the pipe in a figure eight pattern, trying to bank down the fire and heat. Engine Thirty-two's pipeman tried to pull Mitch and the hose back down the stairs. Mitch dug his heels into the stairs. "Nooo." The blistering heat burned his back through the Kevlar.

He heard a blast of water from another hose line. The heavy stream of water cooled his back. A deep voice behind him said, "We got backup. Let's go."

The heat and dwindling air from his near-empty bottle sapped Mitch's strength. He handed the line off. The companies pounded the flames, one line working to hold back the fire from the fully engulfed third floor and the other working on the stairwell fire. They couldn't advance any farther or they'd be trapped by the fire below. The two lines barely kept the fire in check.

The boss shouted up the stairwell, "Engine Fifteen. Get to the stairwell. We can't hold it much longer." His shouts were muffled by his mask and the roar of the fire.

They went silent to listen for any sign from the trapped crew. The wailing of the pass devices didn't change.

Oh, God. No. Please.

Mitch sucked in as much air as he could, ripped off his facepiece, and hollered with everything he had. "Nic, we're on the stairwell. Get out. Now."

Silence. Then rumbling from above. The wails of the pass devices got louder.

One body pushed by him, then another, and another.

Thank you, God.

Mitch slid the mask back over his face. The warning bell stopped ringing. No air. His legs gave out. He collapsed on the stairs.

Cool, fresh air flowed into his mask.

"Stay close," the deep voice said. "We're both working off my bottle. Let's go."

They stumbled through the rear doorway, greeted by cheers. Mitch was startled to see the deep voice of his buddy-breather didn't belong to the giant he imagined in the darkness, but a short, wiry black guy. The crews of Engine Thirty, Engine Thirty-Two, Ladder Nine, and the battalion chief crowded around.

The chief said, "Goddamn nice job, son." He turned to Lieutenant Laubner. "Get your crew checked, then I want to see you. The rest of you get the water towers up. Surround and drown this miserable pile of lumber and brick."

Mitch removed his helmet and mask. The brim of the helmet had drooped from the heat, the white frontpiece blackened. He was alive. His crew was alive. Before he could get the turnout coat off, Nic pulled him close, her face smeared with soot. She pressed her forehead against his. "You are fucking amazing, Garner. I owe you."

"No, I owe you."

She kissed him hard. "You okay?"

"I am now." His body shook as it all sunk in. *Thank you, Ralph.*

Lieutenant Laubner spun him around. The lieutenant's nose was caked with blackened snot. "Garner, I'm putting you on charges for insubordination," Laubner said, spewing ribbons of darkened spittle.

Nic and DeWayne's mouths gaped open.

"You both heard him call me an idiot," Laubner said.

"Didn't hear nothing, boss," Nic said.

"Me neither," DeWayne said.

Mitch wiped the slimy spit from his face and rammed a finger in Laubner's chest. "Fuck you, Laubner. Just fuck you. Pension number 96405. Make sure you spell my name right, you waste of skin."

"I'll have your ass." Laubner stomped away, leaving the crew behind.

* * *

Laubner was gone by the time Mitch and the others got to the MED rig to have their carbon monoxide levels, oxygen levels, and vital signs evaluated. They all checked out and were told they could go back to work.

When Mitch pulled on his turnout coat, the paramedic asked, "Isn't your back burned?"

The back of his canary colored coat was blackened and reeking of smoke. "I'm fine."

His back stung like hell but no way was he going to the hospital and then be off work again on medical leave. No. He'd let Miss Bernie treat the burns. They had plenty of Silvadine ointment left from Jasmine's burns.

Laubner wasn't at the rig when they got back. They sat on the tailboard waiting for him. Crews milled around the fireground watching the aerial ladders blast thundering torrents of water down onto the crumbling building from their master stream nozzles.

"I can't believe that dickhead," Nic said.

"I don't want you guys lying for me. Let him put me on charges."

"That asshole almost got us killed. He should be kissing your ass."

"I should have ignored him and grabbed a line when we went in."

She stood and faced him. "Holy shit. You actually blaming yourself? I can't fucking believe it."

"Firefighter Armbruster," Chief Kowalski, said from behind her. "Can you act as lieutenant for the rest of the shift? Laubner won't be back."

"Yes, sir," Nic said. "He okay?"

"Take your crew and get another line on the east exposure." The white-haired chief marched off, shouting orders into his radio.

* * *

A tall man and a petite, attractive woman were waiting for them inside the firehouse when they returned late in the afternoon. As soon as the rig pulled to a stop, the man and woman ran to the boss's side of the rig. The man yanked open the door and said, "Nicky, you scared the hell out of us."

Nic jumped down and was immediately embraced by both of them. Her mother was a striking, mature version of Nic. Her dad, Chief Armbruster, could be the mold for how an off-duty chief should carry himself with his short-cropped hair and polished appearance.

Nic pulled back and pointed to Mitch. "This is Firefighter Garner."

"I know who he is. Chief Kowalski told me what happened. Let's go to the office." This was a man used to giving orders. He escorted Nic and his wife to the office.

Mitch, DeWayne, and the blue-shift driver went to work sanitizing and checking the masks and preparing the rig for the next run.

Fifteen minutes later Chief Armbruster stormed onto the apparatus floor. He approached Mitch, looking like he was ready to punch somebody. He clasped Mitch's hand and shook. "I don't know how I can thank you, son. What you did is…I don't even know how to say it." Lowering his voice, he said, "Thank you."

Nic's mom embraced Mitch, inflaming his back. He winced and saw the tears pooling in her eyes as she stepped back. Nic stood behind them, watching him with an embarrassed grin. He felt awkward. All he could think was that he was fucking their daughter.

Her dad's face pinched into an angry scowl. "C'mon, Sheila, I got some business needs taking care of downtown."

Chapter 41

Mitch couldn't sleep. Chills racked his body as his mind spun with the images and emotions of being trapped, of coming so close to a horrific death. Every time the image of diving into the wall of flames materialized, his heart raced. He couldn't believe he actually did it. And then, he charged back up the stairwell into the fire to save his crew or die trying. He proved himself. That's why he left the farm. Why didn't he feel like a hero? Why wasn't this enough? The round wall clock in the dorm showed three-ten. He went to the joker stand to listen to late night dispatches and wait for their next run.

The old chair creaked as he sat. The office door cracked open. "I can't sleep either," Nic said. "C'mon in."

Since Nic was the acting boss, she got the office.

Her face was puffy, eyes red and swollen.

"You okay?" Mitch asked.

"Never came that close before. All kinds of crazy shit went through my mind."

"Yeah, I know. Me, too."

She rolled the high-backed office chair around the desk so they were sitting knee to knee. "What were you thinking up there?"

"It's weird," Mitch said. "I was terrified when I realized we were trapped. I knew we weren't going to make it. Then I got real calm, almost like I was okay with dying. But it hit me that I wouldn't be around to help Jasmine and the kids anymore. I'd never see the farm again."

"And Jen?"

Mitch lowered his head.

Nic lifted his chin. "You were thinking about her. Right?"

"You should be with somebody who loves you."

"That'll never be you, will it?"

Mitch couldn't answer.

"So that's it?" Nic said. "Goddamn you, Garner."

"Sorry. I just think it's time we ..."

"Why can't you be more of a dickhead so I can hate your fucking guts?" Nic punched him in the chest.

Before she could hit him again, he cradled her trembling fist.

Her smoky voice cracked. "Know what I was thinking up there? That my life was over and I haven't done shit. Felt horrible." She rubbed the side of Mitch's face with her free hand. "I crawled through that room, looking for you. I knew we were going to die and wanted to be next to you. Then I heard my name over the sickening sound of that fucking fire. It was you, calling for me. I'll never forget that incredible feeling." Her eyes misted. "Anyway, I need to stop screwing around and get on with my life. I need to find someone who looks at me like you look at Jen. Maybe have kids someday." Her lips quivered. "You know how much I love kids."

Mitch squeezed her hand.

She kissed the top of his hand. "Think we can be friends?"

"Damn right."

"Does that mean you'll stop by once in a while for a sip of Jack and some best-friend talk? Maybe give me advice on my latest boyfriend?"

"Bank on it."

"So, what about Jen?"

"I don't think she'll want to leave Milroy. And I can't move back there. Jasmine needs me here and working with these inner-city kids feels like I'm doing something important." He paused. "Probably don't matter. She's done with me."

"You're wrong. Not with the way she looked at you in the hospital. Hey, what did you mean at the fire when you said you owed me?"

"That basement fire we had a couple months ago? I was scared shitless. You didn't let me back out. If I had, I could never have faced my crew. I would have quit the job."

"Glad you stuck around. Laubner would have killed us all today if you hadn't been there." She grinned, her eyes sad. "Plus, I know what kind of man I'm looking for now."

They embraced. Mitch held back a painful groan as she ran her hand over his raw back.

* * *

Ralph was the first one on duty in the morning. He cornered Mitch in the upstairs washroom. "What the hell were you thinking yesterday?"

"I wasn't."

"No hose line?" Ralph scowled. "Am I wasting my time?"

"I know. I know. It was stupid. Should never have listened to Laubner."

"We're rid of that dickhead. Nic's old man went downtown and raised holy hell. Demanded Laubner be shit-canned. Chief didn't want a fight with the union, so he offered Laubner the choice of being reassigned or terminated. He's now the deputy's gopher."

"How you know all this?"

"Learn from your fuck-up. I can't teach you everything. Oh, and the deputy wanted me to thank you for your little performance."

"You were in my head up there. If it wasn't for you showing me the ropes…"

Ralph waved him off. "Save it, that was all you. Bambi grew a rack. From now on you're Buck."

"Rack?"

Ralph pointed at Mitch's tattoo. "Ain't that what you rednecks call those things?"

Mitch grinned.

"Working today?" Ralph asked.

"No, made trades so I could finish some things at the school."

"Who are you? You save the girl, save the school, save your crew. And, turned a lesbian straight." Ralph laughed, not a loud belly laugh, more like a restrained snicker. "What's next, Middle East peace?"

Ralph headed downstairs shaking his head.

Mitch finished mopping the washroom floor and went down to wash any dishes left from their shift. The red-shift crew and off-going blue shifters crowded around the kitchen table. Kenny went to his knees when he saw Mitch and bowed, "We're not worthy, oh, Master Buck." The room erupted in laughter.

Captain Reemer pointed the tip of his pipe at Mitch. "Somebody get our hero a cup of coffee."

"Let me, let me, oh please let me," said Kenny.

Ralph scowled at Kenny. "Get Buck some coffee and stop acting like a jag."

Kenny stood with hands on hips. "Well, I never."

The crowded kitchen echoed with more laughter. Mitch laughed along, lifted by theirs.

Copies of the *Milwaukee Journal Sentinel* newspaper with a front-page photo of him were plastered on the kitchen walls. Every copy had green antlers sketched on his head. Wherever he was mentioned, "Firefighter Garner" was replaced with "Buck" in bold green marker. Mitch soaked it in. He was one of them, a professional firefighter. A brother.

* * *

By the time he left for home, his back was a throbbing mass. Too many pats on the back. He had eight days off. Plenty of time for Miss Bernie to work her magic on his burns.

Alexus and Jasmine were gone to school when he got home. Miss Bernie met him on the porch waving the morning paper. "Oh, my Lord. Says here it was a miracle." Miss Bernie wagged her finger at him. "The good Lord surely has more work for you."

Mitch peeled the bottom of his shirt from the oozing blisters. "Can you bandage my back?"

"Oooh, that's an angry mess."

Miss Bernie led him to her room and had him lie down on her bed. She applied the cooling Silvadine burn ointment. His phone rang. Miss Bernie said, "Get that later."

He dozed off before she finished.

He woke in the late afternoon to the *Sponge Bob Square Pants* theme coming from the living room. He pulled a fresh T-shirt on over the burn dressings. The ointment had taken the edge off the throbbing.

He had work to do at the school. Before heading over, he checked the phone. It was a message from Chris. "Dad's had a stroke. Get home as soon as you can."

He misdialed Chris's number three times. Chris answered on the first ring, "Mitch, you gotta get home."

"How's he doing?"

"Not good." Sniffling. "We're at UW Hospital."

"On my way."

Mitch rushed past Miss Bernie and Alexus. Miss Bernie asked, "What's wrong?"

"Dad had a stroke."

He pushed the old van to its limits on the fifty-mile drive to Madison.

Chapter 42

Seated on the cushioned wooden couch in the waiting room of the stroke clinic were Maggie's parents, John and Betty Hillenbrand, and Chris. They rose together when they spotted Mitch. Chris looked like a lost puppy.

Betty cupped Mitch's face. "Your dad's had a stroke, but they caught it early. Go on in. Let him know you're here."

Mitch crept toward Sid's bed, searching for words. The antiseptic smell reminded him of the burn center. Andy lectured Opie on the elevated television.

"Don't make them like that anymore," Sid said, slurring the words through the right side of his mouth. "Now it's all killing and screwing."

"You doing all right?"

Sid continued staring at the screen, the left side of his face drooping. "Go back, to Milwaukee. I hear you're quite, the hero down there."

"I want to help. What can I do?"

"Don't need your help. Go on now."

"Dad."

"You heard me. Get out." The monitor beeped faster. Sid's face reddened.

"Okay. I'll let you get some rest." Yesterday he was embraced as a hero. Today defeated, crushed by Sid's angry words.

Back in the waiting room, Chris stared at the laminate wood floor. Betty must have seen the look on Mitch's face. "Mitch, he's not thinking straight right now. Give him time."

Chris's chest quivered. Mitch slid next to him. "Hey, brother, he'll be all right."

"It's bad."

"We should go," Betty said. "Let you boys talk."

John followed Betty out.

"He's a tough old bird," Mitch said. "He'll bounce back."

Chris collapsed back on the couch. "We got papers from the bank. If we don't catch up on our bills by the middle of June, they're foreclosing. That's what got Dad so pissed. He was screaming at the papers. Made me drive him to the bank. And did he go off on them. That's when he went down."

"Crap. How much?"

"If we don't come up with over forty thousand by then, they'll call in the whole six hundred thousand."

"They're not taking the farm."

"Even if we could stop them, we don't have money for seed corn, and we're running low on feed. It's been awful. Dad's temper's getting bad. It's hard to be around him."

"Isn't milk bringing in enough to cover costs?"

"That drought killed us. The money from your truck kept the bank off us for a while, but I just couldn't make it work."

Chris's sad hound-dog eyes and thinning hair tore at Mitch's heart. "Why didn't you tell me?"

"Hey, I saw the Milwaukee news this morning. Said you rescued some firefighters. Man, that has to feel good."

"Yeah, feels great," Mitch said, trying to sound cheerful.

Chris stood. "I should get back to the farm. Getting dark. Already late for milking."

"No. Stay. I'll take care of chores."

* * *

The headlights washed over the house and barnyard when Mitch swung the van into the drive. Gravel crunched under the tires as he approached the old farmhouse. The farm hadn't changed, but it seemed foreign. He felt a tug in his chest. He stepped from the van and was bowled over by Billy. The dog frantically licked at Mitch's face with his coarse tongue. This was wonderfully familiar.

The cows crowded the milking parlor gate, bellowing to be let in. Mitch gave Billy a proper rub down, then went inside the parlor, flicked on the fluorescent lights, and breathed in the soothing smells of manure, urine, and iodine. The cows fidgeted impatiently to be drained, their swollen udders dragging close to the ground. Mitch went to work and fell into the ritual of wiping down the rubbery teats with orange antiseptic and attaching the cups, moving from cow to cow. The ritual comforted him.

After milking and feeding, Mitch retired to the couch in the living room. If he could figure a way to save the farm, Sid would have to forgive him. Forty thousand. And that was just the start. They'd need a lot more to keep the farm running through the summer until harvest. He'd think of something.

* * *

Mitch woke to the smell of bacon. Chris was at the table working on a pile of scrambled eggs, fried potatoes, toast, and bacon. Through a mouthful of food, he asked, "What's with the ratty old van? And what's an Odyssey School?"

"Hey, watch how you talk about my pride and joy."

Chris pointed at the platters of food, enough for a family of four. "Might as well dig in before they toss us off the farm."

Mitch was suddenly ravenous. He had never eaten yesterday. "Why don't you take care of chores and I'll work on the fields?"

"If they're taking the farm, why bother?"

"That's not happening."

Chris frowned. "What you got planned?"

"When you finish with chores, go check on Dad."

"Getting pretty bossy there, big brother."

"Don't tell him I'm here."

"Sure, whatever, boss man."

* * *

Mitch got a good look at the farm in the daylight. The side of the house was still blackened from the fire. The bare field across from the house was half-plowed. The massive John Deere 8200 tractor and twenty-foot disc plow waited in the field where Chris left off. Mitch trotted to the tractor. He grasped the cold metal rails, pulled himself into the cab, and settled into the cushioned seat. He was reuniting with an old friend. The tractor roared to life, spewing black smoke from the tall stack. He engaged the transmission and headed down the row, the discs of the plow churning the ground. The loamy scent of freshly tilled soil floated into the cab. The tractor chugged toward the end of the field bordering the woods. Mitch sucked in a deep breath and sighed. The majestic oak still stood guard over the burned-out trees and brush. Steel cables that once supported his treehouse swayed in the morning breeze.

His thoughts turned to Jennie. If Nic was right and she still loved him, there was hope. Tomorrow he'd go see her. Then he'd go to the bank to see about a loan extension for the farm.

Mitch plowed until well after dark. When he finally pulled himself away from the comforting solitude of working the soil, Billy met him on the porch, licking his hand as if he had never been gone.

He rinsed off the sweat and grime in the mudroom and headed to the kitchen. Chris was at the sink scrubbing a cast-iron frying pan. Mitch pulled a chair over to his old spot at the table and assembled a BLT from the tomatoes, lettuce, toast, and bacon Chris had left out for him. His mouth watered as he slathered on the mayo.

Chris dried his hands on the soiled dish towel. "So, what's your grand plan?"

"No grand plan. Just catch up the mortgage payments, get the fields planted, and get Dad well."

"Why didn't I think of that?"

Mitch took a huge bite of the sandwich and washed it down with cold milk. "How was Dad today?"

"Ornery as ever. I had to check in at the billing department. The insurance will pay for physical therapy but not for him to stay at the clinic for more than thirty days. After that, he has to come home." Chris plunked a chair backward next to Mitch and hung his arms over it. "Who's gonna stay with him when he comes home? I gotta work the farm."

"Don't suppose you've seen Jen around?"

"She stopped in to see Dad while I was there. She's a nurse now. Works right there at UW in the cancer unit."

"Say anything about me?"

"Told Dad and me she'd help with anything, just let her know."

"Chris, she say anything about me?"

"When we came down to see you in the hospital, she cried all the way back to Milroy." He went back to the sink. "You still going with that smoking hot chick in Milwaukee?"

"I'm gonna go lay down."

* * *

Mitch gave up on sleep and was back plowing at three in the morning using the powerful lights of the tractor to illuminate the fields.

Jennie *must* love him. She had cried over him all the way back to Milroy. He'd tell her that it was over with Nic. They'd get a nice house on the far south side of Milwaukee and raise a family. She could come back to Milroy as much as she wanted; it was only a one-hour drive. And he could make trades to be off during the planting and harvesting seasons to help with the farm.

By the time he came in for breakfast, he was giddy. Mitch wolfed down a bowl of Cheerios and headed to town.

* * *

Jennie's black Ford F-150 pickup was parked in front of her apartment. Before knocking, he took a few seconds to calm his nerves. She answered the door in sagging camo pajama bottoms and a loose fitting Green Bay Packer T-shirt. The right side of her face was rosy and creased.

Mitch went blank.

Her jaw dropped. "Jesus, it's you."

"I get you up?"

"I see you're as perceptive as ever. Sorry, that was mean. And sorry about your dad. That's tough." She hugged him.

"Oww."

"What?"

"Burned my back in a fire three days ago."

"Yeah, I heard. Whole town's proud of our hero."

"You too?"

"C'mon in. Let me see your back."

Her apartment smelled like a bakery, triggering memories of cinnamon buns, sex, and early morning talks.

"Sit. I'll make coffee." She went to the counter, and he went to the card table. A pair of men's slacks hung from a folding chair. Mitch stood at the table staring at the pants, breathless, feeling like someone punched him in the gut.

222

Jennie lifted the slacks off the chair and tossed them in a clothes hamper. "Here, sit," she said. "Take off your shirt."

Jen, I love you. Tell her now. He lifted off the shirt.

"It's oozing. You need to change that dressing every day. Mitch, you hear me? You need to change it every day."

"Yeah, every day." The words came out flat.

"You have ointment?"

"In Milwaukee."

"I can take care of it at the hospital when you visit your dad today if it's after three. I'm on second shift."

"He doesn't want to see me."

"That's crazy talk."

Mitch stared at the clothes hamper.

"Look, Mitch. I don't know what—"

"He staying here?" Mitch rose to face her.

She clamped her arms over her chest and tilted her head. "She staying with you?"

The inches between them became an impassable ravine.

"Mitch, why did you come?"

"I don't know."

"I don't know either."

Chapter 43

The bank president said the farm's been falling farther and farther behind on payments over the last year. The board of trustees was forced to file foreclosure papers six months ago. As much as he would have liked to help, he couldn't override their votes. In two months, on June 10th, the farm would be sold off at auction. If Mitch could come up with the back payments before then, they'd call off the auction and foreclosure.

First Jennie, now the bank. He could leave this all behind again. All he had to do was head back to Milwaukee.

At the farm, he headed to the John Deere and went to work on the field, struggling for ideas. He thought of how Brother Williams said hope and faith can overcome impossible odds, but Mitch was running on empty. He plowed through the afternoon and into the early evening, going numb with exhaustion.

Chris met him on the porch. "So, what's the plan?"

The blood drained from Mitch's face. "The bank's selling the farm off in sixty days."

"All I know is farming." Chris's voice cracked. "What me and Dad gonna do?"

Mitch coughed to clear the knot. "You and Dad can stay with me in Milwaukee."

"I don't think Dad would go."

"I can't blame him for hating me."

"You need to see something." Chris led him to Sid's sparse bedroom. Against the back wall was a queen-sized bed with a solid walnut headboard. Across from it, an antique dresser covered in a thick layer of dust.

Mitch sneezed. "Smells pretty funky."

"This is what you need to see."

Chris pulled open the top drawer of the dresser. Inside was a copy of the *Milwaukee Journal Sentinel* newspaper with the story of Mitch's heroic attempt to rescue Jasmine and another edition with the follow-up story. There was also the issue covering the Odyssey School and how Mitch got the fire department involved. At the top of the pile was the program Chris brought back from Mitch's graduation from the Fire Academy featuring a portrait of the recruit class. Mitch stared at Jamal and LaMont's beaming faces. *Rot in hell, DeAndre.*

"I don't get it. Why would Dad want these?" Mitch asked.

"That's not all. C'mon out to the shed."

He followed Chris across the yard with Billy trotting behind.

Chris swung the wide doors of the rebuilt shed open. He flicked on a flashlight and shined it on an antique red Massey Ferguson tractor.

Mitch gasped. "My old tractor?"

"After you left, Dad went to the auctions and swap meets. He found parts to rebuild it and had it painted."

Mitch took the flashlight from Chris and ran his hand over the smooth red fenders. The pile of charred metal bound for the scrapheap had been resurrected. "I don't get it."

"Go ahead. Start her up. Runs great. Dad put a lot of work into her."

He crawled onto the polished metal seat and hit the ignition. The rhythmic *chuk—chuk—chuk* was the sound of hope.

* * *

Mitch worked the fields through the night trying to understand what the hell all this meant. "Things aren't always what they seem; assumptions bite you in the ass," Crusher liked to say. It was sure true about Ralph. Was he wrong about Sid all this time? And about what?

The newspaper articles got him thinking back on the last year. So many times he was tempted to give up. Fighting fires with a veteran crew taught him you don't give up. Ever! An unrelenting fire might force a change in tactics, but the Red Devil was always snuffed out, defeated. He was not going to give up on Sid and the farm.

Mitch returned to the house before sunrise and had a stack of pancakes and sausages waiting for Chris when he came downstairs.

"What's the occasion?" Chris asked. He mounded a plate with hot cakes and slathered them with butter and maple syrup and dove in, shoveling forkfuls into his mouth while moaning. "Who taught you to cook?"

"Always have sex with your food?"

"Never heard you come in last night."

"Got an idea. I should be finished with the fields by Sunday. Monday I'll drive to Milwaukee. I need to get some things. It's weird wearing your underwear. Kind of tight for me down there." He grinned. "I'll put in for a leave of absence from the department. At least enough time to get us through planting season."

"What about Dad?"

"I'll get a loan from the Credit Union in Milwaukee to cover the back payments and enough for seed and feed. Now that I've got my year on, my credit should be good."

"But what about Dad?"

"I should get back in the field."

"Wait. Jen told me I need to change your dressing every day."

Jen.

Chapter 44

First stop in Milwaukee was Orchard Manor to check on Kyle. Mitch told him about the farm and how he'd be working there and wouldn't be able to visit for a while. Kyle's head did nonstop figure eights while Mitch talked.

Next stop was the Milwaukee Fire Department Bureau of Administration where he asked to see the Deputy Chief in charge of personnel. This was the same chief who berated Lieutenant Laubner for nearly losing his crew in the fire. The chief didn't hesitate to grant Mitch as much family leave as he needed but explained family leave was unpaid. He told him his job would be waiting for him whenever he was ready to come back. The chief informed him he'd be receiving the department's highest commendation, *The Class A Award for Heroism*, at the awards banquet in the fall.

On the way to the elevator, Mitch noticed Laubner seated at a desk in the back corner of the outer office. Laubner narrowed his eyes at him. Mitch gave him a one-fingered salute.

Next stop was the credit union. The plan was coming together.

Mitch waited across the desk from the slick branch manager while the man clicked away on his keyboard. The manager's eyebrows knit together. "Haven't you ever bought anything on credit?"

"My dad always made me save for things I wanted."

"Without a credit history, we can't grant an unsecured loan for sixty-thousand dollars."

"How much *can* you loan me?"

"We could go as much as ten thousand since you're on the fire department. But you've only been employed for a year."

So much for Dad's great advice. "I'll take the ten grand."

Mitch had been so sure of his plan. Now what?

227

He headed to Miss Bernie's to get his things. Before he got up to his flat, Miss Bernie stepped into the hallway. "Mitch Garner, don't you dare take another step. We been worried sick over your daddy."

"I really need to get back to Milroy."

"Get yourself down here."

He had no energy to argue.

"My Lord, Mitch, your daddy pass?"

"No. Things got complicated."

"From that look on your face, I thought he surely did. How bad the stroke?"

"Not bad, but it'll be a while before he can work."

Miss Bernie's face clouded. "This an awful time to add to your troubles. I'm terrible worried about Jasmine. She cut herself on the wrist."

A jolt shot up his spine. "You mean, she tried to…"

"The other night she was washing dishes. She been wearing long sleeves all week in this crazy heat. I could see she trying to hide something. I pulled her hand out the water and there on her wrist was cuts." Miss Bernie exhaled loudly. "I ask her what that was all about. She pull her hand away and ran to her room. Well, I follow her in and kept at her. That child clam up tight. Didn't know what to do, so I call Brother Williams."

"Did you call 911?"

"The cuts were healed. Just red marks. Brother Williams, he come over and she don't talk to him neither so he called that woman who works with them troubled girls. She gets here and spends a good hour in there with Jasmine."

"How was Alexus handling all this?"

"That woman told us Jasmine wasn't trying to hurt herself. Told us some young girls suffering with shame and miseries do this cutting on themselves. Says this gives them relief. Never heard of such a thing."

"What are we supposed to do now?"

"They got her on some pills." Miss Bernie sighed. "Poor Alexus can't figure why her sister so sad all the time. I don't know what to tell the child."

"I should be here."

"You got family needs you. Me and Brother Williams will look after Jasmine."

"I wish I knew…"

"Lord knows, we all do. We surely do. Now go. Take care that farm and your daddy."

* * *

Mitch got back to the farm after dark. He found Chris in the barn loading the hay wagon. Evening milking was done and the cows were waiting in the pasture for the hay.

Chris wiped the sweat from his brow with the back of his yellow cloth glove. "Any luck?"

"Take a break. The cows can wait." The brothers sat on the rear gate of the wagon. "Here's what we're gonna do. I got a loan for ten thousand dollars from the credit union."

"That's not enough."

"I stopped by the Hillenbrands and asked John if he could order extra seed so we can get started with planting. We'll pay him back after harvest."

Chris wrinkled his sweaty brow. "Dad won't be happy. Kills him to ask for help. Kind of like someone else I know."

"Yeah, I'm working on that." Mitch grinned. "Anyway, screw Dad. He'll lose the farm over his stupid pride. John had no idea we were in trouble."

"What should I tell Dad?"

"The seed'll be delivered tomorrow. I'll start in on the planting. You take care of chores and milking."

"What about back payments? And Dad? What do we do with him when he comes home? That's only three weeks away."

"Don't know. I do know if we don't get the crops in there's no hope. Remember the movie *Field of Dreams* where they said 'build it and they will come'. That's what we're doing."

"Now you're hearing voices?"

If you only knew. "Let's get the crops in for now."

"We'll be planting corn for the bank."

"See Jen today?"

"Yeah, she stopped in to check on Dad. She's the only one can make him smile."

Mitch envisioned her contagious smile, the type of smile you can't resist smiling back at. Every time he thought of her his stomach knotted. "Yup, she's good with that."

"So what do we do about Dad and the back payments?"

"Pray."

"Think it'll do any good?"

"Some think so."

Chapter 45

The gnarled wicker chair creaked in protest to Mitch's fierce rocking. Billy lay curled at his feet. They waited on the screened porch for Chris and Jennie to bring Sid home. Mitch had stayed away from the hospital the last month to avoid angering Sid.

The plan was for Mitch and Chris to take shifts staying with Sid while the other took care of chores. The days would be long, but they had no one else to stay with him. Jennie volunteered to drive Sid to the stroke clinic on her way to work for the physical therapy sessions in the afternoons. One of them would have to come get him. Help was in short supply in the farming community during spring planting. Mitch and Chris were on their own.

Mitch had intended to get to Milwaukee once a week to see Jasmine and Alexus and to help Miss Bernie and Brother Williams, but with spring planting and equipment breakdowns, the month flew by. He called Miss Bernie every night praying for encouraging news. He only got yes's and no's when he tried talking to Jasmine. When he ran out of things to say, Jasmine handed the phone off to Alexus who chattered on as long as Mitch let her. The calls left him crushed.

Miss Bernie had told him she tried to tell the therapist the pills were making Jasmine worse. The therapist told her they can take time and sometimes dosages have to be adjusted. Miss Bernie wasn't so sure.

* * *

A red Camry turned into the drive. Jennie was driving her boyfriend's car. Mitch took a deep breath and went to greet them. Billy followed. The car pulled to a stop in front of the house, stirring up a dust cloud. When the dust cleared, Sid was glowering through the back passenger window, the left side of his face drooping. Chris popped the trunk. "We got a wheelchair to get him around for now."

Jennie stepped past Mitch and opened Sid's door, never making eye contact. Chris unfolded the wheelchair and Jennie unstrapped Sid's seatbelt.

Mitch couldn't take his eyes off Jennie. "I feel pretty useless. What should I do?"

"Hold the wheelchair while we slide him out," Chris said.

Sid's face twisted into a crooked scowl when Mitch pushed the wheelchair up to the open door. "What the hell you doing here?" The words came out slow and slurred.

Mitch took Miss Bernie's advice and ignored Sid's anger. "Just here to help."

"We don't need your help."

"Yes, we do, Dad," Chris said. "I can't work the farm alone. Mitch has been here helping the whole time you were in the hospital. He built that ramp and set up a bedroom for you on the first floor."

Sid jabbed his right index finger into Chris's chest. "Tell him to get off our land."

"It's his farm too."

"Not anymore."

Chris leaned into Sid. "Then we lose the farm."

Mitch was shocked to hear Chris raise his voice to their dad.

Sid turned back to Mitch. "I—don't—want—you—here."

"I'm staying until you can get out of that wheelchair and chase me off. Deal with it."

Sid's face and bald head went from red to purple.

"Let's get you inside and settled," Jennie said. "Then you boys can get back to your pissing match."

Sid instantly calmed and gave Jennie a lopsided smile. "Yes, ma'am."

Jennie rolled him up the ramp with Chris and Mitch following. Sid clenched his lips while they moved him to the rented hospital bed. He held his right hand to his chest in a tight fist as if he were ready to punch somebody. His left arm hung limp.

Jennie glanced from Chris to Mitch. "Give me a few minutes with him."

When she returned, she said, "He's resting. The trip home wore him out and that little blowup didn't help."

"Are we supposed to ignore the hollering?" Chris said.

"Yes. Yes, you are. Unless you want him to have another stroke. And the next one could be catastrophic. So yes, ignore him."

"Jen, thanks for doing all this," Mitch said.

"Your dad's a good man, in spite of that temper."

"Think sometime we could…?"

"Oh, just so you know. I told him to behave himself. Said if he raises hell with you boys, I won't be happy."

"Thanks."

He stared at the road long after she disappeared over the hill.

* * *

Mitch slept downstairs on the couch in case Sid needed help to the bathroom during the night. He wasn't ready to sleep in his old room.

Late that night Mitch heard a crash from Sid's room. He found him crumpled in a heap next to the wheelchair.

"Don't touch me," Sid croaked. "Tell Chris to get in here."

"You okay?"

"I said, tell Chris."

Mitch slid in behind Sid and slipped his arms through Sid's armpits.

Sid shook his good fist. "Get your goddamn hands off me."

Mitch ignored his own building anger and hefted Sid into the wheelchair.

The right side of Sid's lower lip stuck out like a pouting child. "Why you here?"

"To help Chris with the farm."

Sid struggled to straighten himself in the wheelchair. "Bullshit. It's Jen, ain't it?"

Mitch flared but didn't respond. He wheeled Sid to the bathroom where he pulled Sid's shorts down and sat him on the toilet. He'd never seen Sid naked below the waist. The pasty legs were far too skinny for his short, stocky torso. The sight of Sid's sagging genitals was something he could have gone his entire life without seeing.

Tears streamed down Sid's face. "Goddamn humiliating," he said as Mitch wiped him.

Mitch's anger faded to gloom. His dad, a powerful bull of a man, had been reduced to this whimpering, frail stranger.

When he got him back under the covers, Sid said softly, "Why can't you just leave?"

Because I don't know how to give up. "Get some sleep. Next time call for help."

In the morning, Mitch fed Sid pancakes and tuned his bedroom television to the *Turner Classic Movie Channel*, then headed to the hayfield after letting Chris know.

When Mitch came in for lunch, Chris told him he found Sid on the floor. He bruised his hip.

Mitch approached Sid's bed. "You okay?"

"Go the hell back, to those people, you love so much."

"Those people?"

"Goddamn welfare bastards."

"The blacks?"

"Damn right, the coloreds."

Mitch tried but couldn't hold back. "So, you're quite the fucking expert on black people. How many you know?"

Sid's eyes bulged. "Get the hell off my farm."

Mitch was stewing at the kitchen table, mad at himself for letting Sid get to him when a soft hand rubbed his neck. "How you holding up?" asked Jennie.

"Okay, I guess."

"This must be tough, eh?"

Mitch nodded, lost in her smile.

"How's the burn healing?"

"Okay, I guess." *Jesus, that all I can say?*

"Let me take a look. Got some time before I take Sid to the clinic."

He couldn't get his shirt off fast enough.

She unwrapped the gauze. "These burns should have healed by now. Where's the ointment?"

He pointed to the counter stacked with dirty plates, pots, and a giant cast iron fry pan.

She spread the ointment over the burns in gentle circular motions. Her warm hands on his back sent shivers through him.

"I see you didn't let yourself go."

"Heard you don't like fat guys."

She laughed and pressed her cheek to the top of his head. "Let me change this from now on. How things going with Sid?"

"He can't stand the sight of me."

"Really? You're not all that hard to look at." She grinned. "That's the stroke talking. Give him time."

After she finished, he pulled the sweaty T-shirt back on. "Jen, I need to tell you—"

"I should go. Sid needs to get to the clinic, and I need to get to work."

He helped her wheel a jovial Sid to the car. Jennie had that effect on people.

Mitch and Billy stood in the drive as they drove off. "Just wanted to tell her I love her."

Billy licked Mitch's hand and panted.

Chapter 46

An ambulance sped over the hilltop, red lights flashing. Mitch watched from the cab of the John Deere while mowing hay in the back field. He and Chris had settled into a routine with Mitch taking care of the fieldwork while Chris humped the chores. They took turns checking on Sid. Over the five days since Sid's return, his violent verbal attacks on Mitch intensified. At times Mitch had to walk away.

The ambulance slowed. He couldn't see past the hill. The siren faded. Mitch's chest tightened. He jumped from the tractor and ran over the choppy ground. The blue and white ambulance with *Milroy EMS* emblazoned on the side idled in front of their farmhouse. Red and white beams of light splashed across the house and barn. Mitch raced inside.

Bob, the veteran EMT who was at the scene of Maggie's tragic death, was at the foot of the gurney. They had Sid packaged and heading for the ambulance with Chris following.

"What happened?"

"Looks like a wrist fracture," Bob said.

Mitch stopped Chris. "Why didn't you get me?"

"I was out in the barn when I heard him hollering. Found him on the floor with his wrist flopped in a weird direction. Scared the hell out of both of us." Chris lowered his voice. "And he pissed himself."

"I'll go with him to ER."

From behind them, Sid slurred, "The hell you will. I want Chris."

"Dad. He's an EMT," Chris said.

"I don't care if he's Jesus Christ."

"Chris it is," Bob said. "Shouldn't be long. ER's usually slow Sunday mornings."

* * *

After feeding calves, Mitch headed to the field. Rain was in the forecast the following week. The hay had to be cut, dried, and baled before the rains came or they'd lose the entire cutting if it got wet and moldy.

He came in from the field when the red Camry turned into the drive. Chris and Jennie were wheeling Sid into the house by the time he got there.

"Jen gave us a ride home," Chris said.

Sid's right forearm was covered in a light blue cast. His blank expression spooked Mitch.

"So, what did they find?" Mitch asked Jennie.

"Fractured wrist and some bruised ribs."

After they got Sid tucked in, he followed Jennie to the porch. "Thanks, Jen."

"Sid hasn't even been home a week for crying out loud. You guys need to watch him better."

"We've been trying."

"Just take care of that old man. He's your father."

"Right. Thanks."

The familiar ache in the pit of his stomach flared as Jennie drove away.

Chris moved alongside him on the porch and gazed across the open field. "How we gonna keep going like this?"

"It's bound to get easier. Rehab should help."

"Things aren't getting easier though. They're getting worse."

"So, what should we do?"

Chris sighed. "Maybe a nursing home?"

Mitch clenched his jaw. "Nope. We're not giving up."

"How, Mitch? How? Even if we keep going the bank's gonna take the farm next month."

"We take one day at a time." *And pray like hell.*

Chris walked to the barn shaking his head.

Mitch plodded to the back field. The hay needed cutting. He needed to think.

Chris checked on Sid through the afternoon, allowing Mitch to continue cutting hay until the evening dew set in. The pain pills kept Sid out for most of the day. After he woke, they took turns running him to the bathroom while the other worked his tail off to catch up on chores. Manure had to be cleaned from the milk parlor and barn. The calves had to be fed and pens cleaned, feed had to be mixed for the cows, and hay delivered to the pasture. Tomorrow they'd start all over and do it again along with the fieldwork, milking, and equipment maintenance.

Well after midnight, they quit for the day. Chris dragged himself to bed and Mitch crashed on the couch.

* * *

"Goddamn it. Somebody get in here."

Mitch stumbled to Sid's room shaking the haze from his head. He choked. The room reeked of shit. He went into mouth breathing mode like Kenny taught him.

"For Christ's sake, I've been hollering for over half an hour. You deaf?"

Mitch refused to answer and covered the wheelchair with towels before sliding Sid into it. While lifting him from the bed, Mitch was smeared with Sid's excrement.

"Oh, man. Not again," Chris said, standing in the doorway wearing saggy jockey shorts. His small pot belly hung over the top of the shorts. He was looking more like Sid every day.

"I'll clean him in the tub. Can you change the bedding?" Mitch said.

Sid banged the blue cast on the wheelchair. "Just put me—out—of—my—goddamn misery."

Chris stared at the soiled bed.

"I can do that if you can't," Mitch said.

"No. I got it. Take care of Dad." The words sounded hollow.

Once they had Sid settled, Chris went back to bed. Mitch stayed awake, listening for the old man. In the morning, Chris was milking before sunrise. When he came in, Mitch headed to the field. Rain was forecast for tomorrow.

He fought the drowsiness by drowning himself in coffee and not eating. If he ate he'd pass out. That couldn't happen. Not after what happened with the combine and the fire. He had an alarm clock in the tractor so he could grab short naps to keep going through the day.

Before crashing on the couch after a late supper of Dinty Moore beef stew, Mitch set the alarm to go off every two hours to check on the old man. Sid refused to acknowledge him when he checked on him. The silence had become unbearable. Mitch never thought he would welcome Sid's rants.

The following day, he battled exhaustion, working to get the hay in before the rain came.

Mitch shut down the tractor when he spotted the four-wheeler bouncing over the field toward him with Jennie at the wheel. She skidded it to a stop.

He swung down from the cab.

Jennie motioned him over. "Where were you yesterday when I picked up your dad?"

"I ah…"

"You know these dressings have to be changed every day. Sit. I brought them with me. Got a few minutes before I take Sid in."

"What we gonna do with him? He's like a zombie."

"I'll see if I can get him in to see Doctor Mallory. He's a clinical psychologist at UW."

Mitch closed his eyes while her warm hands moved tenderly over his back. "I think he's the one who came out after I let…after Maggie died."

"Did he help?"

"Not exactly."

She finished wrapping the burns and leaned into him. Her breasts pressing against his back triggered a familiar yearning. She whispered, "By the way, you look like shit. Try to get some sleep." She rubbed his shoulders. "I better get Sid going."

And she was gone, leaving him fantasizing about kissing her lips, making love to her, being with her.

Chapter 47

J ennie's tender massage stayed with Mitch the rest of the day. Images of the two of them together dominated his thoughts as he loaded wagons with the flaxen, bulging bales of hay. He beat the rain. Darkness set in by the time he cleaned and greased the John Deere baler. This was a good day.

After washing up in the mudroom, he went to the kitchen to get a bite before helping Chris with late night chores. He clicked the light on. For a brief second, Mitch thought Sid was slumped over the table, but it was Chris, his lined and haggard face drooping with exhaustion.

"Thought you'd be out working yet," Mitch said.

"I couldn't get in to check on Dad. Had a cow go down."

"You get her up?"

"By the time I got inside, Dad was a mess. He was on the floor. Crapped himself again. It's not right to see your own dad like this."

"He okay?"

"He won't even talk anymore. I'm scared. It's like he's not even here."

Mitch nodded. "I'll stay with him. You take care of chores. I'll think of something."

"We need help."

* * *

Mitch pulled a chair next to Sid's bed after Chris left to finish chores. A shaft of soft moonlight illuminated Sid's face. His right eye was open and vacant; the left in a permanent droop. "Don't give up on us, Dad. We'll get through this, I promise."

Sid's right eye and mouth twitched.

Mitch wiped the spittle from the corner of Sid's mouth. Sid's right eye slowly closed.

Please, God. Help us.

He dozed in the chair next to Sid's bed.

The kitchen phone rang. He rushed to answer it before it woke Sid. The wall clock showed twelve-thirty.

"Oh, Mitch, Mitch, Mitch, that poor child," Miss Bernie said.

"What?"

"We at Children's Hospital. Amblance took her."

A ball of fear swelled in his chest. "Took who?"

"Jasmine took bunch a them pills they give her. She wouldn't wake when Alexus went in to say prayers."

"Is she…"

"Oh, my Lord, Mitch. This terrible. What we gonna do? What we gonna do? Sweet Jesus."

Mitch's knees buckled. He gripped the edge of the counter. "Miss Bernie. Is she…"

"They pump those terrible pills out of her, but she still not awake."

"Who's with you?"

"Just me and Alexus. Brother Williams on the way."

"Tell Lexi I'm coming."

He woke Chris and told him what happened. Mitch jumped in the old van and drove through the late night, his mind numb.

* * *

When Mitch got to the hospital, he found Alexus sleeping on a couch in the waiting room with Miss Bernie and Brother Williams slumped in chairs on each side of her. Miss Bernie pushed herself from the chair and shuffled to Mitch. She clamped her arms around his back and rested her head on his shoulder. She shuddered.

Mitch asked Brother Williams, "She going to be okay?"

"For now. But we're losing that poor girl."

A young doctor came into the room. "Jasmine's awake. You can go in now. She'll be groggy from the overdose."

Mitch and Miss Bernie went to her room while Brother Williams stayed with Alexus. Mitch bit his lip as they entered the sterile room. He needed to keep it together. Jasmine's eyes were barely open. An IV line was taped to her wrist. Miss Bernie smoothed Jasmine's hair from her forehead and kissed her cheek. "Oh, my precious girl."

Jasmine closed her eyes.

They stood by her bed, waiting.

"My stomach botherin'," Miss Bernie said and shuffled out.

Mitch slid a chair next to Jasmine's bed and clasped her hand. He swallowed back the dry knot. "Remember when I told you I know how you felt? It's true. I know why you took those pills."

Her eyes snapped open.

He told her about Maggie and how he blamed himself for her death because he couldn't save her. And how he saw her face when he woke every morning. As he told the story, she turned her face to him, her emerald eyes growing wide. He went on to tell her about the fire that almost took the farm and still might.

When he finished, she continued staring at him. He sucked in a deep breath. "After that my dad hated me, and I hated myself. Couldn't stand the pain." He choked. "I didn't want to be here anymore. I was going to kill myself. Seemed like the only way to stop it. But I didn't. Kill myself that is. Guess that's obvious." He smiled at her. "Instead, I came to Milwaukee and met this amazing young girl who trashed my truck, kicked me, and became my best friend. An amazing young girl who risked her own life to save her sister's. An amazing young girl I would do anything for."

Mitch squeezed her hand. "Don't give up. I promise things will get better."

"I wasn't trying to kill myself," Jasmine said in a whisper. "That true what you told me?"

"You're the only one I ever told."

"Told what?" Miss Bernie said from the doorway.

"Here, sit. I want to talk with the doctor."

* * *

When he got back, Jasmine was sleeping again. He motioned for Miss Bernie to come to the waiting room.

"Here's what I came up with," Mitch said to Miss Bernie and Brother Williams. "I won't leave her like this, and I can't leave my brother alone to take care of my dad and the farm." He paused. "Miss Bernie, you and the girls will come to the farm with me."

Miss Bernie's mouth dropped. "We can't just pick up and leave."

"Why not?"

"The girls still got three weeks of school."

"School isn't doing Jasmine any good and you told me that Lexi's way ahead of her class. I could keep the girls busy. And if you'd be willing to watch my dad while me and my brother do chores, you'd be doing us a huge favor."

"What you think, Brother Williams?"

Brother Williams pawed his chin and broke into a broad grin. "That's the good Lord's answer right there. You all go with Mitch. That just might get Jasmine away from all those painful thoughts. Nothing much gets done those last few weeks of school anyway."

"Won't they keep her here since she attempt suicide?" Miss Bernie asked.

Mitch shook his head. "The doctor said Jasmine told him it was an accident."

"How long you figure to keep them on the farm?" Brother Williams asked.

"They could stay the summer and come back for school in the fall."

Alexus jumped from the couch and ran to Mitch. "We goin' to your farm?"

"Yup."

"Jasmine too?"

"Yup, thanks to you. That was real smart of you to tell Miss Bernie something was wrong with her."

"Yeah, she took too much medicine."

Chapter 48

Billy trotted to the van. Mitch rubbed the dog's ears before opening the sliding door for the girls. He was glad to see the brown Ford Taurus gone. Chris would be on the way to get Sid from physical therapy.

Miss Bernie stepped down from the passenger seat. "Oh, my Lord, that must have been some terrible fire, lookit the side of your house."

He yanked the sliding door open. Alexus jumped out. Jasmine stayed inside. Billy tried to get into the van with her. "Get him away from me," she said.

Mitch pulled the chunky black lab back. "He won't hurt you."

Alexus stroked Billy's massive head, but the dog's attention stayed focused on Jasmine.

Jasmine didn't take her eyes off him as she climbed out. "Don't like how he's looking at me."

"He wants to be your friend," Mitch said. "Go ahead, pet him."

Jasmine grabbed her bag of clothes from the van. "Keep him away from me. He stinks." She plodded to the house.

Miss Bernie scanned the farmyard. "How in the world you take care of all this?"

The van was loaded with half her kitchen and her favorite rocking recliner. She said if she was going to cook for working men she needed to have her things to do it properly. At the end of the day, she wanted her own chair to relax in. The girls didn't have much, mostly clothes along with some dolls and toys for Alexus.

The girls took their things to the spare bedroom upstairs. Miss Bernie insisted on sleeping downstairs so she could keep tabs on Sid. She slept better in her old recliner than a bed. It was easier on her back. Mitch told her he could sleep on the couch to help. She let him know that after working twenty years in the nursing home, she was surely able to handle one little man.

While the girls unpacked, he helped Miss Bernie go through the kitchen and pantry. Pots, pans, and dishes coated with crud lined the counter. When Miss Bernie was satisfied, she said, "Show the girls around while I get supper on and take care of this mess. The way you men live. My Lord."

"Okay, but if my dad gets back before I do, he can be pretty nasty."

"Ain't no stranger to nasty."

* * *

Billy followed Mitch and the girls to the milking parlor, trotting next to Jasmine. He tried to lick her hand. She swatted his nose.

The cows lined up at the parlor for their afternoon milking. Mitch took the girls inside. Alexus wrinkled her nose. "Ooh. Stinks in here."

"You get used to it."

Jasmine scowled at Billy and shoved him. The corpulent dog refused to leave her side.

Mitch gave them a short explanation of the milking process, then took them to the calf barn. The calves bawled, expecting to be fed. Alexus ran to the pen and tried to pet the skittish animals. They scattered, then inched back, stretching their heads toward her, licking at her hand. She giggled. "Their tongues is scratchy."

Jasmine stood back, still scowling, bumping Billy away with her hip. "Make him stop."

"He don't listen to me." Mitch looked away, grinning.

"Can we go back to the house?"

"Let's take a ride first." All kids loved riding in the Gator four-wheeler.

Alexus jumped in the front seat next to him. Jasmine slid into the back seat.

Billy sat on his haunches watching Jasmine as they pulled away. Mitch took them to the back pasture where the stream flowed through their property and widened into a calm pond before drifting on. He parked the Gator on the bank. "That waterhole is where we'd go swimming when I was a kid."

Alexus jumped off the Gator. "Can I go see?"

"You know how to swim?"

"Uh, uh."

"Be careful. It gets slippery."

She bounced down the bank, grabbed a rock, and chucked it into the water.

Mitch turned to Jasmine. "Want to throw some rocks too?"

She shrugged.

"I used to come down here a lot when Mom died. I'd sit for hours watching the water go by. It helped."

"How she die?"

"You can come down here by yourself any time you feel like it. Might help with all you got on your mind." Mitch rested his chin on the back of the seat. "She got real sick."

"Momma got real sick too after my sister died."

They watched Alexus throw rocks into the water in the same place Mitch did when he was a boy.

"You know how to swim?" Mitch asked.

"No water holes by us."

After Alexus got tired of throwing rocks, she climbed into the Gator. They drove out to the endless acres of cornfields with their razor-straight rows of green sprouts. In the distance loomed the woods. Alexus pointed. "Can we go see the forest?"

"It's just an old woods."

Alexus tugged at his arm. "Please, please, please? Never seen a real forest."

"Okay, but it's not that great."

He swung alongside the edge of the woods and stopped. A whispering scent of the fire still hung in the air.

"Why all those wires on that tree?" Alexus asked.

"That's where my treehouse was. We had a bad fire and it burned."

"I wanna go in the forest." Alexus skipped to the woods.

Jasmine stayed in the Gator while Mitch followed. "Okay, we'll take a quick look around and then we better get back. Miss Bernie will be waiting for us."

They trudged over the spongy ground to the giant oak. All Mitch saw was what wasn't there.

"This the best forest ever," Alexus said. "Any monsters in here?"

"Sorry, no monsters."

Chirping sparrows filled trees that had survived the fire. A blue jay squawked. Chipmunks skittered for cover in the charred remains of the treehouse. Branches over their heads rattled with three squirrels playing tag, making *chuk—chuk—chuk* sounds as they jumped from limb to limb.

Alexus twirled. "Lookit all the birds and squirrels and chippies. And all them pretty flowers. Smells lots better than that barn of yours. Your forest fine."

Green buds were sprouting from the upper limbs of the old oak. Most of the trees scattered through the woods also showed patches of green buds pushing through their branches. Purple and white wood violets carpeted the forest floor, layering the musky smell of the woods with their dreamy bouquet. Large and small saplings competed for sunlight. A cherry-red cardinal sang for them. It took a five-year-old girl for him to see it. The fire didn't destroy the woods. It forced it to be reborn.

* * *

The brown Ford Taurus was parked in the drive when they got back. Billy was lying in the same spot on the driveway as when they left. He lifted onto all fours and greeted them, wagging his tail and panting.

"Make him stop looking at me," Jasmine said. "I don't like it."

"He wants to be your friend."

"Just want to be left alone."

"I know."

Alexus hugged Billy's neck. "Well, I love him. Can he be mine?"

Mitch led them to the mudroom. "Try to ignore my dad," Mitch said to the girls. "He had a stroke and isn't thinking right."

"What's a stroke?" Alexus asked.

"His brain got sick."

Alexus squinted at him.

Mitch steeled himself for an ugly scene. He led the girls into the kitchen. Sid and Chris were sitting quietly at the table watching Miss Bernie mash potatoes with the ancient potato masher, their faces showing no clues.

Miss Bernie stopped mashing. "Jasmine, c'mon over and help me put this food on. Mitch, you set yourself down."

Mitch focused his attention on Sid, waiting for the fireworks.

Miss Bernie and Jasmine set out the breaded pork chops, mashed potatoes with light brown gravy, and fresh buttered asparagus. The blend of aromas took his mind off Sid. He was ravenous.

"I found those chops in the freezer," Miss Bernie said. "Enough meat in there to feed my whole church. I found that sparegrass along the side of the house. Now, where you want me?"

Mitch pointed to his mom's chair. Sid's watery, right eye widened and reddened. He said nothing. The girls sat next to her with the men at the other end. Mitch thought it safest to keep some distance between Sid and the girls.

Miss Bernie bowed her head. "Lord, thank you for this bounty we about to receive. We're here to serve You and follow in Your ways. Bless this family during these hard times. Amen."

"Amen," said Mitch and Alexus together.

Miss Bernie reached across the table. "Hand me Papa's plate." She loaded the plate and cut the pork chop and asparagus into bite-sized pieces, then slid it in front of Sid. "Now you don't have to try cutting all that yourself. Just poke it with the fork."

Sid frowned at Mitch. Mitch grinned. "Just poke it with your fork."

Alexus chattered on about all they saw this afternoon.

After the rest of them finished, Sid pushed his untouched plate of food away. "Get me out of here."

Mitch wheeled him into the makeshift bedroom. "Gonna be all right in here?"

Sid's face went blank.

"Okay then. If you need anything, Miss Bernie will be here."

Sid's mouth pinched into a crooked grimace.

Mitch and Chris headed to the milking parlor. Before starting in on the milking, Mitch asked, "So what did Dad say when you told him they were coming?"

"Didn't say a word. Just stared out the front window with a weird look on his face. Gave me the willies."

"Go figure."

* * *

Mitch came in late from chores. The house was quiet except for snoring coming from Sid's room and from the front room where Miss Bernie slept. He went upstairs and entered his bedroom for the first time since he'd been back. Nothing had been moved. A layer of dust covered the charred copy of *A Tree Grows in Brooklyn*. It didn't feel as bad as he thought, but he couldn't open the closet. He changed the bedding before crawling under the sheets. A cool breeze drifted through the open window. He drifted off, feeling good about the day.

* * *

"Aach. Don't touch me," Sid bellowed.

Mitch ripped the covers off and raced downstairs to find Chris standing outside Sid's room. Miss Bernie stood next to Sid's bed with her hands on her hips. Sid looked past her at Chris and Mitch. The words came out in short staccato bursts. "Get that black bitch, away from me. Send her, and those little bastards, back where they belong."

Alexus cowered behind Mitch in her purple Barney pajamas, clutching her black Cabbage Patch doll, looking at him with wide, questioning eyes. He lost it. All compassion for Sid evaporated. He charged into the room. Before he got to the bed, Miss Bernie stuck out her arm. "He ain't in a right mind." She thrust her finger at Sid. "My papa hate white folk about as much as you hate black. That hatred burn inside him 'til nothing left to burn. Destroyed him. You best put out that hatred before *you* got nothing left inside."

"Get the hell out of my house."

"I work for Mister Mitch here. He want me gone, I'm gone. 'Til then, it just you and me while them boys work to keep your farm going, so you best mind your tongue."

"Get her the fuck out of here."

Mitch lost it. He clasped a hand over Sid's mouth. "It's time you shut your goddamn mouth."

Sid's eyes bulged.

Miss Bernie waved her hands in the air. "Enough this foolishness. You boys go on back to bed. Nothing I ain't heard before."

Mitch backed away.

Miss Bernie leaned over Sid. "Now if you need to go, you gonna have to go in that bedpan. You got nothing I ain't seen plenty times at the nursing home. And I can't be lifting you into that wheelchair. You mess yourself, you gonna lay in it 'til morning. Your choice." Miss Bernie straightened and clamped her arms over her chest. "Your choice, old man."

Mitch kneeled in front of Alexus. "Don't listen to him. His brain is sick."

Miss Bernie slid the bedpan under Sid's sheet.

Chapter 49

Mitch traipsed to the milking parlor before the sun came up. Chris shouted over the hum of the compressor and the steady *kachink—kachink—kachink* of the milking machine, "Miss Bernie sure ripped into Dad with that ghetto talk."

"She might talk ghetto, but that lady's the wisest person I've ever known. It's scary how she knows things. It's like she can read minds." Mitch laughed hard. "Better not be fantasizing about Becky Johnson when you're around her."

Chris blushed.

They went to work moving around the parlor like two veteran dance partners anticipating each other's moves. Before going in for breakfast, Mitch patted Chris on the back. "I missed this."

"We doing all this for nothing?"

"I have appointments at three banks in Madison this afternoon. If none of them give us a loan, I'll keep trying. Plenty of banks around."

Miss Bernie and the girls were at the table waiting for them along with platters of bacon, biscuits and gravy, scrambled eggs, and potatoes pan-fried with onions and paprika in bacon fat.

"You boys must surely be hungry. Get Papa and we'll get started."

Mitch wheeled a stone-faced Sid to the table. Miss Bernie filled their glasses with cold milk from a sweating glass pitcher. She had a plate prepared for Sid with scrambled eggs, cut-up sausage, bacon, and chunks of biscuits and gravy. The smell of fried onions and potatoes in the bacon fat along with the freshly baked biscuits and brewing coffee had Mitch swallowing back saliva.

Miss Bernie took her seat. "Mitch, can you say grace?"

"Yes, ma'am." They all bowed their heads except Sid. "Come, Lord Jesus, be our guest, and let these gifts to us be blessed. Amen."

"Amen," said Miss Bernie, Alexus, and Chris.

Mitch spooned heavy white gravy, thick with sausage and chipped beef, onto the steaming biscuits, and dove in. This was not the anemic SOS (shit on a shingle) he and Chris made with hamburger and cream of celery soup spooned over toast.

"Dad, try the biscuits and gravy."

Sid clenched his lips into a lopsided scowl.

Mitch groaned. "Why do you have to be so damn stubborn?"

Sid's lips tightened.

Miss Bernie waved her fork. "His belly'll get to gnawing at him soon enough."

After they finished, Miss Bernie and the girls cleared the table while Mitch and Chris discussed plans for the day. Chris would show the girls how to feed calves while Mitch cultivated corn.

Miss Bernie took Sid's untouched plate to the sink. "Suit yourself."

* * *

Mitch worked through lunch so he would have time to go to Madison. He felt a rush at the sight of the red Camry parked in front of the house and vaulted up the steps to find Jennie and Miss Bernie talking on the screened-in porch. He glanced from Jennie to Miss Bernie. "Don't know if I'm liking that look on your faces. You talking about me?"

"Maybe we were," Miss Bernie said. "Now let me see that back. Miss Jennie says you didn't tend to it proper and it infected."

"It's fine."

"Just get that shirt off so I can see."

Jennie snickered.

He peeled off the sweaty T-shirt.

Jennie ran her hand over the top of his back, sending a shudder through him. "This is where it got bad."

"Settled down nice. Lucky to have this woman looking after you."

"She's the best."

Jennie pulled her hand back. Her smile faded.

He wanted to pull her into his arms but instead asked Miss Bernie, "Where are the girls?"

"They in the calf barn since lunch with that dog of yours. He's been following 'em around all day. He angers Jasmine something awful."

"Dad cause any more grief?"

"Him and me, we'll figure things out."

"I better get Sid to therapy," Jennie said.

After she left, Mitch went to the calf barn and peeked in. Alexus stood in the middle of the pen giggling, surrounded by calves licking at her hands. Jasmine watched from outside the pen with her arms hanging over the top rail. Billy sat on his haunches next to her.

Everything was under control. He headed to Madison.

* * *

The answer was the same from all three. The farm is overleveraged. There was no way they could extend them a loan.

Mitch found Miss Bernie and the girls working the garden in the side yard when he got back. Billy watched Jasmine from the grass. Miss Bernie had a light purple headscarf wrapped around her hair. Jasmine had her brightly colored Kente scarf covering her neck and Alexus had a pink *My Little Pony* baseball cap on. They were on their hands and knees digging holes for tomato plants and mounding dirt over the roots.

"You ladies need help?"

Miss Bernie wiped her brow. "This our work. You tend to yours."

"Jasmine and Lexi, how about I let you ride my pony when you finish?"

Alexus sprang to her feet. "Yay. I never been on a pony. Is he nice?"

"The best."

Jasmine kept digging.

* * *

Mitch had Bert saddled and ready for them when they came around the side of the house. "Who's first?"

"Me, me, me," Alexus said. "I'm kinda scared."

He lifted Alexus onto Bert's back. He led Bert around the farmyard with a very happy girl on his back.

"Go faster," Alexus shouted.

"Kick him with the back of your shoes."

Bert broke into a trot with Mitch running in front, holding the reins. He looked back at the bouncing girl and was reminded of Maggie bouncing on

Bert's back at her fifth birthday party, her last. How could anything feel so good and so bad at the same time?

After two laps around the yard, they stopped in front of Jasmine. "Your turn," Mitch said.

"Think I'll go in now. See if Miss Bernie needs help." She trudged to the house, her shoulders slumped, and head down. Billy followed.

Chapter 50

The rest of May, Mitch continued crisscrossing Dane and Jefferson counties with the papers for the farm. The bank managers and credit union managers all read from the same script. The farm was overleveraged. They were sorry they couldn't help. The land, animals, and machinery that had been Mitch's life would be sold at auction to the highest bidders. Mitch imagined the sadness in the eyes of his grandfather if he were alive. The weight of generations of Garners who worked the fertile land of this Wisconsin valley for close to a hundred years rested on Mitch's shoulders.

* * *

Mitch refused to give up. He had appointments with five more banks in the afternoon.

Before heading into Madison, he had a fuel pump to rebuild. From the machine shed, Mitch watched a Jefferson County Sheriff's squad turn into the drive and stop in front of the house. He recognized the officer from high school. He had wrestled for rival Jefferson High School. Mitch defeated him all three years.

Mitch met him in the drive, wiped his blackened, greasy hands with a shop rag, and extended a hand. "Hey, what's up?"

"Might not want to shake my hand when you hear what I got to say."

Mitch nodded. "The auction."

"June 10th. It's been in the papers. Boss wanted to make sure you knew."

"So they're really doing it. Can't believe this is happening."

Chris ran toward them from the milking parlor. "Why's he here?"

Mitch bit his lip so hard he tasted blood. "They're selling off the farm."

Chris flung fistfuls of gravel across the drive. "Fuck, fuck, fuck. This is such bullshit."

The officer handed Mitch the papers. "I should go. Wish there was something…" He ambled to the squad car.

Chris continued hurling gravel around the farmyard and raging profanities as the squad car drove away. Mitch watched, sinking into gloom. After Chris cooled off, Mitch nodded toward the house. "Time for a family meeting."

"What we gonna do? Where we gonna go?"

Mitch didn't answer.

When everyone was seated around the table, Mitch got right to it. "They're selling off the farm next Monday."

Miss Bernie furrowed her brow. "What you mean, selling off the farm? This your farm."

"Won't be next Monday. The bank is taking it over for back payments."

Miss Bernie cupped her hand to her mouth. "Oh, my Lord."

Sid hunched over the table toward Mitch. "Goddamn you. You did this."

Jasmine and Alexus gawked at Mitch. He said calmly, "I have a good-sized apartment in Milwaukee. Miss Bernie lives right downstairs. We can stay there until we figure things out."

Sid slammed the blue cast against the table, sounding like the blast of a shotgun. The words came out loud and slurred. "This is *my* farm. Only way I'm leaving is boots first. I sure as hell ain't moving to the ghetto with those, *people*." He leveled his index finger at Mitch. "Get out. You're no son of mine."

The words stung. Mitch headed to the front room. He stopped when he heard Miss Bernie. "You old fool. That boy been doing ever thing possible for you, and you just keep on with that foul mouth of yours."

"I don't have to listen to some black bitch tell me shit."

"You think you scare me with that foul mouth of yours? You girls go on to your room. Me and this old fool gonna have it out here and now."

Mitch had to see this. He went back to the kitchen entryway. The girls scampered up the stairs while Sid glared at Miss Bernie.

Miss Bernie circled her finger under Sid's chin. "You gone listen."

He pushed her finger away. She stuck it right back.

He tried to spit at her, but it dribbled down his chin. "Get the fuck out of my house."

"I'm not leaving and you gone listen."

Sid's face pinched into a menacing sneer.

Miss Bernie matched his sneer. They were two rabid dogs ready to rip each other's throats out. "I don't know your reason for trying to run your boy off, but I guarantee you'll regret it the rest a your days. My little girl run off years ago and I ain't seen her since."

"Don't give a shit about your miserable brood. Now get the fuck out."

"Shut that mean mouth. I ain't done." Their eyes locked, faces inches apart. "Never a day goes by I don't wonder about her and wish I could have just one more day with her. She never coming back and I got to live with that. And my boy, Jamal, taken from me, killed by the devil. I got nobody left. You hear, old man?"

Sid twisted away from her.

"I won't ever see my sweet Lettie and Jamal again. And it pains me to no end." She clutched his chin and pulled his face back to hers. "I know you hearing me. Those two boys would do anything for you, and you wanna run one off. You do, and you might lose him forever. That what you want?" She shook her head and sighed. "Don't it get tiresome being mad all the time?"

Miss Bernie straightened her back and marched out. Mitch moved out of her way. She said, "I got words for you too, mister. Out to the porch."

He followed.

"Miss Bernie, I don't know how..."

She opened her palms. "Why didn't you tell me about the back payments?"

"Thought I'd figure some way to get the money."

"Still trying to fix ever thing yourself. Why didn't you ask for help?"

"I went to all the banks asking for loans."

"Maybe you knocking on the wrong doors. How much you behind in payments?"

"Around forty thousand."

"Um, um, um. Lot a money."

They sat in silence across from each other in the weathered wicker chairs with Billy stretched between them.

Miss Bernie bent forward. "Need you to run me to Milwaukee tomorrow. If we going back I better get the house in order. Now I best put supper out so you boys can get back to your chores."

After next Monday, there'd be no more chores.

Chapter 51

Miss Bernie didn't have much to say on the drive to Milwaukee which was fine with Mitch. He had been up all night trying to figure out the next move. He'd give some inner-city banks a shot. Maybe they were the right doors to knock on.

Miss Bernie turned up the radio and hummed along to the song *Ain't No Mountain High Enough*.

* * *

"Umm, umm. umm," Miss Bernie said as they pulled to a stop in front of her house. "Will you lookit that? Brother Williams and them school kids been busy."

The small lawn was trimmed and lush. The petunias surrounding the house were thick with deep purple blossoms.

"I'll get the house in order while you go about your business."

He stopped by the firehouse. It was blue shift so his crew wouldn't be on, but Nic would be working. He went to the office and was surprised to find Captain Reemer at the desk. The captain rose from the chair when he saw Mitch. "I see you're getting lots of sun on the farm. Any idea when you're coming back?"

"Might be soon. I got a question. I thought my leave was unpaid? I keep getting checks."

"Nobody told you? When Ralph heard you were going on unpaid leave, he went around the battalion and asked, well more demanded, members take turns working your shift so you keep getting paid. And our girl Nic's been working more of your shifts than anyone."

"Holy crap."

"We take care of our own. You know that."

"DeAndre ever get put away?"

"Not yet. He'll surface. Scum like that always does."

257

"Is Nic on duty?"

"I think she's working out."

He heard the grunts from the top of the stairs. He crept down the stairs to the bench. In her skimpy blue MFD shorts and snug T-shirt she could grace the cover of any fitness magazine. As the bar got to the top of her lift, Mitch grabbed it. "Need a spotter?"

"Holy fuck. Garner." She slid the bar into the bracket, swung up from the bench, and pressed her sweat-soaked T-shirt against him.

She pulled back and checked him out. "Gonna show me your tan lines?"

Mitch grinned. "You haven't changed."

"How things going on the farm? You and Jen back together yet?"

"She's living with some guy."

The fire alarm chimed. She gave him a peck on the cheek. "Stop fucking around. Get Jen back. You know she loves you."

Nic sprinted up the stairs, taking two at a time. Mitch sat on the bench and listened to the rig roar out the door. He thought about the short time with Nic and their torrid sex. If only he could have loved her.

He stopped by the nursing home to check on Kyle. The nurses told him Kyle had a bout of pneumonia and was weak. When Mitch entered the room, the boy was motionless, no constant figure eights of his head. He told Kyle things were going well on the farm. Jasmine and Alexus were feeding calves, planting a garden, and riding Bert. When he couldn't think of anything else to say, he told Kyle he would take him to the farm when he got better.

Mitch left, praying the words gave his little friend some comfort.

* * *

After visiting three inner-city banks, Mitch returned to Miss Bernie's house. He found her at the sink rinsing a plate.

"Miss Bernie, I tried everything." He slumped into a chair at the table. "We're losing the farm."

"The good Lord finally answered my prayers," she said as if Mitch had just told her the best news ever. What could possibly make her this happy with all the crap that's happened?

"Wait here," she said and went to the front room. She came back with a check. He watched her sign the back. *Pay to the order of Mitch Garner— Bernice Jackson.*

She slid the check across the table to Mitch. He turned it over. It was from the City of Milwaukee, made out to her in the amount of $51,545.35. "Jamal's life insurance. I was beneficiary."

"Miss Bernie. I can't take that. Jamal wanted you to have it."

"I been waiting on the good Lord's guidance. My house don't need work, thanks to you. Thought about helping Brother Williams, but plenty donations coming in to run his school, thanks to you."

Her face lit up, sending a warm glow through Mitch.

"Now I won't feel like Jamal's death was for nothing." She patted Mitch's hand. "That money was meant for you, to save the farm. I know that's what Jamal wants. This God's way of blessing you for doing His work." She leaned back with a contented smile. "And *nothing* give me more joy."

"Miss Bernie. With the way my dad's been treating you? You sure?"

"Gotta be some good deep down in that old man."

"But, Miss Bernie…"

She thrust her palm at him. "Don't deny me this joy. This is yours. That's that."

The numbers on the check blurred. "Don't know when I can pay you back."

"Ain't no concern. Now you best stop all that worrying and get on with it."

Chapter 52

Mitch called everyone to the farmhouse kitchen to share the news when they got back later that same afternoon. Chris wheeled Sid to the table while Miss Bernie clattered dishes into the cupboard over the sink. Sid's listless expression matched Jasmine's.

"Miss Bernie, come on over so we can tell them," Mitch said.

"Go ahead and tell 'em. I got work to do."

Mitch thrust his fist to the ceiling. "We're not losing the farm."

"I don't get it," Chris said.

"Miss Bernie loaned us the money to make the back payments."

Alexus sprang from her chair. "We stayin'?"

"Yup."

Alexus clapped her hands, bouncing on her toes. "Yaaay. I get to ride Bert some more and play with them baby cows."

"Dad, you hear?" Chris said. "We're keeping the farm."

"I didn't ask her for any loan," Sid said.

Miss Bernie dried her hands and faced Sid with one hand on her hip and the other wagging a finger at him. "Now you and me partners, old man. Bet you never dream of that: partners with a black lady from the Hood." She bent toward Sid, smiling. "I gotta be your worst nightmare. Ain't that a stitch?" Her booming laughter echoed through the kitchen, the same laughter that had filled her house before Jamal was gone. Mitch and Chris joined in.

Sid's expression softened. "Anyone think of asking me?"

Mitch raised both hands to the ceiling. "Jesus, Dad, we're keeping the farm."

"Ain't right you didn't ask me."

"Okay, you're right. Should have asked. Sorry."

"Good. From now on I need to have a say." He turned to Miss Bernie. "Who you calling old? And we ain't partners."

"Call it whatever you want, old man, but until you pay off my loan, I got a say in how things gonna go."

* * *

Sid continued his hunger strike. Chris told Mitch he was sneaking him sandwiches and chips, so it wasn't much of a strike. Sid was going to show her he didn't have to do what she said or eat what she fed him. She wasn't the boss of him.

Mitch shared this with Miss Bernie who said, "Even an ornery old pit bull smart enough to know where its food comes from. He'll come around."

Miss Bernie kept upping the ante with meals of southern fried chicken, baked ham, roast beef, all manner of biscuits and rolls, and freshly baked pies. The aromatic smells filled the farmhouse from morning till night. Sid didn't stand a chance.

After three days he was back at the table. He dove into the savory chunks of chicken fried steak, the milky-white gravy running down the left side of his chin. From across the table, Miss Bernie gave Mitch a wink and a sly smile. Sid's excuse was that the physical therapist demanded he eat to keep up his strength for the therapy sessions. He was following orders.

* * *

Sid had good days and bad. Fits of anger and frustration overwhelmed him on bad days, but the good days were getting more frequent. Miss Bernie ignored his constant protests, pushing him hard to strengthen his left leg and arm. She refused to get up in the middle of the night anymore, so he either had to lie in the mess or get himself in and out of bed. He could wipe his own ass from now on. During the day she made him struggle with the walker. No excuses. Sid told Mitch the only reason he did what she said was to stop her constant nagging.

Jennie had been coming early to visit with Miss Bernie before taking Sid to therapy. On days Jennie was coming by, Mitch rose extra early to get morning chores done so he could join them.

Jennie was fascinated by Miss Bernie's stories of her life in the inner city. These were stories Mitch already knew but they were just as incredible hearing them again. Along with gripping stories of gang violence or how her mother died giving birth to her, she'd share humorous stories of crazy church friends and quirky neighbors. Jennie shared stories of tragic losses and miraculous recoveries at the cancer center. Mitch joined in with stories of crazy firehouse antics. Jennie's intoxicating laughter and Miss Bernie's booming laugh echoed through the house.

Sid's speech had improved. He was now giving the walker a daily workout, following everyone around the house, pestering them with complaints. Nobody listened. The girls were taking great care of the calves and helping Miss Bernie with the garden and household chores. And Mitch got to see Jennie six days a week.

* * *

The early June rain and warm weather had the crops ahead of schedule, so Mitch had some free time to work on his antique tractor in the afternoon. He was in the machine shed when he heard screams. "Mitch, Mitch. Please, Mitch. Where are you?"

He stepped outside. Jasmine was running toward the barn. "Jasmine, over here. What's going on?"

She flung around and raced at him, breathless. "Lexi's—in the pond."

Mitch clutched her shoulders. She was drenched in sweat. "Is she still there?"

Her green eyes widened. "I couldn't get her."

They jumped in the Gator and sped across the pasture.

Mitch shouted over the wind in their faces. "What happened?"

No response.

"Jasmine. C'mon. What happened?"

Her lips quivered followed by a torrent of words. "She slipped on the bank and went in the water. She was out too far. I couldn't get her." Jasmine buried her face in her hands and sobbed. "I couldn't get her, Mitch. I couldn't get her."

Think.

"Jasmine, hold on to the bar."

They lifted off the seat as they flew over a berm. The Gator wailed, the RPMs pushing redline.

Mitch skidded the Gator to a stop and ran to the pond. It was still and quiet. He hurled himself down the slippery bank, scanning the water for any sign of Alexus. Jasmine slid down the bank behind him. Something rippled in the middle of the pond. He yanked off his boots and tossed his wallet to the ground. He looked back at Jasmine. "Stay here."

He dove into the chilly pond wearing his pants and T-shirt and swam toward the middle. As soon as he saw the tiny pink tennis shoe bobbing on the water, Mitch's insides twisted into a sickening mass. *Think.*

He dove down to the muddy bottom. He felt the smooth rocks embedded in the mud along with long-neck beer bottles he and his high school buddies used to drink. He came up for air. Fighting panic he called out, "Jasmine, see anything?"

Jasmine stood on the bank gripping the top of her head with both hands.

He dove again praying he'd find her but dreaded finding her. He stayed down until his lungs screamed for air. He surfaced. Jasmine hadn't moved since he came up the first time. Mitch scanned the stream that fed the pond. If she got into the current she'd be swept downstream. He was about to tell Jasmine to go back to the house to call 911 when he heard Billy barking from the stand of cattails bordering the open bank. He shouted, "Jasmine, go see what Billy's barking about."

Mitch swam toward shore. Jasmine disappeared into the six-foot tall cattails, the brown tops tumbling as she pushed through. Billy's barks turned frantic, then stopped.

Mitch slowed to listen. "Jasmine?"

The cattails rattled in the warm breeze.

Mitch ripped through the water, swimming to where Billy's barking had been coming from. When he got to the shallow bank, he plunged through the tangled reeds and sucking muck, slamming cattails out of the way. "Jasmine?"

"Over here."

Billy whimpered as Mitch stumbled over him. Partially obscured by the weeds and cattails sat the sisters in the mud holding each other, rocking back and forth. Alexus coughed hard, gagging herself. She looked at him, her hazel eyes clouded. Her hair was matted with black muck and her white shorts and pink top soaked a muddy brown. Mitch wanted to shout to the heavens.

"Lexi, you okay?"

Her lower lip nudged out. "I wasn't careful like you told me."

Thank you, God.

Jasmine held Alexus at arm's length and scrunched her brow. "How'd you get out?"

Barely visible along the collar of Alexus's muddy top was a long row of teeth marks. Mitch looked back at Billy whose thick black coat was plastered to his body, then back at Alexus. A chill washed through him.

"I couldn't breathe," Alexus said. "Got real scared. Then Billy drag me out."

Billy flicked his body from head to toe, showering them with cold pond water.

Mitch rubbed Billy's wet head. "Holy crap. You are frickin amazing." Billy licked his hand and panted. Jasmine stepped between them, wrapped her arms around Billy's thick neck and kissed the top of his head, ignoring his swampy smell. He licked her cheek.

Mitch watched in silence, mesmerized by Jasmine's serene face.

"Lost my shoe and cap," Alexus said.

Mitch hoisted her from the slime and kissed her muddy cheek. "Tomorrow you and Jasmine are learning to swim."

"Good as Billy?"

"Good as Billy."

Chapter 53

Miss Bernie demanded they attend Sunday morning church service at Milroy Trinity Lutheran Church. Mitch hadn't been there since Maggie's funeral and tried to come up with excuses not to go. Miss Bernie was hearing none of it. Said the good Lord deserved an hour of his time. He didn't argue. Not after yesterday.

Mitch paused and took a deep breath before pushing the castle-like doors of the old church open. Inside, the musty smell and warm reds, greens, and blues of the stained glass washing over the congregation brought it all back. He focused on the open space in front of the pulpit where the tiny white casket had been. A hollow ache spread through his chest.

Sid steered his walker to the last row of pews. Miss Bernie kept going.

Sid called after her, "Hey, woman, we sit in the back."

"Suit yourself. Me and the children settin' in front so they pay attention to the word of the Lord."

"Guess we sit in front," Mitch said.

Sid scowled. "For Christ's sake. How come she's the damn boss? It's our church."

Miss Bernie scowled back at him. "Hush your mouth. You in the Lord's house now."

Sid gritted his teeth. "Aach."

Chris covered his mouth, holding back a snicker.

Mitch escorted Sid down the aisle behind Miss Bernie and the girls. Miss Bernie plopped herself in the front pew. The girls slid in next to her with the men sitting at the end.

"Mind if I join you?" Jennie said from the aisle, startling Mitch. Sid's scowl gave way to a lopsided smile. Before Mitch could answer, she slid past him to Miss Bernie and the girls. He was disappointed she didn't sit next to him, but her presence lifted the darkness he felt on the way in.

Mitch didn't hear a word of the pastor's sermon. He was consumed with thoughts of Jennie while glancing down the row at her. She never looked his way.

When the service concluded, Jennie rushed out before he had a chance to talk to her.

* * *

Halfway up the drive, the rich smell of pot roast drifted through the open windows of the van. The beef, potatoes, carrots, and onions had been simmering in the oven since early morning. As soon as they got inside, Miss Bernie pulled the dark blue enamel baking pan from the oven. She thickened the brown juices and poured it over the steaming meat and vegetables. Jasmine set the table. Sid watched Miss Bernie slice the meat. She stopped cutting and waved the knife at Sid. "You Lutherans sure a quiet bunch. Don't know how the good Lord can hear you folks." She went back to cutting the meat.

Through the kitchen window, Mitch saw the red Camry pull to a stop.

Miss Bernie peered out the window. "I told her to come eat with us. Her man's working a double shift today."

Her man. The words slashed through him.

Alexus ran out and led Jennie by the hand to the kitchen, breathlessly telling her how Billy saved her yesterday. Jennie glanced around the table while Alexus told her every detail. Sid reached across the table and snatched a slice of beef with a fork while the others listened to Alexus run on, her arms flailing to show how she splashed in the water.

After Alexus wound down, Miss Bernie said, "Let's say grace before the food goes cold." She frowned at Sid. "At least those of us had the decency to wait."

Sid ignored her and forked meat into his mouth.

Miss Bernie folded her hands, bowed her head, and prayed, "Thank you, Lord, for these blessings we're about to receive. Thank You for giving us your only son, our Lord and Savior, Jesus Christ, to save us from our sins. And for blessing us with Your spirit this morning in church, just pray You might a heard us. And thank You for giving us Billy." She paused. "Who saved our precious Alexus. Amen."

Everyone but Sid chanted, "Amen."

Serving spoons clattered as platters moved around the table.

Jasmine asked Mitch, "Why can't Billy eat with us?"

Mitch considered this for a moment. "Yeah, why can't he?"

Sid banged his fork on the table. "Don't you let that mangy thing in here."

"We're all partners," Mitch said. "What does everyone think?"

"He's not coming in my house," Sid growled. "And we're not partners."

Miss Bernie stood. "I think we take a vote. Who wants Billy to eat with us?"

All hands, but Sid's, reached for the ceiling.

Jasmine sprang from her chair. "I'll get him."

"The hell you will. Goddamn…aach."

Jennie went behind Sid and rubbed his back. "Let it go, Sid. What'll it hurt?"

"Ah, Christ." Sid went back to shoveling hunks of beef into his mouth.

Miss Bernie put a bowl of meat and gravy on the floor between Jasmine and Alexus. Billy gazed up at them before gulping it down without chewing. Jasmine's high-pitched laugh had everyone smiling, except Sid, who stopped chewing and pointed his fork at Jasmine. "Why don't you ever take that ugly scarf off?"

Jasmine gripped the brightly colored Kente scarf. The room went quiet. Mitch balled his fists. Before he could say anything, Jasmine pointed her fork right back at Sid. "Why you so ugly?" Her emerald eyes blazed with a fierceness that had been missing since before she was burned. She slammed her chair back and marched up to him. "Think you're bad? You don't know bad. Don't scare me none with all your hollering." She was in Sid's face, and Mitch was loving it. "Know you hate us, but what makes you any better?"

Sid jerked back and looked past her to Miss Bernie. "This how you teach your kids down there? Call her off."

"Jasmine, let the old man be," Miss Bernie said. "He don't know what he saying. Don't know nothing about your scarf."

"Good," Sid said and went back to wolfing down meat and potatoes.

"As for you, old man. That girl been through more hell than you ever know. Lucky all she did was give you a tongue lashing. Best treat her with respect. Now, let's eat in peace."

Mumbling to himself, Sid said, "Why do I have to give respect? I sure as hell don't get none."

"Got to give it to get it," Miss Bernie said.

Miss Bernie explained the history and meaning of the colors of Jasmine's Kente scarf to Jennie. She told her how Brother Williams gave her the sacred scarf after she was burned in the fire. Miss Bernie had to pause often to let Alexus chime in with her five-year-old excited explanation of things. Sid showed no sign he was listening. Jasmine stroked Billy's back while the story unfolded.

After lunch, the girls went to feed the calves. Chris went to the milking parlor to clean equipment. And Sid hobbled to his room with the walker for an afternoon nap.

Mitch cleared the table while Miss Bernie and Jennie stood side by side at the sink washing dishes and chattering about Jasmine. Miss Bernie filled her in on the murder of Jasmine's older sister, her mother's drinking and men, her molestation, and her agonizing depression.

Mitch was thrilled Jennie stayed, but couldn't shake the words *"her man"*.

"Do the girls have swimsuits?" Mitch asked Miss Bernie.

"No. And you not letting 'em in that water again?"

"I promised to teach them to swim today. They can wear shorts and T-shirts."

"That girl needs a swimsuit," Jennie said. "And she should be wearing a bra." She turned to Miss Bernie. "How old is Jasmine?"

"She twelve."

Jennie dried her hands on the dishtowel. "Only twelve?"

"In our neighborhood, they form early. Their bodies way in front of their heads."

Jennie handed the towel to Mitch. "Mind finishing up while we ladies do some shopping? I'll stop and get my suit so I can help with the girls."

"You bet." He tried hard to hide his elation.

Chapter 54

Jennie stepped out of her loose cutoffs and lifted off her camo T-shirt revealing a modest lavender bikini and her lanky figure. Watching her brought back bittersweet memories of skinny-dipping on hot summer nights and the intoxicating warmth of her body pressed against him in the cool water.

Mitch spread an oversized yellow beach towel on the bank of the pond. The girls slipped off their shorts and T-shirts, revealing matching lavender swimsuits. Jennie was right, Jasmine was no longer a little girl.

Mitch chuckled. "Miss Bernie pick those?"

"She love purple," Alexus said.

He remembered Miss Bernie telling him purple was the color of hope. He could feel it. Then he remembered how his mother loved purple lilacs and his thoughts clouded.

Jasmine carefully unwound her scarf and laid it on the towel. The white gold necklace flickered in the afternoon sun.

"Jasmine, what a pretty necklace," Jennie said. "Some boy give you that?"

"Mitch gave it to me."

"I love that gold leaf."

Jasmine clutched her neck.

"Is that where you got burned? Can I see?"

Jennie gently pulled Jasmine's hand away and ran her fingers over Jasmine's neck. The burns had left light colored, mottled scarring below her left ear and down her neck. "You're such a beautiful girl, nobody'll ever notice. We girls all have things we don't like about ourselves." She pointed at Mitch. "Not like those boys, who think they're perfect." Jennie laughed.

Jasmine caught on fast. She, Jennie, and Billy swam back and forth across the pond while Mitch worked with Alexus. The near-drowning had Alexus petrified of the water. They started in the shallow area where Alexus could touch the bottom, then moved to deeper water where he encouraged her to put her face in the water while he held her. Every time she dipped her face, she panicked, jerked her head out of the water, and gasped for air.

After two hours of patiently encouraging her, he carried her to the shallow water and put her down. "Let's rest for a while."

Jasmine and Jennie were sprawled on the yellow beach towel, soaking up the rays.

Alexus's lower lip quivered. "Guess I won't ever learn to swim like Billy."

"I'm not a good teacher. You need Jen showing you how."

Alexus ran to Jennie. "Miss Jennie, can you teach me to swim?"

"Let's go. Race you." Jennie and Alexus splashed into the pond, giggling.

Jasmine stayed on the beach towel hugging her knees to her chest.

"Jen's right," Mitch said. "Those marks remind me of what an amazing young lady you are. It's like you have a tattoo of courage for risking your life for Lexi. What could be more beautiful?"

Jasmine rested her chin on her knees. Barely above a whisper, she said, "I never thanked you for the necklace."

"Sorry they couldn't find the one from your dad."

"I like yours better." She dashed into the water and joined the girls. Billy followed.

Jennie and Alexus splashed water at Jasmine and she splashed back, all of them laughing hard. It struck Mitch how Jennie lit up around them and how they lit up around her. They had talked a lot about kids when they were going together. She loved teaching the little ones at Sunday school. He ached to be back with her, to touch her again, to be a part of her world.

* * *

The late afternoon sun washed over them, spreading its citrusy hues through the trees, the shimmering rays dancing on the water.

Mitch went to the edge of the pond. "Hey, girls, it's getting late."

They trudged out of the water and plopped onto the beach towel.

"You girls go on. Miss Bernie'll be looking for you to help with supper," Mitch said. "Me and Jen'll take care of the towels."

Alexus hugged Jennie's waist. "You the best teacher ever."

Mitch grinned. "She is the best."

Jennie stepped over Billy and lifted Jasmin's chin. "You are a beautiful, beautiful girl. Don't ever think those marks change that one bit."

Alexus grabbed her sister's hand. "C'mon, we best get back or Miss Bernie be giving us a talking to."

The sisters walked together hand in hand over the pasture with Billy trotting next to Jasmine.

"Think I lost my dog," Mitch said.

"He knows where he's needed."

Jennie dried and fluffed her hair with her back to him. Jennie's willowy body was nothing like Nic's sculpted bronze legs, tight abdomen, and model's looks. When Mitch was with Nic, he saw how people reacted to her beauty and were drawn to her. People were also drawn to Jennie, but it was different. Jennie was pretty enough, but she wasn't drop-dead gorgeous. It was a magnetic attraction that pulled others close. Her gentle smile, absorbing brown eyes, and natural laugh lifted him and anyone else fortunate enough to be in her presence. He thought about Crusher's advice. "Want to be happy? Find a woman you can laugh through life with."

"Thanks for helping, Jen."

"They're both adorable. And Jasmine, that girl is so darn beautiful and she doesn't have a clue." Jennie sat next to him. "What you've done with these girls is nothing short of miraculous. I've been telling Dr. Mallory, the psychologist, about them. He wants to meet them if it's okay."

Mitch nodded. He wasn't thinking about the girls, not with Jennie this close.

"Hey, that was a really nice thing you did, buying Jasmine that necklace." She grinned and said, "How come you never bought me anything like that?"

"Didn't think you went for that type of thing, sorry I…"

She laughed her throaty laugh. "Just giving you crap."

She kissed his cheek. Her knee brushed his thigh, sending a warm ripple through him. He turned to her and she pressed her satiny lips to his. Their tongues danced over each other. Jennie's breathing quickened. Mitch's entire body prickled with desire. They fell back onto the soft beach towel, their bodies remembering, taking over, fitting together like before, but somehow better. He ran his hand along her thigh, up her side, and to her breast. She panted. Her hips pressed against him. Their wet bodies were ready for each other. This is where he belonged, with Jen. He kissed the nape of her neck right where it always drove her wild. She moaned.

He slid the top of her bikini down and caressed her breast with his mouth. She stiffened, pushed him back, and pulled her top up. "No, Mitch, no. I can't. I gotta go, Jason's waiting."

She jogged across the pasture in her bikini, holding her clothes to her chest.

Jason. Her man.

Chapter 55

Bert trotted figure eights around the barnyard with the girls on his back. Alexus had her arms around her big sister's waist. Jasmine's face was tranquil and focused. In less than a month, she had learned to control the pony with reins and her feet. Mitch, Billy, and Dr. Mallory watched from the fence. The men leaned over the rough-hewn fencing on their elbows, each with a leg resting on the lower rail like a couple of cowboys watching a rodeo. They were a strange duo, with Mitch in stained coveralls and the much taller doctor next to him in a tailored gray tweed suit.

"Extraordinary," Dr. Mallory said. "From what Jennifer told me about the trauma these girls have endured, to see them like this is enlightening. And you? Have you found peace? Come to terms with Maggie's death?"

"I'm not as messed up as I was. Working with kids has helped, but, I don't know." Mitch jammed his hands into his coveralls. "Sorry I was such a jerk last time I saw you."

Dr. Mallory grinned. "Jennifer told me what you've been doing in Milwaukee." He paused and studied Mitch. "Embrace the good you've done."

"It never seems like enough. I feel like I'm chasing something just out of my reach. And I don't have a clue what it is."

"What you accomplished with these girls gives me plenty to think about."

The doctor wedged his long frame into the black BMW two-seater and leaned his head out the window. "It might be shadows you're chasing. Talk to your dad."

Miss Bernie and Jennie had been chatting on the porch during Dr. Mallory's visit. Jennie had been coming in the mornings to swim with the girls. After Jennie's rejection last Sunday, Mitch came up with excuses for not joining them.

* * *

At supper, Mitch told Miss Bernie and the others about Brother Williams' call that morning. He wanted to bring some school kids to the farm for the Fourth of July weekend next week. *The Boys and Girls Club of Milwaukee* provided tents and equipment for them to camp. The farm would be reimbursed for any expenses. Brother Williams said they'd like to come a few days early and help with any repairs or maintenance to show off the carpentry skills Mitch had taught them.

"So, what do you all think?" Mitch asked. "We could use some help around here. Maybe have them repaint the house and do some landscaping?"

"Jesus Christ, we'll have the whole goddamned ghetto here," Sid said. "What the hell are you thinking?"

Sid's bellowing had become background noise. Nobody listened.

"What about the rest of you?" Mitch said.

"It would be a blessing for those children to spend some time here," Miss Bernie said. "Most of 'em surely never seen a cow up close before."

Chris nodded enthusiastically. "I could have them help with milking." He raised his brow at Mitch. "Then I can give the orders instead of taking them from my bossy brother."

"And they can help me with the calves," Jasmine said.

Alexus raised her hand like she was in school asking a question. "How 'bout having them fix your tree fort? Then we can play in there."

"That's a great idea," Mitch said. "So it's decided. I'll call Brother Williams and tell him to go ahead."

Sid banged the table and pointed at Mitch. "When those hellions start shooting the place up, it'll be your damn fault. Probably get me shot or knifed in my own bed."

Miss Bernie rolled her eyes.

"Jeez, Dad, they're just kids," Chris said.

"Yeah, we'll see."

* * *

Mitch organized lumber, roofing, and windows at the foot of the oak tree to rebuild the treehouse. His friends, the Bunzell brothers, volunteered to help. Their family had been in the construction business for generations. They'd set up two hydraulic platforms, so the students wouldn't have to work off ladders. Mitch purchased paint for the house. Chris took Miss Bernie to the garden center to select plants, trees, and shrubs for the yard.

The day before the kids were to arrive, Chris took Miss Bernie into town to stock up on food and drinks. There'd be fifteen children along with Brother Williams and two adult supervisors from the *Boys and Girls Club*. She'd be feeding eighteen of them plus the girls, the Bunzell brothers, and the Garners. When they got back, it didn't take long for the old farmhouse to fill with the smell of baking apples, cinnamon, and butter from the apple pies along with the rich smell of chocolate from chocolate chip cookies Alexus was baking.

At breakfast the next morning, Miss Bernie bounced around the kitchen, checking the pantry and moving her pots and pans from counter to counter.

Mitch watched in amusement. "Is it just the kids you're excited to cook for?"

"Wanted to church it up for their first day here." The guilty look didn't match her words. He knew who she wanted to impress. She hadn't seen him since they left Milwaukee.

Mitch grinned to himself. He was excited too. This is what he needed to take his mind off Jennie. Sid watched all the activity with interest and kept his mouth shut. He had learned the hard way that he wouldn't get any pie or cookies if he crossed Miss Bernie.

Mitch stepped onto the porch to see what Billy was barking about. A yellow school bus with bright green bundles strapped to the top inched toward the house.

"Miss Bernie, they're here."

"Oh, Lord, I surely ain't ready."

Everyone but Sid went to meet the bus. Sid watched from the porch, leaning on his walker.

The folding bus door slammed open. The top of a shiny black bald head poked under the low opening. Brother Williams bounded down the metal steps, his overbite stretched in a broad grin. Excited children, most around Jasmine's age, streamed out behind him. Mitch recognized two younger ones from the tutoring group at the firehouse, Alexus's friend Elan, and Spiked Hair's daughter, Peaches.

Brother Williams went straight to Miss Bernie and they embraced. She stepped back and examined his baggy jeans and short sleeve denim shirt. "You sure a sight."

"Come here to work, not preach."

"Looking a bit spare. Best be ready to eat."

"You know that. You're looking fine, though."

"Just hush now."

Brother Williams faced Mitch. "Thanks for making this possible, my brother."

Alexus ran at them. Brother Williams hoisted her to his chest. She hugged his neck. "Now that's what I'm talking about," he said and kissed her cheek. "Where's your sister?"

Alexus pointed. "Over there next to my dog."

The noisy crowd of kids scurried past them toward the barnyard with two young female chaperones trailing. The cows were chomping dry feed and slurping water from the metal troughs. As the onslaught of kids charged the fence, the cows scattered in a cloud of dust.

Brother Williams carried Alexus to Jasmine and put her down. Brother Williams kneeled and glanced at Jasmine's uncovered neck, no longer wrapped in the Kente scarf. "Now that's one fine necklace."

Jasmine pinched the gleaming white gold necklace. "I love it."

"And look at you," Brother Williams said. "You're growing into such a radiant young woman. I pray you can help tutor again when school starts. You're a gifted teacher."

Jasmine's face glowed.

Sid observed all the commotion from the porch, leaning on his walker.

"That your dad?" Brother Williams asked Mitch.

"Afraid so. I'm not sure how he's going to..."

Brother Williams rushed to the porch and up the stairs. "Mister Garner. I want to thank you for allowing us to impose on your good will. You have a magnificent farm."

Sid craned his neck, gawking up at Brother Williams. Mitch wondered how many people assumed him to be an intimidating, violent man; someone to fear. Brother Williams reached out to Sid who lifted his hand as if in a trance. They shook.

Chris moved alongside Mitch and said, "No way."

"I've come to know your son well and must say, he's been a savior and a blessing." Brother Williams released Sid's hand. "Any complaints while we're here, you let me know. These students came here to help with your farm, not bother you."

Sid stood speechless, his hand still open from the shake.

The porch steps creaked under Brother Williams' heft as he ambled down to Mitch. "Where you want the tents?"

"Anywhere on that side of the house. My dad's room is on the other side."

"One more thing, Mitch." Brother Williams turned solemn. "Come on over to the bus."

He had Mitch wait while he went inside. He came back holding a green and gold football jersey with the large "80" on it. "We were planning on Kyle coming along. I know how you loved that boy, we all did." Brother Williams handed him the jersey. "The good Lord called our little Kyle home." He paused while Mitch soaked in the words, shaking his head violently.

Brother Williams gripped Mitch's shoulder. "Find peace in knowing you gave him joy while he was with us. He was a blessing for all of us, students and teachers alike. Although he couldn't respond in any physical ways, we all felt Kyle's spirit, and he lifted us." He paused. "That beautiful boy softened the hearts of students who had been hardened by the street. He taught us about selfless compassion and love. He was our teacher. Watching students take turns helping him so warmed my heart. This was God working through Kyle. I'm sure of it. Praise the Lord."

Mitch turned the soft jersey over in his hands.

"Roberta, the attendant over at the nursing home, said you should have his jersey."

Mitch's eyes blurred as he stared at the jersey, picturing Kyle's bright grin when he gave him that first one.

Chapter 56

The red vintage Massy Ferguson tractor chugged through the
moonlit back pasture, pulling a wagonload of squealing children
as they bounced on bales of hay. Cows bawled at them as they
wound through the herd, the evening air rich with the smell of manure
and ripening crops.

Mitch had promised them a hayride if they worked hard. After the
tents had gone up in the morning, the children were split into groups. One
group went with Mitch and the two Bunzell brothers to work on the treehouse, another with Brother Williams to start painting the farmhouse, and
another with Chris to help with chores and work on planting the nursery
stock around the yard. Jasmine showed the children in Chris's group how
to mix calf formula and feed them. The two chaperones volunteered to
help Miss Bernie prepare the noon meal of scalloped potatoes and ham
with fresh-baked buttermilk biscuits along with chilled pitchers of grape
Kool-Aid. Jennie came early to help Miss Bernie before taking Sid to therapy.

The crews took turns eating lunch. There were too many to eat at one
time. Mitch's crew was the last to come in. Brother Williams and Miss Bernie
went to work on the dirty dishes when they finished. On the way out, Mitch
spotted them through the kitchen window, standing side-by-side at the
sink, gazing at each other and snickering like a couple of giddy teenagers.

Alexus served as the tour guide on the evening hayride, going on and
on about everything she knew about the farm and property. Mitch got a
kick out of listening to this little girl lecture the older kids. She warned them
about Sid, saying he liked to holler a lot because his brain was sick.

Mitch took them to the pond where it sounded like a rainforest teeming
with croaking frogs and screeching night bugs. Alexus launched into the
story of Billy rescuing her from the deep water. With hand waving and

animated facial expressions, she painted a dramatic picture of her near drowning, ending with a stern warning to stay away from the pond.

They continued to the edge of the dark woods where Mitch turned the tractor off. The rustling leaves, chirping insects, and eerie shadows from the bright moon were the perfect setting for a scary story. He told them about an old hermit who lived way back in the woods many years ago and whose ghost had been seen wandering the woods at night. Eyes as wide as Miss Bernie's saucers peered at Mitch from the dark faces of the hushed children.

"Listen," Mitch whispered.

Mouths dropped.

Crashing sounds echoed through the woods, getting louder. Several children shouted, "Let's go."

A figure draped in black, burst from the woods, running toward the wagon, screeching. Alexus and her little friends laughed. The older children shrieked.

Chris threw off the sheet and laughed. "Got you guys."

Mitch had warned the young ones earlier so they wouldn't be terrified.

After a few moments of silence, the kids erupted, accusing each other of being scared. Chris jumped on the back of the tractor, and they headed to the house.

In the middle of the makeshift campground stood an eight-foot pile of wood, stacked like a teepee, reeking of kerosene. Mitch had the children form a wide circle around it. "Firefighters call fire the Red Devil because of the pain and destruction it can cause. Tonight the Red Devil will dance for us."

The fire erupted with a whoosh, the radiant heat forcing the children back while they hooted and hollered. After the kerosene burned off and the flaming pile of wood calmed, Brother Williams moved in front of the fire. "Mitch, come on over. We held a fundraiser at the church sponsored by our school. Our teachers planned it. We put a firefighting boot alongside Kyle's wheelchair so he could be a part of it. You should have seen how people lined up to put money in that boot. I think half your fire department turned out. These children all helped with the food and games."

All eyes were on Mitch, their shiny faces beaming in the firelight.

"Thought you had plenty of donations for the school," Mitch said.

"This was for you, for your farm. Kyle didn't have much of a chance at life, but these children here do, thanks to you. Our school would have been shut down if not for you. You saved our school. We wanted to help save your farm." Brother Williams handed Mitch a check. "This is from all of us at the school and our generous neighbors. And Kyle."

Mitch stared at the check in the orange, crackling glow of the fire, $8,654.25.

A few hand claps sounded, then more until everyone's hands were clapping together in thundering applause. Sid nodded at Mitch.

They spent the rest of the evening singing songs like *Old McDonald* where the children made up their own silly lyrics, howling with laughter. Chris kept busy helping make s'mores and pudgy pies over the fire. As the evening wore on, Mitch made his way around the dying fire, thanking every child.

Alexus, Peaches, and Elan chatted off to the side, away from the older kids. Alexus was doing most of the chatting. When he got to them, Peaches handed him an envelope and said, "My daddy say to give you this. He say to thank you."

Mitch opened the wrinkled envelope and unfolded the note. In the dim light of the dying embers, he read, *"DeAndre back. Stay away."*

Chapter 57

Chris banged pots and pans by the tents. It was still dark. Cows don't wait for the sun to come up for milking and neither would they. The groups rotated activities each day so that by Saturday they'd all have a chance to help with the different projects and all have the wonderful opportunity to see the sun come up. The treehouse crew and painting crew were allowed to sleep in until breakfast, but most were milling around well before. Brother Williams had to rein the kids in occasionally when they got loud and rambunctious.

The crews worked to exhaustion on Thursday, determined to finish the landscaping and painting. Friday morning, the Fourth of July, they all pitched in to complete the treehouse. The Bunzell brothers helped put the finishing touches on it and headed home to celebrate the Fourth with their families.

Mitch and Brother Williams stood on the elevated platform in the shade of the giant oak tree's broad canopy. They watched the children chase each other through the woods, the boys hiding behind trees and chucking pine cones at each other. Chris was in the middle of all the commotion, laughing and hollering right along with the children.

"That's the same stuff we did with our friends," Mitch said. "Chris had a pretty good arm. I still have marks."

Brother Williams nodded. "Pine cones better than bullets."

Miss Bernie pulled up in the Gator with Sid next to her.

"Now that's a sight," Brother Williams said.

"She's all over the farm with it. And she's been hauling Dad along. He bellyaches about her driving but goes along."

"Will miracles never cease?"

Brother Williams banged a hammer on the steel rail. "Everyone, come on over."

Miss Bernie and Sid stayed in the Gator while the kids ran to the tree, shouting and laughing. Brother Williams pounded the hammer on the steel rail again. They went quiet.

"Mitch, I don't know how many times I've thanked you." Brother Williams' deep voice resonated through the woods. "I can assure you, not enough. What you did for these children will go on changing lives." He stretched his open palm toward the children below. "As these children grow and raise their families and help others in our community overcome their own challenges, the good you did will live on."

Mitch's face blazed with embarrassment.

Brother Williams continued, "Since I don't want to bore everyone here with a sermon I'll resist the urge, unless of course, these children demand one."

"Nooo," echoed off the trees and thick brush.

Brother Williams grinned and gave Mitch a small slab of cedar siding and the hammer. "This glorious edifice was created by the love of every one of these blessed children. Our hope is that you will find peace here and feel their loving embrace. Now complete it with this last piece of siding."

Mitch's old treehouse was pretty elaborate, but this was like a cottage in the sky with cedar shake siding and shingles, windows on all sides, a skylight, and finished interior walls, three painted light purple and one left white.

He drove the last nail through the slab of siding and the children went wild, clapping and cheering. Once Mitch cleared the dry lump in his throat, he waved at the children, quieting the loud ovation. "You all know, I'm not much of a talker. Miss Bernie can tell you that." Laughter rippled through the children. Miss Bernie waved her finger at him. "Anyway, you guys taught me more than I ever taught you. Working with you has changed my life. It took a while for this to sink in because, well, some say I'm pretty hard-headed. Just ask my brother." Mitch grinned down at Chris.

"Only one with a harder head is the one in the Gator over there," Chris said, nodding toward Sid. "Right, Dad?"

Sid's face tightened. "Damn right."

"You guys did a super job," Mitch said. "Now I have a surprise for all of you this afternoon."

* * *

They all gathered in the barnyard after lunch. From the roadway came the rumble of what sounded like semi-trucks climbing the other side of the hill. Two gray diesel pickup trucks hauling twenty-foot aluminum horse trailers crested the hill and turned into the drive.

Mitch and Chris greeted the three Kiekafer girls and helped unload eight sleepy quarter horses and a spirited thoroughbred. Mitch had arranged for the Kiekafers to bring their horses over for the afternoon so everyone would have a chance to ride. Mitch introduced them to the children and explained they would be giving riding lessons. Once the children got checked out they'd get to go on a trail ride, one group at a time.

Mitch and Chris went to the barn to put up hay while the Kiekafers worked with the excited, but squeamish children. When Mitch and Chris finished in the barn and returned, the air was thick with swirling dust as the Kiekafers walked the horses and young riders around the barnyard. Every child's face was plastered with a wide smile as they bounced across the yard. Mitch spotted a white van parked down the drive with *UW Health* printed in red letters on the side. The red Camry was parked behind it, sparking hope he'd have some time to talk with Jennie today. He *had* to tell her how he felt. If she loved this Jason, he'd have to accept that. But not until they stopped playing games and got everything out in the open.

Dr. Mallory was at the fence dressed in jeans and a white polo shirt. Alongside him were two shorter, well-groomed men dressed in business suits.

"Happy Fourth," Dr. Mallory said when Mitch approached. "Hope you don't mind us dropping in. These are two colleagues of mine."

"You came out on a holiday?"

"I told them about Jasmine." The two doctors shook Mitch's hand while Dr. Mallory continued. "We're not used to seeing this kind of drastic improvement in children suffering from PTSD."

"Hey, Mitch," the oldest Kiekafer girl shouted from across the barnyard. "I'd like to see what Jasmine can do on Durango. That okay?"

"Have at it."

She shot him a thumbs up and helped Jasmine into the English saddle of her glistening dark brown thoroughbred show horse. Jasmine worked the athletic horse in crisp figure eights, her long braids bouncing off her shoulders. Jasmine's soft posture, focused expression, and command of the horse radiated confidence and pride. The doctors grinned at each other as if they had discovered the cure for cancer.

Jennie trotted down the porch steps and headed toward them. Mitch swallowed hard. Now or never. He took a step toward her and stopped as Jason emerged from the porch.

"What's her fucking boyfriend doing here?" Mitch said through clenched teeth.

All three doctors' heads snapped around.

"You mean her fiancé?" Doctor Mallory asked.

Fiancé. The sliver of hope gone in a single word.

The two doctors focused their attention back on the children and horses.

Dr. Mallory studied Mitch. "Sorry, I didn't realize..."

Jennie and Jason came toward them.

"I got work to do." Mitch spun, grinding his boots into the gravel and headed to the barn.

Inside the barn, he looked for anything to throw.

"Lose something?" Jennie said from behind him.

He whirled. "Why didn't you tell me?"

"How'd you know?"

"Mallory."

"I wanted to tell you myself."

"You have to bring *him*?"

She closed the gap between them. "Thought it was time for Jason to meet everyone."

"I'm not interested."

"So, we can't be friends?"

"Do you love him?"

"I don't know why you're so pissed." Her voice rose. "You're the one who pushed me away and left, remember?"

"You don't know what I was going through."

"How could I?" She jabbed him in the chest. "I waited for your calls, wanting so bad to hear you missed me and were coming home for the weekend. But no. When you did call, it was always an excuse about why you couldn't. How was that supposed to make me feel?"

"You know how shitty it feels to hear you're getting...?"

"Oh, really? What about when I came to the hospital and saw your gorgeous girlfriend at your bedside? I can't compete with that." Tears formed at the edges of her eyes. "So, yeah, I know what shitty feels like."

"I'm not seeing her."

"Took me a while to realize there was no future for us. My life is here and yours is in Milwaukee." Her voice softened as she reached for him. "Can't we stay friends, please?"

Mitch stepped back, pushing her away. "You never answered, do you love him?"

"You haven't changed." She bolted out of the barn.

I have changed.

Chapter 58

The yellow bus inched down the long drive. Smiling faces and waving arms crowded the open windows. Mitch, Chris, Miss Bernie, and the girls waved back from the top of the drive with Sid watching from the porch. The shouts of the children faded as the bus turned onto the road and shifted through the gears.

Once the bus disappeared from sight, Miss Bernie and the girls went to the house, Chris went to the barn, and Sid settled into a wicker chair on the porch. Stillness blanketed the reborn Garner farmstead. The house had a fresh coat of white paint and was surrounded again by lilac bushes. Red maple saplings dotted the lawn along with clusters of white hydrangeas, yellow forsythia, and red azaleas neatly arranged by Miss Bernie. And there was the treehouse. All of this at the hands of a group of inner-city children. Mitch should be feeling good, but he couldn't shake the brewing melancholy. *Jason. Her man. Her fiancé.*

Mitch headed to the treehouse. Brother Williams promised it would bring him joy but didn't want him going inside until after the children were gone.

The smell of fresh-cut wood and drying latex paint flowed from the trap door entrance as it slammed open. Mitch saw why Brother Williams insisted part of an inside wall be left white. Inscriptions in phosphorescent reds, greens, and blues were scrawled across it in all directions.

Thank you for letting us come to your farm. I really liked it. Especially the horses. Love Brandon.

I hop we can com bak. I luv your farm. Luv Elan

You the bomb. I Luv you. Peaches

Can I come back and ride horses again? That was fun. Love May.

I want to be a farmer. Can I work on your farm? I will work real hard. Love Gordon.

Mitch's misty eyes were drawn to the perfect blue script at the top corner. *I'm sorry for being so evil when you first came around. I was foul. I can't believe you didn't give up on me. Thank you for making me feel like I'm not so bad. Love Jasmine.*

"I love you too, little girl."

Right below Jasmine's note, written in red was: *Wish you were my daddy. Love Lexi.*

At the very bottom in bright green was: *Thank you, Mitch Garner. You are our savior. May the blessed peace of the Lord always be yours. Love, Clarence Williams.*

Brother Williams was right, he did feel the joy of their loving embrace up here.

Mitch read the inscriptions over and over again, picturing the faces of the beaming children. He decided this treehouse should be a place to remember, not like when his mom died and he went to the treehouse to forget, to escape guilt and pain. Trying to forget never brought him one second of peace. He went back to the house, lifted by the words scrawled on the white wall.

Music blared from the kitchen doorway. Mitch stepped inside to a chorus of *(I Can't Get No) Satisfaction* coming from Sid's CD player on top of the refrigerator. Miss Bernie and the girls danced around the kitchen gyrating their hips, singing along. Miss Bernie was working it. Sid was at the table tapping his foot.

"C'mon, Mitch. We need a man in here dancing with us," Miss Bernie said.

Jasmine snickered and said, "I've seen him dance. It isn't pretty."

"Oh, yeah? Watch this." Mitch sashayed over to them and broke into moves he had seen the kids doing at the campsite. His rhythm was off by half a beat. Miss Bernie and the girls hooted.

When the song ended, Miss Bernie took a seat at the table, huffing and puffing. Mick Jagger launched into *Wild Horses* with Jasmine and Alexus swaying to the smooth lyrics. Mitch had heard the song before, but today the words jarred him. Wild horses should not have been able to pull him away from Jennie. Now it was too late. She was getting married.

Mitch joined Miss Bernie and Sid at the table. They watched the girls move around the kitchen, Alexus copying her older sister's rhythmic moves.

"Mitch, you ain't believing this." Miss Bernie said. "Me and that old geezer finally got something in common."

Sid slapped at the air.

"I found his pile of CDs. Turns out we both love this old music," she said. "Ain't that right, old man?"

Sid scowled at her. "You ain't much younger than me, you old biddy."

"Oh, smooth your feathers." She laughed.

This sounded like the banter around the firehouse table.

Miss Bernie winked at Mitch. "He ain't happy I told him all this rock and roll come from blacks. People like John Lee Hooker were playing rock and roll long before Elvis come along. And old John Lee Hooker got his music from slaves."

"That's a bunch of crap," Sid said.

"Next time I come back, I'll have some of that old black music with me. Then tell me if that ain't rock and roll."

"Can't I listen in peace without your jabbering?"

Miss Bernie smirked. "He knows I'm right."

Mitch smiled to himself. Yes, Sid had met his match.

* * *

Sunday after church and another gut-busting feast, Mitch was drawn to the closet in his bedroom. He had avoided opening it since coming back. The first thing he saw was the sweat-stained John Deere hat, the one he planted on Lydia Hillenbrand's head the day her sister died in the fire. Behind the hat was the blackened fire helmet he wore that day, still reeking of smoke, bringing back his desperate attempt to save Maggie. Every second of that horrific afternoon played out in slow motion with agonizing clarity.

Mitch ran his hand over the coarse charred helmet. A flash of white light exploded in his head as if lightning had struck inches from him. He gasped as pure bliss filled his entire being. There was no way he could have gotten to Maggie through that intense heat with no breathing apparatus. It wasn't his fault Maggie died in that fire. The charred helmet removed any doubt. If he didn't back out when he did, he would have died too. He wasn't a coward. Never was.

He thought back to the fun he and Maggie had together, the joy they brought each other. He could see her beaming face while riding old Bert.

That's what he'd remember, not her soot-darkened face he woke to every day since her death.

Mitch's mind, unshackled of guilt, spun with thoughts and images of the last year: helping to save and rebuild the school, the rescue of Nic and his crew, their farm rescued from foreclosure. Alexus and Jasmine. If he had died in that fire with Maggie…

He had been absolutely sure it was his fault Maggie died and he was absolutely wrong. Like Crusher said, "Assumptions will bite you in the ass."

He rummaged through the closet and found the trophy for winning the Wisconsin State High School Wrestling Championship, the blue ribbon for his prize Holstein at the Jefferson County Fair, and a folder of photos.

He dug through family pictures he hadn't seen since before his mom died. He was shocked by how much he had grown to look like her with her jet black hair, dark eyes, olive complexion, and smooth jawline. In almost every photo he noticed her strained smile.

He found pictures from prom. He stared at the photo of him and Jennie kissing and felt the warmth and softness of her lips. In one photo she was staring at him as if he were the most fascinating person in the world.

Mitch loaded the Gator and drove out to the treehouse. He hung the pictures on the walls along with the John Deere hat and fire helmet. The trophies went on the bookcase the children had built. Yes, this is where he'd come to remember, not forget. And to face painful memories, deal with them, let them go, and focus on the good ones.

Back at the house for another load, he took the charred copy of *A Tree Grows in Brooklyn* from the bed stand and opened it to the last page. *Mitch, when you finish reading this let me know what you liked about it. Love, Mom.*

He closed the book and held it to his forehead. *I love you too.*

The Temptations were singing *My Girl* as he trudged down the steps. Miss Bernie and Jasmine bumped hips to the music while rolling out pie crusts.

"Jasmine, you need to see this," Mitch said.

He set the book in front of her. She opened it, the edges of each page darkened with soot. "I love that book."

"Why's it all burned?" Miss Bernie asked.

"It was in my old treehouse when it burned in the fire. That's where me and my mom would go to read and talk about books." Mitch paused as the memory played in his mind. "We spent a lot of time up there together. "

Jasmine's eyes widened. "Your tree, Mitch. It's like the Heaven Tree in the book."

Miss Bernie folded her hands. "Don't know nothing about Heaven Trees, but my daddy told me about a tree momma loved. A big old oak like yours, Mitch. Daddy said they'd set under that tree after chores was done and talk till bedtime. Told me, after she died, he'd set under that old tree and talk to her." She smiled to herself. "He said her spirit lived on in that tree. Said when people die, their spirit don't go in the ground. It's in the alive things they loved and left behind."

Miss Bernie went quiet. Mitch figured she was thinking about her father and the mother she never knew. Miss Bernie's eyebrows shot up. "Mitch, your momma's spirit in that tree. That's why it refuse to die in that awful fire."

"I believe you're right. Your dad sounds like he was a wise man."

She nodded. "Your daddy wise too in his own stubborn way. He's out on the porch taking a snooze. Worked him hard this morning. He fights ever inch of the way, but he won't be needing that walker by the time we go back."

"How's your back holding up?"

"Don't worry about me none. Brother Williams got one of them bone crackers for me when I get back. He swears by 'em."

"Would you see where Billy is?" Mitch asked Jasmine. "I haven't seen him in a while."

When he heard the screen door slam behind her, he said, "Miss Bernie, DeAndre's back."

"Don't make no matter to me. Got no time for hate. Only feeds the devil."

"Why didn't they lock him up?"

"Brother Williams heard they couldn't find any witnesses. Had to drop the case."

"What about what I told them?"

"You got to let it be."

Jasmine burst into the kitchen. "Mitch, it's Billy. He's laying by the barn. Hurry." She ran out. When he found them, Jasmine was on her knees next to the prone dog. Billy's breathing was labored and eyes clouded. Jasmine buried her face in the dog's thick neck.

"Let's get him back to the porch," Mitch whispered.

He carried the limp dog to the house. Jasmine ran up the porch stairs in front of him. Sid rose from the wicker chair. "He don't look so good."

"He's dying, isn't he," Jasmine said.

Mitch lowered the sick dog onto his porch blanket. Jasmine lay down next to him.

Billy gave her a feeble lick on the face, struggling to breathe.

"He'll be okay," Sid said softly to Jasmine. "Probably got into some raccoon crap."

Sid patted Jasmine's head. "We'll get the vet out here tomorrow. Be hard to find him today."

"He'll be fine," Mitch said, feeling guilty about lying to her. Billy had been with them for over fourteen years, ancient for a lab.

* * *

Mitch stayed on the porch with Jasmine until it was time for chores. "Come get me if he...if anything changes."

Jasmine didn't reply.

God, he'd miss that dog. And Jasmine? How was she going to take it? Billy rarely left her side.

Jasmine stayed on the porch through supper. Billy held on and Jasmine refused to leave him. Mitch brought Jasmine a plate of fried hamburger patties to try to feed him. He sensed she wanted to be alone with him, so Mitch peeked in from time to time to check on them. The hamburger patties remained untouched.

Mitch and Miss Bernie watched the late news together in the front room that no longer smelled like a musty locker room. It smelled of fresh linen with a touch of lavender. Miss Bernie had transformed the smelly old farmhouse into a warm, cozy home. She even had Sid's upstairs bedroom smelling fresh.

"Mitch, I know it hurts, but look what that glorious dog did, lifting our Jasmine out of her misery. That was surely the good Lord working through him and if the good Lord is calling him home, well God bless him."

"He was a good dog," Mitch said solemnly. "Think I'll go check on them."

Before he got to the porch, he heard Jasmine. "You can't die. I won't let you. Mitch is sad too much and I don't know how to help him. I love him more than I ever love my own daddy. So don't you go dying, you hear?"

Mitch coughed a few times before stepping onto the porch. "Jasmine, it's getting late, better come in."

"I'm sleeping out here."

"He'll like that. I'll get you some blankets."

* * *

Mitch rose before dawn. It was his turn to start in on milking. He headed to the porch, dreading what he'd see.

The empty blanket lay crumpled on the rough decking. The plate with the hamburger patties was empty except for a layer of cream-colored congealed grease.

The mercury vapor yard light cast a stark whiteness over the barnyard, the air thick with dew. Jasmine was nowhere to be seen, and there were no lights on in the hay barn or milking parlor. He went for the Gator and stopped when he saw the light in the calf barn. He raced across the barnyard.

Inside the barn, Jasmine was mixing calf formula. At her side, stood Billy with the Kente scarf neatly draped around his neck.

Mitch knelt and stroked Billy's head while the dog licked his face. "How the heck ..."

Jasmine pointed at the scarf.

"Holy crap. Really? The scarf?"

"You love him a lot, don't you?" Jasmine asked.

"What about you?"

"Yeah, he's not so bad."

She went back to mixing calf formula. "These calves begging to be fed. Us farmers never get any rest." They both laughed.

With Billy okay and her giggles filling the small barn, Mitch felt like dancing. "I saw what you wrote in the treehouse."

Jasmine kept mixing the milky liquid with a slight smile.

"If I ever have a daughter, I want her to be just like you."

"Guess you'll be marrying a sister."

Mitch chuckled. "Maybe she could teach me to dance."

"What's with your daddy?"

"What'd he do now?"

"Yesterday he talked all nice and patted my head. He pretending to like me?"

292

"Dad don't pretend."

Jasmine went back to feeding calves, and Mitch headed to the milking parlor.

Mitch cut hay after milking and got back to the house well after breakfast. He stepped into the kitchen. Alexus was next to Sid, holding a whiteboard and going through the alphabet, demanding he repeat each letter. Mitch watched for a while and when they got through the alphabet, Alexus said, "You doing real good. Now let's work on your name."

Mitch went to Miss Bernie at the sink and whispered, "What's going on?"

"Miss Jennie said we need to help the old man learn how to read and write again. The stroke took that away. Lexi's the only one has time, so that's her job."

Mitch grinned. "This is too good."

"No, a big *S* not a small one," Alexus said sternly to Sid, taking the red marker from him. "Here, like this." She wrote *Sid* on the whiteboard. "See? Big *S*, small *i*, small *d*. Now you try."

Sid shook his head. "Can't believe I'm being ordered around by a kid."

Miss Bernie wagged her finger. "That child smarter than all of us. Jasmine had her reading and writing before she was three. Best listen to her."

"This is embarrassing," Sid said.

Miss Bernie smirked. "No more than not being able to write your own name. Might want to close your yap and let her teach you something."

Sid slapped at the air. "Aach. Never let up do you, old woman?"

"See, I'm teaching him just like you teach us at the firehouse," Alexus said to Mitch.

She handed the red marker to Sid, "Now you write your name like I wrote it."

And he did.

Chapter 59

Mitch trekked to the treehouse after supper. He covered the floor with family photos of his mom. Under the luminescent light of the Coleman lantern, he studied every photo, trying to peer back through the years for the faintest clue. Anything.

What made you do it?

Was she struggling with the same feelings of hopelessness and self-hatred that pushed him to the edge of suicide? What could have been so bad? She didn't have to deal with a little girl's horrific death or burning the farmland or with her own mother's suicide.

The photos revealed nothing but her melancholy eyes. He settled into the wooden rocker Brother Williams brought along as a treehouse-warming gift. He rocked for hours waiting for an answer, listening to the loud chirping and screeching of night bugs.

Mom. Why?

When he rose to leave, he took one last look across the photos on the floor. "I hope you're proud of me."

He plodded back to the farmhouse and up the porch steps. Billy opened his drowsy eyes and rose from the blanket. Mitch motioned for him to stay.

The only sound in the house was wall-rattling snoring coming from Sid's room. Mitch cracked the door. Dim yellow light from the front room washed over Sid. Mitch opened it wider. It creaked. Sid jerked awake. "What the hell?"

"We need to talk."

"We losing the farm?"

"I want to talk about Mom."

"I don't."

"Just listen then." Mitch pulled a chair next to the bed. "I can't get over what Mom said to me, that she wished I was never born. It wasn't long after that she killed herself. I keep hearing her say that over and over. I can't stop it. Was I the reason?"

Sid winced.

"Dad, was that it, the reason?"

Sid rubbed his forehead. His speech was slow and slurred. "You blamed...yourself? What the hell did I do?" He choked, struggling to get the words out. "I should...have told you."

"Told me what?"

"Get the lockbox. From my closet."

Mitch brought the gray metal box to him. Sid's fingers shook as he spun the dial of the combination lock. After three tries he shoved it at Mitch. "Open the damn thing. Combination's taped to the bottom."

Inside was a sheet of purple-tinted stationery Mitch's mother used for letter writing. Sid pulled it from the box, examined it, and handed it to Mitch. "Time you knew."

Mitch clicked on the bedside lamp. Sid had the ashen pallor of a cadaver. "Dad, you okay?"

"Just read."

Sidwell.

You must hate me for doing this, but I can't fight anymore. It's not your fault. You've been there through all of this with me, so you have to know how hard I've tried. I really have. I just can't fight it any longer. It's become unbearable, and I find myself lashing out at Mitch. He's such a wonderful boy and doesn't deserve any of this. I've become helpless against this monster inside me that makes me say these terrible things. I don't understand it and hate myself. I love Mitch so much. I can't allow myself to inflict my pain on him anymore.

You're a good man. I wish I could have returned your love. You deserve to have a wife who loves you. I wish it could have been me but it wasn't. I don't know why. Life makes no sense.

I'm so, so sorry to leave you with the boys to raise alone. You will all be better off with me gone. I pray you find happiness again. You deserve it.

Please take good care of the boys. I know you will. You've always been a good father. Raising Mitch as your own was a true act of grace.

I beg you to find it in your heart to forgive me,
Sylvia

Mitch couldn't take his eyes off those words. *As your own?* "Dad?"

"Can you ever...forgive me?"

"Forgive you for what? I don't get it. You're my dad."

Sid propped himself against the solid walnut headboard. "If anyone's to blame, it's me." He ran his hand over his bald head. He continued in short, halting phrases. "I didn't know how, to make her happy, and I hated myself."

"I don't get it."

"Goddammit. I keep, losing the words. Fucking stroke." He took the suicide note from Mitch and stared at it. "We were together almost every day, all through grade school, and through middle school. Kinda like you and Jennie, when you were kids."

Me and Jen.

"Why did you, let her go, Mitch?"

"I'm an idiot."

"What the hell, was I saying?"

"You and mom were close friends growing up."

"Your grandma called us two peas in a pod." The faraway look on Sid's face was the same look he got when looking across a pasture for a stray. "She lost interest in me. In high school." Sid leaned back against the headboard. His head twitched like he was trying to clear the cobwebs. The words came slower. "It killed me, to see her, with other guys. I acted like it was okay, so we could stay friends. She came to me, for guy advice. We'd talk, for hours." His eyelids sagged. "She was so damn beautiful, Mitch."

Mitch nodded and waited for him to continue, stunned.

Sid pushed tighter against the headboard. "After high school, Sylvia started hanging around some bikers, in Madison, the Crusaders. She'd tell me about the wild parties." He paused again, staring at the ceiling like he was waiting for the words to drift down. "I hoped, this was something she needed, to get out of her system. Then she fell in love, with a guy called Drifter. He's all she talked about." Sid's chest heaved. "She always told me, what a good friend, I was. It was damn hard, trying to act, happy for her. I wanted to stay in her life, so I never told her, how I felt."

Mitch shuddered. "Is he my...?"

"The bastard knocked her up and took off. She came to me and I held her, while she cried and cried." Sid struggled to breathe, wheezing with each breath. "God, that felt good, holding her like that."

"Dad, it's okay. We can stop."

"I gotta get this out. Sylvia, was gonna run away. Couldn't face her dad."

The memories played across Sid's face while he fought for enough breath to continue. Mitch had a million questions but didn't dare push. His emotions were a jumble of shock and pity. Why didn't Sid just tell her how he felt? But then why didn't Mitch tell Jennie how *he* felt?

"I asked her if she'd marry me. Promised, to raise this kid as my own. Nobody'd ever know any different. I knew, I could get her, to love me." A lopsided smile crossed his lips. "After all, who could resist a prize, like me, eh? When she said yes, I couldn't believe it."

Sid broke down and wept in wracking sobs. Mitch didn't know how to comfort him. He patted Sid's folded hands and waited.

"After Chris was born, she got real depressed. The doctor called it, some kind of blues, from having a baby. But this, this wasn't no blues. She couldn't hardly, get out of bed." His face glistened with sweat. "You remember her sister, came to stay with us to help?"

"I do remember. When you let me see Mom, she didn't act right, and it scared the crap out of me."

"She never got better. At least, for long. I tried hard, to make her happy. She went through all kinds of therapies. Some worked, for a while, but none lasted. After she died, Ben Rosenberg told me, suicide runs in her family. Nobody ever talked about it." He pointed a trembling finger at Mitch. "It had nothing, to do with you."

"Or you."

"I was her husband. I should have known, how to help her."

"That's not how it works."

Sid stared at the wall, his chest heaving, while Mitch grappled with his emotions, trying to make sense of it all. "So all these years we both thought it was our fault—Damn."

Sid frowned. "I figured, you hated me, for letting her die."

"And I figured you hated *me*."

Sid lowered his head. "When she left me—us—like that, I *did* hate her. I was so, damn pissed. As you got older, you started looking and talking, even walking, like her." Sid's voice trailed off. "Every time, I looked at you, I saw her." He sucked in a deep breath. "Most everything you did, set me off. And when you left, for Milwaukee, I blew. It felt, like you were leaving me, just like she did." He shook his head. "I hated myself, for the way I treated you." He paused, gasping for breath. "I know this don't make a lot of sense. You didn't, deserve any of that. My God, Mitch, I'm so damn sorry."

Mitch was surprised by the relief swelling in his chest. He should be enraged, but he wasn't. Sid didn't hate him. Never did. "Do you still hate her?"

Sid's eyes closed as he searched for words. "Nobody else, has ever seen that note." He opened his eyes. "That shrink, Mallory's, been talking to me, after my therapies." He frowned. "You know the sly bastard, started by asking questions, about the farm, and before I knew it, got me talking about Sylvia." He sighed. "I don't hate her, and don't see her face, anymore, when I look at you. Just a man, I'd be damn proud, to call son. But I don't deserve that."

The bedroom went quiet, Sid's raspy breathing the only sound. Mitch thought back to when he was a young boy and all the time Sid spent with him, teaching him farming and hunting. Sid hugged him a lot back then. He *was* a good and loving father, before his mom died.

Mitch didn't like the sound of Sid's wheezing. "I should take you in. You don't sound so good."

"I looked your father up, long time ago." Sid pulled a scrap of paper from the lockbox and handed it to him.

Instead of taking it, Mitch went to the kitchen and got a box of wooden farmer's matches. He took the scrap of paper from Sid and scraped a match along the emery side of the matchbox, sending a white plume of sulfur-laden smoke into the still air. He lit the corner of the paper and dropped it into a metal wastebasket. Sid's jaw dropped. Mitch took his mother's suicide note from Sid and lit that. "Nobody will ever see those because you're my dad." He dropped the burning purple stationery into the metal wastebasket. They watched the flame flare, then die, leaving a wisp of black ash. Fire had cleansed their guilt.

"We put Mom to rest once and for all."

His dad's breathing calmed.

Chapter 60

Mitch unloaded the last wagon of hay for the season and headed to the house for a cold glass of Miss Bernie's grape Kool-Aid. From the porch, he heard a car pull into their drive. It was Dr. Mallory's black BMW. Mitch met him in the drive. "Ever think of getting something bigger?"

The doctor uncoiled himself from the tiny two-seater. "I have some exciting news."

"Okay?"

"Can we sit?"

Mitch motioned to the porch.

The old wicker chair creaked as Mitch plopped into it. "You look like you won the lottery."

Mallory lowered himself into the chair opposite him. "No, but you did."

"What the heck are you talking about?"

"Let me start from the beginning. At the UW we've been researching alternative forms of therapy for patients who don't respond to standard therapeutic approaches. There are some pilot programs around the country using animal therapy to break through the walls of chronically depressed and autistic patients. They're showing promising results."

Mallory bent forward. "Mitch, the hospital board voted this morning to create a pilot program using horses for therapy. My colleagues were very impressed when I brought them here to observe the inner-city kids. They were especially interested to hear about Jasmine and her amazing recovery."

"Sounds great."

"They want to use your farm for the program. If it goes well, they'd be building permanent facilities here. Psychologists and horse trainers would work together with the patients."

"I don't think my dad would go for that."

"Already spoke to him. He's all for it. You'd get a generous fee from the hospital for the use of a small parcel of your land and use of your facilities. None of this would interfere with the operation of the farm."

"Wish I was here to see it. Now that the farm is back on its feet, I'll be heading back to Milwaukee soon as I get the corn in."

"That'll be a problem. Your dad's come back nicely from the stroke, but the board is concerned about his ability to oversee the farm-side of the project. The board will only use your farm if you're here to manage things. "

Mitch rubbed his chin and leaned back in the hard chair. "Sorry, doc. I gotta get back to Milwaukee. I have kids depending on me. And fires to fight."

"I understand. I do." Dr. Mallory shrugged. "It's just that we'll have to put the project off until we can find another suitable farm. Yours happened to be the perfect fit. And you would have been a wonderful resource for our animal therapy center with your experiences with troubled children and your own depression." He exhaled slowly. "So how's your dad?"

"Yeah, I owe you. He's a changed man. We actually like each other now. He's in the parlor helping Chris with chores, thanks to Miss Bernie. That lady pushes him hard."

"Will you at least give this some thought before I report back to the board? You'd be part of something which will benefit hundreds of suffering children and their desperate families. If you could look into the broken eyes of these children, you'd see how important this work is. I know you'd find it rewarding." Dr. Mallory pushed his long frame from the low wicker chair. They shook and the doctor headed back to Madison.

Mitch lingered on the porch, thinking about what Dr. Mallory said. Miss Bernie was at the table when he went inside, her hands deep in a bowl of hamburger, eggs, breadcrumbs, and secret seasonings. Her fancy meatloaf, Sid's favorite.

"Where the girls at?" Mitch asked.

"Out at that swimming hole with your dog."

"Miss Bernie, if I decided to stay on the farm, would you and the girls think about staying too?"

She stopped mixing and wiped her hands on a towel. "Mitch, honey, why you ask such a thing?"

He told her of the plans for an animal therapy clinic, then added, "At first, I thought there was no way I could leave Milwaukee but if you and the girls stayed on, maybe I could. I don't know. The girls love it here and I think you do too."

"I do love this place, but it ain't my world. My old neighborhood is part of me, good and bad. I want to foster as many children down there as I can handle. Jasmine wants to help too. And she's itching to get back to helping kids at her school with their studies. She knows that's her gift."

"What do you think I should do?"

"You best do some praying. Let the good Lord guide you."

"No chance you would change your mind?"

"Clarence, Brother Williams, asked if he could call on me when I get back." She grinned like an embarrassed teenager. "He kind of young for me, but he's a good man. I made a terrible choice the first time but was blessed with two precious children, so I never regret that. Now they gone." She sighed. "Now I got these precious girls to raise up. Mitch, you want a good life you need love of friends, love of family, and love of someone to share it all with. Brother Williams told me that. Said if any one of these is missing, it's like one of those three-legged stools that can't stand on two legs. I've gone too long without that third leg."

"I should go back too. All those kids are relying on me."

"What you started down there ain't gonna stop if you stay here. Brother Williams will see to that."

Mitch thought for a while and said, "Be hard to leave the fire department. I have some great friends on the job."

"When you told me about your momma and that little girl you tried to save, I understood why you run from here. Now I don't know what went on with you and your daddy, but I saw you two come together this summer. It warmed my bones. Watching you farm this land, I can see it's in your blood. So why you want to run from here now?"

"I do love farming more than anything, but I couldn't stand not being there for Jasmine and Alexus and all the other kids."

"What about a wife and family?"

"I'll find somebody."

She pinched his chin. "You got somebody right here."

"Jen's got a man."

"You love her?"

"God, yes. But she's moved on."

"Let me tell you something. She never talk about her man when we out on that porch. You know who she talk about?" She pointed at his chin. "And when you out in that field working, she never took her eyes off you. I ain't tellin' you what to do, just want to make sure you seeing things clear. Didn't want to say nothing before. Don't like to meddle, but good Lord, Mitch, you must be blind. That girl loves you."

The words sucked the breath from him.

Chapter 61

After the early morning church service, Miss Bernie and the girls went to work in the kitchen, and the men went about chores. When they finished, Mitch followed Sid and Chris to the mudroom to wash up. Mitch opened the door to the kitchen and felt a rush of warm air, thick with the aroma of cinnamon, melted butter, baking bread, bacon, and roasting meat.

The men stood in awe of what they saw: Sid's favorite meatloaf, the girls' favorite scalloped potatoes and ham, Mitch and Chris's favorite fried chicken, along with potatoes fried in bacon fat, buttermilk biscuits, and a steaming bowl of greens with bacon. In the middle of the table was a sweating pitcher of grape Kool-Aid. And for dessert, Miss Bernie's sweet potato pie with whipped cream made fresh from the morning milking. Miss Bernie and the girls had churched it up good for their last day on the farm. School would be starting next week, the day after Labor Day.

Billy waited beside Jasmine, his tongue dripping while they said grace.

There was no chatting while they ate, just clinking of silverware on plates and a few restrained belches from the men.

* * *

The van was packed for the drive to Milwaukee. Miss Bernie kept rearranging pots and pans, glancing around the kitchen like she lost something. The others waited at the table for her to announce she was ready.

She folded her arms and said, "Guess it's time. Which one of you men gonna hug me before I start in on blubbering."

Mitch and Chris went to her together for a three-way embrace. When they finally let go, Miss Bernie leaned back with a single tear track down the left side of her face. "You boys take care of that old man there. He ain't so tough as he thinks."

They all laughed and turned to Sid. He scowled. "Aach. At least I won't have to listen to your nagging anymore."

She reached her arms out. "You ready to hug an old black lady? Or you still think we the devil?"

Sid grinned, the droop gone. "Guess you ain't such a bad one, even if you did work me like a rented mule." He stood and allowed her to embrace him. Mitch and Chris gawked at each other.

Miss Bernie pushed Sid toward the girls. "Might want to thank them if you can bring yourself to thank three blacks in one day. Don't want your head to explode."

Sid grinned. "Never stop, do you?"

He took Jasmine's hand from her side and shook it. "Sorry we got off to such a bad start." He patted her shoulder.

Jasmine raised her brows. "Suppose you aren't such a bad one."

Mitch held back a snicker.

Alexus moved in front of Sid. "You doing real good with your words, but I can't help you no more. So you best keep working."

Sid hoisted her and pecked her cheek. "Come back and check on me, won't you?"

* * *

After a quiet ride to Milwaukee, they unloaded the van. While Miss Bernie and the girls were putting their things away, Mitch slipped out the door. He wasn't ready for any more goodbyes. Besides, he'd be coming back regularly to help out.

Before he got to the van, he looked back at the purple house, stirring images of him and Jamal drinking beer and talking about girls and the fire department on that porch. His thoughts turned to Miss Bernie and the lectures that steered him toward helping inner-city kids and away from his inner struggles.

He headed to the firehouse. Before turning into the back lot, he paused in front of the overgrown field where Jasmine's house once stood. He thought back to the first encounter with an angry, combative Jasmine and all that happened since. He let the memories run their course instead of fighting them. He no longer feared sad thoughts. In the words of Dr. Mallory, "Thoughts are like leaves on a stream. Acknowledge them and let them drift by."

The aluminum overhead door to the firehouse opened. The red and white lights throbbed and siren blared as the rig sped past. Captain Reemer spotted him and waved. A firefighter he didn't recognize rode in the cub's seat, his seat.

Mitch let himself in. The oily diesel fumes and residue of decades of cigar smoke set off snapshots of the last year. He took his old seat at the joker stand and soaked in the visions and emotions playing through his mind. It was over a year ago when he walked through that door the first time as a cub, eager to prove himself. After all, he was the star of the training academy. How could he fail? He laughed at himself. He was so damn naïve.

Thanks to the mentoring of the veteran crew, especially Ralph, he eventually proved himself to them and himself. And learned there were heroes all around him, fighting in the trenches every day to save these children, people like Brother Williams.

He sat for over an hour gazing out the window. He envisioned Jasmine and Alexus rushing across the street to tell him something important. He thought back to Jasmine's selfless act of courage when she nearly died going into her burning home to find her sister. Her courage had taught him how the power of love overcomes fear.

Mitch went downstairs. The smell of smoke-saturated gear and dried sweat of the workout area brought more memories. He lowered himself onto the weight bench and thought about Nic. Why couldn't he have loved her? He thought about how his mom couldn't find a way to love his dad. She was right. Life makes no sense.

Mitch decided when Jennie came by next Wednesday to get Sid for the last therapy session, he'd beg her to give him one more chance, tell her he never stopped loving her. That would give him all day tomorrow to come up with the right words. If Miss Bernie was right and Jennie still loved him, she might just take him back. Miss Bernie was rarely wrong.

He went upstairs and drifted to the kitchen, the heart of every firehouse. And at the heart of the kitchen, the Bunn coffee maker. Nothing had changed, but it felt distant. Mitch put a fresh pot of coffee on for the crew, then took his gear to the boss's office and waited, listening to the radio traffic on the squawk box. He heard Captain Reemer call for a second alarm. Heavy smoke was coming from the auto junkyard eight blocks from the firehouse.

They'd be there for hours spraying down the tangled mountain of wrecked autos and parts.

Mitch filled out a department form and put it in the captain's mail slot, then placed a note on top of his gear along with the key to the firehouse, and his badge.

Captain Reemer,

There's no way I can thank you and the crew enough for all you taught me and did for me. Please have Ralph accept my award at the ceremony next week. He's the one responsible for the save. Without him teaching me the ropes I never would have made it out.

After spending the summer on the farm, I realized that's where I belong. I'm a farmer. My resignation is in your mail slot and this is my gear. Stay safe.
Mitch

He rewrote the note five times. The first ones rambled. He couldn't get his thoughts into words that made any sense.

On the way back to Milroy, Mitch's excitement grew. Miss Bernie was right again. Farming was a part of him. Last Friday he had called Dr. Mallory and told him he'd be staying on the farm and to go ahead with plans for an animal therapy center.

The farm would be alive with young people.

Sid and Chris were all for it.

All that was missing was Jennie.

Chapter 62

Mitch's heart raced as Jennie climbed the squeaking porch steps. He had spent the night in the treehouse planning what to say. He had to get this right, make her understand they were meant for each other, that he never stopped loving her.

Jennie stopped on the top step and took a step back when she saw him. "Whoa. You don't look so good. You're awfully pale."

Mitch felt like he swallowed a beehive.

The kitchen phone rang.

"Jen, you have to know how much I…"

From inside, Chris called out, "Mitch, phone."

"Not now."

"It's Miss Bernie, said she really needs to talk to you."

"Still no cell service out here?" Jennie asked as she plopped into the wicker chair, squinting hard at him. Was it interest or was it skepticism? He couldn't tell.

Mitch shrugged and went inside. This would give his jangled nerves time to settle.

He pressed the cool receiver to his ear. "Hey, Miss Bernie. What's up?"

"Mitch, oh, Mitch. I'm beside myself." Her voice cracked. "Jasmine never come home after school yesterday. Brother Williams out all night looking for her."

His chest tightened. "The police know?"

"They figure she run off." She sniffled. "Mitch, that girl ain't running off."

"Brother Williams have any idea where she might be?"

"Oh, Lord, don't take another child from me."

"Miss Bernie, listen, Miss Bernie. I'm on my way. We'll find her."

Jennie sprang to her feet when Mitch burst onto the porch.

"I gotta get to Milwaukee," Mitch said. "Jasmine never came home from school yesterday. We'll talk later."

"The hell we will. I'm coming."

"Jen, no, I don't want you down there," he said as he brushed past her.

"I'm coming."

He didn't bother arguing.

When Mitch got the Browning hunting rifle from the mudroom, Jennie stared at it, furrowing her brow. "What's that for?"

"Insurance."

Sid paced the kitchen while Mitch filled him and Chris in. When he finished, Sid said, "You go find her. She's a good kid."

Jennie was waiting in the van. They sped toward Milwaukee.

"You ever getting rid of this old wreck?"

"Means more to me than that truck ever did."

"Boy, you've changed." She checked her cell phone. "I have service now. I'll let Miss Bernie know we're on the way."

Her fingers danced over the phone. She put it to her ear and waited. "Miss Bernie, it's me, Jennie. We're are on our way. Can you tell us anything more? Miss Bernie? Miss Bernie?" Jennie lowered the phone. "She's hysterical. Keeps repeating 'please Lord, not again'."

Mitch grasped at reasons for Jasmine's disappearance. She didn't have a group of friends she hung out with and drugs were out of the question. He needed to calm down. Brother Williams would have more information.

Mitch sucked in a loud breath. "Jen, we should talk."

"Not now."

"I'll go crazy if I just sit here and drive."

Jennie raised her eyebrows.

"I'm moving back to Milroy."

"Okay?"

"Mallory talked me into partnering with the UW Hospital for an animal therapy clinic on our farm."

"What about working with those kids in Milwaukee and firefighting?"

"I'm a farmer, Jen. I know that now. That's all I ever wanted to do. Working with kids in Milwaukee was incredible. I can keep doing that right here with the clinic. And I'll get back on the Milroy Fire Department."

Jennie spoke to her wringing hands, "Mitch, you sure that's why you're coming back?"

"Jen. I love you. Never stopped. You have to know that. And I think you still love me. Can you tell me you don't?"

"Mitch, stop."

"You never answered when I asked if you loved Jason. Do you?"

"Please stop."

"Well, do you? Say yes and I'll stop."

"We're getting married next month. We bought a house together."

Her words sucked the wind out of him. When he could breathe again, he softly said, "You still didn't answer."

"You're not putting this on me—why we're not together. Don't you do that. You left *me*, remember, goddammit. Ever since we were kids I dreamed of being your wife and having your babies. Then you got all messed up and left. All you had to do was let me in, let me help, but no. End of dream. I accepted it and moved on. I had to. Now you want it to be my fault we're not together? Damn you."

"I love you, Jen."

"Jesus, Mitch, you have shitty timing. Why couldn't you have said something, like a year ago?" She turned away and crossed her arms. "Damn you."

"So, now what?"

"I can't leave Jason."

"But you don't love him."

She stared out the side window. A tear dripped from her chin.

Chapter 63

Brother Williams vaulted down the porch steps as Mitch and Jennie pulled to a stop in front of Miss Bernie's house. He met them on the sidewalk, his suit badly wrinkled and eyes drooping. "Thank the good Lord you're both here. Bernice keeps asking for you." He paused and shook his head. "She's barely hanging on. It was a long night."

"And Lexi?" Mitch asked. "How's she doing?"

"We got her off to school this morning. She's smart. Knows something isn't right."

"What's being done to find Jasmine?"

"I crisscrossed these streets all night long. I cornered a One-Niner in the back alley off Sixteenth Street, the one with dreadlocks." Brother Williams' booming voice trailed off. "Lord, forgive me, I nearly choked the life out of him. Said he didn't know Jasmine was missing. I demanded to see DeAndre. He said nobody's seen him since yesterday."

"You think this DeAndre guy knows something?" Jennie asked.

"We'll find out," Mitch said through gritted teeth. "That's the bastard who killed Miss Bernie's son."

"Mitch, please. Let the police handle this."

"Here's what we'll do. Brother Williams, go back to your school before it lets out and ask every single kid when they last saw Jasmine and where. Me and Jen will go to the fifth district and convince them to raid the One-Niner's crack house. Then we'll stop by the firehouse and have dispatch transmit a notice for all units to be on the lookout for Jasmine. The boss can call the other companies in the Core and tell them to watch for DeAndre. They all know the scum."

* * *

Jennie waited in the foyer of Police District Five while Mitch tracked down a detective from Jamal's case. After forty-five minutes, Mitch barged out and motioned for Jennie to follow him to the van.

"They raided the crack-house last night. Ran three gang members in for questioning but got nothing." Mitch started the van. "There's no evidence of a crime at this point and they don't have the resources to stake out the house."

"Now what?"

"If anything comes up they'll call your cell."

"I can't fucking believe this. A young girl is missing and that's it? They'll call if anything comes up?"

He put the van in gear and headed to Firehouse Fifteen.

* * *

Nic answered the door. Mitch coughed into his hand and said, "Jen, this is Nic. Nic, this is Jen."

The two women measured each other.

Nic put out her hand. "We finally meet."

Jennie's hand stayed at her side. "Yes, we do."

Nic shrugged and said to Mitch, "Heard you're a civilian now. Sorry to hear that."

"Who's the boss today?"

"Lt Kaminski took Laubner's spot." Nic turned to Jennie. "Let's you and me have a talk while he chats with the boss."

Jennie scowled at Mitch. He headed to the office, leaving the two women alone.

When he returned, the two were talking quietly and smiling.

"Jen told me about Jasmine," Nic said. "God, I hope you find her." She turned back to Jennie and they hugged. "I really am sorry."

When they got back in the van, Mitch asked, "What the hell was that?"

"Said she feels awful for breaking us up. Thinks I should give you another chance."

"And?"

"Nic seems pretty amazing. Shame things didn't work out."

Yup. A shame.

* * *

They spent the afternoon driving the streets and alleys of the Core, all the way from the Milwaukee River out to Twenty-Seventh Street. They talked with children on playgrounds and schoolyards. They stopped people on the street. Some acted concerned and others acted like these two white people were aliens.

Stillness settled over the Core as darkness set in. Jennie called Miss Bernie's house. "Brother Williams? Good to hear your voice. How's Miss Bernie?—Good thing you're there. Any news?—Sure." Jennie handed the phone to Mitch, "Alexus wants to talk to you."

"Lexi, how was school today?"

"When you bringin' Jasmine home?"

"Soon, Lexi, soon. I promise."

"Okay, then. Told Miss Bernie, I'm staying up 'til she gets home. 'Cause she my sister and I miss her. She needs to be home."

"I know." Mitch choked. "Bye." He handed the phone back to Jennie.

He stopped the van and shouted, "Fuck this."

Jennie took his hand from the steering wheel, kissed it, and held it to her chest.

He could feel her galloping heartbeat. "I'm dropping you off at Miss Bernie's."

"Then what?"

"I gotta find that bastard. He knows where Jasmine is. I know it."

"You're not doing this alone."

"Jen, no."

Her face narrowed. "I'm coming along."

"Damn, you're stubborn."

"Just like you."

"You gotta do what I say and not argue."

"We'll see."

Chapter 64

Mitch and Jennie hunkered down in the tall weeds across from the One-Niner's crack house, the same spot where he shot up DeAndre's car and almost shot Spiked Hair. He brought the rifle, telling Jennie he needed the night-scope to watch the house. They took turns watching while the other dozed.

Jennie shook him. "Somebody came out of the house."

He blinked his eyes clear. "What time is it?"

"Almost one."

Mitch peered through the scope. The bright September moon illuminated the street. "Holy crap. Chirelle."

"Chirelle?"

"She can't be back with him."

"With who?"

"DeAndre. He killed her brother for Christ's sake."

Jennie's mouth dropped. "People live like this?"

"I gotta follow her."

"Mitch, this is getting too real. You sure?"

"Go to the van and stay there until I get back."

"Not happening. If we find him, you're calling the cops, right?"

Chirelle headed north, walking fast through the back alleys behind Nineteenth Street. Mitch and Jennie followed, ducking behind dilapidated garages and sheds, many scrawled with the black, scripted "19".

After following for two blocks, Mitch said, "I gotta find out what she knows. Stay back."

"You know what you're doing?"

"Not a chance." He grimaced. "Here, keep this out of sight and stay in the shadows." He handed her the rifle.

313

He trailed Chirelle for half a block, rapidly closing the distance between them. He was almost on her when she snapped her head around, saw him, and bolted. Mitch sprinted after her. She veered into a backyard where he tackled her hard onto the grass.

Her eyes bulged. "Get the fuck off me."

Mitch clamped a hand over her mouth and pinned her to the ground. She twisted and squirmed, trying to sink her teeth into his hand. Whining, guttural sounds came from deep in her throat.

Mitch tightened the grip on her mouth and leaned his face closer. "Chirelle, Chirelle, look at me. You know who I am?"

Her eyes softened and she stopped struggling.

"You know I was your brother's friend, right?"

She nodded.

"Okay, you know I'm not going to hurt you, right?"

She nodded.

"I'm going to pull my hand away. Please, don't scream, okay?"

Her eyes widened as she looked past Mitch to the alley.

"Get the fuck off my ho."

Mitch sprang to his feet, spun, and looked down the barrel of his own rifle and into the coal black eyes of DeAndre. DeAndre's gold teeth glimmered in the silver moonlight. His face was gouged with red gashes. He nudged the gun barrel up and down. "What you planning on doing wit dis? Blow this nigger away?" He cackled.

Spiked Hair stood beside DeAndre along with two others who were barely old enough to shave. All three had AR-15s trained on him.

The silver moonlight clouded to a red haze through Mitch's eyes. "What'd you do with Jennie?"

DeAndre motioned toward a half-collapsed garage with his left hand while keeping the rifle trained on Mitch.

Jennie stepped from the darkness with a knife pressed to her neck. Dreadlocks had her arms pinned to her back, pushing her forward.

Jennie's glassy eyes locked onto Mitch.

Think. "DeAndre, look. We're trying to find Jasmine. That's all. I wouldn't hurt Chirelle."

DeAndre sneered. "Don't know nothing about that shit. All I know, you try to send me away. Should cap your white ass right here."

314

Jennie kicked Dreadlocks in the crotch and bit his wrist. He yelped and dropped the blade. She ran for Mitch. Dreadlocks snatched the knife off the ground. "No bitch gonna bite my ass."

"Gimme the blade," DeAndre barked. "Not here. Don't need to attract no nosey motherfuckers." He pointed down the alley to a house with the second-floor lights on. "Wait 'til we get them to the warehouse."

"What you planning, boss?"

Mitch stepped in front of Jennie. "Let her go. This is about you and me."

"You in my hood. I make the rules. Maybe I take me a taste of your white bitch."

Mitch fought to control the burning hatred rising in his chest.

Think.

Chirelle edged next to DeAndre and rested her head on his chest. She leered at Mitch and Jennie with a sickly smile. That's when he saw the white gold necklace with a tiny gold leaf hanging around her neck.

Mitch's stomach turned to lead. "Where'd you get Jasmine's necklace?"

"That mine. DeAndre give it to me."

The slap echoed off the garages as Chirelle sprawled to the ground holding her cheek. DeAndre kicked her. "Shut the fuck up you stupid ho."

Spiked Hair watched, expressionless. "So what we doing with them?" he asked DeAndre.

"Juice'll get the honky's rat van. We take 'em out to the warehouse on Thirty-Second and torch it with them inside. Ain't nobody hearing or seeing nothing over there." He sneered. "Barbecue their motherfuckin' honky asses."

"Her too?" Spiked Hair said with no emotion.

"We can't let her go, nigger." DeAndre nodded toward Dreadlocks. "Juice, get the van."

Mitch's heart raced.

Calm down. Focus.

Mitch pointed at DeAndre's face. "Jasmine do that?"

"You one ignorant honky, lookin' for my ass all day in my hood and think I won't know? Well, you found me, motherfucker." DeAndre hooted. "Now ain't that a bitch?"

DeAndre handed Spiked Hair the rifle. "Keep 'em out a sight in the yard. Cap 'em both if he moves. I gotta find a shitter." He pointed at the boarded-up house behind them and handed a small flashlight to Chirelle. "C'mon, you get to hold the light." He pushed her toward the dark house.

Think. He faced Spiked Hair. "What did DeAndre do with Jasmine? She scratch his face?"

"Don't know nothin' about that."

"Chirelle's wearing Jasmine's necklace. He has her somewhere."

"Don't know nothin' about no necklace."

"It's Jasmine's. I gave it to her. You must have seen it. Thought you guys liked her? Now you're gonna let DeAndre do whatever he wants with her?"

Spiked Hair's expressionless stare showed no sign of acknowledgment. *Don't give up.*

"You thanked me for helping your little girl. Now you're gonna kill me, and Jen too?" Mitch's question was met with the same blank stare. "You told me the gang wasn't into killing and putting young girls on the street. Said that was all DeAndre. Was that a lie?" Still no reaction. "Your Peaches is a smart girl. She loves you. This what you want for her?"

The two juvenile gangbangers kept their rifles trained on Mitch while glimpsing at Spiked Hair.

Spiked Hair's eyes narrowed. "Need to shut the fuck up."

Without moving his lips and continuing to look at Spiked Hair, Mitch whispered to Jennie, "We can't get in the van. When I say now, you distract them."

"How?" she whispered back, not moving her lips.

"Think of something."

DeAndre strutted out of the darkness of the vacant house with Chirelle trudging behind. He snatched the rifle from Spiked Hair and waved it at Mitch and Jennie. "This a sweet scope. Come in handy 'round here."

"You got Jasmine?" Spiked Hair asked DeAndre.

"What that fool been telling you?"

"Chirelle's wearing her necklace. You shouldn't be messin' with Jasmine."

"Don't need to worry about anyone messin' wit Jasmine."

"Where is she?"

DeAndre fixed his reptilian eyes on Spiked Hair. "She gone."

"Gone where?"

"Listen, nigger. That girl owe me. I carried her saggy-assed ole lady an' her for three years. Kept them in their crib. Kept Benita's crackhead old man high. They all knew the deal. When Jasmine form, I put her on the street. That fine young thang woulda pulled in some serious jack." DeAndre's mouth twisted into a hideous grimace. "Until this motherfucker fill her head with shit."

"Where is she?" Spiked Hair asked, his voice flat.

C'mon tell him. The van would be here any minute.

DeAndre tugged the front of his shirt down. His chest looked like it had been clawed by a wild animal. "See what that bitch did? Won't ever do that again."

Spiked Hair glanced at the red gashes running down DeAndre's chest. "Where is she?"

"Said, she's gone."

Spiked Hair's face drooped. "You kill her?"

DeAndre leveled the barrel of the rifle at Mitch's chest. "Need to end this now."

The blood drained from Mitch's face. Jennie groaned and clutched his arm.

The lights of the van swung into the alley. Mitch heard Ralph's words in his head, *"Control your emotions. Focus."* Mitch slowed his breathing. Calmness set in. No panic, no rage, just razor sharp focus on the devil in front of him. "Go ahead, asshole. Shoot us right here. Core's crawling with cops. They'll be on your ass before you get out of the alley."

"Fuck that."

"He's right," Spiked Hair said. "Take them out here, we all going away."

"Fuck it, I can wait. Van's here."

The van rolled to a stop.

Mitch whispered to Jennie, "Now."

She didn't move.

"Jen, now. Do it."

She shoved Mitch to the side and ripped off her shirt, glaring at DeAndre. "You wanted a taste of this white bitch. Here I am, fucker. Let's see what you got." She narrowed her eyes at DeAndre and went for her bra strap. He lowered the rifle.

Mitch charged DeAndre. The barrel of the rifle swung back up. The rifle cracked, sending a short blue flame from the barrel. Searing pain ripped through Mitch's side.

The recoil of the high-powered rifle lifted the barrel enough for Mitch to duck under it, grabbing DeAndre's arm and wedging his neck in his armpit. He yanked DeAndre's arm down. The pop of his arm tearing out of the socket was followed by a high pitched wail. The rifle banged to the ground. DeAndre went to his knees clutching the limp arm to his body. Mitch tossed the rifle across the yard.

"Shoot the motherfucker," DeAndre screamed.

The young One-Niners on each side of Spiked Hair leveled their AR-15s at Mitch. Spiked Hair pushed the tips of both rifles down.

Lights flashed on in three houses down the alley.

Mitch glared at Spiked Hair. "How the fuck can you live with him killing Jasmine?" He went to Jennie, holding his side with a blood-soaked hand, hunching forward from the pain.

Jennie screamed, "Mitch."

He turned as DeAndre lunged at him, his right arm hanging limp. Mitch saw the flash of the blade in DeAndre's left hand as he slashed at Mitch's neck. He blocked it with his arm, barely feeling the sting. Before DeAndre slashed at him again, Mitch had him around the legs, lifting him high in the air. With everything he had, he slammed DeAndre to the hard asphalt with a perfect double-leg takedown, driving the back of DeAndre's skull into the pavement. The loud crack resonated down the alley. DeAndre's eyes rolled back in his head, leaving only the bulging, yellowish whites visible. A croaking sound belched from his gaping mouth. If the One-Niners weren't standing behind him with their rifles, Mitch would have choked DeAndre off right there. He struggled to his feet. Blood spurted from the inside of Mitch's arm. His knees buckled. He collapsed.

Jennie ran to him. "Holy shit." She gripped his upper arm, squeezing hard. "He got your brachial. And your side's bleeding."

Mitch heard DeAndre gurgling only feet from him. He watched DeAndre's body flop violently, foam spewing from his mouth. DeAndre stiffened. The man's dying gasps faded. The death rattle. *Hell's waiting, asshole.*

Chirelle threw herself onto DeAndre, wailing.

Sirens blared in the distance.

Dreadlocks bolted from the van. He ran to Spiked Hair. "Let's go. Just do them here."

"No. No more."

"What about DeAndre?"

"He fucked." Spiked Hair snatched the kicking and screaming Chirelle off DeAndre and headed up the alley with the others.

"You bastards just gonna leave?" Jennie hollered at Spiked Hair's back. "What kind of people are you?"

Spiked Hair handed Chirelle off to Dreadlocks, then punched at his cell phone and said, "Got a fireman shot in the alley, Nineteenth and Hadley. He's bad. Get a amblance here, fast."

Halfway up the alley, they stopped. Spiked Hair trotted back to Mitch and Jennie. He looked down at Mitch and nodded, then tossed Jasmine's necklace to Jennie. "Make sure Lexus gets that."

In an instant, he was gone, leaving Jennie, Mitch, and DeAndre's limp body in the quiet, moonlit alley.

Mitch tried to move, but his arms and legs didn't respond.

"Stay still, honey. They're coming."

"Don't worry. This is our run, Engine Fifteen. Med Six will be right behind them. They're good."

"Mitch, you were unbelievable."

"Nice distraction."

"Yeah, you men and tits."

Pinpoints of light flickered in his head. "Jen, I never did stop loving you."

"I know. I never stopped loving you either." She kissed his lips. He felt her warm tears on his face. Her face blurred.

"Good," he whispered.

Mitch fought the darkness.

"Mitch, you asked me to marry you once."

"You never answered."

"Offer still stand?"

"Anybody ever tell you that you have shitty timing, Jennifer McAdams?"

"Well?"

"Promise to make me cinnamon rolls every morning?"

Jennie laid her head on his chest.

Let me see her face once more.

Time stopped. He floated into the air, serene and at peace. He saw himself with Jennie draped over him, sobbing.

Jen, it's okay. I'm with little Maggie. She's fine. Jamal and LaMont are here too. And Kyle and Mom. We're all fine. It's beautiful. So beautiful.

"Goddamnit, Mitch Garner, don't you dare die on me." He saw her kiss his lips.

Don't be sad, Jen. I love you.

The crumbling garages pulsed red and white as Engine Fifteen roared up the alley.

Chapter 65

Soft purple lilac bouquets lined the altar and windowsills of Milroy Trinity Lutheran Church, saturating the air with their comforting scent. The small chapel was packed. Dr. Mallory, Big Jim Nelson, and the Milroy Volunteer Fire Department were seated in the back rows behind Captain Reemer, Kenny, Crusher, Ralph—and Nic. Farm families from as far away as Watertown filled the remaining pews. Mitch's lifelong friend Danny was there with his parents. Next to them was Maggie's family: John, Betty, and big sister Lydia.

The silver-haired pastor, who had baptized Mitch and buried his mom, motioned for Brother Williams to join him at the altar. The church went quiet.

Brother Williams looked over the crowd, cleared his throat, and slowly sang a mellow version of *Hallelujah*. His voice swelled with emotion as he reached the chorus. Brother Williams motioned for the congregation to rise. Tissues came out as parishioners swabbed at their eyes. Those who could, sang Hallelujah after Hallelujah, each one louder, until the entire congregation was swaying and waving their hands in the air.

After the last Hallelujah, the pastor stepped forward. "Don't think this church ever experienced anything quite like that. Thank you, Mr. Williams." He motioned for Miss Bernie to join them on the altar.

The pastor reached toward the ceiling and began, "Brothers and Sisters, today we add another soul into the body of Christ—We celebrate the baptism of Jasmine Margaret Garner with her parents and her sponsors, Clarence and Bernice Williams."

Brother Williams and Miss Bernie took their place next to Mitch and Jennie. Together they all gazed at the baby girl dressed in a lacy white baptism dress and bonnet, barely concealing her thick black hair. The pastor began. The squirming baby clutched Mitch's finger while Jennie held her to her chest. Mitch's free arm went around his wife's waist. To each other, they mouthed, "Love you."

Alexus smiled at them from the front pew. Her two front teeth had grown in. She rocked a baby in her arms while Chris bounced a toddler on his knee. Sid was seated between two adolescent boys. Sid, Chris, and Alexus had been placed in charge of Miss Bernie and Brother Williams' four foster children during the service. Alexus was now the Williams' adopted daughter.

After the baby had been properly sprinkled with water and baptized, the pastor motioned for the congregation to stand. He took her from Jennie and held her toward the joyful gathering. "Please welcome Jasmine Margaret Garner into the body of Christ."

Cheers came from the back. The rest of the congregation joined the firefighters with thundering applause, startling baby Jasmine whose wails rose about the applause. Jennie took her from the pastor and calmed her. Mitch caught sight of Maggie's mother, Betty Hillenbrand, dabbing at her eyes with a white handkerchief while stroking her husband's back.

Mitch and Jennie led the others back to the front pew. After they were all seated, the pastor launched into the sermon. Alexus tapped Mitch's arm. In a whisper, she said, "Baby Jasmine need to have this." She unclasped the white gold necklace with the tiny gold leaf from her neck and handed it to him.

Mitch held the necklace in his open palm, staring at it.

Jennie kissed Alexus on the cheek. "Aw, Lexi, that's so sweet."

Alexus went back to rocking the foster baby. "Just make sure she knows about my sister."

"You bet she will," Mitch said. "She'll know all about your sister. And you too."

Alexus nodded. "Good."

Mitch looked up to the thick wooden rafters. *How could I ever forget you?* He closed his eyes and saw her sparkling emerald eyes.

After the sermon and last hymn, the pastor closed by saying, "May the peace of the Lord that surpasses all understanding be with you."

Mitch and Miss Bernie nodded at each other.

The congregation repeated, "And also with you."

Mitch looked up again. *And with you, sweet Jasmine.*

As the congregation filed out the door, Mitch's pager buzzed. "Report of a barn fire, highway Eighteen at Q. Repeat. Report of a barn fire ..."

The End

Thank you so much for investing your time and money in my story. If you enjoyed it and think it's an important story, I would be deeply grateful if you would leave a review on Amazon or Goodreads or both. Smaller publishing houses don't have the funds to promote their books like the major players. So we rely on word-of-mouth and these reviews. Please consider leaving a review even if it's only a few lines or a few words.

Thank you,

Gregory Lee Renz

Acknowledgements

Where do I start? Who do I thank? I could fill pages and pages with the names of everyone who played a part in this eight-year journey to publication.

I'll start with my biggest supporter, my wife Paula, who kept me humble and focused. Her eyes were the first to see my pages and her editorial advice was crucial in keeping me on track. She knew my characters, especially Mitch, better than anyone. Frequently, our dinner conversations centered on whether I was portraying this young man properly.

A huge thank you goes out to the University of Wisconsin Continuing Studies program. Without their creative writing courses, conferences, and workshops, I'd still be plunking away at the keyboard with no idea on how to write a novel. My mentor and coach, best-selling author and screenwriter Christine DeSmet, was there at the beginning of this journey and pushed me to the finish line with her wisdom and insight into this incredibly challenging craft of creative writing. Along with Christine, I have to thank Laurie Scheer for her support and Angela Rydell for her patience in my early creative writing courses. The conferences and workshops offered through the Continuing Studies program always provide a wonderful experience for us writers due to the tireless work, behind the scenes, of Laura Kahl. Thank you, Laura.

I have to thank our writers' group in Lake Mills, Wisconsin, The Writers' Dozen, for energizing me with our monthly meetings. Along with this group are all the Beta readers who read the manuscript and provided honest feedback for improving the story. Every one of you helped polish the story in some way. Thank you all.

I'm grateful to the Milwaukee Fire Department for offering me the best job in the world. This book would not be possible without the twenty-eight years of unimaginable experiences and all the colorful characters I had the privilege of working alongside.

A heart-felt thanks goes out to all the writing friends I've made on this journey. I learned, early in this journey, that we all share the same challenges of getting words on the page and the pain of rejections when we type the end to our labor-of-love. Without this inclusive community of understanding supporters, it may have been tempting to walk away. So glad I didn't.

Finally, many thanks to Kira Henschel of HenschelHAUS Publishing, whose vision and enthusiasm for this story matched my own. Her experienced guidance through the revisions, publishing, and marketing of the novel have been invaluable.

About the Author

Fire Captain Gregory Lee Renz was involved in a dramatic rescue of two little boys from their burning basement. He received a series of awards for this rescue including induction into the Wisconsin Fire and Police Hall of Fame in 2006. When he was asked to share the dramatic rescue at several awards banquets, he was moved by the emotional responses he received and was struck by the power of his storytelling. Gregory has always been an avid reader and thought maybe he could craft a compelling novel if he could learn how to get these stories on the page. Numerous creative writing courses, workshops, and conferences later, he typed *The End* to this novel, his first, which was inspired by two adorable little girls, around eight and five years of age, who lived across from an inner city firehouse he was stationed at for three years. Those two girls stayed in his thoughts over the years, demanding he tell their story. They are two of the main characters in the novel. He hopes he did them justice. After serving the citizens of Milwaukee for twenty-eight years as a firefighter, Gregory Lee Renz retired to Lake Mills, Wisconsin with his wife, Paula.

glrenz.com

CPSIA information can be obtained
at www.ICGtesting.com
Printed in the USA
LVHW011216210721
693234LV00001B/6

9 781595 986887